Over, Under, Across & Through

Book 1 of The Real World Series

Barbara Cutrera

Published by On My Way Up, LLC

Cover art by Lisa Anderson of Barefoot in the Glass
www.barefootintheglass.com

ISBN- 978-0-9858255-3-9
Second edition

In memory of my aunt, Dr. Barbara Cicardo, who was a giving, strong-willed woman and a brilliant English professor

Prologue

Sarah Nash sat in her favorite chair with a book open across her lap. She was having difficulty concentrating that evening. After only a few paragraphs, her attention began to wander. She started slightly, chagrined at finding herself staring blindly into the lace panels that covered the front window.

Illumination from the lamp on the end table made a harsh circle around Sarah in the darkened living room. Gusts of wind stirred the leaves in the trees, and the combination of cold outside and heat inside made the house creak and groan. Ralph, the family's black Lab, snored in canine oblivion on the kitchen floor. Sarah's five-year-old son, Kristopher, slept soundly in his bed. Her husband, Daniel, hadn't made it home, yet.

Molasses, she thought. *Every time I try to think about making a change it's like molasses is flowing through my brain instead of blood. Pitiful.*

It was early November in 1994. The next day would herald her thirty-second birthday. Sarah thought about this upcoming milestone and a variety of other things while she waited for Daniel. She reflected on her life and on her appearance as she grew older. People always remarked that she looked younger than she really was, perhaps because she was so petite. Only five feet tall with auburn hair and hazel eyes, she was generally pleased with how she looked. It really didn't matter to her as long as she remained attractive to Daniel, and he never failed to tell her frequently how beautiful he thought she was.

Thinking that perhaps the simple act of movement might pull her up and out of her malaise, Sarah removed her glasses, put down the book in the recliner, and let the dog out then decided to straighten the living room. If that didn't work, she could always retreat to the pantry and the box of chocolates that rested on the upper shelf. Sighing, she decided that housekeeping was probably better for her than chocolate.

She swore silently as she stepped on a tiny, blue Lego. Pocketing the offending rectangle, she limped over to the coffee table. Heaped on top of the Sunday paper was a pile of junk mail,

1

a *Money* magazine, and a picture of a turtle Kris had drawn at school. Sarah put the newspaper and the junk mail in the recycle bin, tacked Kris's artwork to the refrigerator with a magnet, and positioned the magazine at an acceptable angle on the table.

Hesitating, she slowly surveyed the living room. Except for the book she'd left in the recliner, everything was in order. The couch beckoned to her. She could light some of her candles, turn off the lamp, then lie back and watch the warm glow of the flames reflecting off the pale walls and the white ceiling. It was a soothing image.

"Mom," a drowsy voice called from the back of the house.

"I'm coming, Kris."

She turned from the couch and made her way down the hall. As she crossed the threshold into her golden-haired son's sacred domain, she asked, "What is it, Sweetie?" even though she already knew what he was going to say.

"Will you lay down in my bed? I can't sleep."

"Just for a minute."

Following the routine, she stretched out on top of the comforter next to the boy. Waiting for Kris to doze off again, Sarah stayed motionless and let her eyes roam around the room. She squinted at the familiar tiger picture on the opposite wall. She saw the outlines of the baseball pennants above the shelf where her son's little trophies and treasures rested. A dinosaur opened its mouth in a silent roar in the dim rays of the nightlight.

Once Kris was sleeping deeply again, Sarah rolled off the bed and edged out of the room. She could hear the grinding of the garage door mechanism. The door leading into the kitchen opened at the precise moment that she flicked on the lights. Daniel stepped inside and smiled.

Sarah's husband was tall with graying black hair and dark eyes. He was thirty-six years old, but the strife in his early life had changed his appearance somehow and had made him appear slightly older even when he'd been a young boy. He didn't look haggard as might well have been the case. It was the way that he carried himself, the way he'd grounded himself. He had dug in his heels against hardship and had succeeded in his marriage, his work, and fatherhood.

2

Daniel tossed his keys on the counter and shrugged off his coat, as Sarah said, "What? No passionate 'I'm-home-let's-make-love-on-the-floor' tonight?"

"I'm game if you're interested."

"Kris might walk in on us. *That* would be something to explain."

"True. He is a little young for that talk."

After he'd put down his briefcase and placed his half-finished Coke in the refrigerator, Daniel came over to his wife and kissed her.

"How was that?" he teased. "Passionate enough for you?"

"Very nice."

"Nice? I can see I've got my work cut out for me tonight."

"How was the office?" she inquired automatically, as he moved to get a snack. "Is the financial world doing well today?"

"Very well," came his reply, which was muffled by the pantry door. "How were things at the bookstore?"

"Nothing new there."

Sarah watched her husband prepare the bowl of cookies, milk, and ice cream he would eat while viewing the evening news. She knew that he exercised regularly but still wondered how he could stay relatively slim despite the amount of calories he consumed each day. Sarah, on the other hand, had to watch what she ate or the few pounds she needed to lose would become more than a few. To add insult to injury, Daniel's cholesterol levels did not reflect his love of high-fat foods.

As he settled onto the couch, Daniel glanced at Sarah, who had returned to reading the book she'd left in the recliner. Sitting in the artificial light, the red highlights in her hair glimmered prominently. Although not classically beautiful, she was most definitely an attractive woman. Her skin was exquisitely soft, and he loved to slip his fingers into her auburn curls. She had wonderful curves and nice breasts. Her mouth curled just so when she smiled, and there were little black flecks buried within the green of her eyes. It was the spirit behind those eyes that made her so unbelievably desirable to her husband.

A kindred spirit, he thought. *We're survivors. We never give up.*

When the news ended at 10:30, Daniel let Ralph in. The dog went to his favorite spot in the corner of the kitchen and curled up for the night. Sarah proceeded to switch out the lights and lock the deadbolts. While Daniel fed the fish, she retreated to the master bath to remove her dress. She slipped on a nightgown, brushed her teeth, and turned down the covers.

Sarah nestled herself between the pale green sheets. She savored the sensations associated with getting into bed at night. Each evening this simple act caused her to experience a sense of warmth and security that she could find nowhere else. The feel of the bed linens was phenomenal. She rubbed her cheek into the pillow, making a little hollow for her face. Her leg muscles relaxed, and she curled up slightly and allowed herself to go limp.

A few minutes later, Daniel, wearing his boxers and T-shirt, joined her in the bed. Sarah moved close to her husband, who reflexively draped his arm across her waist.

They spoke casually about their schedules for the next day. The forecast of sleet for the following afternoon led to speculation as to whether or not Kris should wear his thermal shirt under his kindergarten uniform. Sarah reminded Daniel that Ralph was running low on dog food. Daniel remarked that the tube of toothpaste in their bathroom was almost empty. They continued in this manner for several minutes. The list of incidentals was a lengthy one.

Eventually, they stopped talking and made love. They were both tired and swore that they wouldn't draw things out any longer than necessary. Forty-five minutes later, the couple lay entwined, their hair disheveled and the covers twisted awkwardly around them. Daniel smiled in the darkness.

So much for getting to sleep early, he thought, nuzzling his face against his wife's hair. Sarah made a satisfied little sound and placed a hand on his chest. After a time, they drifted apart and then to sleep.

At 2:00 a.m., Daniel woke with a jerk to the sound of thunder in the distance. His heart was racing, and he had to work at unclenching his fists. His temples throbbed in response to the wave of adrenaline he was riding. The muscles of his legs and arms were taut with tension.

4

Daniel knew that he had to do something to distract himself from the dream he'd just had. So, he took a deep breath and tried to think about nothing in particular. This was a trick he'd learned years before: Think of anything except the dream, and some inane subject will present itself.

For sixty seconds, he did some mental arithmetic that related to one of the accounts he was handling at work. Next, he tried to visualize how best to whittle the pinewood car that Kris would need to race for the Cub Scout derby. And so it went for many minutes.

He turned on his side and studied his wife, who lay close to him with her hands tucked under her cheek. She appeared so childlike in sleep. He marveled at how much she reminded him of her father, Tristan.

Physically, they were quite different. Tristan was a giant of a man and was rail thin. Sarah was petite with round curves. Tristan had the Native American features of his Lakota father, while Sarah bore no resemblance to any Native American person Daniel had ever seen. Yet, they shared the auburn hair and the hazel eyes and the expressiveness of their gestures and inflections.

Emotionally, they were very much the same. Both were gentle in nature, yet they were given to occasional fits of temper. Both were blessed with impressive intellect and cursed with perfectionist tendencies and an overabundance of empathy.

Makes them too damn responsible, Daniel thought. *If only they wouldn't weigh every decision like it was the be-all and the end-all.*

Daniel began to breathe easier. Just a few more minutes and then he would get up. He closed his eyes and forced the muscles in his biceps and calves to go slack. Maybe he could get the shaking to subside shortly.

That night, he'd awakened from one of those nightmares that he still had from time to time. This one had been tame in comparison to the others. He'd been about ten and was cornered in a small closet. He could hear his father's footsteps echoing as the man came closer towards the door. It was hardly worthy of notice, he reflected. So why was he still feeling the aftereffects of an adrenaline rush? Why was the anger still burning hot in his chest?

5

As he slid out of bed, he was careful not to wake Sarah. He headed for the home office and sat at the computer desk to pay some bills. Wandering to the living room, he watched part of a special on uncovering the lost city of Troy. He ate a waffle. Ralph, faithful dog that he was, sprawled across Daniel's lap and enjoyed being scratched behind the ears.

On his way back to bed, Daniel walked to his son's room and stood watching the boy sleep. He'd already checked on Kris when he and Sarah had gone to bed. The child lay peacefully on his back, yet Daniel was anxious. Any other time, he would have felt embarrassed at his unnecessary worry concerning Kris, but the dream had left behind a strong sense of uneasiness. Daniel examined the lock on the boy's window and kissed him lightly on the top of his head before returning to his own room and his own bed.

He stared at the ceiling and tried to imagine the other sons and the daughters that he and Sarah would never have. The complications resulting from Kris's premature birth had ended their dreams of having a large family. He wished he could say that his visit to the surgeon for a vasectomy had severed more than their physical ability to procreate. The longing remained, even as the brain never strayed far from the truth.

Movement from beside Daniel jarred him back to the immediate reality of his life. Sarah had turned in her sleep, and the glow from the nightlight in the bathroom cast menacing shadows about her. She looked cold, so Daniel covered her with the bulky white comforter. He wanted to wrap himself around her, but that would only wake her. She couldn't sleep and be held at the same time. He contented himself with lying on his side facing his wife.

Tomorrow, he thought. *Tomorrow I'll take her to the bridge.*

Part One - 1970

Chapter One: Meeting Daniel

"Ah," Tristan sighed with contentment and lazily dragged a French fry through the tiny puddle of ketchup on his plate. "That was good, wasn't it?"

"Mm-hm!" Sarah nodded enthusiastically, her ponytail bobbing up and down with the motion. She took a final sip of the root beer float and listened to the whistling sound as the straw sucked up air instead of drink. "I like cheese."

Tristan smiled across the table at his seven-year-old daughter and asked, "Is that all you noticed? You know there was some meat and bread involved and mayonnaise, lettuce, and tomato."

"Oh, Daddy!" she giggled. "I liked all that too, but it wouldn't have been the same without the cheese."

"No, I guess not." Her father wadded up his napkin and tossed it onto his empty plate before asking, "You almost ready?"

Elvis crooned from the jukebox as they left the Frostop. It was July in Baton Rouge, Louisiana. Not surprisingly this meant the residents had to endure sweltering heat with high humidity. Both Sarah and Tristan had dressed comfortably in shorts and t-shirts, but it wouldn't be long before they'd be dripping with sweat again. Tristan tied his shoulder-length auburn curls back with a black cord, and they set out.

Father and daughter walked hand in hand until they reached Government Street. They meandered past the little shanty houses of the neighborhoods, stopping in front of the Courthouse so that Sarah could remove a pebble from her left tennis shoe. Once the offending rock had been shaken out and tossed near a bush, they continued on. When they reached North Street, Tristan hesitated.

"We could go left by the Old Capitol and the train station, sit on the levee, and watch the Mississippi River for a while." He pointed across the street and proposed, "Or, we could go into downtown and see what we can see."

"Let's go downtown. We went to the levee last time."

They walked down Lafayette Street past the old silo, office buildings, warehouses, and the Capitol House Hotel. Following a straight path, they crossed Florida Boulevard and wandered aimlessly until they reached Latil's and went in to browse through the school supplies that were neatly arranged on green metal shelves. After purchasing a five-cent eraser that was shaped like a puppy, they headed towards the drugstore on the corner.

Tristan didn't bother scrutinizing the marquee at the Paramount Theater since he didn't have the time or money to spare for the features. Instead, he and Sarah wound their way back to North Boulevard. His throat was parched, and Sarah's face was red from the heat. They purchased a Coke from the City Newsstand and shared it in companionable silence as they passed the Old Post Office.

In a building adorned with a sign that read "Collective Expressions," the pair got a taste of what it must have been like to experience shopping in a bazaar. A plethora of artists displayed their works and wares. Tristan struck up a conversation with an artist named Benjamin that lasted for over forty minutes.

Eventually they emerged, blinking in the light of the ordinary world. Sarah complained that she was tired, so her father lifted her up into his arms. They pressed on until they stood in front of the Pentagon Barracks.

"Daddy, what is *pentagon*?"

"Basically, there were five buildings here."

"But there are only four."

"That's true. One was destroyed by fire at some point. Soldiers were stationed here."

The buildings stood vacant and baleful in the July heat. Mosquitoes buzzed noisily around the few tourists who had come to examine the ruins.

"Not much to look at, is it?" Sarah declared tiredly. "Can we go see the flowers now?"

The garden in front of the Capitol was well-tended and included shaped hedges, trees, and seasonal flowers. People crisscrossed the grounds on the interlacing sidewalks and rested on several concrete benches. A huge statue of Huey P. Long dominated the center. Sarah bit her lip nervously when they read that the former governor's body had been laid to rest there after his assassination.

"Our Capitol building is a marvel, both inside and out," Tristan informed his daughter. "I've always loved it, even before I started studying architecture. It's the tallest Capitol in the United

9

States. You see those carvings on the façade? You know why they're there? No? Because it was done during the Depression, and the craftsmen and artists came from all around and did a great job. We get to benefit from what they did."

"So, if they got to work, then why were they depressed?"

"No, no. It was during the Depression. That was a time in U.S. history when the economy…" He struggled to find words she could understand. "Lots of people were poor because there was little money and few jobs. For good or bad, it gave the country cheap labor to build things like the Hoover Dam and our Capitol. People were desperate for money."

"You mean they were poorer than we are?"

Tristan almost stumbled. Almost. He led Sarah to a nearby bench and pulled her up onto his lap.

"You think we're poor?"

"Aren't we?"

"What makes you think that?"

She shrugged, and Tristan wondered what exactly the other children in Sarah's school had to say about her station in life. She seemed to be well-liked by her peers, but he knew that several of their parents had made comments about him within his hearing, and he worried that some of their children were repeating these comments to his daughter.

He knew that they didn't actually have to say anything for Sarah to deduce that she was, indeed, worse off financially than all of her classmates. She heard them talk about their vacations, their toys, their houses, and their pets.

"We have more than others," Tristan said finally. "Some people don't have food to eat or a place to live. Some don't have a coat in the winter. Some sleep on the floor because they have no bed."

"So, we're less poor than some people?"

He sighed. He wanted to tell her what being destitute was really like the way that he had lived it. She was too young for that. There was no need to make her feel any less secure about life than she already did.

"It's okay, Daddy. Don't feel bad. I don't mind."

She squirmed out of his lap and ran towards the steps that led up to the front doors of the Capitol.

"Daddy, look at this! There's writing in the steps!"

Tristan suppressed the urge to go over to his child and continue their talk about money. He decided that it would be better to leave the topic alone for now. He couldn't lie to her and tell her that he wasn't struggling to keep them afloat financially. She would see the deception in his eyes.

"Each step is engraved with the name of the individual states and the date of their inception into the Union."

"What does that mean?"

"When they became states."

"I bet I can run up all the steps faster than you can!" cried Sarah, as she proceeded to get a head start.

There was never any doubt as to who would win the race. Sarah's agility was no match for Tristan's long legs.

"Just once you could let me win a race!"

"Wouldn't be right," Tristan panted. "How could you enjoy winning when you knew I'd thrown the race?"

"Maybe I wouldn't, but how will I know if I never get the chance to find out?"

Inside, the first floor was a treasure trove of marble and bronze. The tour of the House Floor was brief, but it included a trip to the balcony that overlooked the empty chamber.

Tristan muttered, "I wish the House were in session, so we could see them in action."

"What do they do?"

"Make laws. Change laws. Argue a lot."

"I don't see how that would be any fun."

"You'd be surprised," quipped the tour guide behind them. "It can be quite entertaining."

Sarah looked doubtful, but simply nodded and asked the man, "Can we get to the top from here?"

They rode one elevator to the twenty-fourth floor, then were asked to take another miniscule elevator up to the twenty-seventh.

"Why do we have to switch?" Sarah asked a security guard on their way to the top.

"The cable's not long enough to reach all the way," he explained. "You wouldn't believe the size of the room downstairs that holds the elevator cables."

The view from the observation deck was breathtaking. Extending all the way around the pinnacle, the deck provided spectacular views of the Mississippi River, the front garden, the Capitol Lakes, and the rest of the city as far as the eye could see. The wind whipped fiercely at their hair and took their breath away. A light summer rain fell, cooling their skin and refreshing their souls. They went round and round several times before taking the two elevators back to the first floor.

At 4:00, Tristan conceded that it was getting late. He hated to break the spell of the afternoon. He'd enjoyed an entire day of true relaxation and the aura of peace, the first he'd had in many, many months. He and Sarah reluctantly started the trek back towards the university. They agreed to take the long way home.

Actually, any way they went would be the long way home. It was more than two miles from downtown Baton Rouge to their little rented house outside the gates of the Louisiana State University. The tall office buildings jutted up around them, providing them with some shade. Steam began to rise from the pavement as the earlier rain evaporated in the summer heat.

They decided to cut through behind some of the shops and clubs. It was a path they'd never taken. Sarah slipped her small, soft hand up into Tristan's warm, rough palm, and his fingers closed around it. She was safe, a tiny fairy protected by her own personal giant.

As they passed behind one particular bar, the door swung open with a *blam!* and a boy emerged into the alley. He held the heavy door open with his backside while he dragged out some large cardboard boxes. Unfortunately, one of the boxes became wedged between the doorframe and the boy's thigh, and he was forced to stop. He stared at the box, unsure as to what course of action to take. The door wouldn't open any further.

"Need a hand?" Tristan offered. "Or a foot or something?"

The boy jerked up with genuine fear clearly evident in his expression. Tristan frowned. He knew that he was an unusual-looking man with his Lakota features, auburn hair, and hazel eyes. At six foot seven inches, his height could be intimidating, but the kid looked like some cornered stray dog. Well, he was stuck, come to think of it.

"Hey, if you want us to move on, it's no big deal."

He smiled, as the boy glanced down at Sarah. Tristan couldn't imagine that they appeared to be too threatening.

"No...I *could* use a little help." Then, he said more firmly, "Thanks."

It was not as easy as Tristan had thought it would be. They tugged, wiggled, kicked, and pushed the box. Eventually, it caved in under their assault, and they were able to drag it out to the dumpster. Tristan noted the number of boxes there. At one time, all of them had been filled with liquor bottles. Most had already found their way into the large waste bin. The child had probably been responsible for their disposal.

"Thanks," repeated the boy.

"No problem," Tristan assured him. He wiped his grubby hands on his cut-offs then held out the right one. "My name's Tristan Maes. This is my daughter, Sarah."

The boy rubbed his own right hand on his shirt, then on the leg of his jeans. Finally, he must have decided that it was as clean as it would get and extended it. "Daniel Samuels."

From inside the bar, a deep male voice growled, "Danny! Damn it, where in the flaming hell are you?"

Daniel stiffened, and the frightened look Tristan had seen earlier returned.

"I have to go," Daniel mumbled, looking at his feet. "Thanks again."

Tristan doubted seriously that Daniel should be in the establishment. He appeared to be about fourteen years old, although Tristan sensed that he was slightly younger, perhaps eleven or twelve. As the boy pulled on the handle of the metal door, Sarah called out, "We'll see you again?"

He hesitated, turning slightly in their direction before answering, "Yeah, maybe so."

Tristan hoped that his little girl hadn't seen the fading bruise that was on the boy's left cheek.

Chapter Two: Reflection

Tristan and Sarah walked down Highland Road, past the television station, the hardware store, and the bank. They stopped at the A&P for a head of lettuce, a tomato, and a box of macaroni and cheese. Tristan knew that Sarah wanted some ice cream from Baskin Robbins, but she didn't say a word. They'd already had the cheeseburgers and root beer floats for lunch at the Frostop and had shared the Coke they'd bought at the City Newsstand in the afternoon. Still, he felt bad and almost detoured into the ice cream parlor, but he really didn't have the extra money to spend. There were cookies at home, he reasoned.

The image of Daniel Samuels's purple cheek continued to disturb Tristan as he prepared supper for himself and his own precious child. He boiled the macaroni and some hot dogs and washed the lettuce for salad, but every act was automatic. His mind was worrying over the boy, and he wasn't paying attention to what he was doing. Halfway through chopping up the hot dogs and adding the pieces to the macaroni, he cut his finger deeply and had to stop and search for a bandage. The finger throbbed all during dinner, but it wasn't enough to stop him from obsessing about the boy and the bruise.

The problem of Daniel Samuels bothered Tristan as he sat with Sarah in the faded, overstuffed chair and read her a chapter from *A Little Princess*, and it bothered him long after he had tucked her into bed and watched her fall asleep. He looked down on her, the light from the street seeping in through the shade and casting an eerie glow on her skin. Her auburn hair spilled over the pillow and the white lace edging her nightgown ruffled in a circle around her neck.

When his vision blurred with tears, he turned away and began to wander the house. He felt the sudden need to take stock of what he had invested in the place. At least that was what he told himself. In reality, he needed some kind of distraction. Anything to divert his thoughts away from the meeting with Daniel.

Tristan walked down the hall, unlatched the screen door, and pushed against it, emerging on the front porch. He could just make out the glow of the lights from the filling station down the street.

Cars were passing, and his neighbors were coming and going from their apartments and houses. Someone was singing in a drunken baritone in the direction of the university.

Leaning against one of the posts, Tristan studied the exterior of the house. It must have been a nice gray color before time had begun to peel the paint and chip some of the stones. It was still solid, if not attractive. It would need some major repair work soon, but he doubted that the owner would be willing to put forth the amount of money necessary to truly renovate the property.

He walked back inside and entered the living room. The previous tenant had painted the walls a deep blue. It wasn't bad and actually complemented the faded, old, plaid couch he'd inherited from a neighbor who'd moved away the previous year. The bulky flower-patterned chair in the corner could almost have been considered a loveseat. The little black-and-white TV sat on an orange crate across from the couch. A square coffee table and the bookcases had come with the house.

Tristan went across the hall into his bedroom, ostensibly to retrieve a book he'd left on the floor next to his bed. He had been lucky enough to find a decent queen-sized mattress, box spring, and frame at a garage sale for fifteen dollars. There was a built-in shelving unit in the closet, which was good because the bed took up most of the room. A lamp rested on the little stool that was against the wall.

Book in hand, Tristan returned to Sarah's room to check on her. She was sleeping soundly in the twin bed, which was crowded by a three-shelf bookcase and a bedside table. She was guarded by a poster of John, Paul, George, and Ringo on one wall. What few toys and dolls she had were all neatly arranged in their usual spots. They stared blankly at him in the darkness.

He went past the bathroom into the kitchen for a snack. The tile floor was cool under his bare feet. Tristan laid his book on the enormous cable spool that served as a table and opened the refrigerator, bending low to peer inside. He rummaged around, then settled on milk and some of the chocolate chip cookies that he and Sarah had made the day before. Sitting at the kitchen table, he ate and then worked on a paper he'd been writing about safety regulations and building structures. He couldn't get Daniel's face out of his head.

Tristan was now almost certain that Sarah had seen the purple mark. She hadn't mentioned it, but she'd been unusually quiet all evening. She'd also asked her father to stay with her until she fell asleep, which was not part of their normal routine. He sighed and went to wash the dishes in the sink. Later, he went to bed, but not to sleep – not for a long time.

Two days later, he and Sarah caught the bus that would take them down Highland Road to Maxwell Nash's home. Every summer weekday morning, he dropped Sarah off at his friend and benefactor's house so that he didn't have to drag her to school with him. He knew that Max's housekeeper, Lillian, would take good care of his child and that Sarah would be a lot less bored at the house than she would be doodling in one of his classes.

As the bus barreled down the street, Tristan debated on whether or not he should mention the incident with Daniel Samuels to Max. Peripherally, he was aware that they were passing West Parker, then Lee Drive. Sarah stood on one of the blue plastic seats and reached for the cord above their heads. Tristan steadied her so that she wouldn't go flying when the bus driver put on the brakes.

Maxwell Nash's house was older, large, and dignified, just like its owner. The dwelling sat on a sizable piece of property, as did many of those older homes that lined Highland Road. A long driveway guarded by two rows of crape myrtle trees led up to a garage on the left side of the house. The house itself had two stories and was painted white. The shutters were green, as was the trim. A wooden porch ran along the front of the house.

Tristan and Sarah went in through the unlocked front door. Sarah's tennis shoes squeaked on the hardwood floor as they passed the living room and dining room. Once Tristan had gotten his daughter seated at the kitchen table, he went off to find Max. He didn't have much time before the bus would be making its return trip towards the campus. He found the man in his office and proceeded to give him the essential details of what had transpired Saturday afternoon.

"I don't know what to do," he concluded. "I don't know what the real situation is. He could have slipped on something and hit his face by accident. It could be any number of things."

The psychiatrist, who was in his mid-fifties, tall, and rather portly, leaned back in his chair and stroked thoughtfully at his gray beard.

"Do you really believe that?" Max asked mildly in his soft British voice. "At any rate, he shouldn't be in the bar during business hours."

"True." Tristan looked at the clock and said, "I'm going to miss the bus if I don't get going."

"Go, then. We can discuss this further when you come for Sarah in the afternoon. It's over a mile back to campus, and I'm not yet ready to leave. You'll be late for class."

Tristan hurried back into the kitchen, where Sarah was enjoying some scrambled eggs with ham on toast that Max's African-American housekeeper, Lillian, had made for her. He bent to kiss the top of his daughter's head, picking up his book sack at the same time.

Lillian looked askance at him and said, "Tristan, you have got to eat *something*."

"I'm already running behind. If I stick around to eat breakfast –"

"You *have* to eat something. You're too thin as it is. If there were a strong gust of wind, you'd be blown away. Wait just a minute."

Ignoring his attempts to argue, she turned her back to him and proceeded to put some of the egg mixture in between two pieces of toast. Tristan studied her with appreciation as she wrapped the sandwich in a piece of aluminum foil.

Lillian Johnson had dark brown skin and eyes the color of milk chocolate. Tristan estimated that she was perhaps ten years older than he was, which would mean she was thirty-four years old. Most of the time she acted like an old mother hen.

Tristan often wondered why she'd taken this job. Admittedly, she was an excellent housekeeper, and Max seemed to be an excellent boss. However, she was young and attractive and her living there with Max wouldn't lend itself to an active social life. She was isolated at the house. Maybe for some reason she preferred it that way.

She held out the sandwich to him as he headed for the back door then declared, "I expect you to eat this."

He grinned and said, "Yes, ma'am. No coffee?"

The door slammed behind him before the hand towel had a chance to make contact with his chest.

Sarah ate her last bite as her father ran back to the street. She picked up her plate and cup and took them to Lillian, who was washing dishes and pans in the sink. The woman's head was bent down, her elbows out, as she scrubbed at a particularly difficult spot on the iron skillet. Sarah watched her for a moment before asking, "Can I go watch TV in the living room?"

Lillian glanced at the child then went back to scrubbing.

"*May* I. And, yes, but not for long. I have to save the dishes when I'm finished washing them. Once they're put up, we'll go. We have some shopping to do today. I thought we might go to the park afterwards."

Sarah skipped off towards the television set, but she was interrupted by the sound of a knock on the front door.

"It's me, Dearie," came a familiar voice.

The little girl swung open the door. That morning, CoCo Genevieve had outdone herself. The woman, who appeared to be slightly older than Tristan, wore a hodge-podge of clothing and jewelry even more outrageous than usual. She had donned plaid pants, a flowery shirt, a broad-brimmed hat, and tennis shoes with orange laces. Pink earrings and bracelets completed the ensemble. She *whooshed* in and gave the child a pat on the head and a piece of candy, which Sarah put in her pocket. She would throw it away later. Who knew how long it had been in Mrs. Genevieve's purse?

"Sarah?" Max called from his office.

"It's okay, Max," she called back. "It's just Mrs. Genevieve!" She turned back to the woman standing behind her and said apologetically, "I'm sorry. I didn't mean it was *just* you."

"Oh, it's quite all right." The color disaster flounced off in the direction of Max's office. "I know what you meant. By the way, I *adore* your outfit. I'll be back in a flash!"

As the office door closed behind the woman, Sarah looked down at her own clothing. That morning, she wore a sleeveless loose orange top and a pair of blue shorts. She would have thought her outfit a little too tame for Mrs. Genevieve's taste.

CoCo Genevieve had the great distinction of being one of a select group of patients Max saw at his home office. He normally conducted his psychiatric work at an office downtown, but Mrs. Genevieve was an exception. She was his nextdoor neighbor. Also, her husband didn't allow her to drive, which was probably for the best.

Twenty minutes later, Lillian sang out, "Time to leave, Sarah! Are you ready?"

Sarah turned off Mr. Green Jeans's conversation with Captain Kangaroo. She slipped on her tennis shoes and scooted out of the back door with Lillian behind her. They walked around to the garage and got into Lillian's gold Ford Galaxy.

"Sarah, I thought maybe we'd go look for your father's birthday present today. There's less than a week until the seventeenth, and I don't think we'll have time to shop for it again before then. Besides," Lillian went on before the little girl could protest, "you already have four dollars and seventy-five cents saved up. If you need a little more, I can lend it to you until you get your allowance this Friday. How's that?"

Sarah felt a surge of gratitude and wrapped her arms around the housekeeper's waist.

"All right then," said Lillian, putting her arms briefly around Sarah. "We'd better get going."

Sarah knew exactly what she would get her father. They had seen it while they were out on their Saturday adventure. She even had enough money. Well, she would if Lillian would advance her a few cents.

They headed downtown. Lillian needed gas for the car, so they tanked up at the Esso station. The dry cleaning was ready to be picked up at Kean's. There was a book on hold for Max at the LSU Bookstore. A deposit had to be made at the bank.

At last, Lillian pulled the car over on North Boulevard near the Old State Capitol, and she and Sarah set off on foot. It was almost 11:30, so they stopped to have an early lunch at Stroube's Drugstore. Sarah ate her sandwich in a rush, as usual. Lillian fussed a bit but relented and let her order a second Coke to drink while she finished her lunch.

When they set out once more, there was a breeze. It helped to cool them down a little, but the humid air was sticky and thick. Lillian plucked at the front of her dress and peeled it away from her skin as Sarah led her down North Boulevard past the historic

Old Post Office. There, she came to a sudden halt and asked, "Isn't this a nice building? Don't you like the columns and all the carvings?"

"I suppose it is nice. I've never really paid much attention to it before."

"What do you like about it?"

"I like the way it's covered almost completely by vines. It used to be City Hall for a time."

"Daddy said they sold it to a men's club. What's a men's club?"

"It's a place where only men can go. They can eat, read, or play cards together. Whatever they like they can do that there, either alone or with other men. I read a murder mystery once that took place in a men's club.

"Why can't women go?" Sarah asked with a frown. "Is there a women's club?"

"No, I don't believe so."

"But that's not fair," Sarah persisted as she took a few steps away from the building.

"No, it's not. Now, let's hurry and get wherever we're going."

Chapter Three: Collective Expressions

Sarah and Lillian eventually arrived at a doorway that had the words "COLLECTIVE EXPRESSIONS" painted on a sign above the transom. As they walked inside, Lillian was openly amazed.

"I never suspected that a place like this existed in Baton Rouge."

They edged forward, stopping frequently to admire the artwork and handmade goods for sale. There were rugs and blankets and pottery and sculpture and paintings.

Finally, they came to one particular artist, a man with long, black hair braided into a plait down the center of his back. Sarah and Tristan had seen him work two days before and had talked with him at length while he was in-between customers. Tristan had commented on the man's talent, and the father and daughter had been granted the honor of viewing some of his other artwork. Sarah had never met anyone who could draw as well as he did.

"It's here," Sarah whispered, as she turned to Lillian. "If it's still okay for me to borrow the money, then I'd like to get him to draw my picture. I won't be able to pay you the whole twenty-five cents for two weeks though."

Lillian seemed surprised but said, "A portrait would be perfect, Baby. I think your daddy will be real happy with that. Now, go on."

Tentatively, Sarah approached the young man, who was deeply involved in a sketch of a couple who was obviously in love and obviously just passing through. She waited until he'd finished, and the couple had made off with their prized portrait.

"Benjamin?"

He smiled broadly when he saw her and exclaimed, "Sarah! Good to see you, Darling! I didn't figure I'd see you again until next weekend, though. I thought your dad had work and school."

"He does," she admitted. "I came with Miss Lillian. I stay with her and Max every day during the summer when Daddy's got class and I don't have school."

Benjamin rose and took Lillian's hand in his. He leaned forward and brushed his lips against it.

21

"Enchanté," he breathed with a flourish. When Lillian blinked in surprise, he raised his eyes to meet hers and grinned. She couldn't help but smile. He was utterly irresistible, and he knew it.

"The pleasure's mine, Mister...."

"Benjamin will do nicely, but if you must know the last name's Milan." He returned his attention to Sarah and asked, "Now, little princess, what may I do for you?"

After she'd given him an explanation of her intentions, she asked uncertainly, "Should I...fix myself up or something?"

"Why would you need to 'fix yourself up'? You look beautiful! How about sitting on that stool there, and we'll get started."

The process took all of fifteen minutes. When the work was completed, Benjamin signed it with a sweeping script. Sarah got up and moved around to see the finished product.

"Do you still think it'll be a good present, Miss Lillian?" she asked expectantly.

Lillian moved closer and studied the portrait.

"Well, Miss Lillian?" Benjamin prodded. "What do you think?"

"It's amazing," she murmured before blurting out unexpectedly, "What on Earth are you doing here?"

Benjamin laughed, and Sarah smiled at the woman's obvious and uncharacteristic embarrassment.

"Darling, I've asked myself that a thousand times before. I'll get around to leaving the shop someday. Right now, my lady and I are happy here."

"Lady?"

He laughed again when Lillian's expression reflected embarrassment for a second time. Sarah was confused but was reluctant to ask for any clarification. Perhaps her father could explain it to her later.

"I – I apologize," Lillian stammered. "I thought –"

"Don't be sorry, Dear. You weren't far off. I do so enjoy the best of both worlds, you know."

"I...see."

"Where is your lady friend?" Sarah piped in.

They followed his finger with their eyes to a stall approximately thirty feet away and saw a lanky, young blonde woman with a remarkably sweet face and extremely pale skin.

"Her name's Halley," Benjamin volunteered. "Would you like to meet her?"

"Miss Lillian?"

"All right, but we can only stay for a little while longer. I don't think we'll have time as it is for the park."

"That's okay. I want to meet Halley."

As Sarah paid Benjamin for the portrait, he suggested, "All I ask of you is that you get a nice frame for it."

"I don't have enough money for a frame, too."

"Don't you worry about that," Lillian said behind her. "Max and I didn't know what we were going to get your daddy for his birthday. I think that we might be able to buy the frame and have this wonderful picture ready in time. If you don't mind, that is."

Lillian seemed to take the hug for a "yes," and Benjamin carefully prepared the portrait for travel. After handing it to the little girl, who gingerly accepted it, he walked with them to Halley's stall.

Lillian looked dubiously back to his area and asked, "Aren't you worried that someone will take your things?"

"Oh, heavens, no! We watch out for each other down here." He rounded the front of the stall and went over to greet and kiss the young woman. "I'd like for you to meet Sarah and Lillian. Remember I was telling you about Sarah and her dad last night?"

"Of course. Great to meet you."

She rose to greet them, then paled and pitched forward. Benjamin caught her elbows and lowered her into the chair.

Sarah watched as the housekeeper jumped into action. Super Lillian! Sarah would have giggled, but Halley looked sick and probably wouldn't have appreciated her humor.

"Are you ill?" Lillian put one hand on the girl's back and rested the other on the edge of the table, which was full of hand-embroidered pillowcases, napkins, and tablecloths.

Halley swayed and closed her eyes for a few seconds then slowly opened them. Sarah was concerned that the girl was going to faint, but she merely sat and seemed to struggle to regain her equilibrium. Benjamin knelt to one side of the chair and spoke

23

soothingly in her ear, slipping his arms around her shoulders. As Halley folded into his embrace, Lillian pulled a dollar out of her purse and handed it to Sarah, who was becoming increasingly alarmed.

"Baby, would you go get her something to drink? There's a man right over there who is selling sodas."

Reluctantly, Sarah tore herself away from the stall and found her way to the vendor. She felt Lillian watching her as she asked the man for Halley's drink. He looked up sharply and gave her a cup without taking the money. Then, he followed her back to Halley's stall.

Sarah held out the cup of 7-Up and asked, "Will this make it better?"

"Thanks so much. Halley, look. Sarah's brought you something to drink. Why don't you give it a try?" he coaxed. As she accepted it in trembling hands and took a small sip, he said, "That a girl. Try some more."

"Benjamin," interrupted the drink vendor. "Do y'all need anythin'?"

"No thanks, Man," Benjamin insisted. "I think she's pushing herself too hard. I'll get her home in a few. I'm going to pack my stuff. I'll be right back. You stay put, Halley."

Lillian regarded Benjamin's back as he walked away from them. After a slight hesitation, she turned to Sarah and said calmly, "You stay here with her. I'll go help him pack up, so they can get home sooner."

The little girl made a noise that denoted agreement, and Lillian set out in Benjamin's wake. Once Sarah saw that Halley was surrounded by other concerned adults, she followed silently.

"Mr. Milan," Lillian began. "Benjamin? I think that she needs a doctor. Whatever's wrong could be –"

"We know what's wrong, and she has been to the doctor. He told her to rest for a few weeks, but she's afraid that she'll lose the stall if she stays gone that long. At least the worst is in the past, although she won't get rid of some of the little things she was sewing for it."

"She was expecting?"

"Yes. What business is it of yours?"

"It's not my business at all. I only want to help. I work for a psychiatrist, and I do have some doings with the patients occasionally, even if I am only the housekeeper." She smiled gently and said, "Please, accept my apologies, and let me help you gather all of this up so you can take care of Halley."

"Apology accepted," he grumbled. "Thanks for wanting to help."

As Sarah hovered out of sight, the two of them proceeded to put away the supplies and close up the work area. After about five minutes, Benjamin said, "I didn't want it."

"I beg your pardon?" Lillian's hands were in the middle of hooking a leather strap on a box of colored pencils.

"I didn't want the baby."

Looking miserable, he sat down heavily on the floor and rubbed his eyes with the heels of his hands. When he lifted the hands, blinking away stars, his expression was almost pleading.

"I would have done it for her, but God knows what kind of father I'd have made. Halley takes care of things. Oh, I take care of things in my own fashion, but I'm not very good at the everyday stuff. And I'm not very…loyal." He picked up a brush then threw it down and admitted, "I didn't want her to have someone else to take care of besides me. I'm sort of a handful on my own, and I like our life the way it is."

"Maybe you could talk to the man I work for. He's good at his job, and –"

He shook his head and pushed himself up off the ground. His former disposition was in place, and he said, "You'll have to forgive me, Darling. I don't mean to lay it all out like this. If we had some family it might be different, but our families lost interest in our shenanigans long ago. We'll work it out."

Sarah sneaked back to Halley's stall, as Lillian and Benjamin brought everything to the little blue Volkswagen Beetle parked right outside the back door. By the time they returned to Halley and Sarah, they discovered that some other vendors were helping to take Halley's stall apart.

"We've got it, Benjamin," said a plump woman of about forty. "We'll take it back to my place. Just call me tonight and let me know if you want it all back tomorrow or if I should hold it for now." She gave a quick glance toward Halley and added, "It's no trouble."

"Thanks," replied Benjamin as he crouched in front of his girlfriend. "You ready to go home?"

He slipped one arm under her knees and the other under her arm. He proceeded to lift her with an ease that obviously shocked Lillian.

"I hope we get home soon," Halley said tiredly.

"We'll be there in no time."

"I'm sorry to be so much trouble," she said to everyone gathered around. She looked at Sarah and Lillian and asked, "Would you come see me here again when I'm feeling a little more…when I'm better?"

"We will," Lillian assured her and took Sarah by the hand. "But now it's time to go."

They walked in silence for a while until Sarah finally asked, "Miss Lillian? Will she be all right?"

"He – Benjamin, that is – said that she'd been sick. Sometimes, when you're sick, it takes time."

"Yes, ma'am."

Lillian stopped and exclaimed, "Oh, Baby! You must think I've lost my mind. I know you don't have to be told about that."

"It's okay," Sarah whispered in a conspiratorial tone. "We don't have to talk about it if it upsets you."

Lillian bent down and whispered back, "Thank you. That's very thoughtful."

Since it was mid-afternoon there was not as much traffic, and the drive home passed quickly. After they'd entered the Nash residence, Lillian put the portrait in her own room for safekeeping then returned to the kitchen. Subdued, Sarah wandered through the front rooms of the house. She ended up in Max's office. It was open, and Max wasn't back from work, yet. She sat in the rocker, put her feet on the bar that went across the front, and began to rock.

When Max strode into the house thirty minutes later, she was still rocking, back and forth, back and forth. He observed her from the doorway, as she gazed out of one of the windows at the garden on the side of the house.

Suddenly, without warning, she spoke.

"Why do you have a garden right there, Max?"

"It relaxes me."

He walked over to his desk and sat in the leather chair behind it. He took out a folder from the drawer of hanging files and opened it. Sarah continued to rock.

Max wasn't about to push her to talk. It had taken her almost six months to speak to someone other than her father without being asked a direct question first. When she was ready to talk, she would.

Five minutes passed. Ten. Fifteen. And then the rocking ceased.

A small voice said, "Max, I'm…he…Daddy doesn't take care of himself." As if a locked door had been flung wide, her words tumbled out, stumbling over themselves. "He doesn't eat enough, and he worries so much about everything, and I don't think he gets enough rest, and I think he misses Mommy all the time."

The monologue came to an abrupt halt, as her tiny hands gripped the arms of the rocking chair. Max put down his papers and pen and closed the folder. He walked around the desk and stood in front of her.

"Sarah? Would you like to take a walk in the garden with me? Maybe we can talk better there."

He could sense that she was already wondering if she'd made a mistake in saying as much as she had. He held out a hand to her, and she took it. Together, they went out the side door into the fresh air.

Max's garden was a fairly large one. It was filled with trees, azalea bushes, and flowers of all kinds. Day lilies were clustered cheerfully in a sunny corner near a goldfish pond. Carolina jasmine had crawled up and over one side of the fence, and a little gravel path wound its way around the enclosure. Max and Sarah walked down the path until they came to a bench under a Japanese magnolia.

Once they were seated, the psychiatrist began, "You said that you were worried about your father. That's perfectly understandable. Everything you said is quite correct."

Max crossed his arms over his stomach, lifting one hand to stroke his beard. He didn't want to overload the child with questions, but there were things he did need to know. Part of the agreement with the State stipulated that he ensure the safety of this child. He thought for a moment then said, "Your father worries a lot, Sarah. You're right about that. He wants to take care of you…and everyone else, for that matter. It's the way he is. He's a very responsible man." When she didn't respond, he pushed ahead. "A little too responsible, I admit. He has a hard time letting go of things that he can't change."

"I know." Sarah's eyes were shining with tears as she added, "And I'm the same way."

That brought Max up short. That a child of seven could see that so clearly was quite amazing to him. Parent and child were, indeed, extremely similar in many respects. Their only notable difference lay in their size.

A part of Max wondered if her features were those of her mother. Tristan had never shown him a picture of Emma, and he had not felt it was necessary to ask. Yet, he would have liked to put a face on the shadow of the dead girl.

"My dear, you are a completely different person!" Sarah made to protest, but Max held up a hand. "Please listen. You're correct. You and your father are very much alike, *but* you're an individual, as is he. We all make our own choices. Your father is trying to learn how to deal with his life and the choices he's made in the past so that he can make good choices in the future. Perhaps you'd like to work towards the same end?"

Uncertain and afraid, she kicked some gravel and didn't answer him. Finally, she said, "What if it doesn't work? What if you can't help him or me? What if he –" A tremor began in her lower lip at this point. "What if he dies?"

She burst into tears. Max put his arms out and lifted her until her head rested on his shoulder. He rocked her back and forth gently while she cried. He saw Lillian standing at the window. There was probably someone on the phone for him. He shook his head slightly, and she made an acknowledging movement. Max knew that she would take care of things. He closed his eyes, as the tiny body shuddered against him. The crying slowly ebbed to a trickle then surged once more. He felt her small hands balled up on his back, and his shirt was drenched on one side.

Max opened his eyes… and was startled to see Tristan standing about twenty feet away from where they sat. He must have heard them and come directly around to the garden, for he still carried his book sack on his shoulder. The expression of pain on the younger man's face gave Max a sinking feeling. It also made him concerned.

Max had long suspected that Sarah had been holding back her tears so that she wouldn't distress her father. She desperately needed relief and help, but her need might set Tristan back in his willingness to enter into real therapy. They were so attuned to each other's emotions that it actually interfered with their recovery.

Too much empathy, Max thought ruefully.

Separating them, however, was out of the question. They loved each other fiercely, and they'd already lost so much. If only they could work through this period, Max felt that things would balance out for them. At least that was what he hoped.

Tristan's jaw tightened, and he retreated silently to the house. Max wondered if he hadn't heard the footsteps because of the child's sobs or because Tristan had stayed on the grass instead of walking along the path. No matter. It was irrelevant.

Sarah pulled away from Max. Her face was puffy, and she was in dire need of a Kleenex. Max fished out a clean handkerchief from his pants pocket. She blew her nose obediently and took a shaky breath.

"I hate crying." She wiped at the wetness on her face and explained, "My head gets all stopped up."

Max suspected there were other reasons, but he let it go. When he felt the time was right, he said, "Sarah, I think you should come talk with me in the office on a regular basis. Or we could meet here in the garden if you like."

She was on her feet before he got the last word out.

"I...can't...I...have to go."

She backed away; then he took off for the gate, leaving it open in her rush to escape. Max sighed. What had taken place on the bench was a start, but it was only that – a start.

He returned to the office and listened as Tristan and Sarah left for the day. He sat down wearily at his desk. Lillian came to the door. Was it already time for dinner? He glanced at the clock.

She leaned against the doorframe and dried her hands on her apron. There was not much light in the room, but Max could easily make out her familiar movements.

"Tristan wants to come back tonight after Sarah's asleep. He has a friend with a car who can drop him off."

Inwardly, Max was soaring.

She continued, "I told him that I didn't think that would be a problem, and I'd stay with Sarah as long as he needed."

"You're a good woman, Lillian." He opened a notebook and switched on his lamp before adding, "Thank you."

"Dinner will be ready in ten minutes."

Her smile wafted through the dimness of the room as he bent over his papers, the chain from the lamp still swinging wildly.

Chapter Four: The Step

At 9:15, Tristan stood on the third step leading up to Max's front porch. After passing through the entrance to the house, Tristan crossed the oriental runner and headed for the home office.

A short distance from the door, he stopped and leaned his forehead against the smooth surface of the wall. He couldn't seem to take in enough air with each inhalation. He wanted to go home, but the memory of Sarah clinging to Max in the garden dared him to turn away. He pushed against the wall and forced his feet to move forward towards the half-open door.

Max was sitting in a leather chair reading a book. Tristan cleared his throat, and Max shut the volume and put it down on a side table. *Steppenwolf.*

Tristan hung back in the hallway, unable to go the last few inches into the office.

"I thought you'd be reading something more...clinical. You know, some book of high-brow psychiatric observations."

"And you don't think *Steppenwolf* falls into that category?"

"Is this a trick question?"

Max rubbed at his moustache in an attempt to hide his smile.

"Have you ever read the book?"

"A long time ago. I found it slow."

"You might want to try it again. Books may mean different things to us at different times in our lives. You may find it more interesting now."

"I'll have to check it out sometime."

"Please, come in." Max got to his feet then asked, "Would you like something to eat or drink? I know Lillian's not here, but I assure you that I'm not completely helpless in her absence." When Tristan shook his head and shifted nervously from one foot to the other, he went on, "No? Well, then would you like to talk in here or somewhere else? Perhaps in the living room?"

"Here's fine."

Tristan lowered himself into the largest chair in the room. It was not as comfortable as it looked, although Tristan thought that maybe he would find it more appealing if he was sitting in it

31

somewhere else. He stretched out his long legs, crossing them at the ankles. Then, he uncrossed them and sat up straight once more. He realized he was gripping the armrests and made his fingers loosen a little. Looking at Max, who was sitting patiently in the leather chair, he said, "I don't know if I can do this."

"That won't do," said Max in a matter-of-fact tone of voice. "Do you have any other options? I've been placating the Family Services people for the last six months. We really should get to work."

At the mention of Family Services, Tristan stiffened visibly. A muscle twitched on the right side of his clenched jaw. His fingers wrapped tightly around the arms of his chair. This time, he did not relax them.

He was still so close to collapse, Max realized. Physically, he was much improved, but he needed to find some measure of true emotional peace soon. Max decided that if he didn't force Tristan into going through with this now that it might be too late to find an effective treatment in the future. The bluntness of the next sentence caught Tristan off-guard, which was, of course, the point.

"You've been thinking about death a lot, lately?"

"I could never leave Sarah like that!" Tristan shouted defensively, jumping up from the chair. "Maybe you can waltz around and not get involved, but she's my child, and I could never abandon her by killing myself!"

Max had expected this reaction. He'd anticipated this response since the day he'd met Tristan and Sarah. That was one of the reasons he'd fought so hard to keep them together. Tristan had no independent reason to live. Sarah was what had kept him going.

"Did I mention suicide?"

"No."

"Yet, that's the first thing that came into your mind."

"So?"

"Why don't you take a seat?" Max offered, gesturing offhandedly to the chair.

Tristan glowered at him, but he obeyed, elbows on knees and hands clasped together, his back rigid.

"I don't know what to do," Tristan confided as he steepled his fingers and focused on them. "It's like I'm in a boat in the middle of the Gulf of Mexico, and I can't see any land anywhere. I keep floating around, hoping for a glimpse of something solid. I've got no direction. How can I know what to do when I don't know which way to go?"

"I'll hold up a flag to get you started." Max removed his reading glasses and his handkerchief and began to polish the lenses as he asked. "What sort of baggage do you have in that boat with you?"

The younger man sighed when Max continued to wait then said with annoyance, "What do you want from me?"

"Your history from your point of view."

"Fine," he snapped. "My name's Tristan Maes. I'm twenty-four-years-old, a widower with no family other than my child. I'm getting my degree through the architectural program at the university. I've got student loans and a part-time job."

"Tristan, you must go deeper than that, and you know it."

"You want deeper? Okay. Last year, I almost died of an overdose. Sarah came close to dying of pneumonia because of me."

Tristan shut his eyes and turned his head to the side. He stayed that way for some time and worked at maintaining control. Max reached out and put a hand on Tristan's left wrist. With effort, Tristan didn't pull back. He did, however, sit very still.

"You're not alone, Tristan."

"I thought I could handle things by myself. I'm not sure of anything anymore. Some days, I think it's all in the past. Then, everything comes back to me worse than before."

"And so it goes." Max released his wrist and said, "You're an extremely kind and intelligent man. You've been through quite a lot in your young life. Not many men could have handled everything as well as you have. Other men would envy your strength."

"Oh, sure. All the other twenty-something-year-olds out there would love to have my life. Who needs to be captain of the football team when you can be poor, lose your wife, and just about lose your mind? It's a dream come true. I've done a great job. That's why my life is so –"

Tristan paused. Lillian didn't allow swearing in the house, and he tried to respect that. Despite the fact that she was nowhere around, he did a verbal double-take and continued, "That's why my life is such a disaster."

"I mean it," Max insisted. "But if you don't take time to help yourself, everything else will fall apart. You give so much of yourself, but you don't take enough in return."

"I don't know any other way!" He stood and started to pace around the office, which was cluttered with furniture, books, and the massive desk. "Where do I start?"

Max sat forward in his chair and asked, "What's bothering you the most right now?"

"I don't *feel* right," he muttered. When Max raised an eyebrow, he went on, trying to verbalize a feeling that had previously defied description. "I feel disjointed, isolated, apart." Tristan rested his hands on the back of the large chair and said, "I'm so tired, Max. You know, I feel if I don't do such and such, then it won't get taken care of."

"Then what?" Max prodded.

"Huh?"

"I mean precisely what I said. Then what? If you don't wash the dishes, then what's the worst thing that could happen? If you don't complete an assignment perfectly and on time, then will you be expelled from school? If you –"

"I know!" The volume of his answer startled them both, and he lowered his voice before saying, "I know all that. I can't help it. Sometimes, I'm okay for a short while but not for long. I feel so overwhelmed almost every minute of every day."

"Have you always felt like this?"

"To an extent," he reflected. "I guess I've always been a perfectionist, but I didn't go this far with it. And I never let other people see it, not really. People just thought I was very...determined."

"And you are. But with all the upheaval and change you've had in your life over the last few years, the way you feel now isn't surprising. A "perfectionist" – to use your term – whose ability to control his life has been greatly diminished would feel all of the things you're describing. I believe we can get you back to the point where you can be in control again, although I'd suggest that we work on lessening the...well, teaching you how to not be so hard on yourself all the time. The constant worrying and the suicidal thoughts can be managed by learning how to deal with your anxiety and how to distract yourself."

Tristan didn't look convinced.

"Oh, you'll probably always have certain tendencies," Max continued. "That's part of your personality. However, you must learn to see them proportionately. Why don't you start from the beginning, and let's talk about your life in general. Unless you'd rather call it a night and begin another time?"

The younger man shook his head and moved around to the front of the chair. Once seated, he said, "No. Maybe if I start now, then it'll be easier next time."

"Then tell me whatever you like, whatever you feel is relevant or important to you. If I require more information or am confused, I'll tell you."

Tristan leaned back against the padding of the chair, his head tilted up and his face angled towards the ceiling.

"My parents were Tom and Anne Maes. My father was a full-blooded Lakota Indian who was brought up by the priests and nuns at an orphanage. My mother was a nice, Irish Catholic girl, raised by her good-natured alcoholic father. My folks were honest, hard-working, poor people. They were an odd couple, even on the wrong side of the tracks. It never seemed to bother them, so it didn't bother anyone else in our neighborhood. We had all kinds." He closed his eyes and said quietly, "My father was a carpenter, the best I've ever known. He had a lot of health problems after he got back from fighting in the Second World War. Mom did some sewing to help out with the money. We never really had any – money, that is. My dad couldn't do everything like before the War, before I was born. He and my mother taught me by example and pushed me –"

Tristan's eyes snapped open. He appeared shaken by whatever he'd been intending to say, and Max hurried to reassure him.

"I want to hear how you feel. Don't worry about how you say things or what I'll think. Saying something about your parents that's true, although possibly unflattering, is fine in this room. You aren't being disloyal to them by simply talking about how you felt."

Tristan's shoulders slumped marginally as he said quietly, "They pushed me in school. Hard. They wanted me to do better. They told me that if I worked at it enough, I could be a success in life. I never thought of them as failures. It kind of bothered me to know that my father thought that our life wasn't good enough. We had a happy household, and usually a full one, since we'd sometimes take in boarders or overnighters for extra money."

"What kind of a child were you?" Max queried, his professional curiosity kindled by these revelations.

"A scared one," Tristan replied without hesitation. "I wasn't scared of things like climbing the highest tree or not having any friends. I always had lots of friends and took any chance I wanted. I was scared of my own shadow more than anything. I always had a pretty strong imagination, and at night I'd imagine that the cat on the windowsill must be a vampire coming for me. That sort of scared, you know?"

Max nodded and said, "Yes, actually I do know. I imagined very similar things when I was a child."

Tristan's look of incredulity made Max laugh in spite of himself.

"Yes, me. Psychiatrists aren't perfect. As a matter of fact, some of my colleagues are in more need of therapy than their patients, but you didn't hear that from me." The younger man looked genuinely amused as Max added, "Remind me to tell you about the time that a colleague of mine decided to take up papier mache and proceeded to sit on the floor working away in the back of our van on the way to a conference. It was dreadful. Mannequin arms and legs sticking up all over the place."

That did it. Tristan burst out laughing, really laughing.

"Max, you are too much. Maybe I will take you up on your offer of sustenance. Got any cookies and milk?"

Delighted, the psychiatrist rose from the chair and headed for the kitchen.

"I don't know if I'd consider cookies and milk "sustenance," but you're welcome to them."

As he lifted the cookie jar from the counter, Max said, "Why don't you continue telling me about your childhood? I'm sure you were a straight A student who was involved in many extracurricular activities. I'd wager you were well-liked by both teachers and fellow students."

"You got it, Sherlock. I loved school, sports, and playing with the other kids. When I was seven, my father got this old, beat-up piano from some family he'd done work for. They were tired of it and just let him have the thing. Somehow, don't ask me how, my parents paid for lessons for me. I didn't take them long though. My mother didn't have to make me practice every night. I loved it; I still do. That's why I started Sarah on it when she was little. We'd go to the School of Music on campus, and she'd play and play." He made a choking sound and began to cry as he explained, "She loved it, too."

The psychiatrist put down the container of milk he'd been carrying and came over to where Tristan was seated at the table. Pulling up a chair, Max sat next to him and put an arm around his shoulders. Tristan roughly pushed the arm away.

"Sarah can't play the piano anymore," he said miserably.

Max digested this information for a moment then ordered, "Tell me."

"We were with Jamie."

"Not surprising. He has been your best friend for ten years. What happened?"

"Jamie and I were sitting in the laundromat doing some homework while we waited for the clothes to wash and dry. Sarah was reading and coloring; then I noticed that she was looking funny at my open textbook. I asked her what was wrong, and she said that she couldn't read the page. It was all kinds of equations, and Jamie and I looked at each other, and he asked her if she could read the lines in his book. It was chemical equations, not mathematical like mine. So, she tried." Streams of tears were flowing down his cheeks although his voice was steady. "We could tell she was struggling. So, I told her it was no big deal, lots of grown-ups didn't understand all that, just to read what she saw." Tristan put his head down on top of his arms, which were folded in front of him on the old oak table. "She couldn't read it. It was like her brain wasn't making the connection, like she couldn't process the numbers and letters in the equations. That's probably why she's refused to play the piano since she had pneumonia. I don't think she can read the music anymore."

"Music in its written form has its basis in mathematics," Max remarked quietly.

"She told me she was sorry!" After a slight pause, the younger man went on bitterly, "It's my fault. I let her get sick. She'll hate me for this when she gets older. It's…it's not fair to her. If it weren't for me and what I did, then she wouldn't be like this."

"I think we need to stop here and start here. Let us start with thought stoppage."

The young man sat up, wiping at his cheeks with the backs of his hands.

"What do you mean? What's that?" He looked curious and hopeful, not alarmed. Max's calm words appeared to be having some effect after all.

"Whenever you start to find yourself thinking about something negative that's in the past or that's beyond your control, I want you to redirect your thoughts and focus on something that's positive. For instance, Sarah was sick, and you were most definitely responsible for not noticing how sick she truly was. You didn't do it on purpose; you were very ill yourself. But it happened. It's in the past now, and you can't change it."

"So, whenever I have a bad thought, I become aware of it and think about something else?"

"Precisely."

"It can't be that easy," he said, as the chair scraped along the floor and he got up to pace the kitchen.

"I didn't say it would be easy. However, it will get easier as time goes by." Max turned in his chair to face Tristan as he announced, "That's one point we need to concentrate on. Also, if Sarah's having trouble learning in any area, she needs to be tested. There may be some other problem which can be dealt with by a physician or it may be psychological. Either way, we need to know the extent of her difficulties. When did the incident involving the equations occur?"

"Three weeks ago."

"And you've been worrying about it ever since. Correct?"

Tristan stared at the floor and mumbled, "She won't touch my books now, not even to move them out of the way." He raised his head and looked apologetically towards the seated man before stating, "I'm sorry for crying like that."

"Why are you sorry? Is there anything wrong with crying?"

"Nothing whatsoever."

"Do you tell Sarah not to cry?" Max prodded.

"Of course, I don't!" The suppressed anger was granted a moment's release before Tristan locked it down tightly once again and asked, "You think I say things like that to her? Don't forget to brush your teeth and wash your face. Oh, and while you're at it, don't ever let me catch you crying. Oh, yeah. I say that every morning."

"I don't believe you say anything of the sort. And, yet, today was the first time you had seen her cry since her mother died."

It was said reprovingly and rather harshly. Realization and understanding flowed across Tristan's features, and he whispered, "But I never told her not to cry."

"You didn't have to. When's the last time before this evening that you've cried since your wife's death?"

Tristan didn't answer. He bowed his head and studied his shoes. Finally, he said, "I can't remember. At the hospital?"

There was no movement in the kitchen, although there were vague noises from the yard and the street. A dog barked in the distance. A truck roared by as it passed on the road.

Max remained silent as Tristan made his way towards the back door. The young man stopped with his hand on the knob. Without turning, he said, "If I let it all out now, I'll never be able to stop."

The back to which Max addressed his comments was stiff with resolve.

"If you don't start now, you won't be able to go on much longer."

Chapter Five: A Walk in the Park

Tristan pulled the heavy wooden door shut behind him and let the screen creak closed then descended the steps. His chest hurt. Going around to the front of the house, he walked towards the road. The noise of cicadas was all around. He veered right when he reached Highland, ready to head for home. It had rained while he was in the house, and the pavement was shining under the light of the moon and the occasional streetlamp. It came to Tristan suddenly that his shirt was damp with perspiration and that this was not the result of being out in the muggy humidity of the evening.

He'd only gone twenty feet when he heard a car coming up behind him. Cars were passing infrequently at this time of night, so he knew he had better make an effort to hitch a ride with this one. He held out his arm and stuck his thumb in the air. Luckily, the car slowed to a halt. Tristan bent down to look through the open window. A scruffy-looking blonde man was at the wheel.

"Where you headed?" Tristan asked.

"Morning Glory. Still want a lift?"

"Yeah," he nodded. "My place isn't too far from there. Thanks."

Opening the door, he slid onto the front seat of the Chrysler. The upholstery was torn and the dashboard was cracked. The engine clanked loudly as the driver shifted gears. Despite all of that, the car ran more smoothly than many of the other cars in which Tristan had been a passenger, lately.

"You a righteous guy?" the driver asked.

"Righteous?" Tristan repeated uneasily.

"Do you believe in Vietnam and killing or do you stand behind, like, peaceful protest?"

Tristan took in the green army jacket, the tattered yellow shirt with the smiley face on it, and the torn, brown pants.

"Peaceful protest?" he responded, hoping that this was the answer his host was looking for.

"I can dig it, man. Right on! Peace is the way. Love and a little LSD, too. Makes your brain open to all the possibilities. Right?"

It was a relief when the Morning Glory Avenue street sign came into view. Tristan thanked the man as he got out of the car. After he'd watched the Chrysler drive away, he started off toward Dalrymple Drive.

It didn't take him long to reach the intersection. There, Tristan hesitated. He turned right and walked in the opposite direction from his house. He went down the street following the path by the lakes then through the hollow of the underpass. He finally crossed the street and struggled up the hill into City Park.

His mind was confused by anxious thoughts and strong emotions and, above all, desperation. He knew that what Max had said was the truth. He *was* about to break again. The thought of Sarah's being hurt and alone had been the only reason he hadn't lain down to die. Recently, he'd found himself imagining and rationalizing what would happen to her if he did it, and that frightened him.

He stumbled through the balmy July night, past the oaks and the pine trees. Eventually, he sat on a picnic table. He wished it were longer. All he wanted was to sleep, to find comfort in nothingness. There was no comfort, though. Tristan wondered idly if he would throw up.

Instead, he got down from the table and stretched out on the grass. He laced his hands together behind his head, looked at the clouds, and listened as the owls hooted in the trees. He could hear a radio playing in one of the run-down houses behind the park. There was a gentle wind rising from the lake in front of him, and the sour taste in his throat gradually dissipated.

It seemed strange to be there without Sarah, watching her climb on the metal bars or going down the slides with her. He should be pushing her on the swings, not brooding over whether life was worth living.

"I should get home," he said to no one in particular.

"Why?"

Tristan sat bolt upright. He squinted through the darkness and saw someone moving towards him. The figure was obviously a woman in a white top and long skirt. As she got closer, he began to make out some details.

She appeared to be his age. Well, maybe she was a little younger. The woman was about a foot shorter than Tristan and almost as slender. Her hair was a deep, rich color, but he couldn't tell whether it was black or brown or…. She walked through a patch of moonlight, and he saw that it was red, that deep red that one so rarely saw. It fell in waves down her back. The shirt she wore was tailored, while the skirt was flowing at the bottom.

As she approached, Tristan started to scramble up from his resting place. She held out a hand and put it on his shoulder then insisted, "I didn't mean to disturb you. If you'd rather I leave, then I will."

Tristan extended his left arm, palm open and down, and patted the ground next to him.

"No, please. Stay."

The girl sat, her long skirt covering her feet. After a few awkward moments, she looked at her lap and smiled slightly. Tristan couldn't help but smile, too.

"You're staring at me," she said quietly. "It makes me feel shy."

Before Tristan knew what was happening, he saw his fingertips in the air between them, reaching to brush some hair away from her eyes. Mortified, he let his hand drop to his side. When he made to speak, he found that he had no voice. He cleared his throat.

"I'm sorry."

He directed his gaze at the stars. He felt her fingertips on his cheek. She was stroking the stubble on his face with a light touch. Tristan found the movement arousing, almost intoxicating. After a few minutes, he took his right hand and wrapped it around hers, drawing it down between them.

"Please, don't," he said hoarsely.

He wondered how he must appear to her. He guessed he looked presentable by 1970 standards. She would have been beautiful by *any* standards.

She didn't get up, as he feared she might. Instead, she put her left hand over his right and felt his fingers tighten over hers. Nodding her head once, she said, "My name's Vaughn. What's yours?"

Somehow he managed to say it to her. He was finding it hard to think now. He narrowed his eyes and said, "Are you sure I'm not dreaming?"

She laughed, a soft, delicate noise.

"I don't know if *I* can tell you whether or not *you* are dreaming. But I hope not. I was pretty certain that I wasn't a figment of someone's imagination. I get an electricity bill, and I have to pay rent. I do feel a little lightheaded though. I didn't expect to see anyone out here, especially not someone like you." She looked up at a lone bird perched in a tree across from where they were seated. "You feel right to me." When she shifted her focus to him, she continued, "I'm a little unconventional. I sculpt and paint mostly. How about you?"

Tristan smiled and said, "I made a snake out of Play-Doh once. The only kind of paint I've ever used is finger-paint and interior."

"No, silly." She laughed again, that dainty noise he'd heard from her only minutes before. "Oh, you know what I meant."

"Yes. Sorry. I'm working towards my degree in architecture. I have a student job at the College of Design, too."

"So, who *are* you?"

Tristan pulled his hand from between hers. He plucked a blade of grass from the dirt and examined it thoughtfully.

"You're the second person to ask me that tonight. I really have no idea. I've been struggling to figure it out. I guess more than anything I'm a father."

"That's cool," she said sincerely, but he thought there was a slight waver in her tone of voice. "How many kids?"

"One daughter. Sarah."

"Sarah what?"

"Maes."

She laughed, more freely this time.

"I mean does she have a middle name?"

"She has two middle names, Elisabeth and Anne. My wife and I couldn't decide, so we put both of them in, one for her mother and one for mine. We didn't stop to think that her initials would spell '*seam*'."

An image came to Tristan of his wife, Emma. Her eyes were bright with excitement despite her exhaustion as she held a newborn Sarah in her arms. Emma's hair was damp with sweat, and the exertions of fifteen hours of labor were evident in the dark circles under her eyes. However, her expression was so joyous that she had never looked more attractive to the boy who was her husband. She was telling him something in this vision, but there was no sound.

Something brushed against his left arm. Vaughn had a scarf in her hand and was offering it to him. It took him a minute to figure out that his eyes stung with tears and that she'd seen them.

"No, thanks."

She let her fingers snake up to his neck and stroked his collarbone in what he perceived as an invitation to engage in a more physical encounter. "I can't," he said apologetically. "I have to get home."

"Can't what?"

She looked at him questioningly. He couldn't tell if she was being innocent or coy.

"I thought you…that is, um, that you were interested in…wanting to have…that is, to make love…to me…with me. Oh, hell!" He threw his hands up in the air, then rested his arms on his knees. "I'm such a fool!"

"I would like to," she insisted, as the corners of her mouth turned up. "It doesn't have to be tonight, though. I don't want your daughter to be worried."

Tristan was relieved, although he wasn't sure whether it was because she did want to make love to him or because she didn't expect it from him right away. He hadn't touched a woman since Emma had died. He really hadn't been interested until this night, this girl. He pushed himself up then offered Vaughn a hand. They both stretched, stiff after sitting on the hard ground. Tristan realized that things didn't seem so overwhelming at that moment.

"When will I see you again?" Tristan put a hand to his forehead and muttered, "Jesus, that sounded dumb."

"Hey, it's not dumb at all. How about dinner at my place tomorrow night? I live right down the street on Kleinart. My place is on the second floor of the big two-story to the right at the intersection. Go up the side steps."

Impulsively, she stood on tiptoes and kissed him. There was only a brush of the lips. It was not enough.

Tristan wanted to take a step forward and put both arms around Vaughn's shoulders. Instead, he stepped back and inclined his head toward her then said casually, "Tomorrow would be great. What time is good for you?"

Inside, his mind was screaming *No! You have homework! You need to mop the kitchen floor! Your paper isn't finished!*

"Is 6:00 all right?" As he nodded, she said, "You can bring your little girl if you like."

"I think I'd rather come alone. I haven't...I haven't had dinner with anyone since my wife died."

"You must be starving," she quipped, then covered her mouth in embarrassment. "Oops. I sometimes speak without the help of my brain. No offense."

"None taken. I – I'll see you later. Tomorrow."

Tristan turned and walked down the hill, heading in the general direction of his house. The sky had cleared, and he was aware of the stars winking in the heavens as he meandered back past the lakes, following Dalrymple until he reached State Street.

Halfway down the block sat his little, gray-stone house. When he entered through the front door at 11:43, Lillian was not a happy woman. Max had called after Tristan had left. That had been an hour and a half earlier. She scolded him accordingly for worrying her. After profuse apologies and many thank you's, he saw her to the door. He checked on Sarah then went to the bathroom and stripped off his clothes. Once he'd showered, he put on some shorts and called his best friend, Jamie.

"Hello?" a woman's voice answered.

"Oh, hey. I need to talk to Jamie."

He listened absently as the receiver was put down and footsteps faded. Finally, he heard another set of footsteps approaching, and the receiver was picked up.

"This is Jamie," came a sleepy voice.

"What are *you* doing sleeping at the early hour of 12:30?"

It was a good-natured gibe, but it was actually a valid question. Tristan knew his friend all too well.

"You don't know Bunny. She's wearing me out in bed."

"Bunny? You have got to be kidding me. Tell me you're kidding me. Oh, never mind. I've got to ask you a favor."

"Of course, Man." Jamie yawned loudly. "What do you need?"

45

"A babysitter. I think I have a date tomorrow night." When there was no response, Tristan said, "Jamie?"

"Course." He could hear the pleasure in his friend's voice. "No problem! We can work out the details at lunch, okay?"

What Jamie really wanted to say was "Thank God. It's about time!"

Chapter Six: Sheer Terror

Jamie Nesser, candidate for a Master's of Science degree, was in a foul mood as he waited for his best friend the next afternoon. His blonde hair needed a trim, but he didn't have the money for a haircut. His breakfast had consisted of a slice of American cheese. He considered the professor directing his Master's thesis to be an idiot. He'd only slept for three hours the previous night and was exhausted. Tristan had told him that he'd be a little more rested each day if he stopped having sex with every pretty girl he met. It was probably true, but Jamie had always had a weakness when it came to members of the opposite sex. So many girls; so little time....

Jamie was irritated because Tristan was late. And Tristan was *never* late. Jamie had come to depend upon his friend's punctuality and often used Tristan as a walking indicator of the correct time. Jamie had never gotten around to buying a watch, but Tristan could be counted on to remind him of what time it was and where he needed to be.

He should be here, Jamie thought uneasily. *He sounded good last night. I hope he isn't having a slip.*

Jamie remembered all too well how Tristan had begun to drink heavily and experiment with drugs shortly after Emma's death. His behavior had alarmed even Jamie, who'd always been open to moderate use of those substances himself. He'd tried to talk to Tristan about it, but all of his attempts to help had been rebuffed. He kept going back because Tristan had been his closest friend for ten years and because he was worried about Sarah. He knew that Tristan needed help, but he also knew that Sarah would, in all likelihood, be removed from her father's custody if he sought treatment.

Jamie had done what he could. It wasn't enough to prevent the cataclysm that would nearly destroy them the previous January.

At 2:00 a.m. one morning not long after New Year's Day, Jamie had awakened to the ringing of the phone. When he'd answered it, the sound of Sarah on the other end made his heart pound hard with anxiety. She'd had a slight cold a couple of days before when he'd been at Tristan's. That morning, he heard the congestion rattling around in her chest and the feverish tone in her voice. Almost every other word was punctuated by a series of wheezing, convulsive coughs.

"Uncle Jamie? Can…could you come? I feel so bad. I tried to take some medicine, but the bottle slipped and broke on the floor."

"I'll be there in two seconds, Munchkin." Jamie had licked his dry lips and asked, "Where's your Daddy?"

"I tried to wake him up. He won't."

With the inevitable next series of violent coughs, she'd dropped the phone. Then, he heard only the dial tone.

Slivers of fear worked their way through Jamie's mind and body as he'd run from his apartment on Chimes Street to their house, which was one block over. He'd kept telling himself, "It will be okay. It will be okay." By the time their house was in sight, he was fairly certain that it would not be okay. There were no lights on inside, and one window was open despite the fact that it was below freezing outside. The door was ajar.

Jamie had entered the house with a growing sense of panic. He called out "Sarah? Tristan!" but got no answer. He advanced into the living room and shut the window, although it didn't seem to make much of a difference. No heat was emanating from the floor vents. He'd edged through the house, turning on every light as he went.

He'd found Tristan, his face a horrible shade of gray, sprawled unconscious on his mattress. There was a bottle of whiskey on the floor and some drug paraphernalia on the little wooden stool by the bed. Tristan's breathing was uneven, abnormal. Jamie had reluctantly left him and hurried down the hall.

When he discovered Sarah on the floor of her room, she was shivering violently. Not only was she unbelievably hot, she was also spattered in blood. It appeared to be her own, judging from the looks of the gashes on her legs.

"How?" Jamie had asked aloud. Then he'd remembered about the medicine bottle. He lifted Sarah and ran down the hall to the kitchen. Glass and blood covered one area of the tiles. As he glanced back down the hall, he could see the trail of blood leading to the telephone niche and to Sarah's room. She must have fallen on the glass and crawled towards the phone.

"Oh, Lord."

He'd raced to pick up the receiver, which was beeping noisily on the floor. Jamie had pushed down the button and pressed 0. When the operator came on the line, he'd practically screamed at her, "This is an emergency!" and gave her the address. Then he threw down the receiver, not caring where it landed. Still holding the limp child in his arms, he rushed back towards the bathroom. He couldn't help Tristan right then, but he could try to help Sarah.

Jamie attempted to light the gas space heater three times before succeeding. He'd turned on the shower, regulating the temperature until it was not hot and not cold, but cool. He carefully climbed in and held Sarah under the water. She didn't resist or seem to be aware of where she was as the plaid flannel nightshirt she wore quickly became plastered to her skin. A few wet strands of hair clung to her cheeks, while most of the tangled mass hung heavily over Jamie's arm. Sarah had lain against him with her eyes closed, and her godfather had tried to calm himself by speaking softly and reassuringly to her.

Minutes later, Jamie heard the sirens and called out "In here!" when the front door banged open. The sounds of running feet bounced off the walls in the hallway. The door to the bathroom was flung wide, and the tiny room was quickly filled with medics and policemen.

"Hey!" Jamie shouted. "My friend's in the front bedroom!"

Two of the paramedics retreated from the room. The other two came further into the bathroom with a burly policeman and shut the door. Jamie had made no attempt to hide his fear from them as he explained what had happened. While he talked, the medics proceeded to examine Sarah, who was still being pelted by the spray from the showerhead. Finally, they'd taken her out and begun to get her ready for the ride in the ambulance. Jamie could hear urgent voices and noises near the front of the house.

Another policeman, taller and thinner than his fellow officer, came into the bathroom and said, "We'll go with them to the E.R. I'll see you there."

The burly policeman nodded and said, "I'll only be a few more minutes here." He looked inquiringly at Jamie and asked, "You got a car? I could give you a lift. I'll be waiting outside."

Jamie had run to Tristan's bedroom and stripped off his wet sweater and jeans. His teeth were chattering in the chill of the house, and he knew he had to put on something dry. He tore through the neatly folded and stacked piles of clothing in Tristan's closet. The gray warm-up pants and sweatshirt he selected were too big, but they would have to do.

As the medics covered Sarah in blankets, Jamie had shut off the space heater and checked the house for any sign of an intruder. There was none. Grabbing Tristan's keys from atop the coffee table, he'd locked the door on his way out.

"They went to the General," the policeman had told him, as Jamie climbed into the squad car. "You're lucky they dispatched all available officers and medics to the scene. From what I heard, you didn't tell the operator what kind of help you needed or what the emergency was. Next time, you might want to do that."

"I hope there's never a next time, but thanks."

The hospital ordeal had begun the moment Jamie arrived. He had to give a formal statement to the police, and the hospital staff requested information about Tristan and Sarah. He told them what he could, but there was so much he didn't know, such as Social Security numbers, vaccination information, and Tristan's medical history before age fourteen.

"I wish I could tell you more," Jamie had said to the nurse. "Sarah had the chickenpox last summer. I think Tris said he had the mumps when he was a kid, but I can't be sure. I wish I could do more."

From behind him, a male voice said, "You've done a lot already." As Jamie stared blankly at him, the man added, "I'm Sarah's pediatrician, remember? I believe you brought Sarah in for a throat culture a couple of years ago when her parents had final exams."

"How is she?" Jamie asked as he practically leapt from his chair. "Can I see her?"

"She's very ill. Although the cuts on her legs weren't too deep, she's fighting double pneumonia. Most likely, her temperature was so high at the house that she would have died in her room if you hadn't thought to put her in the shower. I'm certain that you saved her life."

I could have saved her from all of this, Jamie had thought. *Tris, too.*

"So, can I see her?" he repeated hopefully.

"Not until she stabilizes."

"Stabilizes?" Jamie paled and nervously asked, "She could still die?"

"We'll know in the next forty-eight hours. The situation's critical at this point."

"Then I have to see her! She'll think she's all alone!"

"She's not cognizant of anything at the moment. I think it would be better for you if you stayed out here until her condition improves."

"No! I have to go to her! And what about Tristan? Where is he? Why won't anybody tell me where the hell he is?"

"Hey!" The policeman who had given him a ride came forward and took hold of Jamie's arm then said firmly, "If you want to stay here at the hospital, then calm down. Whatever the doctor says goes."

The pediatrician tucked Sarah's folder under his arm and said soberly, "If it looks like she's not going to make it, then I'll send for you."

"And Tris?"

"I'll tell his doctors to do the same. From what I understand, the prognosis is bleak." As he turned to go, he added gently, "Try and get some rest."

For two days, Jamie whiled away long hours and ate and slept little in a hospital lounge, as both Tristan and Sarah hovered near death. On the evening of the second day, Sarah's fever broke, and Jamie was allowed to see her. He stared at her, his once-rosy, once-happy godchild, and he knew that he'd failed her completely. It had been his job to see to it that she was taken care of if anything happened to her parents. He had tried to do the right thing, but there she lay, reproaching him with her small, unconscious form.

Jamie had returned to the lounge in a daze and sat in the first orange plastic chair he'd come upon.

They'll take her away from us, he thought. *If Tris doesn't die before, he'll die when he finds out what happened and that they'll take Sarah away. They'll both be gone, and I'll be alone.*

A hand had come down on his shoulder. Jamie had jumped involuntarily and released a cry of surprise.

"I didn't mean to startle you," said an older British man Jamie hadn't known was there. "You look unwell. Shall I call for someone?"

"No." He shook his head, sending the long, blonde strands in all directions. "No, I –"

He hesitated. What could he say?

"May I?" asked the man, gesturing to the chair next to Jamie. "Go ahead."

At that moment, Jamie didn't care about anything except the loss of his hope. Tristan might live or die. Regardless, Sarah would be placed in some foster home. Maybe when she got better, Jamie could smuggle her out, and they could go somewhere else for a while. He couldn't let her get caught in the system.

"My name's Maxwell Nash. Please call me Max. I'm visiting an old friend today." When Jamie didn't volunteer any information, Max continued, "Dr. Elenstraub and I have known each other since our days at college. We both have a great passion for psychiatry."

"Psychiatry?"

"Did I say something wrong?"

"No, I…it's just that…I'm Jamie Nesser."

As they shook hands, Jamie realized what he must look like to this man. He hadn't bathed or shaved in over two days. He'd had less than four hours of sleep. He was wearing Tristan's clothes.

The middle-aged gentleman seated next to him was impeccably groomed. He was marginally taller than Jamie and much heavier. His black hair was fading to gray. He sported a beard and moustache and a suit replete with tweed vest and bow-tie. Even the way he spoke was refined.

Talk about a clash of cultures, Jamie had thought. *Proper British gentleman meets dirt-poor street-wise smart-ass.*

"Can I tell you the situation? I don't have any money to pay you, but I can't think of anyone else to turn to. I mean, you're a psychiatrist. Maybe you can give me some advice. Things look bad, and, if they go down the way that I think they will, then my friend is going to kill himself. If he lives, that is."

"By all means," Max said seriously. He settled back in the uncomfortable chair and went on, "My chosen vocation is to help people with their problems. I've no monetary difficulties at the moment, so don't concern yourself with that. I'd like to hear your story and help if I can."

Jamie proceeded to tell the stranger what had happened over the last year, starting with Emma's death and ending with Tristan and Sarah's present conditions. Max listened patiently to Jamie's story and assessment of the emotional needs of his friend and his godchild.

When the tale had ended, Max asked, "How did your friend's wife die?"

Jamie's throat constricted, and he found it difficult to speak.

"Emma was my friend, too. More than my friend. We're all family, the only family we've got." He'd raised a hand before the apology could come and insisted, "I know you didn't mean anything by it."

The man nodded and persisted, "How did your friend die?"

"She was hit by a car. The kid had just gotten his driver's license. She was crossing the street to go to class, and he ran a red light. Thank God, Sarah and Tris weren't around to see it."

"I'll talk with my associate here, and we can meet with your friend and his child to discuss the situation. If your instincts are correct, then it would be better to deal with things in a more personalized manner than is customary." Something behind Jamie caught the psychiatrist's eye, and he said, "Ah, here comes the good doctor, even as we speak."

Dr. Isabelle Elenstraub came into the lounge, and introductions were made. She was a middle-aged woman, tiny and professional in demeanor. With her white coat and her light blonde hair in a bun, she carried with her a no-nonsense air of authority. It was intimidating. Yet, when she spoke to them, her voice, heavy with a German accent, was soft and kind. Jamie relaxed slightly.

Max turned to his new acquaintance and said, "I'd like to explain events to Isabelle over dinner. Would you like to join us?"

Before he could reply, one of the nurses hurried into the room. Jamie had dealt with this one several times over the course of his encampment in the lounge. She had been very helpful. Under different circumstances, he would have already asked her out on a date.

"Your friend's conscious," she began. "However, he's in such a state of agitation that the doctor's being summoned. He may have to be sedated."

Panic-stricken, Jamie looked to Max, who said, "I don't think this can wait. Isabelle, would you mind if we saw to things now? I'll give you a brief run-down on the way."

By the time the trio had reached Tristan's room, two orderlies were preparing to strap the young man down to his bed.

"Stop that immediately!" Elenstraub barked.

The tone of her voice left no doubt as to who was in charge in the room. Still, one of the nurses protested. Elenstraub glared icily at her.

"Do you honestly think that this man is strong enough to truly injure *anyone*, himself included?"

They released Tristan, who struggled to turn onto his side and rise from the mattress. When his limbs proved uncooperative, he searched the room with his eyes and found his friend.

"Sarah," he rasped. "Where is Sarah?"

Jamie went to the rail and reached through it to put a hand on Tristan's arm.

"She's downstairs in the pediatrics ward. I saw her a little while ago."

"Is she all right?"

Tristan lay rigid as he waited for an answer. There was a yellow tinge to his skin. In the glow of the artificial lights, it was painfully obvious to Jamie how emaciated Tristan had become. The man's body shook, as if it could barely contain his fear. Jamie didn't want to say the wrong thing and exacerbate the man's distress.

He looked uncertainly at Max. The psychiatrist nodded, and Jamie answered, "She's been sick, but she'll be okay."

Dr. Elenstraub ordered the nurses and orderlies out of the room, as the attending physician entered.

Tristan lay back and closed his eyes.

"They wouldn't tell me where Sarah was. I figured she had died, and they were trying to spare me or something. It's my fault."

Although the man made no movement and shed no tears, the excruciating turmoil that was roiling in him was palpable to those remaining in the sterile room. Max closed the door as Isabelle said to the attending physician, "We have a matter here that needs prompt attention."

"Yes," the doctor agreed. "Let's get down to business before the bureaucrats get involved."

When the four visitors finally emerged from Tristan's room, their faces were grim but determined. They went immediately to Sarah's room, where the child lay whimpering in her sleep. Jamie stroked her hair and kissed her temple.

"Daddy?" she murmured, trying unsuccessfully to wake.

"Shhh." Jamie leaned over the rail and took her hand. "No, Daddy's upstairs. Try to sleep, Princess. I'll stay right here. I promise."

"Jamie?" She forced her eyes to open, although they could hardly widen beyond thin slits. "I saw MaMa in a dream. I kept running to her, but she got further and further away, no matter how fast I ran. I couldn't find Daddy anywhere."

Sarah's eyes closed, and she was silent for so long that Jamie wondered if she had fallen asleep once more. He opened his mouth to say something to Max, but the child began to speak again, not fighting to open her eyes this time.

"Daddy wasn't anywhere," she repeated. "And you were gone, too. I went around and around, but I couldn't find you. Daddy wasn't anywhere. I was so scared. There was nobody left but me...."

She floated back into the realm of dreams, as Jamie laid his head on their clasped hands and cried. Emma's sudden death, the emotional strain of worrying constantly about Tristan and Sarah for weeks on end, the stress of the last forty-two hours, and the lack of adequate food and sleep – it was all finally too much.

The three doctors left the room in order to talk in the hall. The attending pediatrician was summoned, and the group adjourned to a conference room. The Family Services people were not in favor of the proposal that developed during the discussion that had followed, but the doctors were firm in their resolve to implement a workable, personalized plan of action.

Over the next two weeks, it was decided that Tristan and Sarah would leave the hospital in the care and charge of Maxwell Nash. They would stay with him until he deemed them fit to go back to their house. He would temporarily pay the rent and work out arrangements with the university so that Tristan would not lose his student job or financial aid while he took off that semester. Therapy would begin for both father and daughter. If Max was not satisfied at any time with the progress of the arrangement, the social workers would be allowed to remove Sarah from her father's custody.

The only reason Max had been granted this leeway was that the man in charge of Family Services for the parish was a friend who was aware that Max was an excellent psychiatrist and a stickler for honesty. He knew that if Max was not comfortable with the arrangement, then he would say so and let the social workers do what was necessary to protect the child in question.

So, on a sunny February afternoon, Tristan and Sarah were taken home to Max's house and to his housekeeper, Lillian. By early April, father and daughter were allowed to return to their house, in spite of the fact that no serious headway had been made in regards to real therapy. Tristan had started summer school in June, and he and Sarah did seem better.

Even though it was mid-July, Jamie sensed that things were still not quite right. Jamie knew that it was nothing personal, but he felt hurt sometimes by the emotional wall that had risen up between Tristan and the rest of the world. He hoped Tristan would open up about things sooner or later. If he ever seriously suspected that liquor or drugs were in the house on State Street, Jamie wouldn't hesitate this time to tell someone. He would tell Max.

Chapter Seven: Vaughn

Jamie's thoughts were interrupted by Tristan's arrival. Tristan actually looked happy, and Jamie's mood was greatly altered. He couldn't help but grin as he reached down to get his lunch out of his book sack. Tristan sat in the chair, facing him on the other side of the table, and smiled.

This was their spot. It was off to the north side of the Union next to the high glass windows. All of their friends at school knew where to find them at lunchtime, and these people would frequently drop by to talk. Not today, though. Jamie was grateful. He wanted to talk with Tristan alone.

As he unwrapped his sandwich, Jamie said casually, "So, what did you do last night? You sounded pretty wired when you called."

Tristan procured an apple from his bag and took a bite. He unscrewed the top of a small bottle he'd filled with water that morning and gulped greedily before answering.

"I had a very traumatic afternoon then I had an even more traumatic evening." He rested an ankle over one knee before confiding, "I had my first real session with Max."

Jamie chewed more slowly, his full attention on Tristan.

"When I left, I was so confused and stressed that I hitched a ride and ended up at the park. I just wanted to clear my head. While I was there, I met Vaughn."

"So, that's her name. Is she a good lay?"

Tristan balled up his napkin and threw it at Jamie, who ducked accordingly.

"I wouldn't know. Jeez, I only met her last night!" He laughed, then said, "I guess I forgot to whom I was speaking." Raising his hands in the air, he pretended to bow to his friend. "Oh, Great God of Love, I supplicate myself to you and your vast knowledge of copulation! Please accept my meager offering of a Twinkie, the closest thing to a phallic symbol that I possess in my lunch bag."

Jamie laughed until he cried. *This* was Tristan. *This* was his best friend. He wanted to get up and give the man a hug. Instead, he said, "Keep the Twinkie. I have my own." Still smiling, he asked, "What time do you want me at your place so you can meet this Vaughn girl? Maybe you should take your Twinkie with you."

Jamie was incorrigible. That night, he was also punctual.

"I feel like I'm a teenager," Tristan grumbled, as he tucked his shirt into his jeans. "This is ridiculous. I didn't get jittery like this when I *was* a teenager."

"Daddy, why are you so nervous? Aren't you excited?" Sarah held out the leather belt he'd been searching for and reminded him, "It's your first date!"

Tristan smiled down at her. He'd been uncertain as to how she would react to his announcement at breakfast that he was going to have dinner with a woman that evening. She'd received the news with ambivalence and had excused herself from the table. Eventually, she returned to the kitchen and climbed onto her father's lap. Neither of them had said another word for thirty minutes.

Now that the hour of his dinner date was fast approaching, his daughter seemed as happy and anxious as he was.

"What's her name again?" she asked, following him into the bedroom. "Vanna?"

"Vaughn," he answered, slipping on his shoes.

"And she's an artist like Benjamin?"

"That's what she said."

"Can I come with you next time?"

"If there is a next time."

"What do you mean? I thought you liked Vaughn."

Her father looked past her at Jamie, who was grinning in the doorway. His friend said, "Let the Great God of Love explain this one. Get moving before your free ride leaves without you. I wouldn't want your coach to turn into a pumpkin."

"Does my babysitter disappear at the stroke of midnight?"

"The fairy godfather will be here whenever you return."

Tristan was ten minutes early when he arrived at Vaughn's apartment. The house itself was an older two-story structure painted brown with white trim. A set of steps wound around one side and led to a door. He went up the steps and knocked, and a few seconds later Vaughn appeared.

Her dress was short with a row of faux pearl buttons running down the front. The emerald green color was a wonderful backdrop for her red hair and luminescent skin. She wore a small, ornate silver drop on a chain around her neck. Matching silver earrings framed her jaw.

"Hi," he said awkwardly.

"Hi," she replied in kind. "Come on in. I hope you like culinary disasters."

She headed across the room – towards the kitchen, he supposed. Tristan closed the door behind him and followed her.

"Your apartment is cool. It's simple, but...beautiful. The furniture's great. Is it antique? The way you have it arranged, it makes the place seem really spacious."

"Thanks. The people who own it live downstairs. Most of the furniture is theirs. They're a nice, older couple who found the house had gotten too big once the kids moved out. They had the top half renovated so they could rent it out and pull in a little extra money."

Vaughn picked up a potholder from the counter and opened the oven. She peered in and pulled the wire shelf out. The dish inside held some sort of casserole. After pushing the shelf back in and closing the oven door, Vaughn continued, one hand on the counter and the other still holding the potholder.

"I lucked out. They had a really bad first tenant. I told them that I was looking for someplace quiet where I could work. After I assured them that I wouldn't get plaster and paint everywhere, they agreed to rent to me for half of what they'd charged the previous girl. They're sweet. I kind of look out for them, and they seem to be happy with me."

"And is it quiet?" Tristan asked.

"These old walls and floors are so thick that no one hears me, and I don't hear a lot of distracting outside noises unless I open the window. Would you like a look-see?"

She led Tristan around the place, which had hardwood floors and old-fashioned crown molding. Her paintings hung on some of the walls, and Tristan admired them greatly. Her sculptures were in a few choice locations, but Tristan had to admit that he didn't care for them. Whereas the paintings were detailed and realistic, the sculptures were smooth and amorphous.

The master bedroom was large, as was the second bedroom, which was what Vaughn used for her studio. A bathroom lay in between the kitchen and the studio.

Vaughn insisted that Tristan wait in the living room while she got everything out of the oven and refrigerator. He studied the painting that hung on the wall across from the couch. In it, two little girls were standing in the middle of what appeared to be a farmyard. He could see a barn off to one side of the older subject, a dark-haired girl of perhaps ten, who was dressed in jeans, unlaced tennis shoes, and a yellow shirt. The younger girl wore a blue sundress but no shoes. Her hair was a familiar shade of red.

The thing that stood out about the painting was not only the skill of the artist, but also the vantage point given to the observer. The girls were looking up at the viewer through a window on the second floor of what one assumed must be the farmhouse. Anyone standing in front of the painting would feel that he or she was that person calling out from upstairs to gain the children's full attention. It was an unusual sensation.

Vaughn leaned through the archway and called, "Dinner's ready!"

Tristan returned to the kitchen and discovered that she'd put a lace tablecloth on the small table in the corner and had placed candles all over the counter. The overhead light was off, and the candles gave the small dining area a soft glow. It was a nice way to make a guest forget how cramped the dining area was.

He sat down to food that was not unappealing, merely different. Vaughn had prepared ambrosia, some sort of lemon chicken, a vegetable and cheese casserole, rolls, and a carrot cake for dessert. A pitcher of iced tea sat on the counter. As he lowered a peach napkin into his lap, Tristan asked about the painting of the girls.

"Oh, that's me and my sister, Kate. Our personalities are real different, but we've always been close. As a kid, I preferred playing inside, but she was just the opposite. So, we'd take turns doing something I liked, then something she liked. Most of the time, it worked." She spooned some of the casserole onto a plate and explained, "Mom would usually lean out of the window if she was upstairs and there was something she needed to tell Dad, and we'd be the messengers and run out to the barn or the fields." She unfolded her napkin and picked up her fork then paused and admitted, "One night, it came to me that it would be a perfect thing to paint."

They continued to talk in an easy manner as they ate, taking their time with the food and the conversation. When their plates were empty and their stomachs full, they rose and headed back to the living room, leaving the dishes and glasses on the table.

As she walked through the archway, Vaughn asked, "Would you like a drink? I have some wine in the refrigerator."

"No, but thanks." He looked down and said with discomfort, "I don't drink anymore. I used to be...." Tristan thought about his sponsor at Alcoholics Anonymous and a discussion they'd had the week before. "That is, I'm a recovering alcoholic."

Without hesitating, Vaughn said, "Okay. How about a Dr. Pepper?"

Tristan hadn't expected that kind of response. No judgments from Vaughn. It was refreshing, but also unnerving.

"Um, yeah. That'd be great."

"Good. I think I'll have one, too."

When she returned from the kitchen, he said, "Can I ask you something personal?"

"You can ask me whatever you want."

"Okay. How do you support yourself? I know you're an artist, but what do you *do*?"

"You mean, do I have a day job? Yes, I work at a gallery downtown as a receptionist. I do make money off my pieces, but not enough to pay my bills, yet. Someday, I hope."

Vaughn got up and put her *Sgt. Pepper* album on the stereo turntable. They sat next to each other as they listened to the Beatles. Vaughn leaned her head against Tristan's chest, and he moved his arm from the back of the couch to encircle her shoulders. When the first side of the album was finished, they listened to the scratch of the needle for a moment before Vaughn pulled back and got up. Instead of flipping over the record, she put it back in the sleeve.

"Would you mind helping me with the dishes?"

They stood together in front of the sink. He washed, and she dried. As he rinsed off the last plate, Vaughn said, "You're pretty good at this."

"Thanks."

Vaughn lowered the plate into the drying rack and draped the towel over the faucet. She turned to face Tristan and said, "You're so...genuine."

"Genuine? What do you mean? I'm just me."

"You are so open about yourself and your life. It's unusual in people. I do it all the time, and not everybody is comfortable with it."

"I'm open with you. Up until yesterday, I wouldn't say I was very open with anyone, not even myself. I'm pretty messed up, to tell you the truth. I'm determined to change that, though." He shook his head and said earnestly, "You seem uncompromisingly true to yourself."

"Sad, but true," she sighed. "I don't know how to act any other way. Sometimes I wish I were more conventional."

"Don't ever wish that, all right? Conventionality isn't all it's cracked up to be."

They kissed then, and she slid her arms loosely around his waist. He spread his fingers behind her back and drew her closer. Continuing the kiss, he lowered his hands and moved his mouth to the curve of her neck. Vaughn lifted her hands and rested them on his shoulders. He took his right palm and brought it to the front of her dress. Vaughn made a soft "oh" sound.

After a while, he drew back. Vaughn looked a little dazed, and Tristan was finding it difficult to remember what they had been talking about before the kiss. He took her hand and led her to the bedroom. Once there, he undid all the buttons on her dress and let it drop to the floor.

"Tristan, wait. I – I have to go to the bathroom."

While she was gone, Tristan undressed and lay down under the covers. He wanted this very, very badly, not simply because he hadn't had it in so long, but because he wanted it with Vaughn. At the same time he felt guilty, as if he were betraying Emma. What if this was the wrong thing to do?

He forced himself to put aside the guilt. He had to move on or die. Vaughn had said that he felt right to her. Well, she made him feel human again. She was so different, so certain of herself. She made him pay attention to what it was like to feel alive.

Vaughn came back into the room and climbed onto the bed. Tristan went to turn off the lamp on the nightstand, but she gripped his arm tightly and said, "No. I want to see you."

Her skin was smooth as he touched her with his hands and his mouth. She ran her fingers tentatively over his chest and his arms. Then, she brought them downward to his hips. Tristan stopped. Her hands were trembling.

"What's wrong?"

He straightened slightly so that he could see her expression. She looked afraid.

"What is it?"

"Nothing," she said shakily.

"Do you want to stop?" he asked patiently. "If you do, tell me now. I don't think I'll be able to stop soon."

"No!" Now, she looked as if she was afraid that he would stop. "Believe me. I want this. Please."

This Vaughn was different from the one he'd come to know in the last twenty-four hours. For the first time, she seemed unsure of something.

Tristan moved up and wrapped his arms around her. He kissed her mouth, then went back to his ministrations. Finally, he put his palms under Vaughn's back, pressed forward, and encountered resistance. Surprised, he propped himself up on his elbows to look at Vaughn. She stared back at him, and he became aware of how tightly she was gripping his shoulders.

"You've never...?" He paused and frowned before asking, "I'm hurting you, aren't I?"

He didn't know what to do. Halting things now would be very difficult for him, but if that was what was necessary....

"Tristan, I told you I want to be with you."

A tear slid into her hair.

Tristan was torn. He had known Vaughn for only one day, but already he knew that he wanted to be with her and only her. It was the same feeling he'd had the first time he'd met Emma eight years before. After her death, he had despaired of ever experiencing that overwhelming passion and love with anyone else. The surge of relief and exuberance was as good as any fix he'd ever had.

But he didn't want to hurt Vaughn either. If they were to go on, there was nothing that could be done about the physical pain

63

that this first sexual experience would bring to her, but he'd been an emotional wreck for a while and worried that he might wreck Vaughn's life, too. What if –

What if? He was doing it again.

Okay, Max, he thought. *I get the picture. I'll try.*

Tristan bent forward and brushed his lips across her collarbone then murmured, "Are you positive you want this? That you want me, my life, and everything that comes with it? My problems? My child? My student loans? Because if you're not, then I'll have to leave right now."

She pushed her hips up slightly, and a second tear fell into her hair. Tristan kissed the salty wetness and put aside his reservations.

She cried afterwards, and he held her, whispering apologies and sweet nothings into her ear.

Chapter Eight: The Present

At 11:00 a.m. the following Saturday, Lillian was busily putting the finishing touches on Tristan's birthday cake. Earlier that morning, she'd spread a white tablecloth over the enormous, old mahogany table. The lace napkins and placemats had been pulled from their drawer in the buffet and had been carefully arranged in front of each ornately carved chair. The Dresden china and the silverware had been set out, and a crystal glass stood next to each blue-and-white plate.

Sarah had wanted to decorate the room, so Jamie had purchased yellow-and-white streamers and helped her twist them together and taped them to the doorframes, hutch, and buffet. As Lillian moved a carnation from one side of the flower arrangement to the other, she viewed the spray of color all around her. It did look festive.

Lillian placed the glass dome over the cake plate then slipped the faded gray apron over her head. She made sure that her hair hadn't been mussed up, since she had decided to leave it loose for the party. She smoothed the front of the periwinkle blue dress she'd pulled from the back of her closet.

Max came into the dining room and placed an elegantly wrapped package on the shelf of the hutch.

"You look very nice," he said admiringly. "That color suits you."

"Thank you. There used to be a time when…well, that's what I was told. I suppose I should wear it more often."

"Quite."

The doorbell rang, and Lillian quickly picked up her apron and opened a drawer to remove a box of birthday candles.

"I believe our guests have begun to arrive," Max said officiously, as he hurried to open the front door. "Hello, Sarah. Hello, Jamie. Where is Tristan?"

"He went to get Vaughn," Sarah said excitedly. "They should be here any minute!"

She was practically jumping up and down in her little pink dress. Max was glad to see that her reaction was so positive, but he was also concerned. She seemed to be accepting the appearance of her father's new companion without hesitation, but what if they didn't get along? What if Sarah became jealous of Vaughn? It was an all-too-common occurrence when a widowed or divorced parent found a new partner.

Max smiled to himself. What if? Now he was doing it.

Jamie headed straight for the kitchen and inhaled deeply before saying, "Mmmmm. Smells great, Lil. Can I have a taste?"

Lillian scowled at him, but Sarah knew she wasn't truly angry. She liked Jamie, although she frequently called him "a scoundrel."

"Get out of there, Jamie Nesser!" She slapped his hand as he picked up a spoon and made to taste the spaghetti sauce from the pot on the stove. "You'll be the death of me!"

Jamie hooted, "I didn't think you'd give me the chance! Must be that sexy dress!"

"Watch your tongue, especially when there are children present. Now, shoo!"

"You look nice, Max," Sarah offered.

"Max always looks nice, whether it's in a three-piece suit or in pants and a shirt like today," Jamie offered. "He'd probably look nice in cut-offs and a Jimi Hendrix t-shirt."

"Maybe I'll try that for Halloween," Max chuckled. "Don't downplay yourself, Jamie. You generally look very nice."

"So, you'd like to try my jeans with holes and the faded Oxford shirt?" Jamie winked at Sarah and declared, "Maybe I could start a new clothing line. People could pay hundreds of dollars to dress like this and be in style."

He sat at the kitchen table, and Sarah climbed onto his lap. Max lowered himself into a chair, and they talked to Lillian as she put away the dishes she'd washed earlier in the day. As usual, she refused all offers of help from the others.

Eventually, Sarah asked, "Miss Lillian? Why do you call it 'saving' the dishes? What are you saving them for?"

"It means to put them in their place."

"Kind of like when Jamie says he has to 'make' the groceries?"

"That actually means to buy the groceries at the store."

"So, you make the groceries, then you save them?"

"Exactly," said Lillian.

There was a knock at the door. Max excused himself then went to the front and opened it. There stood Tristan and a lovely young woman with dark red hair.

"Vaughn Gillebert, I presume? Come in. I'm Maxwell Nash. It's a pleasure to meet you." He gestured for them to enter and added, "I believe you already know Jamie?"

"Yes, sir," she replied, smiling at the approaching figure. "Tristan brought him by the gallery yesterday."

"Hey, Vaughn! Wow. Tris's in style, too."

Max smiled. Tristan wore an outfit almost identical to Jamie's, except that his Oxford shirt was faded green, not faded blue. Vaughn, on the other hand, wore a bright yellow sundress that had a band of appliqued daisies encircling the high waist.

Sarah came down the hall holding Lillian's hand. Max could tell that she was apprehensive as he introduced his new acquaintance to the housekeeper. Tristan moved towards Sarah and picked her up. He carried her to where they stood.

"Honey, this is Vaughn. Vaughn, this is my daughter, Sarah."

Sarah slid out of Tristan's arms and stood before the young woman. She held out a hand.

"It's nice to meet you, Miss Vaughn."

As Vaughn shook her hand, she said, "It's great to meet you, and just "Vaughn" is fine."

Sarah smiled back then impulsively stepped forward and put her arms around the girl's waist. Vaughn didn't pull away. She returned the embrace and patted the child on the back.

After a few moments, Lillian said, "Well, I hope everybody brought their appetite. Lunch is about ready. Why don't you all go to the dining room while I bring in the food?"

Sarah took Tristan's hand and pulled him forward, as the others followed.

"Come on, Daddy. We have a surprise for you. Now, close your eyes." When they reached the doorway, she said, "Okay, open them!"

Tristan viewed the dining room and all of its adornments, then said, "You didn't have to go to all this trouble."

"Of course we didn't have to," said Jamie. "We *wanted* to. Jeez, I think you're worth a few streamers and some fabric and nice dishes on the table."

Lillian came in from the kitchen, carrying a basket of rolls and a bowl of grated cheese. As she placed them on the table and pivoted to go back for more, Vaughn asked, "Would you like some help?"

"Oh, no," Lillian replied, waving her off. "Today's a day when everyone here is a guest. Dr. Nash and I will handle everything."

"Ah," Max laughed. "I think that was a hint. Please excuse us for a moment."

Vaughn, Jamie, Tristan, and Sarah moved around the table to take their seats. Before Vaughn sat to Tristan's left, she slipped a small, wrapped box on the hutch next to the large present and the card Jamie had brought. Sarah seated herself to Tristan's right with Jamie next to her.

Max and Lillian came in with two large covered bowls, which they placed on the trivets on the table. Sarah peered through the glass tops. One bowl held spaghetti mixed with some sauce and the other held only sauce and pieces of chicken.

Her father had told her that chicken and spaghetti had been his favorite meal since childhood. He never made it himself, although Sarah didn't know why. It couldn't be *that* difficult to cook. She decided that she would have to learn to prepare the dish when she got older.

Once the salad bowl had been positioned next to the rolls, Max filled their glasses with Coca-Cola. Lillian sat next to Vaughn and turned towards her employer, who was seated at the end of the table across from Tristan.

"Max, I think you should say Grace before we eat. I know you usually defer to me, but I feel like you should do it today."

"As you wish," he said with a smile.

Once the Catholic blessing had been given, they reached for the food. Tristan had known that the meal would be delicious. Lillian was a good cook and had done well at recreating his mother's recipe. He had no idea how his mother had prepared it. As a boy, he'd been oblivious to the mysteries of the kitchen. After eleven years, it was difficult to recall exactly how the spaghetti sauce had tasted. However, the memory of its singular delectability lingered in his mind, and he'd strained to dredge up the familiar taste of the tomato sauce and herbs. Lillian had forced him to repeat it again and again, making notes all the while. Her facsimile was almost as good as the original. Perhaps it was better, and he'd merely imagined that his mother's chicken and spaghetti was undeniably superior to anyone else's.

"Is it all right, Tristan?" Lillian asked hopefully.

"It's perfect," he said between mouthfuls. "Just like my mother's in every respect."

She looked doubtful, then pleased.

Only minutes after the table had been cleared, Sarah could no longer stand the wait and suggested that they have cake and presents. She placed five white candles in between the icing flowers Lillian had made on top of the chocolate frosting. Max lit them, and they all sang "Happy Birthday" in many different keys. Tristan closed his eyes and blew out the candles, refusing to reveal the nature of his wish.

Sarah insisted that Tristan sit to open presents as Lillian began cutting the cake. Max gathered the coffee things, and Sarah went to the hutch where she carefully picked up the large present. As she gave it to her father, she said, "Don't drop it, Daddy. It might break."

"I'll handle it with care."

He held it firmly with both hands until Max rejoined them at the table. When he pulled away the last of the paper, Sarah said, "I had Benjamin draw it, and Max and Miss Lillian paid for the frame. Do you like it?"

Tristan looked down at his daughter, then looked back at the portrait. He was stunned at how expertly the man had captured the essence of his subject. One could almost touch the spirit that shone through in the bright eyes and the gentle curve of the mouth. The loose curls danced with wild abandon around the intense expression of a child who was wise beyond her years.

"It's beautiful. You're beautiful." He placed the picture on the table and put his arms around her. "Thank you." He glanced up at Max and Lillian. "All of you."

Releasing Sarah, he picked up the portrait once more. It had been placed in an ornately carved, cherry-wood oval frame. The origins of the portrait were explained to Jamie and Vaughn as it was passed around the table.

"He's so talented," said Vaughn, as she examined the piece. "I'd love to see more of his work."

"Why don't Vaughn and Jamie come with us on our next trip?" Sarah suggested.

"Good idea," Tristan agreed. "Let's set a time and place to meet."

"My turn." Jamie got up and walked over to where the card he'd brought lay on the shelf. He handed it to his friend and said, "Here."

Tristan tore open the envelope and pulled out the card. His face immediately burned scarlet, and he made certain he concealed the front of the card with the envelope when he opened it. After scanning the inside, he smiled broadly at Jamie.

"Lil's right. You really are a scoundrel, aren't you?"

Sarah was attempting to peer around Tristan to see the card. Her father closed it and lowered it into his lap to reinsert it into its envelope.

"I wanted to see, Daddy," Sarah pouted.

"It's a grown-up card, Honey. It's not for kids to see."

Lillian put her hands on her hips and snorted, "Trust it to Jamie." She made a clucking noise in the back of her throat. "Will you ever learn?"

"That elegant card isn't all, Tris."

Jamie pushed his hand into his pants pocket and pulled out a small, thin envelope. It was slightly curled, and one corner of the paper was bent from being wedged into such a tight space. Tristan accepted it and lifted up the flap to look inside.

"Jamie...." Tristan pulled out three tickets and announced to the others, "They're for the symphony. You don't have the money to be doing this kind of stuff."

"Hey!" Jamie said indignantly. "What else would I spend it on? Pretty girls?" He gave Lillian a mischievous sideways glance and continued, "I just thought you might enjoy taking Sarah and a new *friend* out for a night of culture. None of us has ever been to the symphony before."

"Thanks, Man."

"I have a birthday present for you, too," Vaughn told Tristan. "I hope that's okay."

She pushed her chair back, retrieved the small box, and brought it over to him. The air in the room was very still, as Max, Lillian, Sarah, and Jamie waited to see what was inside. Tristan examined the box as if it would explode at any moment. Then he carefully peeled back the tape along the edges. The wrapping gave way to reveal a white oblong box. Tristan lifted up the lid and looked at Vaughn.

"You hate it," she said, looking at her hands.

"I love it," Sarah remarked. "Daddy, if you don't like it, *I'll* wear it."

"Oh, good grief!" Max interjected. "What's inside?"

Tristan turned the box so that Max, Jamie, and Lillian could view its contents. Affixed to the cushion at the bottom was a length of black cord. Suspended from the middle was a circle of pewter. A pattern of raised, interwoven lines decorated the circle.

"It's Celtic," Vaughn offered. "It stands for harmony."

Sarah turned her attention to the woman and asked, "What's Celtic?"

"Irish?" Jamie volunteered uncertainly. "Well, not just Irish. A culture that contributed a lot to the world and saved a lot of it, too."

Max was about to give a lecture on Britain and its surrounding areas, but Lillian shushed him and commented that today was not the day for long, drawn-out educational symposiums. Max promised to give the child a proper explanation as soon as possible.

Tristan removed the necklace from its holder and brought the two ends of the cord together behind his neck. He hooked them then sat up straight again.

"I think it looks fitting," Lillian declared. "Any smaller and it would be lost. Any larger and it would look…gaudy. It's just right for your size."

"Thanks, Lil. And thanks, Vaughn. I like the way it feels."

The shrill ring of the phone drew Lillian away from the table. She hurried into the kitchen, listening to the happy chatter of the others as she went. After a moment, she stuck her head through the door and summoned Max, who took the receiver from her hand. He came back to the dining room several minutes later and said apologetically, "One of my patients at the hospital is in need of my attention. Can I give anyone a lift on my way out?"

"That would be cool, but I hate to rush off," Tristan said. "We could stay and help clean up, Lil."

"Nonsense," Lillian replied, stacking some plates to take to the kitchen. "I need to leave in a half hour for a church meeting. I'll pick up a few things and get to the rest later. You take advantage of the ride. It's your birthday, for Heaven's sake!"

Once Max had deposited the little group in front of the house on State Street, the three adults and the child paused on the sidewalk and waved goodbye.

"I think I'm gonna be heading home, Tris," Jamie said, as he began to back down the sidewalk. "I have a date tonight, and I *really* need to get some studying in for that test I have on Monday. See y'all later!"

"See you. Thanks again!" Turning to Vaughn, Tristan asked, "Do you want to come in? I'd like to hang the picture and put up the tickets, and I know Sarah's been dying to show you around."

"Daddy!" Sarah whispered. "You're embarrassing me!"

"Oh. I'll try not to let that happen again."

They mounted the steps and stood on the porch while Tristan unlocked the front door. As they stepped inside, Sarah took Vaughn's hand and proceeded to give her the grand tour. She proudly showed off everything in the small rooms and gladly gave Vaughn background information on most of the furnishings.

Tristan found his hammer and a nail and hung the portrait in the living room where it would be more visible to guests. He sighed as he looked at the picture on the wall. The framed portrait was elegant and highlighted how shabby the rest of the room appeared. Once he finished school, he would have to get some better furniture and a better place in which to put it.

They all sat on the floor playing Monopoly and talking for the rest of the afternoon. Sarah had always loved to draw and color, so she was very serious when Vaughn worked with her and gave her some pointers. Afterwards, since none of them were truly hungry, they snacked on fruit and cheese while watching a rerun of *The Carol Burnett Show*.

By 9:30, Sarah was sleeping, the picture Vaughn had drawn with her taped to her closet door. Tristan emerged from her room, pulling the door halfway closed. He went back to the living room and sat on the couch next to Vaughn. She put her head against his chest.

"Are you...all right?" he asked quietly. "Are you still sore?"

"Hmm? Oh, that."

Tristan couldn't help being amused by Vaughn's attitude. She was so sure of everything, except sex. Why?

"Today it's been fine." She put her hand against his chest once more and admitted, "I'm still scared though."

"What for?" He brought her closer to him and assured her, "Don't worry."

She slipped her fingers inside his shirt, rubbing the hair on his chest in a light, circular motion.

"Why do you do this?" Tristan asked in a tight voice. "Why, if you're afraid?"

"Because," Vaughn said. She pulled out of his embrace and moved her leg over until she was sitting across his lap then explained, "Because I *am* afraid and don't want to be. This part of life is a world I don't know anything about."

"Didn't you date before?"

"Oh, Tristan! Is that what you assume, that every date leads to sex? For your information, I've been out on lots of dates. I dated one guy for ten months."

"Why didn't you have sex with him?"

"I knew he wasn't the one. I knew that when the right person came along, it would all work out. So, I never concerned myself with that."

"But didn't your parents explain things to you?"

"My parents...well, they're great, but they never talked to me about it. I think they wanted to shield me. When my sister was fourteen, she had a baby." All of the color drained from her face before she went on by saying, "Oh, my gosh. Tristan, I didn't even think about that the other night. I wanted to be with you so much that I wasn't even thinking about getting pregnant."

Tristan took her face in his hands, rubbing her cheekbones with his thumbs. In truth, he hadn't thought about procreation at all. It had been so long since he'd had to worry about that. Now, here he was with a girl he hardly knew who might be pregnant from their one sexual encounter. He didn't care. He couldn't. He had enough to deal with as it was. He had no intention of having a future without this woman, so why not welcome any child they might have? Did he have a choice?

All Tristan knew was that he was being reckless and impulsive for once, and it felt good. He could have asked Vaughn relevant questions regarding the subject to try to determine if the topic was even worthy of note. Instead, he sat forward and kissed her.

At first, she responded, but then she drew back and asked, "Don't you understand?"

Tristan was not focusing well. The way she was sitting was so provocative, but she didn't seem to know what she was doing to him.

"You're torturing me, you know."

She looked at him innocently. Could she really be that naïve? Yes, he realized, she could. He put his lips to her neck and spoke between kisses.

"Would it be so bad?"

Above him, he heard her say, "You...you'd be all right with that?" She made a soft noise as he reached the base of her neck and offered, "I don't know if I'm ready to have a baby."

Tristan lowered her down next to him on the sofa. Floors and couches were uncomfortable places to make love, although he'd done it in a variety of more unusual locations. Besides, he didn't want Sarah walking in on them in the living room. He stood and went to check the front door, switching off the lamp as he passed. He paused in the hall and turned back to Vaughn.

"If you want me to call you a cab, I will," he said. "I'd much rather have you stay here with me tonight."

Vaughn finally came in through the doorway to his bedroom. Tristan was lying shirtless on his side. As terrified as she looked, he knew she wasn't going anywhere. She sat on the edge of the bed.

"Will Sarah wake up?"

"She doesn't usually wake during the night. Although the night I...the night Jamie found us, I could have sworn I heard her singing in the hallway."

"Singing?"

"Singing. Max suggested that maybe she was out of her head with the fever. I was pretty out of my head, too. I may have imagined it."

Vaughn reached behind her neck and began to fumble with her zipper. She soon felt Tristan's hands on her back. He undid the zipper and slipped the dress down around her waist. She waited.

Tristan reminded himself that Vaughn had no experience and wouldn't know the basics of sex. It was a new concept to him. He and Emma had both had their share of partners before and after they'd met. They hadn't immediately become a monogamous couple.

In a way, Tristan was grateful for Vaughn's lack of sophistication in the bedroom. It was all new to her. It gave him a different perspective – and great power. He would have to be mindful of it and not allow himself to misuse the gift that Vaughn had unknowingly given him.

He pulled the long hair away from her neck saying, "Don't be afraid. If you're afraid, then it won't be good. I don't ever want to hurt you again."

Vaughn let him guide her as they made love and soon admitted that she couldn't think about being scared or getting pregnant or anything else. She whispered that the sensations that were washing over her were unlike any she could have ever imagined.

The girl's responses gave Tristan more happiness than he would have thought possible. He allowed himself to come when she gave in to her first orgasm. At last, he felt as if he was in control of himself and his life.

He held her in his arms when they'd finished. She didn't cry this time. Rather, she clung to him. Tristan smiled in the darkness. So, she would steady him by day, and he would reach a part of her she hadn't realized existed by night. Let each take what was given and provide what was needed.

Tristan had never had a better birthday.

Chapter Nine: A Learning Experience

The next Saturday, Sarah and Tristan woke early. Once they'd eaten some Cornflakes, Tristan went to take a shower while his daughter watched Bugs Bunny cartoons. It took him thirty minutes to bathe, shave, brush his teeth, and slip on a pair of khaki cut-offs, a white tee, and his huaraches. By the time he emerged from the bathroom, Sarah was already dressed in her jean shorts and a smock shirt that was covered with tiny pink rosebuds.

She'd retrieved her drawing pad and was seated at the kitchen table. Her father joined her there with a textbook and a sketchpad of his own. When he tried to see what she was drawing, Sarah put her arm across the paper and leaned forward so that his view was obscured.

"It's for Benjamin, Daddy. Don't look. I'm not finished."

"Benjamin?"

Tristan opened his book and lifted a pencil from his daughter's pile of supplies. She turned her attention back to the paper and said, "Benjamin drew a picture for me, and it made you happy. Now, I'm going to draw a picture for him. He's sad or missing something. Halley, too. Maybe a picture will make them smile."

Tristan nodded but didn't enlighten his child on the roots of the couple's problems. He had literally bumped into the man and his girlfriend at the A&P and had discovered that they lived only a short distance from State Street down Highland Road. Tristan had been given an open invitation to visit and had taken advantage of it twice in the last week. He hadn't mentioned it to Sarah, because he'd known that she'd be hurt at not being included. It had been nice to sit at the apartment chatting with adults and sipping mint tea for a few minutes before catching the bus to pick up his daughter.

It appeared to Tristan that Benjamin seemed destined for unhappiness, although he was by no means morose. A constant, simmering anger fueled his drive for success and his quest for love. The void in his soul was enormous, and he was incessantly trying to fill it with new relationships, even as he declared his devotion to Halley. For him, devotion and monogamy were not mutually exclusive. One person could never patch the tears in his psyche. He wanted more out of life and people than was possible.

Halley yearned for more from Benjamin than he was capable of giving. She had confided to Tristan that she dreamed of a time when she could provide her partner with all the comfort and peace that he so desperately sought. She grieved for their lost child and would have tried to have another, if she weren't worried that she would lose Benjamin in the process.

Tristan redirected his attention towards his schoolwork. Maybe Benjamin and Halley were two messed up people with complicated lives. Maybe he didn't approve of Benjamin's sexual wanderings or Halley's blind affection for her lover. But they were both friendly and quick-witted, and Tristan was not one to cast stones.

He and Sarah sat together in silence for over an hour until the sunlight shone in so brightly that Tristan knew they had better leave soon or they'd risk being late. He put away his things, while his daughter added the final touches to her project.

"There!" she exclaimed, proudly holding up the picture. "How does it look?"

Her father studied the drawing of their little house. In it, he, Jamie, and Sarah stood on the porch with a woman who had hair that looked suspiciously like Vaughn's. A dog sat on the step. The sky was blue and filled with fluffy clouds and birds.

"Who's that?" he pointed to the female figure.

"Vaughn, of course," she groaned, rolling her eyes.

"And the dog?"

"Oh, it's Rembrandt! You know the man who lives across from Jamie? It's his dog. Couldn't you tell?"

"Now I see it," he said truthfully. "I think it looks cool. Especially the house. You did a good job. You may have a future in drafting."

"You *would* like the house the best," she sighed.

Once she'd rolled up the drawing and tied it with a piece of ribbon, she slipped it into one of the deep pockets of her shirt, and then they were off.

Jamie sat reading with one leg swung over the rusty arm of a metal chair in front of his apartment. He raised his head when he heard Sarah call out his name then shut his book, which turned out to be a volume of the works of Aristophanes. While he went into his place to leave the book, Tristan and Sarah talked with Jamie's neighbor, who was sitting on the porch smoking a cigarette and throwing the ball for his dog. Sarah threw the ball a few times; then they said "goodbye" to man and dog and set out for Vaughn's.

They walked towards Highland, passing by Library Joe's and The Bayou. As it was only 9:00 in the morning, the restaurant and the bar were presently closed. Jamie had visited both the night before. It was not surprising that he was slightly hung over.

"So, Munchkin, are we flying to Vaughn's in our own personal jet?" Jamie teased, as he lifted Sarah into the air, and she squealed with delight.

"No, but close," Tristan answered. "You know my next-door neighbor?"

"That guy with the psychedelic van?"

"The same. He's headed for Government Street, so I asked him if he'd mind dropping us off at the Garden District. Now, we don't have to worry about walking or hitching one way."

"Sounds like a plan to me."

They ended up staying at Vaughn's a little longer than Tristan had anticipated. Sarah was in awe of the large rooms and the high ceilings. She had to examine each piece of artwork and hear the story behind every photo displayed on the bookcase. The studio fascinated her. Tristan knew that she could have explored for the rest of the day, but they were already late. Vaughn promised the child that she could come back very soon and stay as long as she liked. Reluctantly, Sarah agreed to depart.

As they walked towards downtown, Jamie asked, "Will your landlords give you any trouble about us? That van is pretty radical."

"No, they trust me. Believe me, some of the other neighbors have done some really weird things."

"Such as?"

"The guy across the street likes to run out to get his paper without any clothes on. One morning, the door locked behind him. I watched him try to open the windows. Finally, he climbed over the fence."

"You didn't want to go over and give him a hand?" Jamie smirked.

Her face burned, as she quickly tried to change the subject by continuing, "The lady from down the block walks her cats, and there's an old man who sifts through everybody's trash. I guess every neighborhood has a few eccentrics. Doesn't yours?"

This led to a lengthy discussion about some of the interesting habits of the residents of State Street – the drunk who always tried to go into the wrong apartment, the woman who planted dead flowers in her flower pots, the man who moved all of his living room furniture onto the lawn when the weather was good, and the hippies with suspicious-looking weeds growing in their front yard.

Vaughn looked to Jamie and asked, "How about you? What are your neighbors like?"

"Oh, some of them are okay. Some of them are total loons. My next-door neighbor's way out," he confided. "He's a great neighbor and a smart guy. I have no idea what he does for a living. Always willing to help out, though. Real friendly."

"A little too friendly," Tristan laughed. "You better watch your back."

"How can someone be *too* friendly?" Vaughn asked, perplexed.

"What Tris means is that he has *special friends*."

"Special friends?"

"Very close, special male friends."

Vaughn was visibly puzzled by their intimation. Suddenly, understanding became evident in her expression.

"Oh!" she exclaimed.

Jamie threw back his head and laughed with delight. He was enjoying himself immensely. Tristan was more like his old self than he'd been in what seemed like forever. Sarah, too. And Vaughn…Vaughn amazed him. She was sweet, attractive, and more naïve than anyone he'd ever met.

Tristan had talked at length with his friend about Vaughn. He'd even told him of their sexual encounters. Tristan was not the type to brag about his sexual prowess, although Jamie was well aware that the man was no slouch in that area. Tristan might not kiss and tell, but the girls they had known years ago did, including Emma.

No, Tristan had not bragged. He'd simply told Jamie about how much pleasure Vaughn gave him when they were together.

The fact that she knew virtually nothing about sex had shocked Jamie, and he couldn't help but chuckle as Tristan had described to him the varying looks of wonder and disbelief on her face when he performed some technique that was new to her. Tristan found it charming and endearing.

Emma had been quite the opposite from Vaughn. She'd been energetic to the point of hyperactivity and had plenty of practice in the sexual arena before she and Tristan had met and finally entered into a mutually exclusive relationship. According to Emma, the encounters between her and Tristan had been drawn-out high intensity affairs. She hadn't had to tell Jamie. The walls in the apartment had been thin.

Jamie continued his musings as they edged down the hill beside Government Street. They reached the Pastime Restaurant and Lounge and proceeded to go inside and order their barbecue sandwiches, fries, and drinks. Jamie squinted through the murky depths to find a place for them to eat. They sat at the only available table between a group of businessmen and a hippie couple.

In between bites, Jamie asked Vaughn, "Where are you from? You don't talk like anyone around here."

"Neither do you."

"Touché. You first."

She made an unsuccessful attempt to shake ketchup out of the bottle and said, "I'm from Mississippi, but I've worked hard not to have any strong Southern accent. I want people to judge me for me, not for who they think I am. You?"

"I'm originally from this little town near Alexandria called Bunkie, and –"

"Tell her the story!" Sarah interrupted.

"Honey," Tristan said in a warning tone, "You know it's not polite to interrupt."

Vaughn smacked the bottom of the ketchup bottle and asked, "What story?"

Jamie sighed resignedly. He'd told this story dozens of times before, mostly at Sarah's request.

"The town was founded by this man a long, long time ago. His daughter had this monkey, but she couldn't say 'monkey,' so she called it 'Bunkie' and that's what the man named the town."

Vaughn turned towards Tristan, who took the ketchup bottle from her hand, and asked, "So, are you from a town named after an armadillo or something?"

Tristan grinned at her and tapped the neck of the Heinz bottle. The ketchup flowed onto Vaughn's plate.

"I was born and raised near here in Denham Springs."

"Land of the Plaid Shirts!" Jamie declared as he raised his cup in a mock toast.

Tristan ignored him and said, "My parents moved to Louisiana from out West, so my accent is a little different because of the way they spoke, I guess. They settled in Denham before I was born, and we lived there until I was fourteen. We'd only been in Baton Rouge for two weeks when my folks were killed in a car accident. I met Jamie right after I became a ward of the State."

Vaughn dipped a fry and looked inquisitively at the blonde man who explained, "My folks had moved to Baton Rouge because the partying was better here than in Bunkie, which is a sleepy little town. It didn't take the people in our apartment complex long to see that they didn't give a shit about their kids. I'd been in foster care for years before I met Tristan."

"Jamie saved Daddy!" Sarah said enthusiastically.

Vaughn looked questioningly to Jamie for an explanation. Tristan had told her the horrible tale of the night in January when Jamie had saved his and Sarah's life. It didn't appear that Sarah was referring to that incident. In truth, she had never spoken of it and seemed to avoid the topic.

Jamie sighed again. He didn't like to talk about the past, but he couldn't very well deny Vaughn information that he now felt she had a right to know. If things worked out and she was to become a permanent part of his life, then he might as well get this out of the way.

"I don't know if I saved his life. Maybe I was just trying to save my own skin."

"As if anyone would believe that crap," Tristan snorted derisively.

"Do you want to tell it then?"

"Oh, no. By all means, be my guest."

Jamie brushed the hair away from his eyes and pushed his chair slightly away from the table. He took a gulp of Dr. Pepper and then said, "I met Tristan in a group home. We were both fourteen. I was in-between foster homes at the time. Tris was headed for his first. Not many people are interested in adopting teenaged orphans or troublemakers.

"Anyway, within a week, we were inseparable. Within two weeks, I'd convinced Tristan to run away."

"Run away!" Vaughn exclaimed. "But why? You were so young!"

"I knew enough horror stories about foster care. Some I'd heard from other kids. Most I'd experienced or witnessed firsthand." He shrugged and added, "Don't get me wrong. Some foster parents are better than biological parents. My real parents were certainly no prize. They undeniably neglected me and my sisters. When the State workers came to take us into custody, there was minimal protestation from my folks, and they quickly gave up their rights.

"My sisters were adopted almost immediately. People like babies and toddlers. Who wants an eight-year-old smart ass? I got used to being bounced from one foster home to the next."

"You're so calm about your parents not...fighting for you."

"I was better off without them." He ate another fry and sipped his drink before continuing, "So, like I was saying, I was used to living like that. Tris wasn't. His parents had cared about him; that was obvious. He was considerate and thoughtful. I knew that it wouldn't take long for someone so sensitive –" He stopped when Tristan rolled his eyes at this then insisted, "It's true. Someone with your temperament would easily be hardened or crushed by the system." Looking back to Vaughn, Jamie said, "I guess you could say that Tris became the catalyst for my liberation."

"How did you survive?"

"We got by." Jamie grinned at his friend, as if sharing a secret joke. "We found this shabby apartment near McKinley where some older kids I knew from my stint with the State were living. They let us crash there for free until we could find ourselves jobs. They showed us how to register ourselves in school and function on our own without an adult around to help. They moved on one by one, and others moved in. We did the same for them."

Vaughn nibbled at her now-cold barbecue sandwich and asked, "But...nobody in the building turned you all in?"

"You think they wanted to be turned in themselves? Most of them would have been in trouble for a lot worse offenses then skipping out on foster care."

Sarah had finished her lunch and was squirming in her seat, so Tristan said, "We'll have to tell you more about it sometime."

"I don't know whether I want to hear the rest or not."

After they'd stepped outside, the little group walked parallel to the levee past the old train station and began to move on North Boulevard. They turned left onto Lafayette, and Tristan found himself being dragged forward by his little daughter to peer into a darkened shop window across from the Capitol House Hotel. He suggested that the others keep going, saying that he and Sarah would catch up in a minute.

As they walked ahead, Vaughn returned awkwardly to their earlier conversation by asking, "So, where are your parents now?"

"Damned if I know. I could pass one of them on this street today, and I doubt if I'd recognize them. It's been sixteen years. They probably wouldn't recognize me either."

"That's sad."

"Yeah, it is. Tris and me, we've tried hard to be like other people, people with parents and aunts and uncles and cousins. It ain't gonna happen. We're all we've got. I lost touch with both sides of my family when they didn't want to take me or my sisters in years ago. They weren't real winners themselves, you know?

"Tris's parents were both only children, and so is he. So is Sarah. I feel bad for her at Christmas, Thanksgiving, Easter, on her birthday, on Halloween. She should have more than the two of us." He lifted the damp strands of hair up off his neck. "Lil and Max are pretty decent substitutes, but it's still not the same."

"What about Tristan's wife? Didn't she have any family? I'd think they'd be thrilled to help out."

"Don't even go there," he hissed. "And don't ever mention that to either of them. I'll tell you about it some other day when they're not around. Got it?"

Vaughn nodded and began, "If you –"

"We're almost there!" Sarah declared as she came up beside the woman and took her hand. "It's going to be so cool that you'll never, ever forget it!"

83

Chapter Ten: Daniel Revisited

When they got close to Collective Expressions, Jamie said, "Do y'all mind if I stop in here to see Chloe?" He turned to Vaughn and explained, "She's a…friend who works at the gift shop here."

"Can I come in, too?" Sarah asked her godfather. "I like Chloe, and I want to look at the cards and the candles and the flowers. Please?"

Vaughn opted to remain outside, and Tristan selflessly volunteered to stay with her. There was a space between the gift shop and the next building. Tristan pulled Vaughn with him into the shadows.

She glanced nervously back at him.

"It's cooler right here," he explained.

"I guess." Vaughn peered out and asked, "Will Sarah be all right?"

"With Jamie? Sure. He'll take care of her." Slipping his hands around her waist, he went on, "Besides, if she goes in with him, he won't waste time making it with Chloe."

"How can he do that with someone in a gift shop? Wouldn't there be customers?"

"She's not the only one working there, and there's a door leading to the storage room."

As he tugged on her ear with his teeth, Vaughn laid her hands on his forearms and breathed, "Tristan, please."

"Please, huh?" His lips were on her shoulder next to the strap of her halter top as he murmured, "I think Jamie could do it just about anywhere, anyway, anyhow. Bad role models."

"And you?"

"I had good role models. They just didn't stick around long enough."

She was obviously trying to keep her attention on the conversation as she muttered, "No, no, I meant about making it any time, any –"

The bell on the door of the shop clanged. Tristan moved his hands from her front to her back and squeezed her shoulders. He said nothing but edged around Vaughn and took her hand, leading her out onto the sidewalk.

"Hey, Tris! There you are! We wondered where you'd wandered off to."

Jamie smiled at Tristan, as Vaughn bent down to examine the flower Sarah held out to her. Tristan smiled back and motioned for them to follow him.

They went to Collective Expressions and meandered around until they came to Benjamin's portable art studio. He had no customers at that moment and jumped up to greet them.

"Darlings! It's so wonderful to see you! And you brought some friends!"

That afternoon, Benjamin had braided his long hair and tied it with a scrap of cloth that matched his orange silk shirt. Tristan introduced him to Vaughn and Jamie, and he greeted them with much fanfare.

"I tell you what. I'm going to take a break in about twenty minutes when the vendor next to me gets back. I'm watching her stall while she takes lunch. If you can piddle around for a bit, maybe we can grab some ice cream and sit on the levee and talk. I would say let's do coffee, but it's beastly hot out there. I can't even bear the thought of café au lait."

Sarah put a hand on Benjamin's arm and asked, "Where's Halley? Will she come, too?"

He looked down into the girl's expectant eyes and said, "She might. She closed the stall and is supposed to start selling her stuff the day after tomorrow at a place a few blocks over. She's still been feeling tired, although she's much better than she was a couple of weeks ago. Anyway, she said she might drop by for my lunch break, so we'll see."

Placated, Sarah nodded and said, "I brought you something. I hope it's not too bad."

She withdrew the sketch she'd done earlier in the day. Benjamin carefully unrolled it.

"Why, it's magnificent! Do you mind if I display it with my work? You'll be running me out of business soon!"

Sarah giggled but was obviously pleased by his remarks. She took her father's hand as their little group explored the stalls.

At the appointed time, they joined Benjamin and Halley near the door. The girl hugged Tristan in greeting, which Sarah thought was unusual, being unaware as she was of her father's forays to the apartment on Highland.

As the six of them climbed the levee with their ice cream in hand, the wandering foursome learned that Benjamin was from New Orleans and that his parents disapproved mightily of their son, his lifestyle, and his decision to move the year before. He'd run away from his family's expectations and had decided to escape the fate of taking over his father's law practice.

"*You* have a law degree?" Jamie asked in astonishment.

"Oh, you cut me to the quick! I was actually a very good student. I passed the Bar, but I couldn't abide the thought of all those boring legal documents and dreary tomes of wisdom. My father was appalled at my decision. My grandfather took to his bed for two days. Can you imagine anything more ridiculous?"

"Are you from New Orleans, too?" Vaughn inquired of Halley.

"I'm from Grand Coteau," she said softly. In response to the blank stares, she added, "It's between Opelousas and Lafayette. I know you've never heard of it. It's small, and the only industry there is religion."

"I don't understand," Vaughn admitted, cocking her head. "Do they make religious articles there?"

"Not quite. There's nothing in Grand Coteau but a general store, a seminary, several churches, a retreat center, a public school, and a couple of Catholic schools. I went to one of the Catholic schools. It's a beautiful old place with boarders and day students called the Academy of the Sacred Heart. It's been running continuously since 1821. Even during the Civil War, they held classes. It's the only school like that in the U.S."

"Sounds interesting," Jamie said with a grin. "All those Catholic schoolgirls out there in the middle of nowhere with no guys?"

"I miss it sometimes," she said wistfully. "The town's really poor, but it's lovely countryside. But I wanted to go out and make a life for myself, so here I am. My parents thought I was nuts for not marrying the boy next door or going to college right away.

There are times when I'd like to call them and tell them how I'm getting my degree in business as well as working."

"Why don't you?" Tristan asked.

"I'd just get a lecture about how I should have done it before and about my bohemian life here in Baton Rouge."

Benjamin, who was watching her as she spoke, put his arm around her and said, "You sound regretful."

"Never." Edging closer to him, she said firmly, "I'd go anywhere to be with you. Where you are is where I'm at home."

"Let's hope he never moves to the Himalayas," Tristan laughed.

"Or the Sahara Desert," Vaughn giggled.

Tristan leaned over and kissed her. Jamie watched as she slid her hand around Tristan's neck. He cleared his throat and said to Sarah, "How's about another cone of ice cream? I'll race you across the street for it."

Before the others could comment, he and Sarah scrambled up and took off down the side of the levee. Tristan watched anxiously as his daughter darted ahead of his friend, but Jamie called for her to stop before she crossed the road.

When they returned, Tristan remarked that it would soon be time for them to be heading home.

"No, Daddy!" Sarah protested. "This is fun! Can't we stay a little longer?"

"Father knows best," Benjamin advised. "We have to be getting back to the stall anyway. Hope your walk home isn't *too* hot."

Two blocks into their return trip, Tristan stopped and looked at the others. He wanted to go down the alley to his right, but he was worried about what Sarah might see. Trying to talk himself out of it was futile. He gave up and asked, "Do you mind taking a shortcut?"

They made their way through the alley. When they came upon a large dumpster, Sarah tore away from Tristan and ran forward calling, "Daniel!"

The boy jumped and whirled around. The fearful look faded almost immediately as he recognized the father and daughter. He was holding a hose in his hands, preparing to spray some chairs by the looks of it. His upper lip was swollen.

"Hey," Daniel said with a quick and certainly painful smile. "I was hoping I'd see you again."

"Yeah, well, we decided to take another Saturday walk." Tristan tried hard not to stare at the lip and continued, "Today, we even have a couple of friends with us. This is Vaughn and Jamie."

"Hello." He nodded gravely in acknowledgement of their presence before addressing Tristan and Sarah by saying, "Thanks again for your help with those boxes. I didn't know –"

The back door slammed open behind him, and he dropped the hose. A large man with a small potbelly, gray hair, and a graying mustache stormed out into the alley. His brown eyes emanated cruelty and anger.

"What in the hell do you think you're doing? I told you to get your chores done quick before supper. Now, damn it, I find you lollygaging around out here with some long-haired freaks!"

Daniel cringed, but he stood his ground, blocking Sarah from the brunt of the man's aggression.

"They're lost. I was giving them directions."

The man glared at them. His hands were balled into fists. Aware that Tristan was staring at them, he unclenched his fingers and lowered his voice slightly.

"Fine," he spat. "You get directions and stop distractin' him. He's got work to do."

Tristan opened his mouth to say that Daniel should be in the park playing ball, not working.

Jamie moved up next to his friend and said, "No problem."

Daniel looked at him gratefully and proceeded to give them directions to Lafayette Boulevard. Jamie thanked him, and they headed back the way they'd come.

When they stepped out onto the sidewalk again, none of them spoke. Tristan glanced at his daughter, who was staring at the pavement. She looked afraid, angry, and upset. He felt the same way.

"Why'd you do that, Jamie?" Tristan asked hotly. "Somebody should tell that bastard off."

"It wouldn't have done any good. Arguing with him would've made it worse for the kid later. Use your head, Tris."

It had been a mistake to go down the alley with Sarah; Tristan knew that now. He should have anticipated what might happen.

He knelt down in front of his child, ignoring the people who had to walk around them.

"Honey, I forgot to tell Daniel something. I have to go back for a minute."

"What if that bad man is still there?"

"I'll make sure he's not."

"What will you do?" Vaughn asked, looking worriedly towards the dumpster.

"I'm going to give Daniel our address in case he needs a place to go."

With that, he rose and retraced his steps to where the boy was spraying the chairs. The father was nowhere around.

Tristan came up behind the child, making some noise so that he wouldn't spook him. Daniel lifted his head but didn't turn around. Tristan gave his address to Daniel's rigid back. He waited, but the boy made no comment, so he left.

Sarah fell asleep as Tristan carried her, her head resting on her father's shoulder. When they arrived home, he laid her on her bed and pulled the chain on the ceiling fan in her room so that the blades turned faster to combat the stifling heat.

Once he'd kissed his child lightly on the forehead, he went to the living room where Jamie and Vaughn were waiting. Tristan sat heavily next to Vaughn, who was the first to speak.

"We have to *do* something."

"What can we do?" Jamie groaned. "We hardly know the kid. You and I met him today; Sarah and Tris met him at the beginning of the month. What do you think they're gonna do? Let us take him home like a dog from the pound?"

Tears sprang into Vaughn's eyes, and Tristan leaned forward angrily and said, "Give her a break, Man! She hasn't had to live like we have. Since when are you one to give up on something if you know it's the right thing to do?"

"I'm not giving up!" Jamie said through clenched teeth. "I'm only saying that we can't just turn this guy in. We don't exactly have the best track record with Social Services."

There was a long pause. Tristan suddenly asked, "You want to tell me what you were doing running off like that this afternoon and taking my daughter with you?"

"Nothing." Jamie glowered at him and declared, "*I've* been looking out for Sarah since she was born."

He watched the effect his words had on his friend. He hadn't really intended to utter a recrimination, a reminder of Tristan's lapse in parental responsibility. He stood then sat again.

"I think I'd better be going," Vaughn said. When Tristan started to rise, she put a hand on his shoulder and insisted, "No, don't. I can see myself out."

He reached up a long arm and slid it behind her back, pulling her down so that he could kiss her.

"I'll call you tomorrow."

With a small smile she said, "You better." She turned towards Jamie and said sweetly, "It was great to meet you."

"Vaughn, I didn't mean for you to have to leave."

"It's okay. You two need to talk."

She walked to the door and softly opened and closed it as she left. Jamie got up and went to peer out of the front window at Vaughn's retreating back. Behind and below him, he heard Tristan say, "Jesus, what's wrong with you, Man?"

"Hey, you said to give her a break. Well, cut me some slack, too!" He let the curtain drop into place and asked, "You want to know what's wrong? You and Vaughn and Benjamin and Halley...you're so...into each other. You're in love." He laughed bitterly and added, "You're not just in lust, like me. It hit me when we were all on the levee together, and I couldn't handle it. So, I used the ice cream as an excuse and ran away."

"Jamie, I barely know Vaughn."

"But you love her already, don't you?" When Tristan remained silent, he went on, "Don't misunderstand me. I think Vaughn's great. She's right. It's nothing against her at all. I think you can love her in a way you never could have loved Emma."

Before Jamie knew what was happening, he was pressed against one wall with Tristan's hands grasping the front of his shirt. He had never, ever seen Tristan that angry.

Lord, we're both on edge, he thought.

"What are you saying?" Tristan growled. "Are you suggesting that I didn't love my wife?"

"No. I know you loved her." As Tristan let go of his shirt, he continued by saying, "It's not the same kind of love. You and me

90

and Emma, we needed each other to stay alive. When she got pregnant, you got married. So what? I'm not saying you wouldn't have married her anyway...someday. I'm saying who knows? You were both only sixteen years old. She was the mother of your child, for cryin' out loud. Of course you loved her, but love is different when you're a kid than when you're an adult."

"I thought you didn't know what it was like to be in love."

Jamie shrugged and said, "Just because I've never had it doesn't mean I can't appreciate it in other people."

"You'll have it."

"Yeah, well, I don't know about that. With my past, commitment isn't something I feel real comfortable with." He checked the time and clapped Tristan on the back then said, "I better get going. I've got some reading to do, and I know that you haven't been keeping up with school as much as usual, lately."

"You got that right."

Tristan walked with Jamie to the door. They went out on the porch and stood watching the next-door neighbor taking his furniture back into his apartment after an afternoon in the sunshine.

"You know, I was thinking that Max might be able to help you with all this," Tristan offered.

"All what?"

"Uh, what we were talking about." When Jamie made a face, Tristan said, "Just think about it, all right?"

"Okay, okay. I'll think about it."

As Tristan watched his friend walk towards his apartment, he knew that the man had already put aside the idea of therapy as not worthy of consideration. If there was some woman out there who was meant for Jamie Nesser, then he hoped she was up to the challenge.

Chapter Eleven: A Place

Sarah knelt near the mimosa tree in her backyard. She made a small hole in the dirt with her trowel, then wiped at the perspiration on her forehead. There was a slight breeze, but it was still unbearably hot. The cooler weather wouldn't come to Baton Rouge for at least another month.

"Is that big enough, Daddy?"

Tristan put down the hammer and came over to crouch next to his daughter. He poked a long finger into the dirt and shook his head.

"I think it needs to be a little bigger. You don't want a huge hole, but I suppose it's better to give the roots a little upturned soil so they can breathe."

"Oh," she said seriously. "I don't want to squish them."

He laid a hand on the back of her head and smiled before asking, "Are you having fun?"

She nodded enthusiastically and began to enlarge the hole.

"Me, too. When I finish that window box, we can hook it to the sill of the kitchen window. That way, we'll be able to see those marigolds all the time."

"Why couldn't Vaughn come help?"

"She had some sculpting to do today."

"I wish she could live with us."

"You do, huh? Well, you never know. Things have been easier for us, right? We've been seeing Max in his office, and we've both been happier."

"I'd be more happy if you didn't have to work at night."

"The job at Louie's café will only last until school starts. Then, I'll go back to my student job, and that'll be during the daytime. It won't be long."

Sarah smiled and gingerly lowered a plant into the ground. Tristan returned to his hammering and listened to his daughter sing, as she dug another hole. He glanced up to check her progress then swore as he hammered his thumb.

"I'm fine," he assured Sarah. "It's not broken. You keep planting. I'll give it a rest for a minute."

Tristan sat and watched her dig. He'd become very hopeful in the last few weeks. He still had days when depression and anxiety would seize him, and he'd feel as though he was spinning out of control. He tried not to dwell on things when it happened, tried to push forward as Max had instructed. It was a slow process, but it appeared to be working.

He knew that medication might help to fight the depression and anxiety, but he didn't want to go that route because of his past substance abuse. He didn't want to do anything that might jeopardize his recovery.

"Hullo!" Jamie called from the other side of the fence.

"Hullo, yourself! You sound like Winnie the Pooh." As Tristan hoisted the window box in his arms, he said, "The gate's unlocked."

"You started without me," Jamie pouted, as he closed the gate behind him.

"Ha, ha. You were going to spend the weekend with Chloe, weren't you?" He squinted at Jamie and said slowly, "But here you are. What happened? You two have a fight?"

As he walked over to where Tristan was squatting, Jamie patted Sarah on the head. "Hey, Princess."

He lowered himself onto one of the steps. Speaking in a low voice, Jamie said, "I'd rather not talk about it, yet. How was the symphony last night? Did the dress and the suit work out?"

"The symphony was great. Sarah looked beautiful. You'll have to see her dress."

"What did she say when you gave it to her?"

"Well, I went into her room, and she was standing in front of her closet. I could tell that she was aggravated. She had her hands on her hips and this sour look on her face. That was when she told me she didn't have a dress nice enough to wear to the concert."

"I told her that we'd have to remedy that. Then, I walked over to her bed and put the box on top of the spread. She was really curious, so I told her to close her eyes and no peeking. Once her eyes were shut, I took out the dress and laid it on the bed. Lillian did a really bang-up job with the sewing. I put the shoes next to the dress and said not to look until I'd closed the door behind me.

"When she came out a few minutes later, she was beaming. The dress was long and white with pink ribbons. She looked like a little princess."

"What did Sarah do when she saw you in your new suit?"

"She ooh'd and aah'd over it. I had to tell her the whole story about how you and I went to Bates & Thigpen to get it and how Mr. Bates had helped me to select the suit and the tie and the belt and the shoes. She wanted to know why I had chosen dark blue, so I explained to her about using it for interviews and making a good impression. After that, we went to get Vaughn." He took a sip from the glass of lukewarm water that sat next to him and confided, "A friend from my physics class had told me he was painting his place last night, so I asked him if I could borrow his Chevy."

"Cool."

"Yeah, it was. I guess I'll have to start looking for a car soon. Having the suit won't do me any good if I can't get back and forth to work every day."

"I keep thinking the same thing. I'm too busy with my thesis and getting ready to defend it to do much about the car though. I know you've got a few months before that licensing test, but I'm sure that's gonna take up a lot of your time, too."

"The test itself is only four days long."

"Oh, is that all?"

"Seven written tests and two drafting exams. It would help if I got my degree first, since that's part of the deal."

"Daddy, that is so boring!" Sarah called out from her spot in the yard. "You're supposed to be telling him about last night."

"Excuse me for talking about unimportant things like our future."

"You can talk about that anytime. Tell him about Vaughn."

"What about her? Was she wearing her jeans?" Jamie teased.

"No! You should have seen Vaughn's dress!" Sarah said excitedly. "It was some kind of purple –"

"Lavender," Tristan volunteered.

"Lavender," Sarah repeated. "And it was long, and the neck came down like this, and there was a purple ribbon sewn around right here."

She pointed, and Jamie ascertained that the dress must have been high-waisted with a scoop neck.

"But her shoes didn't fit," the child told him. "They were too big."

"The dress and shoes belong to that friend of hers at the gallery," commented Tristan. "The dress was fine, but Vaughn had to stuff some Kleenex in the toes of the shoes."

"Whatever works. Were you on time for the symphony?"

"Barely. When we were on our way down the steps Vaughn tells us that her landlords wanted to see us all dressed up. So, we visited for a little while, and the wife took a picture of us before we left. I guess that's what it must be like to go to the prom."

"Except that most people don't bring their kids to the prom with them."

As if he hadn't heard him, Tristan said, "The symphony was amazing. The pianist played flawlessly. Afterwards, we stopped at the IHOP and had coffee and hot chocolate." He lowered his voice and said, "Vaughn stayed here for the night, and we overslept. Luckily, Sarah overslept, too. Vaughn left ten minutes before Sarah came out of her room. I suppose we timed it just right."

With a satisfied smile, Tristan pried open a can of white paint and picked up a brush. For a time, no one said anything. Sarah continued her planting. Tristan applied one coat of paint to the window box. Jamie sat and looked at the sky.

"Chloe's pregnant," Jamie suddenly announced.

Tristan put down the paintbrush and went to sit by his friend. He hated to ask the next question, but it was unavoidable.

"Is it yours?"

"She told me a while back that I was the only guy. I believed her then, and I believe her now."

Tristan absently picked up the hammer. It rocked back and forth as he circled the neck with two fingers and gently swung it. He had been waiting for this for ten years. As much as his friend slept around, he'd been amazed that Jamie had never gotten any girl pregnant before. Perhaps he had.

"What are you going to do? Marry her?"

Jamie looked across the yard at Sarah and muttered, "I can't, Tris. We're gonna move in together and see what happens when the baby comes. Her parents aren't too ecstatic about it, as you can imagine. We got her stuff from their house this morning. She's at the apartment right now."

"Do you love her?"

"The terrifying part is that I think I do."

Tristan reached out for Jamie's hand and shook it.

"Congratulations, Man."

"Tris, I'm scared. What if I turn out to be exactly like my folks?"

"You won't. Look how great you've been with Sarah from the beginning. Trust me on –"

The next word died in his throat, as they heard Sarah shriek from where she was kneeling underneath the tree. Tristan jumped up and ran across the grass. She'd probably been startled by a lizard. But what if it was a snake?

He came up beside her. The trowel was on the ground, and her gaze was riveted on something to her left. Tristan turned his head towards the gate, and his heart sank.

It was Daniel. Despite the heat, he wore jeans and a jacket with a hood, which he'd pulled up over his head. As he'd leaned against the handle of the gate, the jacket had opened to reveal a shirt stained red with blood from his nose. At least that's where Tristan hoped the blood had come from.

Tristan shouted, "Jamie!" and raced forward just in time to catch Daniel as he fell.

God, let him be all right, Tristan prayed, as he cradled the boy in his arms.

Jamie rushed up next to his friend and ordered, "Get him in the house!"

Tristan lifted the boy and carried him into the kitchen, as Sarah held the screen door open. Daniel's head was tilted back over Tristan's arm, and he began to choke. Tristan stopped and laid him on his side on the floor and the choking subsided. The blood oozed out of his nostrils and spread in a wickedly dark puddle across the white tile.

"Sarah, I have a job for you," Tristan said in a controlled voice that he hoped would not reveal his fear. "Dial the operator and tell her we need an ambulance. Give her the address; then go wait on the porch so they'll know which house it is."

As she ran off down the hall, Jamie carefully undid the buttons on the front of Daniel's shirt. Tristan eased the jacket off the boy's left arm and let it fall to the floor. He couldn't get the other sleeve off without moving Daniel, which didn't seem like a good idea.

The child didn't appear to be aware of his surroundings and lay shaking on the smooth tile. How he'd managed to get all the way from the bar to Tristan's house in his condition was anyone's guess.

Jamie pulled out Daniel's shirttails and undid the last few buttons. Tristan gently slid the sleeve off as he had with the jacket and moved around to see what Jamie was staring at.

"Jesus God."

Daniel's chest was a mass of black, blue, purple, and red. There were scars, fresh cuts, and bruises covering his torso and a swollen area underneath his ribcage on the right side.

"I hope they hurry," Jamie said nervously. "If what I remember of my anatomy classes holds true, then I think he's bleeding internally there."

He brushed his fingers lightly over the area in question, and Daniel made a strangled noise and jerked convulsively.

Jamie took Daniel's left hand in his right and squeezed it gently. Tristan went behind the boy again and carefully put a hand on his upper arm. They spoke soothingly to him while they waited for the paramedics. Neither of them knew if he was conscious of their presence, but they kept talking, trying to reassure him and themselves that help would be there soon.

Then they heard the sirens. Paramedics and policemen entered the house, and Tristan had to hurry to stop his daughter from coming back into the kitchen. The policemen agreed to get a statement in the master bedroom for the sake of the little girl.

Tristan closed the door three quarters of the way and sat on the bed with his daughter. He told the two officers everything he could remember, regretting that Sarah had to hear it but not knowing what else to do with her. At least now someone was listening to him. Now, someone would have to take action.

"And then what?" asked the female officer who was taking his statement.

"And then I talked with a friend of ours who's a psychiatrist. He called Social Services with a tip about abuse. They sent some lady over there, but she said that there wasn't any evidence of abuse. She said that Daniel was living happily there with his parents. The only thing she reprimanded the dad for was letting his son be in the bar during business hours. I don't understand," he said angrily. "How could she not see it? I can't believe that the kid didn't have any marks on him when she talked to him."

Just then, Daniel cried out hoarsely from the kitchen. Tristan could hear Jamie repeating "It's okay. It's okay" over and over. On the bed next to him, Sarah started to cry. Tristan pulled her up onto his lap and rocked her in his arms.

One of the policemen asked, "Was your wife at home? If so, we'll need to get a statement from her, too."

Clearing his throat, Tristan said, "I'm a widower."

The policeman looked chagrined and said, "Sorry."

Sarah began to cry harder and declared, "I – want – my – mama."

Tristan thought he was going to fall off the bed. In the time since Emma had been killed, Sarah had never asked for her. Even at six, she had understood that MaMa was not coming back from Heaven. He'd come to believe that Sarah didn't really remember her mother very well and that she didn't miss her.

Now, he realized that was what he'd always wanted to believe, because he couldn't make things right and change the past for her. He couldn't bring Emma back.

He put a hand over Sarah's ear and held her close while they wheeled the stretcher down the hall and through the front door. The policemen thanked him for his statement and apologized for any trouble they might have caused in the household. It wasn't their fault, and Tristan told them so.

Jamie pushed open the door. Blood was smeared across the left leg of his shorts and spattered across his shirt.

"Tris, they're taking him to the General. I'm going in the ambulance. I'll see you there soon."

Tristan nodded and glanced up at the larger of the two officers still remaining in the room, the one with seniority by the looks of it. His badge gleamed in the glow from the lamp on the stool.

"Officer, could I ask you a favor?"

He called Vaughn and gave her a brief explanation. Then, still holding his crying child, he locked up the house. The policemen took him to Vaughn's and waited while he ran up the stairs, deposited Sarah into her arms with a kiss for both of them, and instructed Vaughn to call Max and tell him to get to the hospital as soon as possible. Tristan folded himself back into the police vehicle, and they sped off down Government Street. He thanked the officers for making the detour as they all emerged from the squad car.

"You and your friend were trying to save that kid's life," the shorter policeman offered. "What's thirty minutes out of our day compared to that?"

The next few hours were a blur to Tristan. There were policemen, doctors, nurses, social workers, Max, and Lillian, who had insisted on coming along. There was emergency surgery for Daniel, who was, indeed, bleeding internally. Once during the surgery, his heart stopped.

The police were dispatched to arrest Zachary Samuels. They found him at home watching the evening news with a whiskey sour in one hand and a cigarette in the other. He resisted arrest.

The social worker who'd visited the residence was promptly dismissed when it was discovered that she'd never personally interviewed Daniel. In addition, his mother had died two years previously and, therefore, could not be living above the bar with him and his father. An investigation of Daniel's public school records would later show that his teacher had documented the child's constant injuries and absences from school. Her recommendations for intervention had gone unheeded.

Daniel was placed in the Pediatric Intensive Care Unit. Tristan, Jamie, Max, and Lillian were allowed to see him before leaving the hospital that night.

No one spoke for several minutes. Finally, Jamie swallowed hard then said, "He looks bad enough as it is but with all those tubes and wires…."

"Hush," Lillian whispered. "Don't say things like that. He might hear you."

"He's been sedated," the nurse curtly informed her.

No pain, Tristan thought. *Not yet. But what will it be like when he wakes up?*

"We'll talk to him anyway, thank you," Lillian said calmly.

"Fine," growled the nurse. "But then you'll all have to leave."

"I will not leave this child alone in the hospital," Lillian declared.

The nurse turned to scowl at her.

"He doesn't even know you're here. You can't stay in the room, so you might as well go home. This is Intensive Care, after all. We know how to take care of the patients." She stared pointedly at Lillian's dark skin, then at the child's pale face before snapping, "He's not even your child. You'd be in the way."

"I'll be in the way then," she insisted. "I'm staying."

She marched over to a chair next to the bed and gave the nurse a nice view of her back. The R.N. stormed out as Max went over to stand beside Lillian.

"Do you need anything? My first patient's not until 9:00. Maybe I should stay. We could take shifts."

Shaking her head, Lillian said, "No. I'd rather stay if you can do without me for a little while. It would be nice if you wouldn't mind packing me a bag."

She reached through the railing on the side of the bed and took Daniel's hand in hers.

"I'm here, Baby," she whispered. "You're safe."

To everyone's surprise, the heart rate on the monitor slowed from its almost frenetic pace. Alarmed, Lillian turned quickly to Max and asked, "Did I do something wrong?"

"No, not at all. I've read about how the heart rates of newborn babies slow considerably when they hear their mothers' voices or feel their touch. It calms the infants. Perhaps there's something similar at work here."

Lillian moved her chair closer to the bed. Resolutely, she said, "We'll be fine. You all go on home."

Tristan and Jamie left the hospital with Max. The psychiatrist drove to the LSU campus and dropped Jamie at his apartment where he immediately went inside and announced to a slightly shocked Chloe that he loved her. They fell into each other's arms as Jamie reached to undo the top button on Chloe's blouse.

Max drove Tristan to Vaughn's and asked, "Would you like me to wait for you? I could take you and Sarah back to State Street before I return to the house for Lillian's things."

"No, thanks. I'll be in touch in the morning. I don't have to work at the restaurant tonight, thank God. Maybe I could get a ride to the hospital and spell Lillian." Sighing, he said, "Vaughn has to work early in the morning, so I don't know what to do with Sarah. Maybe Jamie or Chloe could watch her."

"Enough." Max put a hand on the younger man's shoulder and directed, "Let it go for tonight. You can see to it later. Get some sleep."

Tristan dragged himself up the steps in the darkness and tapped lightly on the door, which was opened momentarily by Vaughn.

"How is she?" he asked, as he stepped inside.

Vaughn looked away and admitted, "She cried in my arms all afternoon. She finally stopped, but she wouldn't say anything. I got her to eat a little soup; then I held her until she fell asleep. I put her in my bed. Don't wake her, Tristan. She was exhausted."

He nodded and collapsed on the couch. His stomach growled loudly, and he realized that he hadn't had any food since 7:00 a.m.

"You have to eat some soup and bread," Vaughn insisted.

"No," he muttered. "I don't want to eat. I feel sick to my stomach after today. I want to curl into a ball and forget what I saw."

"You have to eat," she said firmly, as she joined him on the couch. "You're too thin as it is. If the bones in your hips get any more pronounced, you'll kill me next time we make love."

He stared at his hands and refused to smile.

"Tristan, that was supposed to be a joke. Please talk to me. Don't I even get an 'A' for effort?"

"Yes, you do." He drew his fingers lightly along her jaw. "I appreciate the sentiment behind it. It's only that...I don't want to talk about it, yet."

"Okay, if you won't talk, then your mouth won't be occupied. So, you can eat."

He checked on his daughter while Vaughn heated up the food. Then, he went to the table and forced himself to sip, chew, and swallow until the bowl was empty and the bread was gone.

Afterwards, they returned to the couch, and Tristan told Vaughn everything that had happened at the house and at the hospital.

"But that's so...so...." Vaughn searched in vain for words that could express the obvious horror she felt regarding Daniel's injuries. "It's so abominable! And that his father did it to him. Oh, Tristan! How could anyone do that to his son? It would be bad enough if he'd done it to an adult, a stranger. But his son?"

"I don't know. I can't imagine a parent hitting his own child unless he was drunk, high, or crazy. But some people are plain mean, Vaughn. It was awful, seeing Daniel suffer like that. The feeling of helplessness was so strong. It made me understand what Jamie must have experienced last January." He pulled Vaughn closer and muttered, "Jamie keeps saving everyone but himself. We've been playing this game of life together for all these years. We scramble up until we can just about see the top of the hole we fell into when we were kids. Right when we get to the edge, we lose our footing and plummet back down. It happens over and over again."

"You plummet to the bottom? I'd think that all the dirt that gets knocked down when you fall would build up a bit. One day so much dirt will pile up that you'll be at the top without even realizing it."

"I like that image," Tristan admitted. "I hope you're right."

He tried to make love to Vaughn on the floor, comfort be damned. He had to have some sort of release from the nightmare that had taken over what was to be his pleasant day in the yard with his child. He found that his mind was too clouded with thoughts of Daniel and Sarah and the events of the last day, month, and year. With a deep sigh, he finally lay back on the wood floor and gave up.

Vaughn took him in her arms. She awkwardly took the lead in their lovemaking for the first time. In this initial attempt, she was hesitant and clumsy. Although it was difficult, Tristan resisted the urge to guide her. In her inexperienced grasp, he let himself relax. If he didn't, then she would always be wary of initiating sex in the future.

That night, he slept next to Vaughn on the rug, and the chasm of life, though deep, was not quite so dark.

Chapter Twelve: Silence

Daniel was released from the hospital into the custody of Lillian Johnson on the first of September. She had maintained a vigil by his side during the critical seventy-two hours after his surgery and had been at the hospital as often as possible every day during Daniel's three-week convalescence there. The social workers were all too happy to acquiesce to Max and allowed the African-American housekeeper to be the child's temporary guardian.

"Covering their backsides," Lillian had said.

Physically, Daniel's recovery was progressing well. The pediatricians and surgeons were pleased at how rapidly his wounds were healing. None of them had expected him to survive.

The psychiatrists, including Max and Isabelle, were not pleased at all with his emotional health. Daniel hadn't spoken since he'd regained consciousness. His father wouldn't talk either, at least not about what had happened on that August morning when he'd nearly beaten his son to death. He was in the parish prison awaiting trial.

So, Daniel was safe and cared for by Lillian and Max, but he moved through each day automatically, keeping his eyes lowered at all times.

Sarah was having her own difficulties. Not only was she upset by Daniel's condition and the episode which had preceded it, but she also had to endure a battery of physical and psychological tests to determine what sort of damage she had sustained nine months before when she'd had the high fever. Tristan had told her that it was absolutely necessary, but she'd argued furiously with him and refused to cooperate. Once she realized that he wouldn't back down, she agreed to go but only if Vaughn went with them.

The results of the tests were made available to Max the Friday before Labor Day. Tristan was already scheduled for a session at 4:00 p.m. Max worked through lunch in order to go over the hospital summary and enclosed paperwork. He arrived home at 3:30 and used the half hour that he had to mull over exactly what he wanted to say.

They settled into their usual places shortly after 4:00. Tristan flopped onto the loveseat, and Max rested in his leather chair. Aside from the notepad that he always kept handy during sessions, Max also had a large manila folder in his lap.

"What's that?" Tristan asked, pointing to the folder.

"It's Sarah's test results. I got them back this morning."

Tristan straightened into a sitting position.

"What does it say? Is everything all right?" He shook his head sadly and said, "I know that's a stupid question. Everything's not all right."

"I've gone over the findings rather thoroughly. The hospital team agrees that Sarah's functioning very well emotionally, despite all of the stress she's had to face in the last year or so. Her scores on the intelligence tests are quite high." He shuffled some of the sheets of paper before admitting, "Physically, there was some damage to the brain. She'll face several challenges as she grows. One area in particular was greatly affected."

"The area that deals with mathematical functions," Tristan said flatly. "So, what kind of effects are we talking about here? What can we expect?"

"Basic math skills were acceptable. However, advanced algebra, geometry, calculus, chemistry, and physics will probably be out of the question. She was incapable of answering any of the questions that indicate function in those areas, and she couldn't demonstrate the skills on the manipulative exams that reflect activity in that part of the brain. Retesting will be necessary as she gets older. There may be some form of tutoring or occupational therapy that might help as she continues to develop."

"Anything else?" Tristan asked as he studied his shoes. "Not that that's not enough."

"She showed significant difficulties in following directions."

"Oh, get real!" Tristan snapped. He got to his feet and began to pace. "You could give Sarah a long list of verbal or written commands, and she could do them in exactly the same order."

"Not those kinds of directions. In one series, the doctor asked her if she knew what a compass rose was. When she said no, he explained to her in simple terms about north, south, east, and west. He showed her an example and pointed to the appropriate locations in the room that reflected the four points. Then, he instructed her to repeat his explanation, which she did flawlessly. Next, he asked her to walk south. She walked east. When he told her to go north, she went south. Following that, he asked her to repeat the explanation she had given only moments before. She couldn't remember any part of it. The same thing happened when they tested her on units of measure."

"How will she function? What will happen at school?"

"We can discuss this with the principal and her teachers. At her age, the directional section should only be a small part of her social studies. The measurement issue may be a little more involved, but it shouldn't be too bad. As for the rest, it will be some time before she encounters that level of mathematics."

"And the music?"

"She can still play by ear. I intend to work with her to remove the psychological block that's keeping her away from the piano."

Tristan drew back his foot and kicked hard at the side of the bookcase, causing Max to jerk reflexively as several books toppled to the floor.

"How can I tell her about this?" Tristan wondered aloud. "It's so senseless! What can I say?"

"Keep it brief and straightforward," Max instructed, as he stood and slipped the manila folder in a file drawer. "Most of it involves things she doesn't understand and won't understand. I wouldn't recommend worrying her over something that she can't even fathom, yet."

"It's my fault. What you're talking about will affect her life. It already has. I did this to her."

"Don't obsess. You have to trust that you'll both work through it."

"I'm trying."

"Why don't you and Sarah come here for Labor Day? Vaughn as well. It might help to take your mind off this and may provide a distraction for Daniel. We'll have a cook-out."

"I guess. How about Jamie and Chloe? What about Benjamin and Halley? We could all bring something."

"Excellent," Max agreed, heartened by the younger man's willingness to go along with his suggestion. "A large and lively group may be just the thing we need. Now, let's discuss what you're going to say when you go home to talk with your daughter."

The following Monday, Tristan, Sarah, and Vaughn arrived at 11:00. Tristan and Sarah had baked a pie, and Vaughn had made potato salad. Max went outside to fire up the grill, while Lillian prepared the meat. When it became clear to everyone that the grill wouldn't light, Tristan and Vaughn went outside to help.

"How did it go with Sarah?" Max asked quietly.

"She doesn't understand."

"We'll talk more on it later," Max assured him. "She'll be all right, Tristan."

Inside, Sarah roamed the house. She felt out of sorts, ready to see her old friends but afraid to go back for the new school year. What if she couldn't do something and everyone laughed at her? She had no idea what to expect, despite her father's assurances that it might be many years before she encountered difficulty in certain subjects. She tried to tell herself that third grade wouldn't be so bad.

She found herself standing at the door that led into the guestroom where Daniel was staying. Sarah peered in through the crack and saw the boy sitting in a chair and staring out of the window at the adults who were attempting to light the barbecue pit. From below, there came a triumphant "Yes!" followed by a "Ha!"

The little girl stepped apprehensively into the room. It was larger than her bedroom. The white bedspread had length-wise orange and green stripes alternating across it. There were matching curtains, plus a chest of drawers and a desk. Daniel had taken the chair from the desk and moved it across the room so he could have a view of the yard. He sat motionless in it.

"Daniel?" Sarah took a few more tentative steps. "Can I come in?"

When he didn't respond, she climbed onto the side of the bed nearest to him. Putting her knees to her chin, she wrapped her arms around them.

"This used to be our room when Daddy and I stayed here for a while. They brought up an extra bed for me."

Silence.

"I was afraid they wouldn't let us be in the same room together, but they did. It made me feel better."

Nothing.

"Do you have a pain?"

106

He swiveled his head to look at her. Softly, he said, "I hurt all over." He pointed to his chest and confided, "It hurts here the worst."

"Why?"

"Because I miss my mom."

Sarah got off the bed and went over to him. "I miss mine, too. Sometimes, I don't remember her too well, but sometimes I'm walking down the street and I hear a voice and think it's her. I turn around because I'm sure that she's there."

"But she never is."

"No. Her name was Emma. What was your mother's name?"

"Assumpta."

Sarah had never heard of anyone named Assumpta. She thought it sounded strange, but she wouldn't say this to Assumpta's son.

Daniel twisted a piece of string that was hanging from the seam on his shirt and said, "Now, I have no one."

"You do, too!" Sarah said defiantly. "You have us, all of us. *We're* your family now."

Daniel twirled the string around his finger and lifted his head. "I'd still have my dad if only I'd listened better."

Sarah stared open-mouthed at him, then stammered, "N-no! Why would you want to go back? He – he– It wasn't *your* fault! How could you even *think* that?" She gave him a look that did Lillian justice and insisted, "*You* need to talk to Max." As he shook his head, she protested, "But it would help."

"I don't like talking to adults."

"You can talk to me."

They soon came downstairs hand in hand. The others had arrived, and everyone was sitting outside in lawn chairs, drinking lemonade and enjoying the afternoon. The group fell silent as Sarah and Daniel emerged from the house. Daniel was in his ritual pose with his eyes averted. Sarah led him over to Lillian, who she figured was in charge of Daniel.

"He wants his things," she said plainly. "He doesn't have anything from his room. There's a bedspread his mom made for him and a model plane his grandfather put together when he was little and other stuff. There's a picture of his mom holding him when he was real small."

Max left the grill and came over to stand in front of Daniel, who tensed and tightened his grip on Sarah's hand. Seeing the child's fear, Max moved to stand behind Lillian's chair and said, "There's no need to be afraid. You can ask or tell us anything."

"He's afraid to talk to grown-ups. They might get mad."

Lillian rose from her chair and walked slowly to where the children were standing. She started to put her arms around Daniel, whose expression of terror was deepening with her every step. The housekeeper dropped her arms and took a step back.

"Oh, Baby," she said. "I'm not gonna hurt you. Never."

Jamie announced, "No one here will ever hurt you."

Tristan got up, came over to the children, and stood looking down at the boy.

"I've never hit anyone in my life." He paused to glance at Jamie and admitted, "I have been sorely tempted by certain people." A fleeting smile crossed Jamie's lips, as Tristan continued. "But if anyone ever tries to hurt you again, I will personally kick the shit out of him."

"Tristan!" Lillian exclaimed.

"I'm sorry, Lillian, but it's the truth."

There was a sizzling noise, and Max hurried back over to the grill to turn the meat. Benjamin, Halley, and Chloe sat in awkward observance of the scene. None of them had met Daniel yet, though they all knew what had happened.

"I think I'll go in and get you both some lemonade," Lillian said resolutely to the children. "Why don't you drag up a couple of chairs, and I'll be right back?"

Daniel sat in a chair and stared at the grass. Sarah touched his face and asked, "What's the matter?"

"I don't like lemonade at all."

"Go tell her then."

"No."

"Miss Lillian won't mind. Honest."

"I —"

"Do you want me to tell her?"

Daniel lifted his head and hastily declined her offer. He had a vision of Sarah taking a blow meant for him.

"I'll drink the lemonade, Sarah."

"If you don't tell her, then I will."

His stomach in knots, Daniel rose and slowly climbed the steps to the screen door. As he entered the kitchen, he saw Lillian standing at the counter with the pitcher in one hand and a glass in the other.

"Miss Johnson?"

It was a voice she had never heard before. Without turning around, she said, "Yes, Daniel?"

"I – I don't really like lemonade very much. Sarah said I could tell you, and you wouldn't make me drink it."

"Of course I wouldn't." She put down the pitcher and smiled at him. "Let me get you a Coke from the ice box. Or would you like something else?"

"No, ma'am. Coke is fine."

As Lillian moved towards the refrigerator, her elbow accidentally knocked the nearly empty pitcher off the counter. It made a crashing sound as it shattered on the floor. Between the noise of the window unit and the chattering in the yard, no one outside heard a thing. Lillian looked at the mess and said, "Oh!" Then, she looked at Daniel.

He was flushed and shaking. His next words came out in a rush.

"I'm sorry. I'm sorry. I should have had the lemonade. I'll clean it up. I promise. I promise. I don't need the Coke."

Lillian carefully stepped over the glass and liquid on the floor. She stood several feet away from him and spread her arms in what she hoped would be a non-threatening gesture.

"There's nothing to be sorry about, Daniel. It was my fault. If you'd like to help me clean it up, then that would be fine."

She edged closer, and Daniel stepped into her embrace. He thought of his mother and of how she had held him like that long ago. Soon, the shaking stopped, but Lillian continued to hold him and stroke his hair.

As they cleaned up the glass and spilt lemonade together, Daniel began to relax. They had just finished putting the last of the glass into a bag when the back door opened and the others entered the kitchen. They headed for the dining room, and Benjamin reached above the refrigerator for the French bread he and Halley had brought. Chloe took out a large bowl of salad that she and Jamie had prepared, and Sarah was pleased to see that there were cubes of cheese mixed in with the lettuce, tomatoes, and cucumbers. Lillian brought in her cole slaw and set it down next to the enormous plate of sausage and chicken and the bowl of potato salad.

As they took their seats, Sarah properly introduced Daniel to Chloe, Benjamin, and Halley. Then, they said grace, although Daniel did not participate in the prayer. Everyone ate heartily, except for Daniel, who picked at the bread and potato salad. Lillian held her tongue and reminded herself that he was still weak and had not eaten much of anything for some time. Maybe later he would accept some grits or scrambled eggs, anything that wouldn't be difficult for him to digest.

Late in the afternoon, there was a mass exodus of guests. The house seemed too large suddenly. Max puttered around in the garden, while Lillian hemmed some pants and watched television with Daniel. The boy was still very quiet, but he appeared to be more at ease in their presence, a change for which Max was eternally thankful.

By 8:00, the child was pale and tired, so Lillian suggested, "Why don't you go on upstairs? You've exerted yourself more in this one day than you have since you got out of the hospital. You should rest now."

Half an hour after he'd gone up, Lillian went to check on Daniel, who was sleeping stiffly on his back. His doctors had said that he might feel uncomfortable on his side or stomach indefinitely. She pulled the sheet up a little and softly kissed him on the forehead. Max padded into the room and stood behind her.

"How could anyone hurt a child like that?" she asked in a hushed voice.

"The situation for parent and child isn't normal," he answered quietly. "The parent comes to believe that he's doing it for the child's own good. Soon, he has the child convinced of that as well. Tragic, but not as uncommon as one would like to believe."

Chapter Thirteen: Reluctant Acceptance

Daniel stirred in the bed. Lillian motioned towards the door, and she and Max began to walk in that direction.

"Dr. Nash?" came a sleepy voice. "Miss Johnson?" Daniel sat up, bleary-eyed and stiff, as the two adults walked back to the bed. "Will I…stay here with you?"

"Yes, Baby," Lillian murmured in a soothing tone. "That is, if you want to."

"I want to."

"Then it's settled," Max said affably. "Tomorrow, I'll go and get your things from Social Services, and you can make this room up any way you like. Well, within reason."

"Will I go to school tomorrow?" Daniel asked, focusing on one orange line of the bedspread.

"Not tomorrow," Lillian replied. "The doctors say you need one more week. Next Monday, you'll start at St. Aloysius, where Sarah goes to school."

"St. Aloysius?" Daniel's head jerked up. "But I don't want to go there."

"Why not?" Max inquired with concern. "You don't have to worry about the expense. I do make a good living as a psychiatrist, and I do like to feel that I'm making a difference. Even if I couldn't afford it, that would be where Lillian and I would want you to go. They have scholarships for the children like Sarah whose families can't afford tuition. It's a good school run by caring priests and nuns."

The boy simply stared at his hands and wound the edge of the sheet around his index finger. It was evident that he wanted to say something but was reluctant.

Lillian looked at Max and asked, "Would you leave us for a minute?"

Once Max had gone, she reached out and took Daniel's hand in hers.

"Now," she said. "Why don't you tell me what's really the matter, Baby?"

111

Max heard her footsteps some twenty minutes later. She came into his office and fell into the high-backed chair. He raised an eyebrow in an unspoken question.

"He doesn't believe in God," she said with a hint of pity in her voice. "His mother was a religious woman, but no matter how much she prayed, things were always bad for them. Then she died, and he kept praying, but things only got worse."

"I will *not* have him going to a public school," Max said gruffly. "He needs extra attention as well as a solid educational base. As for the spiritual aspect...." He hesitated. "As a psychiatrist, I understand. As a devout man myself, I can only pray for him and try to give him guidance."

Lillian rose and headed for the hall with the words, "Then pray for Sarah, too. I do."

"Sarah?"

"She says she doesn't know if there's a God." As Max leaned back and put his pen down on the desk, Lillian continued, "She doesn't hate God or blame Him for any of her misfortunes. She just finds it hard to accept that He's there, that it's all good and well if He is, but that it's up to her to take care of herself. God simply doesn't enter into it."

Max was unnerved by Lillian's words. He had honestly never considered talking to Sarah about her religious beliefs. They were all Catholic, as were the majority of those living in southern Louisiana. Tristan took the child to the Catholic Church on campus every Sunday, and the girl had been baptized as an infant and had received her First Communion the previous May. She'd attended St. Aloysius since kindergarten. According to her school records, she always had well above average grades in every subject, including religion.

"She told you all that," he said incredulously.

"Over the last few months, yes," she sighed. "I've tried to...to change her mind. She always listens politely, but I don't think she can believe in what I tell her. She says she wishes she could and that sometimes she tries to believe, but it feels wrong to her. I pray every night that she'll find some faith." Lillian gave Max a tired smile. "I guess I'll have to be praying for Daniel, too."

"Does Sarah tell you anything else you think I should be aware of? I don't want you to break a confidence, but the child's welfare is my concern."

"She seems to be perfectly open about the religion question. And, no, not that I can think of. Except...."

"Yes?"

"Well, I've been considering how to answer this one for a while, but I didn't feel you'd be the one to ask."

"Come now. You know you can talk with me about anything. You've been working for me – or should I say with me? – for four years."

Lillian stood in the doorway and stared at him for several seconds then looked away.

"Sarah wants to know why we don't get married," she said finally.

"What?" Max asked dumbfounded. "What did you tell her?"

His housekeeper came back and sat in front of the desk. She placed one arm on the smooth top and ran her thumb along the edge.

"The first time, I told her that you were my boss and that I was your housekeeper."

"And she replied –?"

"What difference did that make?" Lillian went on, "The second time, I told her that you were white, and I was black."

"And she gave you the same response."

"Yes. The third time, I told her that you were more than twenty years older than I was and that all of those things put together were not usually accepted by other people."

"And what did she say to that?"

Lillian got up and went to the door once more. She put her hand on the doorframe and spoke her words into the hall.

"She said that none of that should matter when two people love each other like we do."

With that, she walked out of the office. Max could hear her slowly ascend the staircase.

The truth of the matter was that he did love Lillian very much. He had loved her almost since the day he'd interviewed her. He suspected that she felt the same way about him. Although their relationship as employer and housekeeper would have been of little concern to two people in love, the difference in their ages and skin color could not be ignored. They were respected in both the black and white communities. An open relationship within or outside the bonds of marriage was likely to cause an uproar. They had never spoken of their feelings, but there seemed to be a mutual agreement to maintain the status quo.

And now the innocent and intuitive questions of a child had upset the balance to which they'd become accustomed. Of course Sarah would not understand. She was a very open-minded little girl who had a strong belief in what the Catholic Church called social justice. The belief had been encouraged over the years by her parents, Jamie, and the Catholic school. Unfortunately, Southern society as a whole did not share many of those ideals. Many businesses and organizations touted them publicly, but reality was still another matter entirely.

Tapping his pen on the desk, Max wondered what he should do. Lillian had told him while Daniel was still in the Pediatric Intensive Care Unit that she wanted to adopt the boy, and Max didn't think that Social Services would object. Yes, it was a biracial adoption, but it would effectively take a big problem off their already over-worked hands. The fact that she was a live-in housekeeper for a well-known psychiatrist didn't hurt either. If he married her, would that make things better or worse for Daniel?

Max straightened in his seat. This line of reasoning was nonsense. He knew it was foolhardy to even consider the possibility that he could marry Lillian. However, now that the subject had been broached, it was too late to stop thinking about it. He decided that tomorrow he would have a talk with Isabelle. She would give him the right advice, a counselor counseling a counselor.

The next day, he and Lillian went about their business as usual, except for the tension between them that hadn't been there before. The conversation was stilted at breakfast, and Max hurried off to work fifteen minutes early. He was two miles down the road before he realized he'd forgotten his briefcase, and he had to turn around and return home for it. He ended up being ten minutes late for his first appointment.

Max didn't have anyone scheduled after 3:00, so he made plans to meet Isabelle at Mike Anderson's Restaurant at 5:00 On his way, he stopped and retrieved Daniel's things. The four boxes were sealed, and the psychiatrist did not open them. They were not his property.

Max pulled into the parking lot of oyster shells an hour early. He stayed in his car until 4:30 then entered the restaurant and requested a table slightly isolated from the others.

Isabelle was late. Once she was seated and their food had been ordered, Max set about explaining to his friend the source of his distress. She listened to him ramble on while they ate and drank. He completed his exposition as she took her last bite of trout. He had hardly touched his food.

"As I see it, you have five choices," Isabelle stated calmly. "One – fire her."

"I don't want to do that."

"Two – carry on an illicit relationship with her."

"Isabelle! I can't do that! It would be unethical, against my religious beliefs, and completely –"

"Maxwell, I am giving you the facts. Listen to the stereotypical German Jewish psychiatrist for a moment." There was a twinkle in her eyes as she teased, "You are a terrible patient."

"Go on."

"Your third choice is to continue on as you are at present."

"I don't see how that can happen."

"All right. Then marry her, and be open about it. To hell with society and all that."

"That might ruin both of our lives."

"Fine. Marry her, and do not tell anyone, at least not for a while. Personally, I think this may be the best option. Stop sputtering, and hear me out. You love her, but you do not want to have sexual relations with her outside of marriage because of your faith, etcetera, etcetera. If you marry her, it could bring shame to both of you, personally and professionally. But if you marry and do not make it public, you can enjoy the closeness of marriage while still maintaining your social standings in your own communities." She took a sip from her steaming cup of coffee then said, "Tell me your objections."

"She's in her thirties. What if she conceives a child?"

115

"So, do something to prevent it." She made a dismissive gesture and stated, "I know what you are going to say. Personally, you do not believe in using birth control. That should be left up to God. So, if she conceives, then you go public."

"And receive recriminations for having secretly married her in the first place and having a mixed-race child?"

"Pessimist." She looked at him sternly. "You asked for suggestions. I did not say they were perfect solutions. Go on."

"What about Daniel? If we were to secretly marry, he would certainly notice that we were sharing a bed. Either we tell him the truth and ask him to conceal it, or we try to hide it from him for the next decade or so."

"Why not wait until he is grown?" she asked sarcastically. "Then you might not have to worry about having a child either, since Lillian will be in her forties."

"Don't be trite, you taskmaster. Now that this has become an issue, I don't think that we can dance around it for the next several years. Plus, the boy needs a stable home. Let's say that I fire Lillian or she leaves. What sort of housekeeping job could she get as a black woman with a white child? Who else would hire her?"

"Pshaw! If you recommended her, I can think of several well-off people who would snap her up in a minute. The truth is you don't want her to leave."

"No. And Daniel needs help. My help. If she leaves, would he get the psychiatric assistance that's required in order for him to become a well-adjusted or even halfway-adjusted adult?"

"I would help him if it came to that." Isabelle brought the conversation back to the main topic by saying, "Really you have two choices. Either way, you marry her. It is whether or not you want to take a chance and make it public."

"It's only...." Max stuck his spoon into the bread pudding in front of him then withdrew it and looked soberly at Isabelle before admitting, "I never thought I'd marry again."

"Gwen has been gone for fourteen years. Come to think of it, you were never able to have any viable children with Gwen. Perhaps you're incapable of fathering a healthy infant. That would solve one of your problems."

"If you'll recall, we had a child."

"I did say *viable*."

"And it should comfort me that I may only be able to father babies who don't survive?"

"Of course not. I apologize." She crumbled some of the crust of her cheesecake with her fingers and went on, "Gwen did have other serious health concerns."

"But –"

"Maxwell, you know as well as I do that nothing is certain in life. Maybe you are meant to be with this woman and to have a large family in your later years."

"I seem to have acquired a large family over the last few months without having relations with anyone."

"True," Isabelle agreed and smiled fondly at him. "And why is that? You have never failed to be a caring psychiatrist, but you have really gone out of your way to help these particular young people. Are you thinking about opening a home for wayward juveniles and adults? Or do you merely enjoy taking your work home with you that much?"

"I suppose that my motives are not entirely selfless. I'm getting older. Perhaps I was beginning to want more from my life than a constant rotation between office hours, Knights of Columbus functions, and gardening. Perhaps I saw my younger self reflected in Tristan Maes and Jamie Nesser that first day I met them at the hospital. Or, perhaps, I'm overanalyzing things."

"Perhaps. It is amazing what a mid-life crisis can do to people, is it not? You told me yourself last year that you did not think you were doing enough to help the underprivileged. Enter Jamie Nesser and Tristan and Sarah Maes." Isabelle paused as a waiter refilled their coffee cups, then she said more quietly, "And, for your information, the combined personalities of Tristan and Jamie remind me very much of you as a young man. They are also good at problem-solving for everyone, except themselves."

"You must admit that Tristan is a bit taller than I." Max added some cream and sugar to his coffee, then said, "I do hope they surmount some of the emotional obstacles they've set in place for themselves."

"And I hope that the extra thirty years or so of life experience that you have had counts for something. Do not revert back to boyhood and run from commitment as Jamie does now. You have got to take care of things at home if you are ever going to look forward to a mellow old age."

"What would you do?"

She patted his hand and said, "Talk to Lillian, of course."

Chapter Fourteen: New Day

Max did not talk to Lillian. For the next three days, his schedule was booked solid, and in the evenings he found himself working through dinner just to update patient records. He knew that he could have made time to talk with his housekeeper. He wasn't sure how to approach the inevitable conversation. It was simply easier to avoid the topic altogether.

On Saturday, he awoke to the sound of a knock on his bedroom door. The clock read 10:17.

"Yes? Lillian?"

Through the door, he heard Sarah's muffled voice.

"It's me. Is it okay if I come in?"

"Sarah, of course. However –"

Before he could ask her to wait until he'd put on his robe, she was in the room.

"I *had* to talk to you," she said plaintively. "Miss Lillian's at the store, and Daniel's watching TV."

Max gestured for Sarah to hand him his robe. He slipped it on over his pajamas and stepped out of bed. After tying the belt, he moved over to sit in one of the two chairs positioned in front of the fireplace at the far end of the room. Sarah took the other chair. Suddenly, she seemed uncomfortable.

"You're like your room," she said.

Max knew that she was stalling, but there was no reason to rush the child.

"How so?"

Sarah looked around the huge master bedroom. There was a four-poster bed that was complemented by a matching armoire, chest of drawers, and dresser. The oriental rugs were old, but not worn. The chairs they occupied went well with the other furniture and looked no less antique. The oil painting of a pastoral scene that hung above the fireplace was beautiful and dignified.

"Everything's in its place. It fits. It works."

At the moment, Max did not feel as though his life had much balance, but he didn't say this to the girl, who asked, "Where are you from, Max? I mean, really."

"I was wondering when you'd ask me that question." The older man smiled down at her and said, "I was born in Cornwall, which is in England. My parents came to this country when I was about your age."

"Where are they now?"

"They passed away some time ago. A few years after they died, my brother moved out to the West Coast. He lives in Seattle."

Sarah mulled over this newly imparted information then asked, "Do you miss him?"

"Yes, but we talk on the phone. We get along very well. I just wish that we lived closer."

"Do you miss England?"

"I became an American, and Baton Rouge has been my home for almost half a century. I do miss the countryside of England. It's stunning, with cliffs and the pounding of the waves and deep green grasses in the springtime."

"You should go back to visit."

"Yes, I probably should." He stroked his beard absently and prompted, "Not that I'm unhappy to see you or to discuss my past experiences, but what are you doing here on a Saturday morning?"

"Oh, that." She started to swing her feet and said, "Daddy had some important thing he had to write for school, and my next-door friend's mom who watches me sometimes had a baby, so I can't go over there today. She had a boy. I bet he's cute. He's twenty inches long and weighed ten pounds. That's big."

"It is."

"Daddy said I wasn't even six pounds when I was born. I was seventeen inches long. That's much smaller than the new baby." She hesitated then asked, "Isn't it?"

"It is."

The child chewed on her lower lip and stared pensively at her lap.

"Sarah, what was it you wanted to talk with me about?"

"Daniel."

Her legs continued to swing back and forth then slowed to a stop.

"Daniel…he thinks that maybe he should leave."

"Leave?"

Over the last week, Daniel had seemed to improve. He never said much to Max or Lillian, but he didn't appear frightened anymore. Max had decided that the boy needed some time to adjust before he began his therapy and had intended to talk with him that afternoon about having a session the following week.

"Yes, he says maybe it would be better if he left. I don't know how he can think that."

"But why does he feel he needs to leave?"

Sarah studied the circular pattern she was making with her right foot. Soon she was making a continual figure-eight.

"He says that maybe things aren't right between you and Miss Lillian because of him, and if he left, you would be like you were when he first came here."

"Is that why he hasn't opened the boxes filled with his things?"

"Part of it. I think he's scared to open them, too. It'll make him think about his mom…and his dad." She flashed him a look of pure guilt then asked, "Do you think he can hear us? I mean, the living room's right below here and all. I don't want him to think I'm tattling or anything. I figured it was important, and you should know. I don't want him to run away or something. It's not like when Daddy and Jamie ran away. He should be here."

"The floors in this house are thick, as are the walls. You definitely did the right thing in telling me about how Daniel feels. And, no, it has nothing to do with him. I'll talk to him about it later." Sarah bit her lip and looked alarmed, so he quickly added, "I won't mention this conversation, and I won't say anything that might alert him to the fact that I know what's bothering him. I'm glad that Daniel feels it's safe to tell you things he can't tell anyone else, but I'm also glad that you know when something is important enough that you need to tell a grown-up about it. All right?"

"Okay," she said seriously, as she hopped down from the chair. "I better get back. I told him I was trying to find some paper and crayons. We were going to draw some pictures."

"Run along then. I'll be down as soon as I dress."

While Max brushed his teeth, he stewed over this new development regarding Daniel.

The situation between Lillian and me is becoming more problematic each day that we don't address it, he ruminated, as he combed his hair, moustache, and beard. *Should I tell Lillian about Daniel's perceptions of our difficulties and how they're affecting the dynamics of the household?* As he tied his shoelaces, he thought, *How odd that Lillian should leave the children here and not wake me when she left the house. I guess it goes to show just how seriously this has affected us.*

When Max entered the living room, the two children were sitting on the floor with their heads bowed over their artwork. With their attention focused on their efforts, they both seemed much younger than twelve and seven. Perhaps it was the high ceilings and the massive bookcases or the heavy pieces of furniture that dwarfed them.

Max shrugged mentally and asked if he could critique their pieces when they were done, got a "yes" from Sarah and a nod from Daniel, and went to eat some toast and drink some hot tea. Then he went to work in his office.

Forty-five minutes later, Lillian came into the room. He lifted his head but didn't lift his pen from the paper.

"Lunch is ready."

"Lillian –" he began.

"Daniel and Sarah are in the kitchen. I have to get back."

By the time Max got to the old oak table, the children were halfway through with their sandwiches. He sat in front of his plate and listened to Sarah chatter on about the things she'd drawn. He reminded her that he would still like to see what they'd completed. Sarah put down the piece of apple in her hand and ran into the living room to get the artwork. Uncharacteristically, Lillian didn't scold her for leaving the table before she'd finished eating.

Sarah held out her picture to Max. It was a landscape scene, full of clouds, birds, and trees that were loaded with fruit and flowers.

"Very colorful," he remarked. "I particularly like this bird here."

"That's a dove. Isn't she pretty?"

"Quite attractive. And where is her mate?"

"Her what?"

"Her mate. Doves are usually mentioned in pairs."

122

"I don't know. Maybe she flew ahead to make a nest."

Sarah took the picture from him and went over to tack it onto the refrigerator with a magnet. Then she returned and put Daniel's drawing into Max's hands.

It was a dark picture done mostly in black, brown, and red. A purple border edged the drawing. The center consisted of black shadowy angles and red shapeless blobs. To the right, there was a large dark blue mass that resembled an oval rock. A brown, spidery design hovered in the upper left-hand corner.

Behind Max, Lillian was busily putting away the rest of the groceries. Max looked up at Daniel and realized that the boy must have been staring at him for several minutes.

"Daniel, what is it?"

The Adam's apple in his throat bobbed as he swallowed and said, "Nothing." He pushed his chair back and stood before asking, "Can I be excused?"

"*May* I be excused?" Lillian corrected. Her voice had an unusually harsh edge to it, and Daniel took off running down the hall.

"Daniel was right," Sarah said softly. "Something *is* wrong."

Guilt began to sweep over Lillian. She wanted to go to the boy and tell him – what? That she was sorry that she and Max were human and, therefore, imperfect? She took several steps forward and walked across to where Max sat at the table. He held out the picture, and she took it from him.

"Very disturbing," Max nodded, as her face was clouded with even greater concern. "Very illuminating."

"What's 'illuminating'?" Sarah asked nervously, as the back door swung open.

Jamie and Tristan ceased their casual banter as they came into the kitchen. It was apparent that something was amiss. Max got up, excused himself, and went out the back door.

Tristan looked to Jamie, who said, "Why don't you and Sarah head home? I'll give you a call later."

"Good idea. C'mon, Honey."

She took his hand, and they said goodbye to Lillian on their way out.

"Daddy?"

"Yes?"

123

He was heading for the front, taking long strides, and she was having trouble keeping up. With effort, he slowed his pace.

"I think Max is in the garden. Should we go talk to him?"

Tristan stopped and crouched down in front of her then explained, "Everyone has to have time alone now and then. Let's see what Jamie says tonight. Why don't we do what he suggested and head back to the house? We can swap stories about school on our way to getting an Icee at the 7-11."

They walked toward Highland Road, as Sarah proceeded to tell her much-relieved father that third grade was "neat."

Inside the house, Jamie asked Lillian, "What's going on? I know I haven't seen you in four days, but that's no reason for everything to fall apart."

Lillian tried to smile. Jamie took a seat at the kitchen table, and she lowered herself into the chair closest to him. He reached down and picked up Daniel's drawing and carefully examined it. Lillian averted her eyes after a brief glance.

"I – that is, Max – that is to say that Max and I are having a…problem." I was tense and spoke a little more forcefully to Daniel than I should have.

The screen door creaked open, and Max trudged into the room. Facing Lillian, he proclaimed, "He thinks it's his fault and that he's the reason for the discord between us."

"Would someone please tell me what the hell is going on?" Jamie asked in frustration.

Lillian opened her mouth to protest, but Max pressed on, pretending that he hadn't noticed.

"Lillian and I…have feelings for each other. However, we've never spoken of these feelings to anyone, even between ourselves, until Monday night. Ever since our conversation, there's been unease overshadowing the usual atmosphere of the household. I think Daniel blames himself for this change."

"Is that all?" Jamie asked with a shrug. "So, get married." He grinned and added, "I know. Here I am unable to make a commitment like that, and I'm telling you to do it. But you should."

"How?" Lillian interrupted, questioning Jamie's solution while focusing on Max. "How could we get married? There are so many differences in age, race, status and with living in the South like we do."

Jamie looked back and forth between the two of them, then said, "You get married for Daniel." As they stared at him, he continued by saying, "Daniel's been through a lot. He needs a good home life with a mother and a father present. You're getting married for *his* sake. At least that's what you tell other people. Tell Daniel the truth, but let them think that you did it to help a poor abused kid. People will admire you for it and accept the marriage as it is. Then they'll get used to it."

A hint of a smile touched Max's lips as he asked, "Jamie, have you ever considered a career in psychiatry?"

"It's always easier to give advice than to take advice. Wouldn't you agree?" Jamie leaned back in his chair and peered down the hall then asked, "By the way, where's Daniel?"

Lillian jumped up and cried, "Oh! He's in his room, I'm sure. I was heading up there before."

Jamie rose quickly, and they followed Max down the hall and up the stairs.

"I hope he hasn't locked the door," Lillian said as they climbed.

"He hasn't," Jamie assured her.

"How can you be certain?"

"If you're used to somebody beating up on you, you know that locking the door only makes it worse. Even if you're lucky and they don't kick it down, they'll take it out on you harder when they get to you the next time."

Max stopped suddenly, causing Jamie to bump into him. Lillian completed things by running into Jamie. Max twisted slightly and searched Jamie's face.

"You speak from experience?"

Jamie didn't turn away but said with an acid tongue, "I told you I was in foster care for six years. You didn't forget, did you?"

He pushed around Max and stalked angrily towards Daniel's room. Max and Lillian hurried up the last few steps, as Jamie stood in front of the door and forced himself to relax. He tapped lightly on the door. When there was no response, he turned the handle and motioned for Max and Lillian to wait outside. Daniel was nowhere in sight.

Jamie wandered around the room. Finally, he bent down and lifted up one side of the bedspread. Daniel was curled in a ball on the floor. Leaving the spread pulled up, Jamie sat on the cool wood and leaned his back against the mattress.

"Nobody's mad at you, Dan. Lillian and Max are in the hall worrying about you. They're having some troubles, and they're upset because they think you might be feeling like you're somehow to blame." Jamie drew up his left knee and rested his arm on it before stating, "You're not the problem, and neither Max nor Lillian is gonna come in and pop you one. Like we said on Monday, nobody here will ever hurt you like you were hurt before. So, try not to freak out about it, okay?"

There was no movement from under the bed.

"Why don't you come out of there so we can talk better?"

Slowly and stiffly, Daniel slid out and sidled up next to Jamie. He still made no effort to speak but did reach down to twist his shoelace around one finger.

"Look, I've been there. If you ever want to talk about it with somebody who's been through it, then you can talk to me."

The boy's eyes went wide, and he said in disbelief, "You? But you seem so normal!"

"Normal?" Jamie laughed. "Yeah, right. Tell me another one."

He held out his hand. Daniel took it, and they shook.

"It helps to meet other survivors, don't you think?"

Daniel's head was spinning. He had never considered the idea that others might have experienced the same things that he'd endured. It was comforting but also frightening.

"Was it your dad, too?"

"My dad wasn't interested in me enough to beat me. I was in State custody for six long years. Some of the people were real caring, but some were only concerned about getting their checks. You slept in your clothes on the floor, and if you got in their way they'd kick you like you were some mangy dog."

"Do you have scars, too?"

"Three."

The shoelace was wound so tightly around Daniel's finger that the skin was purple.

"Could I...see?"

"Sure." Jamie reached up and pulled off his t-shirt, tossing it on the desk chair before saying, "Here's one."

Daniel squinted at the faint white line that extended for approximately three inches across Jamie's ribcage on the left side of his torso.

"How did you get it?"

"I fell, of course."

Daniel almost smiled at the inside joke.

"I got slapped and knocked into the metal edge of a tool chest. You know those big ones that stand about three feet tall? No? Well, anyway, I didn't get any stitches until the next day. The scar would have faded by now if I'd had it sewn up right away."

"What about the other two scars?"

"Right here."

He scooted sideways so that Daniel could see the two pink circles on his upper back. Daniel didn't have to ask. He had an identical cigarette burn on the right side of his back.

"Does Tristan have scars, too?" Daniel asked in a whisper.

"Nah. Tristan's parents took really good care of him until they died. Then, I took care of him. I don't know if I did a good job or not," he said, reflecting on the last ten years. "It's kind of tough when kids raise each other. I'd like to think we were better off on our own, but it's always preferable if you can have a real family. I think Max and Lillian would like to give you that opportunity. I wouldn't turn it down if I were you. Give them a chance."

"But if I'm not the reason things aren't right around here, then what is the reason?"

In the hallway, Lillian began to tremble. Max pulled her closer to him. They didn't dare interrupt the conversation that was taking place on the other side of the wall. Daniel was not only talking; he was responding openly and without fear.

"Lil has worked for Max for a long time. I guess they love each other, but they're afraid to follow through because of what people will think. They've ignored it until they couldn't ignore it anymore. You happened to be here at the wrong time. Or the right time. Anyway, I was telling them that you probably wouldn't mind having a mom and dad and that they could get married and say it was for you. It would be, but it wouldn't be, too. You

127

understand? After a while, people might get used to it, but at first the fact that they really love each other and all would have to be a secret. Do you think you could help them out?"

"Yes," Daniel said slowly. "I want to. It's been so many years since I haven't been afraid all the time." He let the shoestring unfurl. "I guess I know they won't hurt me, but I can't help it and get scared sometimes." He glanced at Jamie and asked, "How long was it before you weren't afraid?"

"Ages. I still have nightmares about it. Not as much as when I was a kid, but they still come for me once in a while."

"I have nightmares, too," Daniel admitted. "All the time. I wake up, and I want to scream, but I can't make any noise. I don't want Lillian and Max to hear."

As he got to his feet, Jamie said, "At least you have Max. Tristan and Sarah think he's a pretty good shrink, so give him a break. Lillian'd make a good shrink herself if she didn't say what was on her mind so much."

Daniel looked up at the blonde man and asked, "So, why don't you go talk to him? Or her?"

Chuckling, Jamie reached down to help Daniel up and conceded, "I might someday. I've been putting it off for so long that I got in a rut about it. I'll get around to it. Don't you make the same mistake I did. And, remember, I'm always a call away if you want to talk about things."

"Thanks."

Daniel went over to the desk and removed a piece of paper and a pen. He brought them to Jamie, who wrote down his phone number. Then, he handed Jamie his shirt.

"I gotta go. Chloe and I are going to hear this kick-ass band downtown, and we'll be late if I don't get a move-on. We're supposed to be meeting up with Tris and Vaughan and Benjamin and Halley." He looked back at Daniel and advised, "Remember what I said."

As he emerged from the room, Jamie went over to Max and Lillian, who were now standing apart. Max mouthed the words "Thank you," and Lillian hugged him before going into Daniel's room.

Chapter Fifteen: What Lies Ahead

Jamie gave in and enjoyed the feeling of satisfaction that was washing over him. It had been hard to talk about his former life and those scars, but it had been worth it. He let himself out and started for the road where he caught the bus that would take him home.

Jamie found it amusing that he'd never thought of the apartment as "home" until Chloe had moved in. He wondered what life would be like when the baby was there with them. He was thankful that he would be finished with his degree in December. He would then start studying for his Ph.D. He wanted to be the best biochemist he could. Teaching and research were Jamie's professional loves. There was so much knowledge to be passed on to those who were interested. He was also fascinated by the idea of exploring possible cures for diseases within the plant world and was intent on working towards gathering materials for a new grant.

The possibilities that lay before him were endless once he got a job. He hoped that he could get a position at the university upon graduation. Usually, they didn't hire their own graduates, but it had been rumored that they would make an exception for him.

He couldn't leave Baton Rouge. With Tristan and the others he had a place in the universe, and he knew that Chloe's parents would calm down after a few weeks and accept the concept of him and a baby. Chloe was their only daughter, and her older brother was off fighting in Vietnam.

Jamie was so lost in thought that he almost missed his stop. He hastily grabbed for the cord, stood waiting at the doors, then stepped down onto the corner of his block. He reached his apartment in less than a minute, jiggled the key in the lock, and let himself in.

"Looking good, Chloe," he said, as she came into the cramped living room wearing bell-bottoms and an embroidered chambray shirt.

"Thanks. Do you like the shirt? Halley made it."

"It looks damned good on you."

"It's loose enough so that I ought to be able to wear it even when I get bigger." As Chloe struggled to insert a hoop earring, she confided, "I think Halley's sad. Every time we talk she's so sweet, but I feel, like, guilty for being pregnant."

"Not your fault."

"I know. If only they'd try to have another one. Halley said –"

She stopped in mid-sentence, and Jamie put down the book he'd picked up from the floor.

"Halley said what?"

"I guess it doesn't matter whether or not I tell you," Chloe sighed. "Halley said that she and Benjamin had a gigantic argument two days ago. He says that he's never going to father another baby, that it would be a disaster, and that he's going to have it taken care of."

"He's probably too squeamish to go through with a vasectomy. You know how he is. Will she stay with him if he does it?"

Easing herself onto his lap, Chloe put her arms around his neck. Her feet dangled almost to the ground over his left leg.

"I'm sure she will. She's so loyal to him. But I think she really wants a baby, *his* baby. I just don't know. He'll never give in. At least I don't think he will."

"Don't think!" Jamie said. "Let's both not think for a while."

They stayed on the couch and kissed until it was past time for them to leave. Jamie's neighbor was smoking on his section of the porch. As they locked the door behind them, Rembrandt loped over and wagged his tail. Chloe stooped down to scratch him behind the ears, and he shut his eyes in ecstasy.

"You want to come out with us tonight?" she asked the dog's owner.

"Yeah," Jamie grinned. "Hey, why not? It'd be cool."

The man took a drag, then spoke, sending out clouds of cigarette smoke with his words.

"Thanks, but I think Rembrandt and I are gonna commune with the universe right here on this front porch tonight."

"You *always* commune with the universe on the front porch," Jamie remarked.

"Every night," Chloe added.

"Yup," the man said, as he ground out his cigarette. "Life's beautiful, ain't it?"

Leaving him to stare at the stars, Chloe and Jamie walked down Highland to Benjamin's apartment. Halley greeted them with a sigh and a frown.

"He's *still* not ready," she groaned. "He's changed his shirt a hundred times. I give up!" She shouted back towards the bedroom, "You know women are the ones who are supposed to take forever to get ready! I've been dressed for hours!"

Jamie's stomach lurched, as they walked into the living room. The décor never failed to make him feel slightly nauseous.

The place was a conglomeration of different styles. Beanbag chairs, a Navaho wall-hanging, Chinese pottery, and tartan throws were jumbled together along with the other bric-a-brac that was spread throughout the apartment. Halley had mentioned that Benjamin had done most of the decorating. He was partial to so many patterns and pieces, and he wanted to enjoy them all. Thus, it was all displayed simultaneously. Jamie wondered how Halley could stand it.

The trio walked into the bedroom and viewed Benjamin, who was shirtless, rummaging through his closet. His long, straight hair was loose, and he kept pushing it out of his face as he tossed pieces of clothing from one side of the closet to the other. Chloe sat on the mattress and fell back onto the brown furry bed covering. She closed her eyes against the visual deluge and breathed a sigh of relief.

"Tell me when we're ready."

Ten minutes later, she woke to Jamie's light kiss and Benjamin's jeans and green T-shirt. His hair had been restored to its usual braid, and he'd tied it with a bright red rubber band. Halley grabbed her purse, and they left for Tristan's.

When Tristan opened the door, it was clear that he was nowhere near ready. He wore shorts and a tie-dyed t-shirt that had seen better days. He was a pale shade of yellow.

"Tristan!" Benjamin cried. "You *must* hurry or we'll be late!"

"Benjamin, I can't believe you!" Halley cried. "You are such a hypocrite!"

"I'm not going. Sorry, guys."

"What's wrong? Where's the Munchkin?" Jamie peered around his friend into the empty hallway and called, "Hey, Princess!"

"Sick. She threw up about five times an hour ago. Must be a virus, 'cause I did the same thing thirty minutes later. When I called Vaughn, her landlady answered and said Vaughn had been throwing up all day and had finally called them because she was feeling so weak. She was in the bathroom the whole time I was on the phone. I tried to call Jamie, but y'all must have left already." He turned to Benjamin and complained, "If you'd get a phone, it would really help sometimes. So, anyway, none of us will be going out anywhere tonight." He looked at Chloe and said, "Speaking of going out, you'd better get out of here. You're only supposed to be throwing up in the morning. I don't want any of you guys to get this."

"Call me tomorrow, Tris."

"Sure thing, Jamie. I hope you have a good time tonight."

"Tristan?" Halley stepped forward slightly and asked expectantly, "Would you tell Sarah that we hope she feels better soon?"

"I will. Thanks."

Tristan shut the door behind them and went back to his room. Sarah was tossing in the bed. She looked as bad as he felt. He dipped a rag in the bowl of cool water that rested on the little stool. Folding it, he placed it over her throat.

"Daddy?" she moaned. "I don't feel good."

He took another rag, wet it, and wiped his daughter's face. The look of misery did not abate, but she did close her eyes and relax slightly.

"I know, Honey. I don't feel good either. It'll pass after a while."

She made a little whimpering sound. He was finding it difficult not to throw up again himself. He lay down next to her and put a rag over his own throat in an attempt to ease the discomfort.

He would have stroked Sarah's hair, but she always lashed out when anyone attempted to hold or touch her while she was trying to sleep. The only exception was when she fell asleep while being carried. She had never been like that before the previous January. He wondered if she would ever allow it again.

Tristan woke in the middle of the night and discovered Sarah huddled against him, his shirt gripped in her small hands. He didn't dare move. She must be deep in sleep to not notice that she was against him in the bed. He closed his eyes and dreamed of Emma.

They were standing on the wooden bridge near City Park. Tristan had never met anyone as beautiful as Emma. Even at fifteen, she'd been undeniably gorgeous.

"I was watching you," she chirped.

"How come?"

"You don't know?" she laughed. "Because you're so *you*."

"Oh." He glanced around, then asked, "Are you waiting for someone?"

"No. Actually, my dad told me to leave this morning and never come back. I liked the bridge, so I thought I'd stop and not think about where I'm going next."

Tristan started to ask her why her father had put her out on the street, but he changed his mind. Instead, he said, "My father used to tell me that bridges were like life. Sometimes, the bridge you need to cross is blocked, so you have to try different methods to get where you're going. You might have to go over, under, across, or through in any given situation. And any one of those solutions might be right or wrong on any given day. It's up to you to figure out which one's the best."

"Can a person ask for help in getting across?"

"Sure."

"Do you know a place I can sleep, at least for tonight?"

"You can stay with me and some friends. We get by."

"Thanks!" Her expression was radiant as she exclaimed, "That would be great! Is it far?"

In his dream, Tristan reached out his hand and put it against her hair, which was cool to the touch. It was like reaching through thousands of silk threads, and he wanted to bury his face in the mass of hair and breathe in the deep aroma of flowers forever.

And then he was putting flowers on her grave, tears streaming down his face in sleep as he had not allowed them to at her funeral.

"Daddy! Daddy, wake up!"

133

He opened his eyes and saw the anxiety in Sarah's face. He could feel the dampness on his cheeks and in his hair. He remembered his conversation with Max a couple of months before and looked at his child, who appeared to be so frightened by his tears.

Let her see them then, he thought.

"I was dreaming about Mama," he explained. "Sometimes I still miss her so much."

She took the now dry rag from his throat and wiped his face.

"It's okay, Daddy. I miss her, too."

He could see the dark circles under Sarah's eyes. Neither of them had slept well or long.

Suddenly, she said, "Do you love Vaughn?"

He blinked in surprise but didn't hesitate to say, "Yes, I do."

"Then why don't you marry her so we can be a family? She makes you happy, and she makes me happy. Why do we have to live apart? Does she…not want me?"

"That's not it at all," Tristan assured her. He sat up quickly and a wave of nausea hit him. Lying back, he said, "You're right. What am I waiting for? The only thing is I don't have a ring, and we don't have the money for me to buy one for a while. Gold and diamonds are expensive. You were two years old before I had saved enough money to buy your mother a gold band with a tiny diamond."

Sarah pondered this obstacle. She almost suggested that her father give her mother's ring to Vaughn. She reasoned that her mother wasn't using it, and she would have wanted Tristan to be happy, wouldn't she? However, for some reason, she sensed that this idea would cause her father to become upset. There had to be some other answer.

"Does it have to be gold like Mama's with a diamond? Vaughn always wears silver. Why don't you get her a silver ring? Do they cost more than gold?"

"It would cost less for a silver ring." He smiled and touched her cheek then asked, "You'd go right away, wouldn't you? Even though we're both wracked out."

"Oh, please, Daddy!"

"No. Not today. We've been too sick."

Her lower lip stuck out when she pouted. It reminded him of Jamie.

"We're going to sit around and eat chicken broth and plain spaghetti and toast off and on. This afternoon, we might even try to get some homework done. Tonight, we'll go to bed extra early, and tomorrow we'll take it easy."

"But when will you look for the ring?"

He pushed a stray piece of hair out of her face and replied, "Next weekend we can look together. Until then, it's our secret, okay?"

Her eyes were bright and expectant. Tristan was momentarily gripped by fear of the uncertainty of life. He forced it down and got up to make some soup.

Chapter Sixteen: First Day

Daniel suddenly realized there was a pattern. First, the rainwater would drip from the right side of the window. Then, two drops would fall from the spout on the left. Next, a drop would come down from the center. Then, it would start all over again.

"Daniel."

Although his name was spoken gently, his heart rate increased involuntarily as he turned around. He was undeniably and understandably going through a bad phase at the moment. He hated Max and Lillian for sending him to the Catholic school. He hated the principal for knowing what had happened to him and for telling the teachers to be extra nice to him. He hated his mother for dying. He hated Tristan and Jamie for not letting him die. He hated himself although he wasn't sure why. For his father, there was only fury, but what good was fury without direction?

"Daniel."

He looked up at the nun. She was a big woman with a soft, soothing voice. Her smile was nice. He couldn't remember her name.

"Daniel?"

He started, surprised. He must have drifted off again.

"Yes, Sister?"

"Why don't you turn to page twenty-one in your religion book? Perhaps you could read the prayer out loud today."

Daniel closed his science book and noticed that the other children already had their religion books out and open in front of them. He slid the one textbook under his desk and reached for the other. Slowly, he turned the pages until he came to twenty-one. He opened his mouth then closed it. Sixteen heads turned to look at him.

Finally, he said, "I'm sorry, Sister. I can't read this prayer."

"You can't?" Lines appeared on her forehead as she asked, "Why not?"

His eyes drilled into the "Hail, Mary" at the beginning of the page, as he said, "Because my mother…well, this was what she always prayed."

From the desk behind him came the voice of the boy Daniel would later find out had been the school bully since the previous year.

"What, did she beat you, too?"

Daniel was out of his desk in an instant. He flung himself at the boy and hauled him up by his shirtfront. In a matter of seconds, he had the bully pinned to the ground.

Punching him felt good. All of the anger Daniel had held inside was channeled into his fist. He heard the teacher in the background, but he couldn't make out what she was saying. He couldn't have cared less.

It didn't take the boy long to recover. He was almost a head taller than Daniel and had obviously had a hearty appetite for some time. He grabbed Daniel's arm with one hand and punched him in the stomach with the other. One of the girls screamed, and Daniel gasped and fell away from the boy, who scrambled to his feet.

The teacher hurried back into the room with the principal. Daniel hadn't been aware that she'd left. The two adults knelt beside him as he tried to ignore the knife-like pain that was stabbing into him whenever he inhaled. He focused on the ceiling and began to take very shallow breaths.

The principal bent over him and asked worriedly, "Daniel, can you hear me?" Then, "Sister, I think we should get the school nurse right away."

The teacher nodded and turned to one of the girls hovering with the rest around their fellow student.

"Go to the nurse's office. Quickly!" As the girl took off through the doorway, the nun leaned over Daniel and asked, "Are you all right? What happened?"

Daniel refused to respond. The principal looked sharply at the boy who'd punched Daniel.

"Something tells me that Mr. Samuels here didn't start a fight with you for no reason. Please go to my office and wait for me there." After the boy had gone, the priest stood and asked, "Would anyone like to tell me what happened?"

"I heard it, Father," volunteered a short, blonde boy.

"Yes, Mr. Taylor?"

The priest waited, hands folded behind his back. Robert Taylor stared down at Daniel, whose eyes were now fixed intently

137

on him. Daniel concentrated and directed his thoughts at his classmate's brain in hopes of some miraculous telepathic communication.

Don't say it in front of everyone. Please.

"He, um, made a rude comment about Dan's mother."

Daniel gave the boy a grateful nod in order to convey his thanks and hoped the priest wouldn't ask for more details.

The nurse arrived and instructed the students to leave the room. The teacher ushered them out and closed the door behind her. The principal retreated to the window and politely turned his back as Daniel was examined. After several minutes, he said, "Well?"

"I think he's all right, but he should go to a doctor to make certain there's no real damage."

The man nodded then said, "Please contact his guardian and his physician. I'll wait here with him."

Once the door had closed behind the nurse, the priest sat on the edge of the teacher's desk and shook his head. Daniel's heart pounded as he lay helpless on the floor.

"I apologize, Mr. Samuels," the principal said kindly. "I imagine you're wondering how that classmate knew about your family situation. The fact of the matter is that his mother is the school secretary. Let me rephrase that: She *was* the school secretary until this afternoon. She's broken the confidentiality rule of this Catholic institution and will now be dismissed. This isn't her son's first offense, and he'll be expelled."

"Will I be expelled, too?"

"You will not. However, I have to give you a written reprimand. Fighting is something that isn't tolerated at our school. I'll make an exception in this instance, but it can't happen another time. Is that clear?"

Lillian arrived a short while later and helped Daniel to the car. He sat hunched in his seat during the drive to the pediatrician's office. The shame began to well up inside of him. Hitting the bully had felt good. Was that what his father had felt when he'd hit Daniel and his mother? Was Daniel destined to be an abuser like the man he'd hated for so long? If so, then Daniel vowed that he would never, ever get married and never, ever have children.

He lay listless on the sofa all afternoon and waited for Max. His stomach was in knots, not because he was afraid that Max would hit him but because he was certain that he had disappointed the man.

"You're extremely lucky," Max remarked when he returned home that evening. "If he'd hit you on the other side, he could have killed you."

"He would have done me a favor."

"And why do you say that?"

"I'm a bad person. I deserve to die."

Max lowered himself onto the ottoman and said firmly, "You are not a bad person. You're a victim. You deserve respect and love."

"I can't be like *him*. I'd rather die than hurt someone like he hurt my mom and me."

"That's why we need to talk regularly. You'll return to school tomorrow. Perhaps this weekend we can get down to brass tacks and begin your therapy."

"But –"

"No buts. Now, why don't you go wash up before supper?"

"I'm not hungry."

"Sarah and Tristan will be joining us."

"Can I go to my room instead? I don't feel much like eating."

Sarah appeared after dinner and climbed onto the foot of Daniel's bed. He pretended to be asleep, but he soon realized that she wasn't so easily fooled.

"The kids from your class were asking about you," she told him. "Especially Robert Taylor. He wanted to know all about you."

He opened one eye and asked, "Why?"

"He likes you. They all like you. They were worried."

"When did they talk to you?"

"At recess. I was sitting with my friends at the old tree stump. We were playing that Barbie and Ken had a house like Tarzan and Jane. That's when Robert and some other boys came over to find out about you."

"What did you tell them?" he asked anxiously.

"That you wanted to be friends with them."

"Nothing else?"

She shook her head and said, "It's better not to talk sometimes. People don't understand how things can be."

"Like what?"

"Like me and Daddy. My friends don't care about where I live or that I don't have a mom. They don't care that Daddy was sick. Their moms and dads care. They won't let them play at my house or sleep over. I have to go to their houses. They think Daddy might let something happen to their kids."

"That's ridiculous."

"If I was a mom and didn't know Daddy then I'd maybe feel the same way."

"So, you go to their houses?"

"Yes. Sometimes they try to give me food or clothes to bring home, but I don't take them. It makes me feel bad."

"Because they try to give them to you?"

"Because I don't take them. I don't want to hurt their feelings. They mean well."

"Thanks for not telling the others about me."

"Will you be their friend when you go back?"

"I'd like to, but I don't know if I can."

"Robert is nice. His mom's Olivia and his dad's Bob. Did you know Bob is short for Robert?"

"Yeah. How do you know their names?"

"They came to see me and Daddy when we were sick. Everybody else from the school was too embarrassed to come, except the principal and the teachers. Miss Olivia gave me a teddy bear, and Mister Bob gave Daddy some money, even though Daddy told him he didn't want to take it. Mister Bob has lots of money, and he said he wanted to help."

"Your dad told you that?"

"No. I was supposed to be asleep. I'm a good pretender."

"Better than me, I guess. What about Robert? Did he come with his parents?"

"Yes. He makes jokes. He made me smile a little. He makes jokes at school, but he gets in trouble for it sometimes. He gets called to Father's office now and then, but Father likes him. Sister Elizabeth calls him the class clown."

"Sister Elizabeth?"

"Your teacher. I wonder if she gives everybody a nickname."

"I hope nobody gives me one. I doubt if it would be anything good."

The following morning, Daniel carefully slid into his seat as the other children tried not to stare. He studied the top of his desk, while Sister Elizabeth described the enormity of the Milky Way Galaxy. He was having an inordinate amount of trouble concentrating. Outside noises and movement in the halls were constant sources of distraction. Daniel would open his book and then either lose interest or become so absorbed that he'd forget what page he was supposed to be reading.

By lunchtime, he was exhausted from his efforts. He wanted to pay attention; he *needed* to pay attention; and, yet, he couldn't pay attention. He filed out of the classroom with the other students and followed them to the cafeteria.

Once he'd filled his tray, Daniel took a seat at the end of one long table. To his surprise, he was joined momentarily by Robert Taylor.

At first, it was awkward. What had happened the day before combined with Daniel's feelings of inadequacy and shame to make him nervous and unsure of himself. After a few uncomfortable minutes, Robert sighed and began to push his fish sticks around until he'd formed an off-kilter rectangle. As Daniel watched, the boy scooped up his peas and deposited them into the center of his mashed potatoes.

"What are you doing?" Daniel asked, as Robert's Jell-O jiggled in response to the prodding of his knife.

"Playing with my food. You've never made stuff out of your food before? It makes eating more fun."

Daniel thought about what his father would have done to him if he'd played with his food. He remembered what Sarah had told him about revealing too much and asked, "How's it make it more fun?"

"I dunno. You can use your imagination and go wild."

"Go wild?"

"Go ahead. You do it."

Other boys began to join them at the table as Daniel stared at the food on his tray. All he saw was food. He felt the eyes of his classmates upon him, as he reached down and began his construction. Within moments, he'd fashioned a precariously balanced teepee out of fish sticks and a mashed potato fire surrounded by rocks made of peas.

"That's great," Robert said encouragingly.

Daniel smiled and admired his campfire scene. Suddenly, he heard Robert say in a stage whisper, "Man, Davey, you've got balls!"

"That's not all he's got," another boy remarked.

All of them looked at the boy's tray. His mashed potato snowman was anatomically correct.

"He's hung like a bear," one boy said in a voice low enough not to be heard by anyone except those gathered at the table. "That's some fish stick, but he's got raisins for –"

"Sister Elizabeth's coming!" Davey yelped, as he quickly pulled the snowman's appendages from his body.

"Yeow!" Robert exclaimed. "He's not a holly, jolly soul anymore, is he?"

Wiping the tears from his eyes, Daniel rubbed at his sore abdomen and said, "I haven't laughed this much in…in forever."

"This is nothing," one of their classmates confided. "Robert could make anybody laugh, even Micky's mom!"

Another boy, obviously Micky, threw a crumpled napkin in mock irritation.

"Don't believe him, Dan. My mom's not like Sister George at the office! *She* really doesn't have any sense of humor."

Daniel listened intently as the boys regaled him with stories of past mishaps and mayhem in previous grades. He was reeling from the shock of their quick acceptance of him. He left his food untouched and spent the remainder of his time in the cafeteria talking and listening to these boys who were fast becoming his friends.

On Daniel's third day back at St. Aloysius, Sister Elizabeth moved Robert so that he sat directly across from Daniel to the right. From that moment on, Daniel's behavior began to improve. He continued to have trouble paying attention for long periods, but the other children caught on quickly as to how they could help him. Softly saying his name in order to bring him back to whatever topic was being discussed got the best results. It took some time, but he responded to them and to his teacher. The need for reminders tapered off, and his circle of friends expanded.

Daniel soon unpacked the boxes that had been stacked in the corner of his room. He discarded most of the clothes, some sheets, and several torn and faded throw pillows. He displayed his model airplane on his desk. Lillian brought him a hammer and a nail, and Daniel hung a picture of two Labrador Retrievers standing at the edge of a pond. The striped bedspread was removed and replaced by the quilt that Assumpta Samuels had stitched for her son a decade earlier. Lillian took down the existing curtains and replaced them with some that she had sewn to match the blue and white quilt.

Daniel had a home.

Several evenings later, Lillian burst into Max's office and stood smiling near the doorway.

"You're grinning like a Cheshire cat," Max observed, as he replaced a book he'd just removed from the bookcase near the window. "You look quite pleased, actually."

"Pleased? I'm overjoyed!"

Her attitude was infectious, and he began to grin broadly himself.

"Why? What happened?"

"I told Daniel that it was time to go upstairs. He said he wasn't ready for bed and asked why couldn't he stay up longer? He almost argued with me!"

With a chuckle, Max said, "I never thought I'd hear you excited by the prospect of a child questioning your authority. It's rather refreshing."

"It's normal for a child to question authority sometimes. This is wonderful!"

"Yes. The fear that dominated his every waking hour does seem to be receding."

"He asked me today about our wedding. I explained about talking with the priests and that they had agreed to perform the ceremony here in the garden next month."

"How did he react?"

"He wanted to know why it couldn't be sooner. I took that to be a positive sign."

"Most definitely. Perhaps we'll discuss it during our session tomorrow."

143

"Maybe I shouldn't go to Ville Platte to my sister's for the weekend. The child's only been here for three weeks. I know he's better but...."

"You'll be leaving in the morning and coming back the next evening. Daniel and I will be fine." With a twinkle in his eye, he asked, "Is it that you don't trust me?"

"I can still remember the chaos when I first arrived here at the house. No, I don't trust you alone here. It took me quite a while to straighten the mess before."

"How much damage can we do in two days' time?"

"You shouldn't tempt fate. You're asking for trouble."

Chapter Seventeen: Unearthing the Truth

Once they'd seen Lillian off the next morning, Max and Daniel walked to the garden. The temperature was below eighty for the first time in months.

"It's perfect weather for relaxing outside, don't you think?" Max asked, as they settled onto the bench.

"I don't feel very relaxed."

"How are you today?" Max began. "Enjoying your room?"

"Yes. I put some things out. Some of it is still in a drawer."

"Such as?"

"A couple of books. This little stuffed bear I had when I was a baby. A picture of me and my mom."

"The model airplane is quite well-constructed. Your grandfather must have been very handy."

Daniel shrugged, but Max couldn't miss the proud smile.

"I think Lillian is envious of that quilt. She never did master the skill herself. Perhaps this will push her to learn. Did your mother quilt often?"

The smile flickered.

"That was the only thing she ever made that I can remember."

"No wonder it's so special to you."

Daniel nodded, and the smile was gone from his face.

"Tell me about the picture of the dogs."

"I saw it at the TG&Y when I was five or six. I liked it a lot. Mom bought it for me." Daniel reached down and picked up a stone before adding, "She didn't get permission."

"Hm." Max stroked his beard and leaned against the back of the bench then asked, "And what happened because she didn't get permission?"

The boy threw the stone as hard as he could and said, "You know."

"Yes, I suppose I do."

"What will happen to me? I know that Lillian said you were going to get married in October, but what about afterwards?"

"We'd like to adopt you."

"But I'm not an orphan. My dad is still alive. How could you adopt me?"

"After the arrest, your father surrendered all of his parental rights."

"He did? Why?"

As the psychiatrist reached out to lay a reassuring hand on Daniel's knee, the boy shrank back automatically. Quickly withdrawing the hand, Max stood and went to examine a cluster of miniature roses.

"It was probably a plea bargain or an attempt at one. He could offer to surrender his rights in order to get a reduction in sentence. I'm not certain in this case."

"He only cares about himself," Daniel said angrily. He picked up another stone and rubbed it between his fingers then muttered, "This happens every time."

"Every time? Could you explain that?"

"My mom was sick, but he didn't bring her to the doctor."

As he continued to examine the tiny bushes, Max asked, "How long was she ill?"

The rock Daniel had been holding bounced on the grass near Max's feet.

"A while."

"What was wrong with her?"

Leaning over, Daniel wrapped the long stem of a weed around his finger and twisted it. He unwound the stem then twisted it again.

"She'd never say. All that last day she was the same, but that night she.... It was bad. She laid on the bed with her knees pulled up. I don't know what was wrong, but she died later that night."

"You don't know?" Max asked incredulously. "Your father never said? No one ever told you why your mother died?"

"No."

"Would you like for me to find out?"

Tugging upwards, Daniel pulled the weed from its niche in between the rocks of the path.

"I guess so."

Removing the handkerchief from his pants pocket, Max asked, "Do you have any objections to our adoption plans? Neither Lillian nor I would ever attempt to replace your parents."

"I'd like to be here with you. You can replace them any time." Jaw clenched, he added, "My father surrendered his rights, so that might make it easier for him. Will it make it easier for you to adopt me?"

"Without it, the process could have dragged on for years, and you might have eventually been returned to your father. As it is, the adoption should be completed by March or April."

Daniel rose wordlessly from his seat and walked slowly back to the house. Max waited for a few minutes then went to his office. He called a friend of his who worked for the parish medical examiner. Within the hour, Assumpta Samuels file had been found, pulled, and read to him.

Max sat stunned in the office for some time once he'd thanked his friend and hung up the phone. Finally, he rose and climbed the stairs to Daniel's room.

The photograph of Assumpta Samuels and her son was in the third drawer he opened. Max stared at it for a long time, not knowing if he would ever see it again. Then he carefully replaced it in the drawer and went in search of Daniel.

The boy was seated in the kitchen. Several sheets of loose-leaf paper were scattered on the table beside a plate of cookies and a glass of milk.

"Book report?" Max said, attempting to sound calm in spite of the tumult in his mind. "What title did you select?"

Daniel laid down his pen.

"You found out, didn't you? What was it?"

"Peritonitis."

"What does that mean? How did she get it?"

Sitting in a chair, Max explained, "An injured area becomes infected. If it goes untreated, then peritonitis sets in. Once that happens, a person must be treated immediately. Discomfort increases with movement, and fever escalates. The way you described your mother, lying in bed in terrible pain with her knees pulled up, is indicative of peritonitis. Within a few hours or days, the organ systems shut down." He leveled his gaze at Daniel and asked, "Would you like for me to contact anyone about looking into her death?"

Daniel turned his head and raked his fingers through his black hair. Then he asked thoughtfully, "You've already called someone, haven't you? What did they say? What would they have to do in order to prove that my father had anything to do with it?"

"It might be difficult to prove foul play," Max admitted.

"How would they find out? My mom's been dead for a long time."

"Her body would have to be exhumed."

Daniel stared blankly at him.

"They would have to dig up the coffin and perform another autopsy."

Daniel looked away. Max waited for more questions, but the boy merely pushed back his chair and left the room. He climbed the stairs to his bedroom and shut the door. He did not come down to dinner.

In the middle of the night, Max woke with a start and became aware of Daniel standing mutely beside his bed. As he struggled to rise and turn on the light, Daniel put out a hand and touched his arm. It was the first time that the child had ever voluntarily come into physical contact with him.

"You don't have to turn it on," he said quietly. "I only wanted to tell you that I made a decision about what you told me. I can't let them dig her up and...do that to her. They'd make me talk to everyone about it and maybe even say things in front of a judge. I'd have to defend her for staying with him, and I can't. It might not even do any good, and it won't bring her back."

"And if he was responsible?"

The boy stood silently in the stillness of the room then went to the foot of the bed. With his back to Max, he said, "I know he was responsible for her death. But so was she. How many times did he beat her, and how many times did she take it? After she died, he started beating me, and I took it. Well, I'm not gonna take it anymore."

"You don't have to."

"My father doesn't want to have anything to do with me, and I feel the same way about him. I don't want to have to go over my whole life again and again and again with anybody. It was bad enough to live through it for the first twelve years without having to relive it for the next twelve."

"I'm afraid you have to discuss it with me if you want to put it all in perspective."

"I can live with that. But that's about all I can live with."

And with those words, he left the bedroom. Thus ended Daniel Samuels's former life.

His new life truly began on Max and Lillian's wedding day. The ceremony was to be held in Max's garden, since there had been an uproar in the congregation when the marriage banns had been posted. Daniel thought that there could be no better place for his parents to get married than at the old Nash house.

Max's brother, Milo, flew in from Seattle to be his best man. Until then, none of them, except for Lillian, Isabelle, and Sarah, had known that he had a brother. Lillian's younger sister, Carrie, was to be her maid of honor.

The 2:00 ceremony consisted of an abbreviated version of the Catholic Mass. The vows were brief and to the point. As their family and friends looked on, Max and Lillian pledged to love and honor one another for the rest of their lives. The only invited guest not in attendance was Isabelle, who was in bed with the flu.

Once the license had been signed, Tristan suggested, "Why don't you all come hang out at our house?"

"That sounds like a splendid idea," Max declared. "It seems a fitting day to 'hang out,' don't you think, Lillian?"

"You take the keys to my car, Tristan," Lillian insisted. "Milo or Carrie can drive it back when we're ready to come home."

"Can you all fit in the Ford?" Max asked. "You could take the Oldsmobile."

"Nah. We'll manage fine," Jamie assured him. "The girls'll just have to sit in our laps. We've squeezed into smaller cars before."

"We'll close up the house and join you shortly," Lillian told them.

As the guests walked out, Sarah called back, "Don't change your clothes! You have to stay dressed up until tonight!"

They assured her that they would not change before going to her home. Carrie and Milo waited in the hallway, while the couple checked around the house to make sure that no lights were left on, that the back door was locked, and that the faucets were not dripping.

"She's always been like this," Carrie offered. "She has to make sure that everything's in its place. It all has to be in order."

"Him, too," Milo said. "I used to swear that he had the most organized room in the world when we were in school. After his first wife passed on, that part of his life became less important to him for several years. I think Lillian got him back on track when it came to keeping things straight."

There was an awkward pause, as they tried not to stare at each other.

"So," Carrie cast about for some topic of conversation. "What do you do in Seattle?"

"Landscape design. And you?"

"I work for an insurance company."

Milo rocked back and forth on his heels. Carrie adjusted the sleeve of her dress for the tenth time.

"I hope this works out for them," Milo confided. "It's not going to be easy."

Carrie moved to stand at the bottom of the stairs, peering up to make certain that her sister was not within earshot.

"It wouldn't be so much of a problem if we lived in New York or Chicago or somewhere like that. Lillian's lost so much already. If only –"

She turned, flustered, as her sister and Milo's brother came across the landing and began their descent to the first floor. Milo looked questioningly at Carrie, but she shook her head and walked past him towards the door.

When Max pulled up at the Maes' curb, Sarah ran out to greet them. She took the newlyweds by the hand and eagerly pulled them forward. Once they came through the front door, they understood the reason behind her excitement.

On the square table in the living room there were several small trays of sandwiches, cheese, crackers, and relishes. Sarah and Jamie had decorated with paper streamers again, but this time they were all white and were accented by peach-colored balloons.

Lillian scanned the room and stammered, "I – I don't know what to say."

"Don't say anything," Sarah told her.

"Not till you've seen the kitchen," Jamie added.

The house was small, so it didn't take them many steps to get to the kitchen. As they walked with Tristan in front of them, Max ruminated on how cramped the younger man must be here, like a giant who lived in a dwarf's cottage. Then he saw the kitchen table, and he couldn't think of anything except how touched he was.

There, on the top of the spool table, sat a three-tiered wedding cake. It was white, and fresh pink roses cascaded around it and circled the bottom layer.

"Exquisite," Max murmured.

"Chloe made it!" Sarah volunteered. "She says she wants to do it all the time."

"I think you've found your calling, my dear," Max said with genuine enthusiasm.

"Do you really like it?" Chloe asked uncertainly. "Really?"

"Like it?" Lillian hugged the girl and said, "It's beautiful. Thank you."

"We all wanted to do something for you," Tristan admitted, as he ushered them back to the living room. "It's only that we didn't have a lot of money to spare, so we decided that we'd each give you something special. Chloe offered to make the cake, so Jamie donated the roses from a bush he's been tending at school. This is from me, Sarah, and Vaughn."

He held out a large, white box tied with a wide, pink ribbon. Lillian and Max undid the bow and removed the top of the package. Inside was a simple, yet elegant wooden box. It had been painted white and detailed with intricate patterns along the lines of tapestry designs. When Lillian opened the top, she saw that a piece of green velvet had been laid inside.

"It's for keepsakes," Vaughn suggested.

"Daddy made the box, then I painted it, then Vaughn painted all the pretty things on it," Sarah piped in.

"It's wonderful," Lillian said, running her index finger along the edges.

"Before you get too mushy about all this, you'd better open our presents," Benjamin said, holding out an envelope to Max, while Halley passed an ornately wrapped shirt box into Lillian's hands. The box contained a tablecloth, embroidered with birds and flowers and vines that had been sewn by Halley. Enclosed in the envelope was a blank piece of paper. Everyone looked inquiringly at Benjamin.

"I couldn't very well do a portrait without any subjects. It wouldn't be right. I figured I'd wait until you were in your wedding suits. My things are in Tris's room. I'll get them in a moment. It won't take but a sec."

Milo stepped forward and said, "Well, I was going to wait until later, but I suppose there's no time like the present for a present."

As Max opened the envelope, he said, "Another blank piece of paper?"

"No, three plane tickets to Seattle. I hope Thanksgiving's all right for you to take a vacation."

Max smiled up at his brother. He hadn't had a vacation in years.

"My turn," Carrie announced, as she moved to one side of the couch then came forward and held out a basket filled with loads of tissue paper cushioning something white inside of it. "I wasn't sure what to give you, Lillian. I hope this is something you'll both like."

She had crocheted a delicately patterned white bedspread for the master bedroom. Lillian had no idea how she'd done it in such a short amount of time, especially since she often stayed late at the insurance company to help the owner, who was trying to make the business a success.

Daniel stepped into the center of the room and proclaimed, "I have something for you, too."

It was a photo album covered in dark blue velvet. Two holes accented the side of the album, and blue cording had been slipped through the holes to hold the book together. Tassels had been attached to the cording, and a strip of blue lace edged the left side.

"Daniel, it's lovely." Lillian squeezed his shoulders and added, "It's perfect."

Max took the album from her and examined it.

"Yes, it's quite different. I've never seen one like this before. Where on earth did you find it?"

"Robert's mom made it. I told her that I couldn't find what I was looking for and told her I wanted you to have an album to keep pictures of the wedding. So, one day when I was over there, she said that maybe she could make one.

"We went to Hancock's, and she told me what materials she wanted to use and asked me to pick out what I wanted. I paid for them with my allowance, and I bought her a rose to thank her for making it. I think it turned out pretty okay."

Vaughn said, "It turned out better than okay. May I see it?"

As she ran a finger lightly along the lace, Max said, "I'm sorry, Daniel. I didn't even think to ask you if you wanted Robert and his parents to come today."

In fact, he hadn't thought about much else besides work, Daniel, Lillian, and the wedding.

"Again," Max said, "I'm sorry."

"It's okay. It's no big deal."

"Yes, it is. I think it's high time we really got to know Robert's parents. I've only met them once, and you two have been going back and forth to each other's houses for the last few weeks. Do you want to call and see if they'd like to come over and celebrate with us?"

It wasn't long before the Taylors' car pulled into the driveway. Tristan met them at the door. Bob and Olivia greeted him warmly, as Robert dashed in to find Daniel.

They're "good people," Tristan thought. He smiled, but it was a smile tinged with sad remembrance. His parents had been "good people" like the Taylors. He stepped back and ushered Bob and Olivia inside.

Vaughn had borrowed the camera from her landlords, and everyone was busy either taking pictures or posing for them. The food they had all contributed disappeared, and the cake was cut and served.

"I hope we have as much fun at our wedding!" Vaughn called out to Tristan from across the room.

Milo, who was deep in conversation with Jamie, tore himself away long enough to ask, "When are you getting married?"

"January," Tristan answered happily. "Vaughn's parents and sister are coming in for the ceremony."

"Just think of how great this is," said Halley. "Max and Lillian got married today. You and Jamie will graduate in December. You and Vaughn will be getting married. Daniel will be adopted. Chloe and Jamie will have their baby. I'll be heading into my senior year of college, and Benjamin will be opening up his own studio."

"A veritable whirlwind of activity!" Milo exclaimed. "Bravo to all of you!"

Tristan looked around at his friends. It was going to be all right. Things had been bad, but they would be wonderful now. They were all on their way.

Part Two - 1979

Chapter One: The Confrontation

The streets were hot, damp, and very dark as sixteen-year-old Sarah Maes made her way back home. The peach-colored summer dress she wore kept sticking to her stomach and upper back as she perspired in the humid August Louisiana air. She looked at her watch. It read 4:37.

Normally, Sarah would have been afraid to be out so late alone. She was only five feet tall but had the long auburn curls, full breasts, and shapely hips and backside that drew attention from the boys at her school and from grown men. She would be an easy target for someone who wanted to take advantage of her in any way. However, that night, she felt no fear of predators, though she knew she would be virtually defenseless against an attacker. She simply didn't care and walked on, feeling impervious to the dangers of the night and detached from her sense of self-preservation.

As she turned the corner, Sarah saw her house. She'd always loved that house, the dwelling of an architect and an artist and their two children. It was a blue, two-story structure with white trim. The old glass windowpanes were hand-blown and had a slightly rippled appearance. The rooms were large, and the multitude of windows gave every space the impression of being light and airy during the daytime. At night when the curtains were drawn, the hardwood floors and colorful walls and furnishings combined to give the house a comforting, welcome feeling.

That morning, Sarah detected none of that wonderful atmosphere emanating from the house. It looked deserted and foreboding. She thought of the neighbors, who were asleep in their beds or watching the late, late show or waking up to get ready for an early shift. She wished she could go to one of their houses instead of to hers.

Her heart flip-flopped for the first time. Was her father inside waiting for her? Was he asleep? Angry? Indifferent? Should she go somewhere else? But where?

No. Running away from this isn't the answer, she thought. *If only I knew what the answer was.*

Sarah cut across the yard and walked up the steps to the porch. The bulb above the door was burning brightly, if not invitingly. She reached forward and slipped her fingers through the pull on the storm door, which swung back dependably. With a turn of her key and a shove on the smooth wood, Sarah opened the door and crept into the hallway. Maybe her father was asleep after all.

Easing off her shoes, she tiptoed towards the stairs.

"I was wondering when you'd get home."

Startled, Sarah froze, dropping her shoes, which clattered to the floor. When she turned to peer into the blackness of the living room, she could clearly see Tristan's profile. He was sitting in what she liked to call "the Comfy Chair." It was her favorite piece of furniture in the house, a place where she could curl up to do homework or read and relax. Tristan rarely occupied it, preferring to stretch out on the couch or to push back in the recliner. Why had he chosen to sit in it just then?

The better to see you, my dear, she thought with a shiver.

Her father rose from his seat and twisted the tiny knob on the lamp, as Sarah's heart thudded woefully in her chest. She didn't want to fight. All she wanted to do was to climb into her bed and close her eyes. It didn't look as if that was going to happen.

As Tristan walked over to where she was standing, Sarah observed that his clothing was in terrible disarray. His jeans were dusty. His sneakers were covered by grass clippings. One white shirttail hung limply over his left pocket. His buttons had not been inserted into the proper buttonholes.

Tristan's person was also in need of some attention. His complexion was sallow, and a sheen of perspiration covered his face. His long hair was loose, and the neglected curls shot out at odd angles. He was sorely in need of a shave.

Halting in the archway in front of her, Tristan towered over his daughter and began to speak, quietly at first.

"When you didn't come home by 8:00, I got scared."

Sarah clenched her hands but said nothing and studied the edges of the hall runner. One of her shoes was lying on its side next to a William Morris leaf pattern that had been woven into the carpet.

"I called around," he continued. "You weren't at any of your friends' houses. So, I went out to try and find you." He paused and ran his fingers through his disheveled hair and declared, "I wandered the streets from 8:00 to 10:00. I was frantic, Sarah. I imagined all sorts of horrible things – that you'd been mugged or raped or murdered."

"Why didn't you call the police?" she asked with mock innocence, as she raised her eyes to meet his.

He gaped at her. She made no excuses, offered no denials, and gave him no apologies. With a single question, she was deflecting the blame from herself to him. The tragedy of it was that she had every right.

As Sarah moved to retreat to her room, Tristan reached out and took hold of her arm. His grip was a fraction too tight, and she winced.

"Where were you?" he demanded. "Tell me!"

"I was with Billy Baudoin, if it makes any difference to you."

Tristan's grip tightened, and Sarah tried unsuccessfully to disengage her arm.

"You know I don't want you hanging around with –" Abruptly, he stopped, pulled her towards him, and muttered, "You were *with* Billy?"

"Daddy, stop!" Sarah's cheeks flushed as she insisted, "It's no big deal."

For a long moment, Tristan stood stupefied in the hallway. In an anguished tone of voice that she'd never heard him use before, he blurted out, "How long have you been having sex?"

Sarah's cheeks and neck went from pink to red. Her anger flared, and red tinged the perimeter of her vision as well. The injustice of it all flooded over her, and she completely lost her temper with her father for the first time in her life.

"How *dare* you judge me! For your information, tonight was the first...I had never...It's none of your business!"

"Of course it's my business!" Tristan shouted. His hand fell away from her arm, leaving five white lines. He threw both hands up at the ceiling and cried, "You're my daughter! You're sixteen! What if you got an infection and didn't know what to do? What if you got pregnant?"

Her eyes stinging with tears, his child admonished, "What do you care? All you care about is yourself and the drugs and drinking yourself into oblivion!"

Tristan veered back towards the living room, not wanting to hear this or acknowledge that it was finally being said.

"And so what if I get pregnant?" she went on. "You got my mother pregnant when she was younger than me! She could prostitute herself with you, but I can't –"

Tristan whirled around with his right arm raised upwards and backhanded her. Perhaps the blow itself wouldn't have been so bad if Tristan had not been such a large man and his daughter had not been so small....

He came to awareness standing over her, gazing at his hand as if he didn't understand what it had done. His vision blurred. He lowered his eyes then focused them on the form of his daughter, who was lying stunned on the floor. Blood was trickling out of her nose.

A howling was rising within him, and it was all he could do to stop it from coming up out of his throat. He knelt next to his little girl, who was crying quietly at his feet. She cowered and proceeded to cry harder.

"Sweet Jesus, Sarah. Talk to me."

"You swore when I was small that you'd never drink or do drugs again!" Sarah brought her hands up to her face and said angrily, "You lied to me!"

Unable to go on, her sobs increased in intensity, and Tristan began to shake. When he made to touch her, she flinched.

"Oh, God. Sarah, no."

Tristan rose from the floor where he'd been crouched next to his daughter. He walked over to the telephone. As he went to pick up the receiver, Sarah's voice stopped him.

"P-please, Daddy! Don't c-call the police. They'll take me away! They'll put you in jail! I-I-I..."

She was getting hysterical. In all of her life, Tristan had never seen her so distraught. His heart breaking, he went back to her and took her in his arms. She only flinched for a moment before she let him lift her up against him. Once there, she curled up next to him, the blood from her nose staining his shirt and shaming him again and again and again. He held her to him and rocked her back and forth.

"But you're right," he whispered into her hair. "About all of it. That I could hurt you like this proves it."

And then the guilt and sadness overwhelmed him, and the tears came. He wondered how he had let things go so wrong. He had thought that it could never happen again. Maybe it would be better if he did call the police.

In the end, he called Max and told him in broken sentences what had happened. Sarah was balled up in the Comfy Chair, not hysterical now but still crying freely. Tristan's own face had never dried.

Within forty minutes, Max, Benjamin, and Jamie were at the house. None of them had been in the same room all summer. Max, who was now in his early sixties, looked virtually unchanged. In their mid-thirties, Benjamin and Jamie didn't appear much different than they had the previous May when they'd all gotten together for Memorial Day, although both had cut their hair short since Sarah had last seen them.

"Sarah, I believe your nose is fractured," Max said, as he took a seat on the couch. "We should have it x-rayed. Don't you think so, Tristan?" Tristan sat unresponsive next to him, so Max repeated, "We should have it x-rayed."

"I don't want to go to the hospital," Sarah said wearily.

The pain, the crying, and the lack of sleep had exhausted her. She wanted the others to go away, all of them, even her father. Especially her father.

"I hurt all over," she mumbled. "I don't care if my nose is broken. I'm so tired." She began to shiver and added, "I'm so cold."

"You're in shock, my dear," Max said gently, as he removed the afghan from the back of the sofa and brought it over to her. "You should be seen by a physician."

"You're a doctor."

"Sarah –"

"I'm not going to the hospital!"

"Let's wait for a while before you make any final decisions."

They listened to Benjamin fumbling around in the kitchen, as he wrapped some ice in a hand towel. He returned to the living room and held the small bundle out to Sarah, but she kept her arms folded protectively across her waist. He lowered his backside onto the arm of the chair and carefully rested the towel on her nose.

"I'm sorry, Darling. I know it must hurt, but your nose is already swollen. Is that too bad?" He waited for a reply, got none, and went on. "Why don't you lean your head on the chair?"

Sarah felt her temple press against the soft fabric of the upholstery. Normally, she would have scrambled for a rag. Her nose was still bleeding intermittently, and red droplets fell onto the cream-colored afghan and the flowery material that covered the chair. What did it matter? Both the afghan and the chair would always remind her of the confrontation she'd had with her father. She never wanted to see either of them again.

Jamie left the room and came back with a glass of water. Sarah sat up slightly and tried to drink, but she couldn't breathe properly through her nose. She kept having trouble swallowing.

"Sip it," Jamie prodded, as he helped her to hold the glass. "Just a little at a time."

There was a knock at the door. Sarah looked wildly at Benjamin, who said, "It's probably a Jehovah's Witness or a couple of Mormons." He forced a smile and added, "Just trying to lighten the mood."

"I don't think it's working," Jamie grumbled. "You're an artist, not a comedian."

Max went to the door, and they heard him say, "Hello, Son. I was concerned you wouldn't get my message."

"I was jogging down Perkins Road when you called. Robert left the apartment and drove to pick me up and take me back to our place. I took a five-minute shower, threw on some jeans, a shirt, and shoes, then sped over here."

Daniel followed Max into the living room. At twenty-one, he was close to six feet tall with short black hair and a toned body. He avoided looking at Tristan while he walked towards the overstuffed chair. Standing in front of Sarah, he offered her his hand.

"Will you let me help you upstairs?"

Sarah allowed herself to be pulled up and led back into the hall. She gripped Daniel's hand as they ascended the stairs in the early morning light. The laughing faces in the family pictures that dotted the wall gave the despair inside of her a foothold, and embarrassing tears rolled down her cheeks. As she passed the framed sketch Benjamin had drawn of her when she was seven, she

161

wondered ridiculously if the last eight years of happiness had been a farce or if recent events were simply some sort of cruel joke.

"Don't fight it, Sarah."

"Fight what?"

"You're trying not to do something. I'm not sure what it is, but –"

"I need to be sick." Covering her mouth with her hand, she struggled to push away the rising nausea. "I don't want to throw up."

"You won't give up that control, not even to your own body, not even for a second. Give in for once. It won't kill you."

She gave in.

Sarah huddled next to Daniel on the floor afterwards and wept in his arms. Once she'd quieted slightly, he sat her on the edge of the tub and turned on the water. After adjusting the temperature, he pulled up the shower lever.

"I'm going to get you some nightclothes."

Sarah undressed and shoved her dress, bra, and panties into the wastebasket. She climbed into the tub and let the warm water run over her, washing away some of the blood and the pain. Daniel came back when she was almost finished and laid one of her nightshirts and some underwear on top of the counter.

When she emerged from the bathroom, he was standing outside the door. He put one arm around her shoulders and slipped his free hand under hers. Once he'd steered her into the bedroom, he sat next to her on the side of the mattress. For a long time, he held her loosely and said nothing.

Eventually, Daniel asked, "What do you want to do?"

Pulling her arms up closer to her chest, Sarah replied, "I don't know what to do."

"I don't mean about the whole thing. I mean, what do you want to do right now? Maybe you should lie down."

She was trembling in his arms. Her voice was barely audible as she said, "I want to call Vaughn."

Sarah had been rehearsing her speech during the shower. She had intended to say, "Vaughn? It's Sarah. Listen, Daddy and I are having some problems, and we could really use you around. I know you've got a lot to deal with at your parents', but I think it would help if you came home."

As she reached for the phone, Jamie came into the room and said, "No, Sarah."

"What do you mean, no?" Daniel asked with irritation. "What can it hurt?"

"It can hurt a helluva lot. Remember why Vaughn went to spend the summer with her folks? You think she took Sarah's little brother and headed over there for a vacation? Things were a mess between her and Tris. She's in the middle of a dangerous pregnancy. Her sister is dying. Her parents were worried sick about everyone but couldn't leave the farm. In the state she's in, Sarah can't call and tell any of them about this crap over the phone."

"But I need her here," Sarah insisted. "I want to call."

"No," Jamie said firmly. "You're too upset, Princess. One of us should call."

"What if she doesn't want to come back?" Sarah asked hoarsely. "I have to tell her how things are. I need Jim and Helen. They're the only grandparents I've got."

When Jamie shook his head, she began to cry. As Sarah buried her face against his chest, Daniel glared at Jamie and said, "You call Vaughn then. What are you going to say?"

"Damned if I know." Jamie knelt in front of Sarah and asked gently, "When's the last time you talked to Vaughn?"

"We t-talk every Friday night."

"How're things at the farm in Mississippi?"

"Aunt Kate's getting worse. Will's having fun playing and fishing."

"How about Jim and Helen?"

"They're...they're like you'd imagine people would be when one of their kids is dying of cancer and the other one is having problems with her marriage and pregnancy."

"Vaughn shouldn't have run home to them," Jamie declared. "Not that all the arguing that she and Tris were doing was helping the pregnancy."

"I thought the arguing they were doing was because she wasn't following doctor's orders about the baby," Daniel put in.

"It's a moot point now," Jamie said. "She should have gone to marriage counseling like Tris asked. She shouldn't have left to get her way. But Tris also didn't have to fall back into addiction and

163

worse. It's everybody's fault and nobody's fault." As he reached for the phone, he asked Sarah, "You want me to make the call downstairs?"

Shaking her head, she said, "I want to talk to her after you do."

Jamie was relieved when Vaughn answered the phone. He was brief and vague as he spoke of Tristan's addiction and the confrontation that had taken place between father and daughter that morning. Vaughn was horrified at the state of affairs, but she took the news more calmly than he had anticipated. She promised she would be on the first flight to Baton Rouge.

"One of us will pick you up at the airport this afternoon," Jamie assured her. "Look, Sarah wants to talk with you. Hang on."

Sarah had steeled herself for this exchange. She hadn't wanted to upset Vaughn and threaten the life of her unborn brother or sister, who wasn't due to be born for at least three more months. Yet, she couldn't control her tears and found herself unable to do anything except hold the receiver and cry.

"Oh, Honey. I'm here."

"Are you coming h-home?"

"Of course I am."

"Are Helen and Jim coming, too?"

"I don't think they can," Vaughn said soberly. "Even if Kate weren't so sick, I can't bring your brother home right now. Kindergarten doesn't start for another couple of weeks. Hopefully, things will be straightened out enough by then. If not, he'll have to stay on with Grandpa and Grandma a little longer."

"I wish they could come. I wish they could have been here. I wish you had been here."

"I'm so, so sorry I wasn't. I'll be there soon, all right? I love you, Sarah."

"O-okay. I l-love you, too. Just please hurry."

Chapter Two: Arrival

Benjamin was thirty minutes late to meet Vaughn at the airport. Although he'd opted for a more subdued look over the last few years, he still had a flair for the dramatic. That afternoon, she spotted him easily in his jeans, loafers, and a white shirt that looked like something Errol Flynn might have worn in a pirate movie of the 1930's. However, his usual flamboyant attitude was severely in check, and he said little as they gathered the luggage and went to his gold Firebird. Jamie was asleep in the backseat.

"You left him in the car?" Vaughn asked incredulously. "It's a hundred degrees in the shade!"

"He insisted on coming then fell asleep on the way over here. We're all fucking exhausted. I wasn't about to wake him up."

"I'm up," Jamie insisted blearily. "I'm up."

"Go back to sleep," Benjamin instructed. "Take advantage of the peace and quiet."

Vaughn asked, "Where's Halley?"

"I don't want to talk about it, Darling."

They rode for a while in uncomfortable silence. Jamie lay quietly with his eyes closed and waited for Vaughn to ask a million questions about Tristan and Sarah, but she surprised him by asking instead, "Does Halley know about what happened at the house?"

Benjamin replied that she did not.

"You could call her."

"I can't. She's with another man now. She wants another baby, and I don't. The end."

Vaughn sighed and admitted, "I love you as a friend, but, as Halley's partner, you're a pathetic failure."

"So, I'm a failure, and you're not? At least I didn't run away from my relationship. It may have taken me a while, but I had the guts to finally end it."

"You know you didn't end it," Jamie muttered. "She couldn't take it anymore is all."

"Shut up, and go back to sleep," Benjamin growled. "It's not my fault I met someone else I couldn't live without. If Halley hadn't made me choose between her and him, plus demanding a baby, then we'd all be living together right this minute."

Vaughn suddenly exclaimed, "You missed our exit! Where are we going?"

"I – I guess I passed it. I'm glad you said something, Darling. I would have driven all the way to Denham Springs. Maybe even to Hammond. Shit, maybe that would be for the best."

"You're scaring me," Vaughn admitted. "How are they?"

He exited at Sherwood Forest Boulevard then made a slow left turn and eased into the right lane saying, "Dan and Max are with them at the house."

"Where are Lillian and Chloe?"

"Lillian's sister went into labor yesterday morning, so Lillian went to Jackson to be there and help her and her husband with the new baby and the three-year-old. Jamie's brood has the chickenpox, so Chloe's housebound."

"Stop stalling," she said insistently. "Tell me what's going on."

Benjamin turned into the parking lot of an A&P and parked near a cluster of shopping baskets before shutting off the engine and twisting around to face her.

"Max got one of his doctor friends to call in an x-ray on Sarah's nose. I swear the man has more connections than President Carter. Anyway, she has a hairline fracture, but there's nothing to be done for it. It'll just have to heal on its own." He took a deep breath and exhaled then confided, "She's pretty shaken up by this. We've all been so busy this summer while you've been gone. None of us have seen much of each other. Perhaps if we had, we would've known something was wrong. Maybe we did know, but we didn't want to acknowledge it."

Vaughn studied the metal handle on a nearby shopping cart before asking, "And Tristan?"

"He's definitely been using, although we don't know what it was. Jamie searched the house but came up empty-handed. We're certain Sarah knows, but she won't tell anyone anything. From what we can ascertain, she's been covering for him. Max found a letter from the firm granting Tristan extended leave. With pay, I might add. It was dated a month ago and is good through the end of the calendar year."

"And you think Sarah wrote the original letter requesting leave."

166

"Or went to the boss to ask for it. You know how much he values Tris, not just as an architect or a partner but also as a friend, and he's got a soft spot for Sarah. Could you turn her down? Anyway, Max wants to contact the boss to check it out."

"Good." Vaughn turned to Benjamin and asked, "How is Tristan? You've told me everything and nothing. Please."

He twisted back to face forward and admitted, "He's a walking basket case. He wasn't fit to go with Sarah to the hospital for the x-rays, so Jamie and I stayed at home with him while Max and Dan went with Sarah. He sits or paces. When he speaks, all he does is berate himself." He glanced at Vaughn and raised the key to the ignition before confiding, "He won't look at Sarah."

Vaughn put her hand over the keyhole and demanded, "Wait. That's not all. We've known each other for too long. What aren't you telling me?"

He let his hand drop to the seat, the keys making a little *clanking* sound.

"Maybe Jamie should tell you instead."

Propping himself up on his elbows, their friend said, "Coward. Christ, Man." Looking at Vaughn, he admitted, "Sarah didn't get home until something like 4:30 this morning. Tris was out of his head with worry, but he had been drinking and all, so he didn't call the cops. He went looking for her, but he couldn't find her anywhere. He eventually returned to the house in case she came back."

"*4:30?*" Vaughn repeated. "That's totally unlike Sarah. Jamie, why didn't you tell me any of this when we talked on the phone?"

He paused then said, "She was out with Billy Baudoin and his crowd."

"Billy? Until 4:30?"

Another pause.

"They were at some party, and she and Billy ended up in one of the bedrooms."

"But...but Billy –"

"Is bright, charming, and very much emancipated," Benjamin put in. "He's a handsome devil."

In a small voice, Vaughn asked, "Is she...okay?"

He gave a quick nod and started the engine as he said, "If she's straight on her cycle and dates, she will be. Max is trying to talk her into seeing a doctor to make sure everything's all right. Maybe she'll listen to you. I think Dan's pretty upset about it."

"Of course he is," she said softly.

Benjamin couldn't add anything to that. When they crossed Old Hammond Highway, Jamie listened to the hum of the engine and the sound of the gears, as Benjamin slowed and turned left onto Goodwood Boulevard. They were almost home.

Despite the fact that there were four people in the house, all was quiet when Vaughn, Jamie, and Benjamin entered through the front. Vaughn put her keys down on the hall table, and Benjamin shuffled past her to bring her blue-gray suitcase and carry-on bag to the master bedroom. As he began to climb the stairs, she took a deep breath and followed Jamie.

Tristan tried to remain calm as his wife studied him from across the room. He was agitated and shaking. A veil of sweat covered his pallid skin. He still wore the bloodstained shirt and pants from the morning. Ringlets of long hair had worked their way out of the black cord that he'd used to hold the auburn mass together at the base of his neck.

He stood looking at Vaughn with that wild hair, the filthy clothing, and with remorse and fear in his eyes. He prayed he wasn't scaring her as much as he was scaring himself. As she approached, he sank to his knees in front of her, bowed his head, and closed his eyes. He was shutting down completely.

Vaughn turned to Jamie and asked, "Would you help me?"

With his support, she knelt in front of Tristan. She lifted her hand and cupped his cheek. His flesh was hot. He didn't acknowledge her proximity or her touch. Alarmed, she looked up at Max.

"His body is craving the substances he's been feeding it," he explained. "He's experiencing a bit of a breakdown as well. I've been trying to guide him through it, but it's been rather difficult. The physical after-effects will pass eventually."

Jamie was acutely aware that he'd said nothing about Tristan's emotional recovery.

Vaughn glanced back and forth from Max to Jamie. Only then did she see how tired and ragged they looked. She faced her husband and leaned forward, raising her lips until they were next to his ear.

"Tristan? I'm here."

He nudged her palm with his cheek then turned his head and rested it against her shoulder. Vaughn slid her arms around him and rubbed his back, just as she'd done with their son to sooth him when he'd been fussy as a baby.

After several minutes, Max said, "Why don't we try to get him to bed? I don't think he'll sleep long, but he's been awake for at least thirty-six hours. With everything that's happened, he needs to rest, even if it's for a short while."

"No," Tristan moaned.

"It's all right. I'm here," Vaughn repeated. "I'll be right here in the house with you and Sarah."

Jamie came around and aided his friend in his attempt to stand. Tristan opened his eyes and stared down at his wife.

"You'll stay with me after what I've done?"

He looks so defeated, Jamie thought. *Does he mean will she stay with him tonight or is he asking her if she intends to file for divorce?*

Vaughn got awkwardly to her feet, then laid a hand on his chest and felt the rapid beating of his heart.

"I love you, Tristan. You have to get some rest right now and some help."

"Will," he said suddenly. "Where is Will?"

"He's still at the farm with my parents and sister. I told him that you and Sarah were sick. Now, come lie down."

Tristan allowed himself to be guided upstairs to the master bedroom. As Jamie stood nearby, Vaughn asked Max to step outside into the hall; then she unbuttoned her husband's shirt and slipped it off him. He was painfully thin. She unfastened his pants and let them drop to the floor. Then, she led him to the bed and urged him to lie down under the covers. He shut his eyes as Vaughn went back to the door where Max was waiting.

"I need to see Sarah now."

"I'll stay with Tris," Jamie volunteered.

"And I'll come with you," Max offered.

Sarah appeared to be asleep on her side. Daniel sat holding her hand, while Benjamin watched them from the window seat.

Vaughn leaned down and kissed her stepdaughter on the temple. Sarah's eyes popped open, and she abruptly let go of Daniel's hand then sat up quickly and swayed slightly, raising her hand to her forehead.

"You came."

Her nose was bruised, and there was a tiny Band-Aid across the bridge. Vaughn observed the marks on her stepdaughter's arm and a purple splotch on her cheekbone. She took the girl in her arms and kissed the top of her hair.

"I think we ought to give them some time alone," Max suggested.

Once Daniel had pulled the door closed behind him, Sarah pulled back from Vaughn's embrace and asked, "Have you seen him? How is he?"

"He's been better." The woman lifted her fingers to touch Sarah's cheek, but the girl jerked away. "How are you?"

"I've been better." She began to shudder as if she were having the chills then admitted, "Max says I'm in shock, and I guess I am. It doesn't make sense! How could Daddy do something like this? Why? He was fine for so long! It's not fair to anybody!"

"How long has he been sick? How have you managed? Why didn't you tell me?"

"How could I?" Sarah cried. "Aunt Kate is dying, and they said your baby could die. How could I call and tell you about…about this? What if you lost the baby and died because of it? What, then Daddy and I could both share the blame?"

"Sarah, don't say that!"

"But it's the truth! It's the first true thing I've said all summer!" She laid her cheek against Vaughn's shoulder and murmured, "It's been so hard. At first, I didn't catch on. I thought that he was out of sorts because you and Will were gone. But then I started to remember things I'd made myself forget. That's when I realized what he was doing.

"He hardly ate and was up at all hours and kept sleeping through the alarm. Mr. Mason from his work would call and ask to talk to him, and I'd tell him that Daddy was sick. Finally, I had to go to Mr. Mason and tell him Daddy was stressed and needed some time off."

"And he accepted that without talking to Tristan first?"

Sarah hung her head and said quietly, "I learned how to manipulate people to get what I wanted when Daddy was like this the first time. It's not difficult. You have to be creative and convincing, and it works ninety-nine percent of the time. I haven't had to do it like that for years. I didn't know if I could do it after so long."

"But you did. How?"

Sarah huddled against her and went on, "I thought maybe he'd stop or that I could make him quit before you came home. I paid all the bills and typed some letters that had to go out. That way, no one would know that he was…that he couldn't…that…."

"Shhh. I should have been here."

Sarah leaned heavily against her stepmother and asked, "Is the baby healthy? Will it be all right now that you're home? Will you and Daddy start fighting again like before?"

"Things are still a bit dicey with the baby, but I'm going to try to keep us all positive from now on. Will you work with me on bringing our family back together?" When the girl didn't reply, she asked, "Sarah? Are you still awake?"

"I keep seeing his hand come down at me," Sarah mumbled. "It gave me the worst feeling in the world. I actually heard the bone in my nose crack, and then I got disoriented when I hit my head on the floor. It was horrible. I don't ever want to begin to try and figure out what it must have been like for Daniel with his dad." Resting her head on the pillow, she said again, "It was the worst feeling in the world."

When Vaughn emerged an hour later, Sarah was asleep, Tristan was awake, and everyone else was drained.

"I think I may have talked her into seeing a doctor tomorrow," Vaughn said, as she entered the living room. "We'll see what she says in the morning."

Tristan left the room, followed closely by Max. Moments later, he was back. If anything, his anxiety appeared to be building. Vaughn stepped towards her husband in an attempt to do *something* to comfort him, but he shrugged her off.

From behind them, Max said, "I believe he needs to be hospitalized until I can start him on some medication to relieve the withdrawal symptoms and treat the anxiety and depression."

"Don't talk about me like I'm not here!" Tristan flashed angrily. "Why give me anything? When I had trouble before, you didn't want to give me medicine once I was out of the hospital! Why do it now?"

"New medications have become available since then," the psychiatrist replied calmly. "I think they should be utilized this time. You suffered from depression and withdrawal before, but you still had a measure of control, no matter how thin it was. I don't see much evidence of control this time."

"No! I don't want that!"

"Do you have another suggestion, Tris?" Jamie asked wearily. "I'm sorry, but I can't watch you do this again."

Everything was still, and then Tristan said quietly, "I don't think I can live in a world where people feel like this. If I can be okay for years and then feel so…off, then what about the people wandering the streets who are like this day in and day out? There are men and women out there who are more disturbed than I am. What if one of them had jumped Sarah last night? What if one of them breaks into the house? What if –"

"Stop," Max said firmly. "You have to take the first step again or the anxiety you're feeling will overwhelm you. You have family and friends who love you and are depending on you."

"How can I take care of anyone else when I can't even take care of myself?!?" he shouted. "I'm tired of taking care of everybody! I don't want to take care of *anyone* anymore!"

He stumbled towards the bookcase and leaned against it, turning his back to the others.

"What do you recommend?" Benjamin addressed Max. "Can he be treated at home with medication and therapy?"

"It's a possibility, but I don't see how. You, Jamie, and I have to work. Dan has school. Vaughn is in no condition physically to handle him if the need should arise. It would be unreasonable to ask Sarah." He rested one hand on Vaughn's upper back and suggested, "You should sit down. You have to continue to take care of yourself."

She sat, put her head against the back of the recliner, and said, "If you hospitalize him, won't they find out about what happened this morning?"

Max stared at his hands.

Finally, Daniel asked, "Could we manage until Lillian gets back? I know she'll be tired, but she could take care of things during the day and maybe we could take shifts at night."

Jamie nodded and said, "That could work. How long do you think it'll take to get things stabilized?"

Max moved over to Tristan and placed two fingers on the younger man's wrist then glanced at his watch in order to get an accurate pulse rate and stated, "It could be weeks. It could be months."

As the others discussed what options were available to them, Sarah lay dreaming. In her dreams, she was walking on a dirt road with a man about her father's age. He wore jeans, a brown leather belt, and a denim shirt. Sandals were on his feet. His unbound hair was brown and went past his shoulders. He had a moustache and a beard.

The day was warm but not hot. They continued on the road and came to an alley made of oak trees. The stranger took Sarah's hand, and they strolled over to a blanket that had been spread on the ground. There was a picnic basket filled with food. They ate and talked, although she couldn't remember what was being said from moment to moment.

When they'd finished eating, she walked back across the road and through a gate. She saw some swings that had been hung from a large metal frame further down past two rows of pine trees. Sarah chose one and sat. The stranger pushed her higher and higher. She thought of how nice it was to feel the wind in her face and her hair flying behind her, and she laughed.

"Sarah?" Someone was shaking her. "Sarah, wake up!"

She opened her eyes and looked at Daniel's worried face. She had never felt more at peace in all of her life. Somehow, even in the dream – vision? – she'd known who was walking beside her. It was God.

She couldn't pretend that it hadn't happened. Anyone else would be down on her knees. And, yet, she still doubted. Why? Sarah wondered what was wrong with her. She felt as though God had given her a glimpse into a world she'd never seen, and she still couldn't accept it.

I'm a Doubting Thomas in girl's clothing, she thought.

"What is it?" Daniel asked with concern.

173

"I think I had a religious experience."

Daniel's face became a mask, and he turned away. She rested a hand on his wrist and sat up in the bed.

"Oh, no. Daniel, no." Sarah took his hand in hers and said earnestly, "I meant it literally."

"You?"

She nodded.

"So, are you going to speak in tongues now?" His tone was harsh and biting. "Or maybe lay hands on people?"

Sarah looked away, and her eyes filled with tears.

"You don't have to be that way. And no, I'm not. I still can't believe it. Are we *that* cynical?"

"Yes. That and other things."

Sarah gingerly blew her nose and winced at the pain.

"I'm sorry if I hurt you. I've just been so alone all summer and so scared, and you weren't here. There were so many nights when I wanted to call and tell you everything that was going on, but I couldn't. I've tried hard to keep it together, but by yesterday I'd had enough. So, I left the house. I met up with Billy and his friends, but I wasn't having any fun. Billy knew it. He suggested that we walk and talk."

Daniel snapped, "I don't really want to hear this."

"You have to," she insisted. "I needed somebody, *anybody*, and there was nobody there. If it makes you feel any better, it hurt when we did it. A lot."

Daniel slid his arm around her shoulders, and she leaned heavily against him.

"Of course it doesn't make me feel better. I never want to see you hurt or unhappy. Today, I've seen both. It's only that I wanted to be the one you –"

Her left hand came up over his mouth.

"Please, don't say it. I can't handle any more tonight. Will you stay with me? Please?"

They lay back on the bed, and she rested her cheek against his chest. He spoke to her in a hushed voice that made her feel both sleepy and secure.

Twenty minutes later, Jamie found them lying apart and fast asleep with Sarah under the covers and Daniel on top of the comforter next to her. He watched them for a minute then retired to the guestroom in order to try to find some solace in sleep.

Chapter Three: The Cross

Daniel's breath came out in white clouds. It was well below freezing, not exactly the norm for southern Louisiana in October. He had on jeans, a t-shirt, a sweatshirt, his band jacket, a scarf, gloves, thick socks, and his tennis shoes, and he was still cold. His ears hurt. If Lillian had been present, she would have been giving him a lecture on the importance of wearing a hat.

Sarah didn't look much warmer. She'd donned similar garments, except that she wore a turtleneck instead of a t-shirt and a lined leather jacket, not a wool one. Her nose was red, and her hair was being whipped around by the icy wind.

"Come on!" Daniel called, as he took her hand and pulled her along past tent after tent. "This way!"

She shouldn't be out here, he thought. *I have to get her someplace warm.*

She'd insisted upon attending the Celtic festival and had dismissed her stepmother's argument that a recent cold combined with laryngitis should be a deterrent. Nobody else was crazy enough to come out with her in weather like this, except Daniel.

So, there they were, being pelted by wind and occasional raindrops. They looked at jewelry and artifacts and applauded performers. Daniel had no idea what she would have done without him since it was an effort for her to speak loud enough to be heard over the noise of the crowd, music, and wind. When she needed to speak, Sarah had to put her mouth close to Daniel's ear and force out whispered words or questions for him to pass along to the vendors or artists.

He dragged her into one of the larger tents that housed food and drinks. Daniel got them each a cup of hot chocolate and made Sarah sit on the ground near one of the food warmers. They huddled together and drank the steaming liquid.

Once his teeth had stopped chattering, Daniel asked, "Are you having fun?"

Sarah looked up at him and smiled. Daniel reflected on how odd it was not to hear her talk. She had always been extremely sociable in the past. Admittedly, that hadn't been the case since the end of the summer. Tristan's attack on his daughter seemed to have broken more than her nose.

The worst of it for Daniel had been seeing Sarah suffer and knowing that she hadn't felt as if she could turn to him for help. He'd tried to be there for her, but what had happened between her and Billy had put up a barrier between them that they couldn't get around. That day was the first time they'd been alone together since August.

Sarah put her head next to his and said as loudly as she could, "I feel like I'm having an adventure!" She paused, and he waited. He knew it hurt her throat every time she spoke. "It is cold, though. Let's go to that booth with the Christmas ornaments; then we can leave. Is that okay?"

They returned to the holiday merchandise then quickly walked back to Daniel's old yellow Volkswagen Beetle. It was holding up well, but it had no heat. It would be a chilly ride back from New Orleans to Baton Rouge. Daniel flipped on the radio, and they settled back in their seats for the hour-and-a-half trip.

As they approached Baton Rouge, Daniel turned to Sarah, who had her hands stuffed in the pockets of her jacket. She hadn't said that she needed to return home immediately. He thought that maybe this would be a good time to attempt a reconciliation.

"Do you want to come and see my new place?"

"Sure."

She didn't even know where the apartment was. He and Robert had only moved from their old complex the weekend before, citing noise from the frat boys as the major reason for needing to relocate. The apartment they'd chosen had been further from campus. Olivia and Bob Taylor had been opposed to the move for that reason, but Max and Lillian had been more responsive. As long as Daniel did well in school and seemed happy enough, they said they didn't care if he moved every semester.

Daniel pulled the VW into the parking lot of what appeared to be a cluster of four-unit complexes. It was nothing fancy, yet not too shabby either. He and Sarah shivered their way to the third unit from the street. His apartment was on the second floor, and they hurriedly climbed the metal steps.

Robert was studying at the table with a cup of coffee close at hand. He looked up as they came in.

"Hi!" he said brightly, slamming his book shut. "You two are exactly the distraction I need. You look like you could use some coffee. I just made a fresh pot."

He walked from the tiny dining area into the tiny kitchen and filled two mugs then refilled his own. Sarah got milk from the refrigerator and added a liberal amount, plus three sugars. Daniel accepted the cup of black coffee Robert handed to him and took two large gulps.

"How can you drink it with all that milk and sugar?" Daniel asked mildly.

"How can you two stand to take it black?" she retorted hoarsely. "It's like drinking motor oil."

"It keeps the parts lubricated," Robert suggested. "I'm glad you came, Sarah. I wish I didn't have to head to my study group. Maybe you could come over for pizza soon. Thursday night's double coupon night here at our place. Lots of cheap, bad pizza and great conversation. You should try it."

"Thanks. I will."

Once he'd departed, the two remaining friends sat in silence for several minutes. Daniel began to twist a piece of string he'd found in his jacket pocket, while Sarah sipped at the dregs in her coffee cup.

"So, I guess you're not pregnant."

Sarah practically flew off the couch. She slammed down the mug on the coffee table and glared at Daniel.

"I told you –"

"You told me!" Daniel interrupted and got to his feet. "You didn't trust me enough to call me, is that it? So, you went to *him*?"

"No! I –"

Her abused throat protested, and she coughed for over a minute. She looked exhausted.

"You never called either," she flashed accusingly. "Were you that busy with the summer session?"

There was an uncomfortable pause, and Sarah went to the window and turned her back to Daniel.

"I had a girlfriend from college."

"I expected you to have girlfriends from college. You had them in high school. You never hid them from me. You never had to. We've always been open about the fact that we dated other people."

"This one…things were a little more serious."

Gazing intently at a crack in the sidewalk below, Sarah said, "You were sleeping together. You think I didn't know? Did you think I was that stupid, that I couldn't figure it out? How dare you! You make snide comments about me and Billy? *You* want to make judgments about *me*?"

The gist of the conversation seemed vaguely familiar to her. Sarah realized that it was almost exactly what she had said to her father in the hallway that terrible August morning. She suddenly began to feel claustrophobic in the small living room.

"Daniel, I told you I never meant for it to happen. I needed someone, and he was there."

Daniel couldn't miss the intimation: *And you weren't.*

As she hurried past him, Sarah grabbed her jacket and bag. Clattering down the steps, she ran all the way to the corner.

The corner of what? She hadn't been paying attention during the ride to Daniel's apartment. There was no street sign. Her heart began to race, and it seemed as though she couldn't breathe properly. How would she get home? Which way should she go?

Don't have a panic attack over this. You're a big girl. If you can't figure out where you are soon, then you can use somebody's phone to call for a ride.

Sarah wiped at her eyes and leaned forward to look first left, then right. She was somewhere on Perkins Road. On a whim, she went to the left, cursing the fact that her sense of direction had been somehow skewed all those years before.

What difference does it make if I'm lost? I don't want to go home anyway.

She decided that she could go to Benjamin and Halley's, then caught her mistake. Halley had moved out, and Benjamin's friend, Quinton, had moved in. Halley had rented her own place and was seeing some businessman named Xavier. Sarah didn't want Quinton or Xavier to see her upset. She didn't want to see them, period. She didn't even know them.

179

She couldn't go to Jamie and Chloe's either. Jamie had flown somewhere to examine a rare type of plant that was supposed to have medicinal purposes for cancer patients. Sarah couldn't remember the exact location, only that it was someplace exotic. Chloe and their three children had gone with him.

I have a key to their house, Sarah thought. *If I could find it, then I could hide out there for a while. Maybe. Well, no.*

Sarah waited for the traffic to pass so that she could cross the street. Once again, she pondered the problem of where she was going. She couldn't wander aimlessly all afternoon.

Max and Lillian's? No. I don't want a therapy session, and I don't want to talk to either of them about sex and Daniel.

Sarah stopped and looked around. Wherever she was, she had been here before, but it had been years. The apartment complex across the street – that was it. She'd been here with Max and Lillian and Daniel once when Tristan and Vaughn had taken a belated honeymoon to Cancun on their third anniversary.

As a gust of cold air took her breath away, she crossed the street and ran up to the doorman. She was relieved to see that he was a congenial, elderly man. In her experience, men like that were the ones who knew everybody and everything in buildings such as these. She explained her dilemma, and he knew instantly the person in question.

Leaving her standing in the small lobby, he went to an intercom located in a glass office. After an exchange that Sarah could not hear, he came back around to where she was waiting.

"She's on her way," he said pleasantly. "If you'll excuse me, I'm needed out front."

Sarah thanked him and began to examine the pictures on the wall. Moments later, the elevator doors opened behind her, and Isabelle Elenstraub emerged. She looked older to Sarah, even though it had only been several months since Sarah had seen her last. The woman greeted her warmly, and Sarah strained to tell her about the laryngitis. Isabelle held up her hand in protestation.

"Do not speak. You sound terrible. Come upstairs, and I will make you some hot tea with honey. Then, we can talk."

They stepped into the elevator, and Isabelle pushed *4*. Sarah tried not to stare at the older woman. She'd never seen Isabelle dressed so casually before. She hadn't thought people in their sixties wore jeans. True, Isabelle also had on a very expensive-looking violet silk shirt and her pearls, but Sarah continued to be slightly disconcerted.

They stepped out when the elevator doors parted, and Sarah followed the psychiatrist to the third door on the right. They entered a spacious apartment done in a minimalist style. Sarah didn't like it.

The apartment was too bare for Sarah's taste, not that she craved frills and tassels. Staying at Benjamin's for extended periods always gave her a bad case of sensory overload. Her own taste landed her somewhere in between the two extremes. Still, at least this place was neat and clean, unlike Benjamin's haven of confusion.

Sarah sat at the table in the breakfast nook, while Isabelle put on some water for tea. That started, the older woman joined her at the table and asked in her still-thick German accent, "Does anyone know where you are? No? Let me call your parents and tell them that we're visiting."

"No," Sarah rasped. Then, "I don't want them to think I don't want to talk with them. I just can't."

Isabelle tilted her head and considered.

"They will be worried. Please, let me handle it. I will not give you away."

Not quite convinced, Sarah gave her the phone number. She listened as Isabelle told Tristan that they had bumped into each other on the street and Isabelle had invited her in for tea, and would that be all right? Assuring him she would see to it that Sarah got home safely, she rang off and went to get the tea. After putting the two cups and container of honey on the table, she resumed her seat cattycorner from Sarah.

"He'll know," Sarah said. "We can sense things about each other, he and I."

"I remember that very clearly from when you were a child. You two were always highly attuned to each other's moods and feelings." She added some sugar to her tea and remarked, "It cannot be helped. I could hardly allow you to stay and have them fretting about you. Would you like to tell me why you are here? Not that I am displeased at seeing you."

"I guess I wanted someone to talk to. Someone objective."

Isabelle snorted and admitted, "I do not know how objective I will be, but I am more removed from things than your family and close friends."

"I assume that Max has told you about what's been going on at my house. Things are better, although we still have bad days. I can talk with Max about all that. The problem I can't talk with anyone about involves Daniel and me. Normally, I could talk to Vaughn, but she's already overwhelmed and not feeling well. I don't want to bother her with more of my problems."

"I understand, but what if you are upsetting her by *not* talking with her?"

"Oh. I hadn't considered that."

"You can talk with her later. You are here. Talk to me."

Chapter Four: A Mutual Agreement

"I love Daniel."

Sarah straightened in her chair. It was not what she had intended to say. Isabelle repressed a smile and pretended not to notice.

"Yes?"

Taking a sip of her tea, which was wonderfully rich and soothing, Sarah said, "He was too busy with school and some girl, and I turned to this guy. We had sex. Daniel and I can't get past it. I don't think it'll ever be the same between us.

"This morning, we went to a festival in New Orleans, and, for a while, it was like old times. But that didn't last long." She wiped at the corners of her eyes with the heel of her hand and took another sip of her tea before confiding, "I hate it."

"It will never be the same," Isabelle agreed. "That does not mean that you can never be close again. You may find you become closer than before." When the girl looked doubtful, she continued. "I know this sounds clichéd, but these things take time. Talk with him about it."

"I've tried. All we do is fight."

"Try again."

It was said so sternly that Sarah raised her head. Isabelle's eyes were filled with determination.

"Let me tell you a story. Maybe it will illuminate things for you."

Sarah rose and said, "I think I need to use your bathroom first. I've had hot chocolate, coffee, and tea. If I don't go soon, I'll explode."

Isabelle nodded and led her down a hallway to the bathroom. Shutting the door behind her, Sarah slumped against it and sighed. She was so, so tired.

When she emerged, the psychiatrist was sitting in a chair in the living room. The girl took a seat on the sofa, and Isabelle began her story.

"Once upon a time, there was a young girl named Isabelle. She was one of the few women of her day who went to college for an advanced degree. Back at home, she had left a boy she had loved since childhood. They had promised to write every week and to wait for each other. He had gotten his law degree and had begun to practice at a local firm, while she continued her studies. They were both lonely, but circumstances prevented them from being together.

"One day while comforting a male friend who had just received some troubling news, Isabelle invited him back to her rooms. One thing led to another. You get the idea? Later, she was ashamed, and so was her friend, who knew that she loved someone else.

"Soon, she stopped writing her letters to the man back home. When the man's letters stopped coming, she was very melancholy." Isabelle paused at that point then said thoughtfully, "For five years, I threw myself into my work trying to forget about the man I had loved for so long. It did not help. Then my aunt died, and I went home for the funeral. He was there."

"He was?" Sarah leaned forward in anticipation. "What happened?"

"We went out for coffee after the service. We talked about everything, except our relationship. Finally, he asked me why I had stopped writing, and I told him."

"What did he do?"

"He got down on one knee and asked me to marry him. He said that he had also committed an indiscretion with someone while I had been away. He had been mortified and afraid to tell me. When I stopped writing, he decided that it was for the best. That was why he had stopped writing, too."

"What did you do?"

"I married him."

Isabelle rose and went over to the bookcase. She picked up a frame and brought it back to the sofa. Sarah examined the middle-aged man's portrait.

"Jacob and I were married for twenty-one years before he died."

"What about your friend? The one you...you know."

"Oh, Maxwell and Jacob became great friends."

Sarah's jaw dropped, and she sputtered, "M-Max?"

"Yes, Max," Isabelle said, patting Sarah's hand. "My friend."

The girl shook her head in disbelief.

"Did you and Jacob have any children?"

Isabelle touched the glass in the frame.

"I conceived three times, but I miscarried early with each one. It is too bad. I would have liked to have had a child with Jacob. It was never meant to be for whatever reason."

Sarah looked at Jacob's smiling face. It was a nice face. She murmured, "I wish Max and Lillian had been able to have children."

Rising, Isabelle said, "Perhaps it is better that they did not. I'm glad they had Dan. I know he was not a baby, but he is their son as much as any child they might have had together. And they have had you and the other children in their lives." She returned the picture to its place of honor on the shelf and repeated, "As I said, perhaps things worked out for the best."

"You're right, but Lillian and Max deserved a baby of their own."

Isabelle sat next to her and said seriously, "The point I'm trying to make here is that Jacob and I wasted years that we could have spent together because neither of us would admit to our transgressions. If you do love Daniel, and he loves you, then do not fritter away your time skirting the issue. You might lose more than a few years. You need to really talk with him about it, whether you end up arguing or not. Resolve it one way or the other."

Sarah steepled her fingers and stared at her knee, then asked, "Would you mind taking me back to his place? I know the name of the complex, but I don't really know if I can get back there on my own. I'm not always so good with directions."

"Of course," Isabelle agreed. "Let me call your father first and tell him that you are headed for Dan's."

They only took one wrong turn and were soon in the parking lot near Daniel's apartment. As Sarah climbed out of the passenger side of the white Volvo, Isabelle said, "Call me or come by if you would like to talk again or if you need a ride home. Here." She held out a business card and told the girl, "This one has my home phone and address on it."

"Thank you," Sarah said, as she pocketed the card. "And thanks for your help. I really appreciate it."

Sarah closed the car door and moved towards the steps of Daniel's building. She climbed slowly to the second floor. When she got to the right apartment, she knocked three times on the door before Robert opened it.

"Hi, Sarah!"

He was a little too cheerful, Sarah reflected.

"I thought you had a study group," she blurted out.

"I did. We finished up, and I came back for a book. I was just on my way to the library, but Dan's still here. Come on in."

He stepped back, and she noticed that he did actually have on his jacket, and his book sack was slung over one shoulder. It was almost as if he had been anticipating her return.

"Tell Dan not to wait up for me. I've got a big paper due Monday, and I haven't even started. See ya!" he called, as he pulled the door shut behind him.

Daniel was not in the living, dining, or kitchen area, so Sarah walked towards what she assumed were the bedrooms and bathroom. One door was open, but she recognized some of Robert's things and continued down the hall, passed by the bathroom, and stopped at the last door, which was closed. She tapped lightly on it.

"Daniel?"

"Come in, Sarah."

He was leaning against the window frame with his hands in his pockets. The mask she'd seen earlier was in place, but his eyes couldn't conceal the darkness of his mood.

"I want to talk," Sarah declared. "We have to talk."

He gestured for her to sit on the bed then sat beside her.

"Okay. What did you want to say?"

Feeling confident that she could handle this confrontation, Sarah took off her jacket and tossed it on a chair before answering him. Pushing the hair out of her face, she looked straight at Daniel.

"I wanted to say that I'm sorry."

Unexpectedly, she started to cry.

"I'm so sorry," she admitted. "I should have called you, no matter what. I was scared that if I called, *she* might answer the phone."

She buried her face in her hands. She hated crying in front of others even now. Daniel put his arm around her shoulders and scooted closer to her. She pressed her face against his chest so that he wouldn't see her tears.

"Why didn't you call Liesl?" he asked softly. "She's been your best friend since fourth grade."

"She moved in June. After her dad died, she wasn't the same."

Sarah put her hands on Daniel's chest, and he brought his other arm around her waist and hugged her to him. He struggled with conflicting feelings of protectiveness, love, anger, and longing. The familiar scent of rose perfume wafted up into his nostrils.

"I pushed it away, Liesl's leaving. And I was putting a lot of effort into making things good at home, but nothing was working."

"You couldn't fix it," he murmured. "Only Tristan could change things."

"I know, but I had to try to do *something*. It was horrible, standing by and watching it all go to pieces. At least when I was small, I didn't understand what Daddy was doing to himself. It was terrifying this time, watching him and knowing what was happening. I tried so hard to make him stop at the beginning. I hid his stash so many times," she said quietly, as her tears cascaded down the front of Daniel's sweatshirt. "But he'd find it every time. Then he stopped going to work, and Mason called, and I begged him to give Daddy some kind of sabbatical. I lied and told him that Daddy was getting help. I didn't know what else to do."

"Shhh." He rubbed her back and told her, "It's not your fault, you know that. None of it. And you not wanting to call me? That's my fault."

Sarah pulled away and regarded him dubiously.

"It is," he asserted. "I – I made a mistake. I wanted to be with you, but I didn't want to take advantage of you or anything. I mean, you're still only sixteen, and I'm twenty-one. It was difficult for me, and I really messed up by sleeping with another girl."

"Can we start over? Do you want to? If you don't, then let me know and –"

He reached out to brush some of her hair back behind her shoulder and said, "I love you."

She turned her head slightly away from him and said quietly, "I know."

Daniel touched his index finger to her chin and guided her face back towards him. He bent to kiss her then lowered her back on the bed. Sarah stiffened immediately.

"We can't do this," she protested.

"We're not. We can kiss and touch all we want. We'll just stop things there."

As he spoke, he slid one hand under her upper back and the other around her waist. She maneuvered herself under him until his hips rested on top of hers. They were still fully clothed, but Sarah was wavering in her conviction that they could go no further.

"Maybe –" she started, but Daniel stopped her.

"We can't take a chance," he said firmly. "You're only a junior in high school, and I'm not done with college. We do *not* need to have a baby right now."

"But it might not happen."

He rolled off of her and lay on his back. She put her head on his shoulder and nuzzled against him.

"I want to know what making love is really like."

"Not until you're eighteen."

"Eighteen! But that's over a year! I don't want to wait."

"I won't endanger your future because of what I want or even because of what you want. Just think, we'll have something to look forward to until next November."

"What if...you can't wait."

"I'll wait until it's right."

Softly, she prodded, "You didn't wait before."

His fingers rubbed against her shoulder as he assured her, "I will this time."

Propping herself up on one elbow, she asked, "Do you promise?"

Daniel pushed himself up off the bed and walked over to his desk. Pulling out the bottom drawer, he reached inside and removed a small white box. He came back to the bed and handed the box to Sarah.

"I want you to have this."

Sitting up, Sarah carefully opened the top of the box. Inside, there was a tiny gold cross on a delicate chain.

"I bought it for you the day after…the day after you had the dream, but then things weren't going so well, and I didn't get to give it to you. So, I put it away."

Sarah gently lifted the necklace from its cushion. The chain was not long. She smiled sadly and said, "The atheist gives a cross to the Doubting Thomas."

"If you think you had a visitation, then I believe in the possibility. Will you have faith in me, that I'll wait for you?"

"I can try."

Chapter Five: Willing and Able

Bringing the ends of the chain together behind her neck, Sarah hooked the clasp then went to look in the bathroom mirror. Daniel stood watching from the doorway.

"I'm afraid," she said to his reflection.

"Me, too."

"I don't want to wait."

"Me neither. But we should. You've got enough to deal with now. Give it some time. I want you to enjoy being with me for what it is, not use that as a tool to try and forget your problems at home." The corners of his mouth twitched, as he added, "Dating probably wouldn't be a bad idea either."

"Dating?" Sarah raised her eyebrows in surprise and said, "We've been together for years. What would make a date different from any other time we're hanging out?"

"Let's try doing something we've never done. How about if I take you to an Al-a-Teen meeting?"

Putting her hands on the edge of the basin in front of her, Sarah said sarcastically, "What a romantic first date *that* would be. Should I wear my best dress? Can we dance the night away in front of a bunch of other troubled kids? Then they can all clap for us and give us loads of encouragement. That's a date every girl dreams of."

"Stop trying to hide behind a wall of sarcasm for once in your life," he said, as he walked over to her and took her hands in his. "Will you admit how hurt you are by what Tris has done to you, himself, and the rest of the family?"

She chewed on her lower lip and studied Daniel's fingers as they caressed hers. She was unable to speak for fear that she would begin to cry again.

"Let me take you to a meeting, Sarah. Afterward, we can go somewhere for dinner, someplace special." He brought his left hand up and lifted her chin before asking, "How about this week?"

Sarah leaned against Daniel's chest and asked, "What time? What day?"

"I'll find out, and we can set it up."

"Okay. Would you take me home?"

"Sure."

She raised her head, and they shared a long, languorous kiss.

"It's going to be a tough year," Daniel sighed.

They talked easily during the ride to the Maes' house, and Daniel sang along with the radio, which made Sarah laugh because his pitch had always been terrible. Then he turned on the windshield wipers, then the hazard lights. By the time they had pulled up in front of her house, they were both laughing uncontrollably and wiping the tears from their cheeks. Sarah was also coughing convulsively.

Daniel gasped for air and said with chagrin, "I forgot about your cold."

"Don't worry about it. I needed that." She leaned across the seat and gave him a quick kiss before saying, "Call me about our date."

She stood on the porch and watched him drive away, then stayed where she was and studied the stars. With nightfall, the chill in the air was worse, but the evening was clear, and the stars were bright. She heard the door click open behind her, but she didn't turn around. The sky was too engaging.

"Sarah?"

"Yes, Vaughn?"

"Are you okay?"

Sarah tore herself away from the heavens and turned to look at her stepmother, who was seated on the porch swing. She sat next to Vaughn and leaned against her, and the woman put an arm around her shoulders.

"I'm getting there," Sarah muttered. "Are you?"

"I think so. I'll be a lot better when I hold this baby in my arms. She sighed and declared, "Never again. This pregnancy's not only risked my life and the baby's but it's also nearly destroyed our family."

Neither of them spoke for a long while. Finally, Sarah asked, "Have you painted at all since you got back?"

"I haven't had the time. You remember when I was so productive in April? Well, that was it. My poor little studio in the back's been deserted. I haven't painted or sculpted since way before I went to the farm with Will. Since I got back, I've been so caught up in everything. After the baby is born, I doubt if I'll have time for several months."

"You need to paint, not only because that's what you do. You need some sort of break from all of us."

"I took a break all summer, and look where that got us."

"I wouldn't exactly call it a break. I can watch the baby and Will, so you can work. We can figure out a schedule or something. You've been keeping us going, and it's wearing you down. Let me do this for you."

"On one condition."

"What?"

"That you work things out with your father."

Sarah shifted so that she faced the street. She rubbed her nose absently, a gesture that had manifested itself since the break two months before.

"I've had a rough day."

"It doesn't have to be today, but I do want it to happen. Tristan told me about Isabelle's call. Did you have a nice visit?"

Her tone was not accusatory, but Sarah felt guilty nonetheless.

"Vaughn —"

"Hey. Things have been strange, lately. I figured you thought that I was a little too close to the problem. I am sleeping with the enemy so to speak. I think talking with Isabelle was a good idea."

"It helped a lot," Sarah confided, as she went to stand by the porch rail. "She told me some stuff, and I knew that I had to get things straight with Daniel if I was ever going to get everything else together."

"And did you get things straight with Dan?"

"It looks like it. I'd like to tell you all about it later, if you're not too tired."

And she does look tired, Sarah thought. *Very tired.*

"I'd like that. Now, if you can help me off this thing, I think I'll go inside where it's warm."

Five-year-old Will ran towards them and jumped into Sarah's arms.

"Sissy! Did you have fun?"

His sister smiled as she saw the peanut butter in his brown hair and the pieces of Play Doh embedded in his sweater.

"The festival was great. Maybe you can go with me next time, if it's not so cold."

"Did you bring me anything?"

Her laughter and the resultant coughing spell echoed down the hallway.

"Did you think I could go to a festival and not bring back some treats?"

Sarah slid the bag off her shoulder and rummaged around in it for a moment. She withdrew a stuffed sheep toy made of real wool that had a metal bell tied around its neck. She handed it to Will, who was fascinated by animals of all kinds. He threw his arms around her then flew up the stairs to introduce his new friend to his other stuffed companions.

Sarah looked up at Vaughn. She had one hand in the bag, not certain as to whether she should pull out the matching brooch and bracelet she had chosen for her stepmother. She wanted to give it to her right then, but she reasoned that she'd purchased it for Christmas and had used all of the money she'd saved to buy Vaughn's gift. Sarah decided to let Vaughn make the choice.

"I have something for you, but if I give it to you now, I won't have anything for you for Christmas."

"Then hold on to it. I don't want to spoil the surprise." As she headed for the stairs, she asked, "Would you bathe Will for me and put him down tonight? I think I need to lie still for a while."

"No problem. Call if you need something."

Sarah's stomach complained loudly. It was 8:00 p.m., and she hadn't had anything to eat since the morning. She picked up the bag and carried it with her down the hall. She walked into the kitchen and found her father reading at the table with a cup of coffee close by.

She forced herself to go into the room but avoided eye contact. Placing her bag on the table, she went across to the pantry and got out a can of Campbell's soup. She was in the process of dumping the contents into a small saucepan when Tristan said, "Potato?"

His daughter jumped, dropping the now-empty can on the counter. It clattered to the floor and rolled under the table.

They stared at each other. Sarah was shaking, and Tristan was visibly horrified by her reaction. He stood but didn't move towards her.

193

"I was only asking what kind of soup you were making. I thought that if it was potato, then I could mash up the potato chunks like I used to do when you were little."

His daughter remained silent. Tristan cast about for some way to say what needed to be said.

"How many times can I apologize? How many days before I can walk into a room without scaring you? I won't hurt you again. Ever."

"How do you know?" came the strained whisper. "When I was small, you said you'd never...that I'd never have to suffer again because of your addictions. And here we are."

She stiffened as he picked up the can and brought it past her to the trash bin.

"I won't ever let it happen again. If I feel like I can't handle things, I'll go to Max or my AA and NA sponsor first thing. What can I do to convince you?"

"Nothing." She shook her head gravely and added, "I know you mean what you say, but I can't believe it. I see you upset, and I want to go to you, but my body won't listen to my brain. Or maybe it is listening to my brain. I know it's not rational."

"And I want to go to you and give you some sort of comfort, but every time you see me, you withdraw. I know that I'm responsible for it, and it makes me feel helpless. At the beginning, I thought a lot about ending things and –"

He stopped. Neither of them moved. No one had known about that, except Max. Tristan had sworn that he would never say it aloud to anyone else. Mentally, he kicked himself for letting it slip.

"Oh," she said in a small voice.

Sarah stepped forward, her lower lip quivering. Tristan stood stock-still. Only when she stood in front of him did he embrace her. She was trembling slightly, but at least she didn't pull back.

"Don't leave me," she said quietly. "I've missed you so much already."

"I've missed you, too."

Will suddenly burst into the room.

"Daddy! Sarah! Mama needs you!"

Sarah felt Tristan tense, and they stepped away from each other. The children ran beside him, but Tristan's long legs soon carried him well ahead of them. He found Vaughn lying on top of the bedspread. She looked ill and afraid. Tristan sat beside her then reached out a hand to stroke her cheek. She smiled nervously at him then frowned at the door.

Tristan turned to Sarah, who was anxiously standing near her brother, and asked, "Would you and Will mind waiting in his room? I'll be there in a minute."

Taking the little boy's hand, Sarah said, "I think they want to have some grown-up talk. How about if we play blocks?"

Reluctantly, he went with his sister, glancing over his shoulder at his parents.

Once they'd gone, Tristan turned back to his wife and concern flooded his face again.

"What is it?"

"I don't know. I feel...so wrong." She drew in a shaky breath and said, "I think I need to go to the hospital. Now."

"I'll call your doctor; then we can leave." He stood and called out, "Hey, Sarah? If Will's situated, will you come see? Vaughn and I need to leave in a minute."

She hurried back to the room and told him, "I'm going to stay here with Will and get him to bed. Do you want me to call anyone else?"

"No," Vaughn said with certainty. "Your dad and I will let you know if you need to call anyone later. It'll be all right."

Tristan left the room, returning minutes later with the words, "The doctor'll meet us at the hospital. He says we should hurry."

He helped his wife stand, and they headed for the doorway.

When they had reached the landing, Sarah cried, "Wait!"

She ran back towards the master bedroom and hurriedly went into the master bath. In thirty seconds, she was walking back to where her parents were standing. She held out the cylindrical container that held Tristan's medication.

"Take them with you," she instructed. "Please. If you don't, you might miss a dose."

Tristan stopped and went back to his daughter. Bending down, he leaned over and kissed her on the cheek. She didn't turn away. Relieved, he accepted the bottle of pills from her then guided his wife down to the car.

Chapter Six: Kate

Sarah was beyond exhausted.

Will had been clingy ever since their father and Vaughn had left for the hospital, and, although she understood why, Sarah had been more than ready for him to fall asleep. Unfortunately, after his bath he'd wanted a peanut butter and jelly sandwich, some milk, and a story. Then he had wanted a glass of water. Then there was a trip to the bathroom. She'd had to stay by her brother's bed for an hour before he'd finally dozed off.

By midnight, Sarah was nervous and tired of waiting by the phone. Her bones ached, and her cough had worsened. After gulping some Robitussin DM, she went to the kitchen to heat more soup.

On her way to the living room, she retrieved her English textbook from her book sack with the intention of reviewing for a chapter test. Changing her mind, Sarah deposited the book on the coffee table and proceeded to search for the local National Public Radio station on the tuner. As the soft strains of Mozart wafted through the air, she lowered herself into the Comfy Chair for the first time since that summer.

At Vaughn's request and against Sarah's wishes, Halley had cleaned the bloodstains from the upholstery on the chair. When Vaughn had asked her friend if she could clean the afghan as well, a pale and tight-lipped Tristan had intervened, going to the couch, lifting the cream-colored throw, and tossing it into the garbage can.

Vaughn's mother, Helen, had sent a new afghan the next week. It was a jumble of pink, green, and cream. Sarah had left it on the couch during the daytime and had taken it up to bed with her in the evenings.

Sixteen years old and I need a security blanket, she thought, as she wrapped the afghan around her and slowly drank her soup.

At 1:17 the phone rang. Sarah sprinted to answer it before the noise woke her little brother.

"Daddy?" she rasped, setting off another coughing fit.

"Honey, you sound a lot worse," her father said worriedly. "You shouldn't have been out in the cold today. Well, yesterday."

"Never mind that. What's going on?"

"Vaughn started having contractions on our way over here. According to her doctor, she was also coming down with the flu. Unfortunately, between the labor and the virus, she's not feeling so good right now. They tried to stop things, since she's not due for several more weeks, but she was so far dilated that it couldn't be done. They're getting ready to take her into Delivery, but I wanted to call and let you know that she was doing okay."

"Thanks."

"Any time."

"Call me when you can."

"I will. I've got to run." He paused then added, "I love you so much, Sarah."

"I love you so much, too."

Knowing that he probably wouldn't be calling for a while, Sarah went up to her room and stripped off her clothes. She put on an old-fashioned, long, pale pink nightgown that Helen had given her the previous Christmas. It was pretty and soft, and it made her feel warm inside and out. She pulled on some socks, returned to the living room, and curled up in the overstuffed chair.

When the phone woke Sarah, she had no idea what time it was. Light was beginning to filter through the curtains, so she assumed it must be just after dawn.

"Hello?" Sarah offered, as she rubbed her neck, which was stiff from her awkward position in the chair.

"Sorry it's taken me so long to call you back, but things got rough on this end," Tristan said. "I couldn't get to a phone until now."

"Rough how? Is Vaughn okay?"

"Vaughn will recover, but we're not having any more kids."

"The baby?"

"They say the baby will be all right eventually, but the delivery was kind of hard on her. She's not very strong. The neonatologists said she'll have to be in the infant I.C.U. for a while, but that would be for the best anyway since Vaughn is sick." He sneezed and added, "I think I'm getting it, too."

"Her? It's a girl? What's her name?"

"We don't know what to call her. She looks like a Belle to me, but Vaughn says she looks like her sister, Kate, and wants to name her that. Neither of us feels like addressing the question today."

"Katie Belle," Sarah said absently.

"What?"

"How about Katherine Belle? We could call her Katie Belle." She rubbed at the bridge of her nose then muttered, "Forget I said that. It's stupid."

"Actually, I think it's great. I'll talk to Vaughn about it when she wakes up. Anyway, don't worry about calling anyone. Your voice sounds better, but I know your throat must be killing you and –"

"Are you kidding? I won't be able to stand it! What time was she born? How much did she weigh? How long was she?"

Tristan knew only too well how impatient his daughter could be and told her, "Call then, but be brief. 3:43. Four pounds, four ounces. Twelve inches long. I'm sorry to have to saddle you with Will today. I know you're tired and fighting that cold, and you have that English exam."

"I'll manage. What about you? You sound like you got run over by a truck. Are you going to get some sleep?"

"I guess. I'll come home later this afternoon if everything continues to go well here."

"Get a doctor to check you out, why don't you? And don't forget to take your medicine."

"Yes, ma'am."

Sarah blushed and was about to apologize for being bossy when he said, "Honey?"

"Yes?"

"You'll always be my little girl. No matter how old you get. No matter what happens."

Blinking back tears, Sarah hung up the phone and decided to shower and dress before her brother awoke. If only she could take him to see Vaughn and the baby, that would make both of them happy, but she knew that was impossible. She had a cold; Vaughn had the flu; her father most likely had the flu; and the baby was in intensive care. Seeing his new sister connected to a bunch of wires and tubes would only scare the boy. Will would be better off at home, but Sarah couldn't abide the thought of sitting around studying and playing with toy soldiers all day. They'd have to find something innovative to occupy their time.

"Sissy! Is my baby here, yet?" Will asked excitedly when he came down at 7:00.

"Yes, she was born last night."

"Is it a brother?" When Sarah shook her head, he cried, "But I told God I wanted a brother!"

"Don't start," Sarah snapped. "Vaughn and Daddy went through a lot of trouble to have the baby."

"But –"

"Don't you tell Vaughn that you wanted a brother."

"Why not?" he pouted. "Maybe they could give this baby back and ask for a different one!"

"If anything happens to this one, they won't get another one!" Sarah said angrily.

He hugged his stuffed sheep and said in a small voice, "Sissy?"

"Yes, Will?" she said tiredly with a hint of guilt in her voice.

"Why do you call Mommy *Vaughn*?"

Sarah took a deep breath and sat at the kitchen table then motioned for him to climb onto her lap. Once he was seated, she hugged him and wondered if there would ever be a good time to explain the situation to her little brother.

"Your mom isn't my real mom," she began. "When I first met her, I knew her as *Vaughn*, so that's why I still call her that. Daddy married her when I was eight. Together, they had you and now our baby sister."

He sat quietly for a time before asking, "Where's your real mommy?"

Sarah hesitated then said, "She's in Heaven."

"My teacher says that Heaven is a pretty place."

"I'm sure it is," Sarah agreed. "I'm sorry I was mad at you a minute ago. I don't feel very good because of my cold."

"That's okay. Can I have eggs and toast, Sissy?"

"Sure. Maybe after I make some phone calls, we can do something exciting and go up to the attic."

"Can I bring Mr. Sheep?"

Sarah created a list of people to call. After breakfast, she telephoned them one by one, talking with Daniel, Benjamin,

Halley, Max, and Lillian. She left a message at Jamie and Chloe's. There was no answer at Vaughn's parents' farmhouse, and this bothered her. She decided she would try them again after lunch.

"C'mon, Will," she told the boy. "Let's put on some sweaters and go upstairs."

When they'd moved into the house four years before, Sarah had explored the empty attic. It had seemed like an enormous, magical place that ran along the entire top floor of the house. That morning as she and Will mounted the last two steps of the pull-down stairs, Sarah realized that it looked much smaller, although it was by no means cluttered. Tristan and Vaughn were organized people, and the boxes which edged the walls were all labeled clearly. *Christmas ornaments. Income Tax – 1975. Extra light fixtures.* None of them looked too exciting.

Will was having a grand time simply running around. Sarah had to remind him to stay on the right side of the attic so he wouldn't fall down the steps and break his neck. She was about to tell him that it was time to go back downstairs when she noticed a box she'd never seen before. It had no label.

Sarah glanced at Will, who was contently drawing patterns with his fingers on the dusty floor, and pulled out the box so that she could sit next to him. It was medium-sized, made of cardboard, and had a lid that folded over and slid in upon itself. She put her thumb in the depression at the front and pushed up.

For several seconds, all she could do was stare into the shadows of the box. After casting another glance at Will, Sarah carefully reached in and pulled out a small, wooden train engine. She put it on the floor next to her, and Will happily pounced on it. Marbles rolled around at the bottom of the box, but she dared not show those to her brother lest they disappear into the attic's dark corners and be lost forever.

Something glinted in the light that was streaming in through the dormer windows. Sarah stuck her hand into the center of the pile and touched metal. Wrapping her fingers around the object, she tugged and pulled out a set of dog tags.

Thomas W. Maes

Underneath the name was her grandfather's serial number, next of kin, street address, and city and state. A chill ran down her spine as she examined the other objects in the box: a rosary, a compact, a hammer, some beads, a slightly crumpled baseball pennant, a mitt and ball, and some sort of book. Putting the other items aside, she randomly opened the book and realized that it wasn't a book at all. It was a journal.

Sarah's mouth was dry as she read the page that lay open to her:

October 24, 1944

The house was quiet when I got home tonight. My father-in-law was out cold in his bed, but I can always talk with him tomorrow anyway. Right then, I wanted to look around at a place I never thought I'd see again. Nothing had changed, not really. The small rooms were still orderly. The old chairs looked a little more worn. There was a stain on the rug in front of the kitchen sink that hadn't been there when I left. It was a dark stain, probably grape or blueberry juice or something that wouldn't come out. It reminded me of blood, so I walked around it and went to our bedroom. There were flowers on the dresser. Anne said the Landreneaux children had picked them for me to welcome me home. I sat down on the bed next to Anne. I know she's worried about me. After eighteen months of duty and being wounded, I know I must look a sight. And the ride on the C-47 didn't do much for my beauty sleep. I was so tired that I asked Anne if she wanted to go to bed with me. Then, like a fool, I told her that I hadn't meant that, not that I didn't want to go to bed with her, I just wanted to sleep. I felt like I was stumbling over my words, but she understood what I was trying to say. We lay back on the bed, and I held her in my arms again and smelled the scent of her powder. We did go to bed, and now I feel like I can go on.

There was a sound in the direction of the pull-down stairs, and Sarah looked up and saw Tristan watching her. Will, waving the train excitedly, ran to his father and cried, "Daddy! We came to play in the attic! Did you bring my baby home with you? Is Mama here?"

"Let me help you downstairs, then I can come back and help Sissy," Tristan said, his eyes never leaving his daughter's face. He darted a glance at the wooden train then said, "Will, you can play

201

with that for this afternoon, but you must promise me you'll be very careful with it. My father made it for me."

"This was your train? And your daddy made it?"

Tristan nodded and proceeded to carry his son from the attic, telling him on the way down about Vaughn and his baby sister. Sarah heard them walk towards Will's room. Then all was quiet.

Several minutes later, Tristan's footsteps could be heard coming back in Sarah's direction. She closed the book but didn't put anything back in the box. She wanted to hide somewhere but felt that was foolish. She wasn't exactly afraid of physical violence, and that thought consoled her somewhat. What she feared now was that she'd hurt her father by inadvertently finding this box and by going through it without his permission.

The stairs creaked as he came up, and Sarah wondered why she hadn't heard Tristan climb up only minutes earlier. He emerged from the netherworld of the second floor and promptly bumped his head on a crossbeam.

"Damn!" he swore, rubbing his head. "I always forget about that."

Sarah didn't move. Normally, she would have smiled, because he did tend to forget about his height and the fact that the world was built for people not quite his size. Just then, she was too tense to smile.

He stooped down and came over to her then lowered himself to the floor. Peering into the box, he nodded, then surveyed the items scattered around her.

"I see you found it."

Tristan wiped at his face with one hand, leaving smudges of dirt across his cheeks. They reminded Sarah of war paint.

His daughter said apologetically, "I didn't know what it was. I should have asked before I took everything out." She swirled two fingers over the bumpy surface of the journal cover and asked, "Why?"

"Why didn't I ever show these things to you? That's an excellent question."

As he took out a handkerchief and blew his nose, Sarah said, "You're sick, and it's cold in the attic. Let me put these back then we can get warm."

"I'm sick?" Tristan reached out and pulled her to him before continuing, "And you? Are you immune to the cold that you can be sick and come up here yourself?"

"Daddy, I'm getting over a cold. You're coming down with the flu. There's a difference."

"Maybe. Either way, we can't leave things like this. You want the truth about the cardboard box? I forgot about it. No, really. When Jamie and I made our great escape, I insisted on bringing it with us. What you see there is all that I'd been allowed to take when they placed me in State custody. These few things are all I have of my childhood."

Still holding her, he leaned forward and studied the various items on display.

"The rosary belonged to my mother's mother. The pennant was from a baseball game we attended. I think the man selling them felt sorry for me, so he let me have it for a penny. I didn't care, but my parents would have had a fit if they'd found out that I had taken charity like that."

His face had a faraway look that Sarah had seen before. It was the same look he got whenever he spoke of her mother.

"I loved the game, so my mom and dad saved their pennies – and I do mean pennies – and bought me a glove and ball for my ninth birthday."

"And the other things?"

"The compact held my mother's face powder that she wore on Sunday to church. The marbles were from my days as the Seventh Ward school champion. Hey, don't look so shocked. The dog tags and the hammer were my dad's. The beads were from a Lakota ceremonial bracelet someone had given my dad when he was a young man. The journal was my father's, too. He started it when he was released from the service after he was hurt. The entries stop in 1946, right after I was born." He chuckled and added, "Babies don't leave parents with a lot of time for things like journals, I suppose." He pulled the rim of the box so that it tipped towards them and muttered, "There should be something else in here." He rummaged around with his free hand then exclaimed, "Ah! Here it is."

"It" was a white glove. Tristan brought it to his nose, closed his eyes, and inhaled deeply.

"Your mother's?"

He nodded and handed it to her.

"I can still smell the perfume she wore. Gloves, powder, and perfume were only for Sundays. That was all she ever wanted for Christmas. Every year, she got a bottle of perfume. I'm sure it wasn't even really perfume. What do they call that other stuff? Some kind of scented water...."

Sarah looked at the glove and raised it to her own nose then said, "I'm too stopped up. How can you smell anything being sick?"

"I can't. I just remember," he said with a rueful smile. "Why don't we go downstairs? We can take these things with us."

"We don't have to if you don't want to."

"Nah. It's been too long since I've gone through this box. When I was a kid, I used to look through these things and imagine what my life would have been like had they lived. It'll do me good to see it all again. Besides, it's your history, too. You should be able to sort through it somewhere warm."

"Do you still miss them?"

"Yes," he admitted, as he replaced the items she'd removed from the box. "And your mother, too."

"Is there a box with her things? Or a journal?"

Tristan hesitated, then rose carefully from the dusty floor and walked over to a corner of the attic. Sarah held her breath as she watched him move a few boxes and reach down into the darkness. He removed a large hatbox and carried it back across to where his daughter waited. He placed the box in front of her and sat once more.

Sarah stared at the box. She hadn't really expected him to have anything. She was surprised and confused and more than a little shaken.

"I didn't mean to keep it from you," Tristan said quietly. "I should've told you about this before, but it was painful to me, and I kept telling myself that I'd show this to you someday. Every year, I forgot about it until her birthday, then I'd put it off again."

His daughter slowly stretched her arm across the top of the hatbox and curved her fingers around the rim. Pulling up, she removed the top and peered inside.

Flowers filled the box. There were pictures cut from magazines that were curled from years of heat and humidity. There was a barrette with tiny, porcelain flowers glued all over it. There were pressed flowers and sketched flowers and a flowered scarf.

"Not much I know, but we didn't have much back then, except each other," offered Tristan. "But the flowers made her happy. I think they reminded her of the pretty things she'd had as a child. It was so easy to make her happy with flowers. When she was down, I'd pick wildflowers and bring them to her, and her face would light up like something you'd never seen. Flowers always make me think of her."

"Why didn't you tell me?" Sarah asked, as she studied his expression. "It must be so painful for you to come to my room. Rose wallpaper. Roses on the bedspread. Roses everywhere. How horrible."

Tristan kissed her on the top of her head and said, "Those are your flowers and yours alone. She never had roses. I don't know why." He picked the barrette out of the melee in the box and fingered it as he confided, "You were our rose. We used to call you that when you were a baby."

Boxes in hand, they backed carefully down the steps. They went to check on Will, who was covered in washable finger-paint. As Tristan opened his mouth to order a bath, the phone rang.

"I'll start cleaning this up, Daddy, if you'll get the phone."

Tristan went into his bedroom, set the cardboard box down on the floor, and lifted the receiver to answer the ringing. It was his mother-in-law, Helen. She and Jim had just come back from the hospital…without their daughter, Kate.

Chapter Seven: Concealed

"Z-E-B-R-A," Sarah read aloud to Jamie's oldest daughter. "That's great, Abby. You're getting so good at Scrabble. The only word I can make this turn is R-U-N."

"Sarah?"

"Hm?"

"What's a bastard?"

Sarah was startled, but quickly recovered herself and said, "Where did you hear it?"

"One of the moms was talking to another mom at carpool while I was waiting for Papa to pick me up yesterday. She said that me and Ally and Abe were bastards. What's that?"

"That means your mom and dad aren't married."

"It sounded bad when she said it. Is it bad?"

And people think babysitting is all about playing games and changing diapers, reflected Sarah. *What do they know?*

"Some people think anything different is bad. That mom is the one who has something wrong with her, not you."

"Oh. Should I tell her little boy? He's in my class."

"It might make him get angry at you since it's his mom. Just try to ignore it. Why don't you tell your mom or dad?"

"I can't."

"Why not?"

"Because something's wrong with them. I can tell."

"Maybe you should talk to them about that."

"No." The little girl placed two tiles on the game board and said, "N-A-P."

"That's six points." As she jotted down the child's score, Sarah glanced across the table at Abby Nesser's somber expression, sighed, and leaned back in her chair before querying, "What makes you think something's wrong with your parents?"

"I may be only eight, but I'm not stupid," the younger girl replied indignantly.

Sarah shrugged and studied the letters in front of her. She rubbed absently at the bridge of her nose then said, "Nobody would ever call you stupid, but if you don't tell me anything, then how can I help?" She smiled, then whistled softly and read,

"Conceal. C-O-N-C-E-A-L. Not bad, if I do say so myself. It's a triple word score, too." As her hand moved through the pile of letters to her right, she prodded, "Your turn."

"What does *conceal* mean?"

"To hide."

"That's what he's doing. *Concealing.*"

A shrill cry erupted from the back of the house, as Sarah was about to ask "Who? What?"

"Let me take care of Allison, then you can tell me all about it. Be thinking of your next word."

The baby's diaper was unbelievably wet. Once she had been changed, she gave Sarah a drowsy, toothy grin.

When Katie Belle's a year old, will she look like this with pink cheeks and brown curls? No, not brown, Sarah thought, as she laid the baby in her crib and left to check on Abe. *Red maybe.*

At that point in time, Sarah's little sister had only a few strawberry blonde strands. She was four weeks old and in very poor health. Her parents had brought her home from the hospital three days earlier.

Maybe it would have been for the best if Vaughn had miscarried at the beginning. What kind of life will Katie have? What if she doesn't outgrow being sick all the time? What if she dies? What will that do to all of us? Maybe she should never have been born.

Guilt wrapped itself around Sarah's heart and squeezed. She pushed the thoughts away and looked in on four-year-old Abe. No problems there, except that he was uncovered and curled into a tight ball on the mattress. She pulled up the blanket and tucked it under his chin then returned to the den.

Abby was fast asleep. Her head rested on her arms, which were folded on the table in front of her. Sarah hoisted her up, carried her to her room, and placed her in the twin bed across from the crib. She carefully eased the barrette out of the straight, brown bob and laid it on the dresser.

As she passed the telephone table, Sarah stooped down and pulled her worn copy of *Interview with a Vampire* from her purse. She sat and started to read, and time stopped, as it always did when she became engrossed in a book.

All at once, she realized that she had been staring at the word *Louis* for some time. Sarah pulled a piece of Kleenex from the box next to the couch and folded it neatly. Once her place in the novel had been marked, she rubbed the grit out of her eyes and looked at the clock. 10:41. She'd been enthralled for two hours. What had distracted her?

Abby.

What Abby had said earlier was true. Her words had been bouncing around in the recesses of Sarah's mind, and they had finally pushed themselves to the forefront. Something was wrong in the Nesser household.

The key turned in the lock of the front door. Sarah listened as Chloe and Jamie came in and divested themselves of their coats. Chloe's heels clicked in the foyer. Sarah turned around on the couch as Chloe asked, "Did they give you any trouble?"

She came over and sat on the ottoman. The velvet dress she wore was red. Her eyes were red, too.

"Allison wouldn't eat her peas. That was it for the out of the ordinary tonight."

"Good."

Jamie remained standing in the archway. He looked very dapper in his dark blue suit. His jaw was tight.

"How – how was the party?" Sarah stammered. "Jamie?"

"Fine. Wonderful. Stupendous."

"It was very nice," Chloe broke in quickly. "Here, let me pay you; then Jamie can drive you home."

Sarah watched as Chloe fumbled around in her handbag. She had always retained a very youthful appearance but suddenly seemed older than twenty-six. Of course, she had three young children, and she was always busy at her catering job. Perhaps the extra weight had taken some of the youthfulness out of her features.

Twenty pounds wouldn't make her look that much older. Would it?

Sarah accepted the money, hugged Chloe, and grabbed her leather jacket. She stuffed the novel into her purse and walked out the door ahead of Jamie, who was slipping his left arm into the long gray sleeve of his coat. He pulled the door behind them then locked it.

"I want to walk," Sarah declared. Before he could voice his objections, she added, "It's only a few blocks, and it's not as cold tonight as it has been. Please?"

"Fine," he snapped. "I'll walk you home. Whatever."

Tears came to Sarah's eyes, but she said nothing as they set out for her house. He'd never lost his temper with her. Never.

"Jamie?"

He kept walking, and she struggled to keep up.

"Are you and Chloe…all right?"

He stopped walking, and she skidded to a halt to avoid running into him.

"We're all wrong," he said bitterly. *"I'm* all wrong."

A streetlight shone not far away. Sarah tried to read his expression, but he wasn't focusing on her. She couldn't fathom the seriousness of the situation when she couldn't see into his eyes.

Suddenly, he looked directly at her, and a series of knots began to weave themselves around her intestines.

"There's someone else," he said matter-of-factly. "I have to leave Chloe."

The knot twisted and snaked upward into Sarah's throat, strangling the words she'd intended to say. Stupidly, she asked, "What's her name?" Then, sarcastically, "Or is it a guy like with Benjamin?"

"Winter," he said, ignoring her sarcasm. "Her name is Winter."

The anger began to burn and fray the knots of panic. In a caustic tone, Sarah barked, "Can Spring be far behind?"

"Munchkin –"

"Now is the Winter of our discontent?"

"That's enough!" Jamie jammed his hands into his pockets and muttered, "C'mon, Princess. Don't do this to me."

"I didn't do anything to you! You're doing it to yourself! Why?"

Sarah started to edge away. She wanted to be home.

"You know I'm not good with commitment. Chloe knows that I still love her and the kids."

"Almost a decade and three children doesn't equal commitment? How long have you been with this other woman?"

Jamie squinted up at the bulb above them and admitted, "Two months. She's a secretary at work. She's really great."

"Is she worth your children's happiness? Is she worth Chloe's love? I thought you didn't want to neglect your children. You think you can really be there for them when you're living with someone else?"

Sarah didn't wait for an answer. Instead, she turned and ran all the way back to her house.

Her lungs were burning by the time she reached the driveway. Helen and Jim's blue Toyota sat cold behind her father's truck. They must have arrived not long after she'd left for the Nesser home.

As quietly as she could manage, Sarah entered the house. Her father had left a light on for her in the living room. She went to turn it off so that she could go up to bed.

"Hello, Sweetheart."

Startled, Sarah spun around. Helen was sitting on the sofa with a romance novel in her hands. A handsome woman in her mid-fifties, she had platinum-blonde hair that had been braided and draped across one shoulder. She wore a light pink robe and beige slipper socks.

"I couldn't sleep, so I thought I'd stay up and read for a while," she explained. She patted the cushion next to her and said, "Come here, and let me give you a hug."

Obediently, the girl sat and leaned over to hug the woman who had been her de facto grandmother for eight years.

"When did you guys get in?"

"At about 6:00. We were a little late leaving the farm. A friend's daughter is going to look after it for us, and we had to show her this and that. It hasn't been a working farm for so long; you'd think it wouldn't have taken any time at all." Helen drew back to look at Sarah and said firmly, "I'm glad we're here now. I'm sorry that we couldn't be here sooner."

"Not your fault. I'm sorry we couldn't be there for Aunt Kate's funeral. I offered to go."

"I know you did. I appreciate it, but your father was right. With you and your parents sick and the baby in such a precarious state…. No, you needed to be here for yourself and for them. Jim and I understood."

"Did you get to see the baby awake?"

"For a while. We were so touched that she's named after Kate. She sleeps quite a bit, doesn't she?"

"It's because she's sick. Did Vaughn tell you that the doctors were wrong, that she wasn't really early?"

"Yes, Vaughn said her low birth weight and weak lungs had thrown them off somewhat. She wasn't developing at a normal rate, and that's why they miscalculated."

"I still think they should've been able to tell," Sarah remarked.

"Doctors aren't God, although many of them seem to think otherwise."

"Katie's got all sorts of other problems, too. Did you know they wanted to keep her in the hospital even longer?"

"No," Helen admitted with surprise. "Why?"

"Because she wasn't growing fast enough, and her immune system's underdeveloped."

"If that's the case, then why bring her home?"

"Vaughn insisted. She said that the baby would do better here than in some sterile hospital setting. She and Daddy had a big fight about it."

Sarah withdrew a Kleenex from her pocket and ostensibly blew her nose in order to hide the tears in her eyes. The fight had distressed her more than she was willing to concede. In a moment of panic, she had envisioned a repeat of the decline in her father and the break-up of her family.

"Daddy disagreed with Vaughn, but then he said that she could bring Katie home if she promised to take her to the pediatrician every day until he declared her okay or whatever the term is. Released her."

"I didn't know any of that," Helen admitted, attempting to keep her voice level. "I think your father was wise in that the baby probably would have been better off in the hospital. You know Jim and I have sided with your father regarding Vaughn's handling of the pregnancy."

"You have?"

"That shocks you?"

"I figured you'd take your daughter's side, no matter what."

"Even when we think she's wrong?"

"A part of me thinks she was right, at least about Katie's coming here. Being connected to a bunch of machines isn't a lot of fun, especially when you're a helpless baby. She is a cute baby, isn't she?"

"Yes," Helen nodded. "She's like a little peach."

"She's almost that size," Sarah added morosely. "I wonder if she'll ever grow and blossom. That's so poetic and dumb. I wish I could explain it."

"You think I don't know what you're feeling? You wonder if she'll die and if she should have survived in the first place. You're afraid of what it might do to your father and the family if she dies now."

"How did you know? I haven't told anyone. I only thought about it myself tonight while I was at Jamie and Chloe's."

"Sweetheart, don't lie to me or yourself. I'm sure you've been thinking about this off and on since Vaughn began to have trouble last spring."

Sarah mumbled, "Maybe. I'm horrible, I know."

"You're not. You're a scared girl who wants to save her family. You don't believe that what you're thinking didn't cross my mind almost every day from April on? Not that I knew about what you and your father were going through, but I was petrified that something would happen to Vaughn. I was going to lose one daughter. I couldn't stand the thought of losing the other, too."

"You thought about it, too? Do you still think about it?"

"I'm not afraid for Vaughn anymore, but I am concerned about the baby. I want so much for her to thrive, and I pray that she will."

Helen lifted a finger to brush a large curl from her granddaughter's forehead and grazed Sarah's nose in the process. Automatically, Sarah jerked back violently, raised her arms, and knocked Helen's fingers away.

Sarah grabbed at the sleeve of Helen's robe and said, "I'm sorry. It's just that…well, I don't like for anybody to touch it. Not even Daniel."

"Then I won't do it again, Sweetheart. Really, Sarah."

The girl stared at the floor and tried to conquer the sense of shame that was building in her then said, "Look, it's not…I'm kind of tired. Can we talk more tomorrow?"

Helen picked up her book and said, "Of course we can. You go on upstairs. I'm going to finish this chapter. Felicity may find true love with Antonio yet."

Sarah hugged her again and climbed the steps to the second floor. She passed Will's room and the bathroom and entered her own bedroom. Switching on the lamp, Sarah sank heavily onto the edge of the bed. She wanted Daniel there, holding her.

With a deep sigh, she rose and went to the dresser for a nightgown, choosing the one that Helen had given her. She was beginning to think of it as a comfort nightgown, since she only seemed to wear it when she was weary or anxious.

There was a young woman in the mirror, not at all the same girl who had been there the previous spring. The cotton nightdress looked childish and out of place. The dainty gold cross glinted in the lamplight. The image mocked her mercilessly, and yet she wanted more than anything for it to be right.

Sarah saw her father clad in sweatpants and an undershirt reflected in the shiny surface in front of her. She looked at him questioningly and asked, "Insomnia?"

"Katie Belle," he volunteered. "12:00 feeding and medication." He stretched out on the top of her bed and laced his fingers behind his head before remarking, "She may be tiny, but, God, she's feisty. You ought to see the way she fights me when I'm trying to get the medicine down with that dropper."

"The medicine probably tastes disgusting," Sarah said irritably. "Would you want to swallow it?"

"If it was a choice between life and death, then I would. I'm certain that it's got to be better than those gamma globulin shots."

"You mean that she's got to have all that? But, Daddy, they're supposed to be so painful! She's only a little baby!"

"As I said, Honey, when it's a choice between life and death, you do what you have to. It's not something I'll be happy about, but I want her to live, okay?"

"Okay!"

In the stony silence that followed, Sarah removed the gold cross and laid it on her dresser. She tossed her watch on the nightstand and unwound her hair. Grinding her teeth, Sarah wondered whether or not she and her father were about to engage in another argument. All that she wanted was to be left in peace.

Chapter Eight: Run Away

"How was babysitting?" Tristan asked, attempting to diffuse the tension between them.

"Fine. Wonderful. Stupendous." She paused and studied the strands of hair tangled in her brush before declaring, "My walk home with Jamie was terrible."

Tristan propped himself up on one elbow, his concern evident, and asked, "What happened?"

"You don't know then," she murmured dully. She went to the bed and sat within the right angle of his bent knees and hips. "No offense, but men are such jerks."

"Not that I'm contradicting you, but in what way?"

"Jamie's leaving Chloe and the kids for some secretary."

"So, that's what it was."

"You did know? Why didn't you say anything?"

"I didn't exactly know what was going on," he said, taking her hand. "But even as mixed up as I've been lately, I've known that something's been off with Jamie for a while. He wouldn't tell me what it was, said I'd just try to talk some sense into him. It was maddening. It made me understand a little better how he must have felt in August and years ago when I was so messed up."

Sarah rose, went to the window, and said, "Daddy, please don't talk about that. Any of it." Pressing her forehead against a cold pane, she closed her eyes and asked, "How can he do it? Chloe and the kids will hate him for it."

"No. Chloe will forgive him. Always. The kids, too. Oh, there'll be resentment, but they'll forgive him." Rising, he walked over to stand behind her. "We're all human. The people we love let us down with alarming frequency. Those of us who are lucky enough eventually receive absolution."

Sarah listened as he went back to his room and shut the door. Then she went to bed but immediately realized that the afghan was not in its usual spot. She had forgotten it downstairs.

Don't be such a baby. You can sleep without it.

Suddenly, she was wide-awake. She tossed and turned in the bed. She kicked the blanket off. She threw the covers up over her head. She pulled the sheet up under her chin. Nothing worked.

At 1:00, there was a light tap on her door.

"Sweetheart?"

"Yes?"

"I thought you might be cold. Mind if I tuck you in like I do with Will?"

"You don't have to."

"I know I don't have to," Helen said with a twinkle in her blue eyes, as she placed the afghan she carried onto the rocking chair in the corner. She straightened the sheets, blanket, and bedspread. Spreading the afghan across the top of the bed, she said, "Humor me. You all grow up so fast."

"Daddy used to tuck me in when I was a child. He used to watch over me…."

Sarah was asleep. Helen lowered herself into the rocker and watched over her for an hour. It was the least she could do.

When his wife climbed into the guest bed at 2:00, Jim woke and was instantly alert. He raised an eyebrow and asked, "What is it? What time is it?"

Helen smiled affectionately at his tousled gray hair and replied, "I'm just coming to bed. It's about 2:00."

Jim moved closer and pressed against her, trying to take away the chill on her side of the bed.

"Well? Did Felicity find true love with Antonio?"

"No, she ended up riding off to Wyoming with Cord."

"You win some; you lose some."

"I've been with Sarah. Oh, Jim. My heart bleeds for her. She's so young and yet so old. She's so in charge, and yet so out of control emotionally. I've never seen her act like this."

"Are you sure you're not talking about Tristan?"

"I might as well be."

"Go to sleep, Helen. Things will look brighter in the morning."

"A lot of help you are, Pollyanna. You'll see for yourself tomorrow."

The next morning Sarah was subdued when she came down to breakfast. Vaughn was feeding the baby and talking with Helen at the kitchen table. As Sarah went to the pantry for a Pop-tart, Helen sprang from her chair. It reminded Sarah of something Lillian might do.

215

"No, indeed! As if I'd let you eat a Pop-tart when I'm here to make you one of my famous omelets!"

"Don't worry about it, Grandma. You're the guest."

Helen ignored her and went to the refrigerator to remove eggs, ham, cheese, green onions, milk, and mushrooms.

"Sit," she ordered. "It'll only take a minute."

Sarah sat.

"MOM!"

"Not again," Vaughn sighed and shook her head. "Yes, Will?"

"MOM!" he cried, running into the kitchen. "There's a white plane on TV like the one I flied at John's party! It's only $5.95!"

Vaughn made an acknowledging, yet noncommittal movement and said, "Maybe for your birthday. Can you write the numbers on a piece of paper the next time it comes on?"

"Yes!" he cried then darted back towards the living room.

As Helen clattered about behind her, Sarah asked, "Where are Grandpa and Daddy?"

Vaughn pulled the half-empty bottle from the baby's mouth and raised Katie to her shoulder.

"Grandpa's in the backyard working on the lawnmower, and Tristan went to talk to Jamie."

"MOM!"

"Coming, Will," Vaughn sighed. "Sarah, would you hold Katie Belle while I go see this white plane?"

Sarah extended her arms for the baby and the bottle. Vaughn disappeared down the hall. Sarah talked sweetly to her sister, not really aware of what she was saying, just cooing at the infant as the level of formula slowly dropped in the bottle. The back door swung open behind her, but she didn't stop or turn around. Katie was much too tiny and much too adorable.

Daniel stood watching Sarah. From his vantage point at the door, he could only see her back, her profile, and Katie's little head. It was such a gentle moment that he was transfixed. He wondered if his mother had been like that with him. Surely she had.

The screen creaked behind him, and Daniel obligingly stepped out of the way.

216

"Hello!" Jim crowed. "Good to see you! And there's my angel!"

Sarah twisted slightly in the chair and called out, "Grandpa!" Then, more naturally, she said, "Hey, Daniel."

Helen turned from the stove and said, "Why, hello there, young man. Look at you! I wouldn't have recognized you!"

Daniel stood uncomfortably off to one side of the room. As usual, he hated being the center of attention. Sarah decided to spare him.

"Would you hold Katie so I can give Grandpa a hug? Thanks."

She proceeded to rise and come over to him, depositing the baby in his arms.

"Sarah, wait!"

"Don't have a cow. You've held lots of babies before. I know between Carrie's kids, Jamie's kids, and Will, you've changed a few diapers and mixed formula. What's the problem?"

"The problem is that she's the smallest baby I've ever seen. I feel like if I hold her the wrong way, I'll break her."

"Trust me, you won't."

She went to Jim and hugged him tightly. Being near him made her feel safe, yet there was still some fear lurking inside of her. It seemed as though every man she'd known and loved had betrayed her trust. Jamie was leaving Chloe for Winter. Benjamin had left Halley for Quinton. Max had slept with Isabelle years before, and he'd known she'd had a boyfriend. Daniel had been with someone else. And her father....

"What are you thinking, pretty lady?"

Jim looked so genuine. She wanted to say that it was nothing, but she couldn't lie to him.

"I'm wondering if I'll ever be able to trust any man ever again," she admitted. "Can I trust you, Grandpa? If you say I can, then can I believe you?"

Daniel didn't lift his eyes from Katie's face. Jim looked over to Helen, then back to his granddaughter. He reached up to brush the perpetually loose curl from Sarah's face. Helen made as if to say something, but she was too late. Sarah stepped back and pushed roughly at his hand. Her face burning with embarrassment, she rushed out through the backdoor.

Fifteen minutes later, Daniel appeared in the garage and found Sarah near the old wooden trunk where Vaughn kept the paper goods. Her hands were wrapped around her knees, but he couldn't tell if she was scared or just cold.

"Is Grandpa mad at me?"

Daniel shook his head and went to join her. He took off his jacket and covered her with it as best he could.

"He's worried about you. I'm worried about you."

He bent down and kissed her lightly. She slid her hand behind his neck and kissed him back hard.

Clank.

Tristan stood at the far end of the garage. His foot had come into contact with a wrench that Jim had left on the floor. Moving slowly, he came over to where they sat and lowered himself onto the concrete.

"I am *not* having a good day," he declared, bringing his knees up slightly and resting his elbows on them. Clasping his hands together, he continued, "I had a bitch of a fight with Jamie, and it didn't accomplish a damned thing. Then I come home, and I find out that Jim had to eat your omelet. Helen said she'd make you another one if you wanted."

"Right now, I feel like I'm going to throw up."

Actually, she had felt like she was going to throw up since the previous June, but her father didn't need to know that. Neither did Daniel.

Tristan picked up a stray pine needle that had made its way into the garage and asked, "You want to give Max a call?"

"No."

"Do you want a doctor?"

"What I want is for everybody to leave me alone."

"We can't do that, Honey."

"And we can't call Max for every little thing for the remainder of our natural lives either, Daddy."

"So, why don't you and I get away for the day? Maybe it would do us both some good to have a change of scenery."

"What do you suggest?" Sarah asked warily.

"Let's see what we can come up with." Tristan asked hopefully, "Any ideas?"

"I – I'd like to go to The River."

"The river?" Daniel echoed. "Why do you want to go there? Isn't it a little chilly to go stand on the levee and look at brown water?"

"Not the Mississippi. I want to see a place near where Daddy grew up. He told me about this creek while we were going through that stuff we found in the attic."

"I thought you said it was a river."

"It was a river to me," Tristan explained.

"Like that makes any sense," Daniel muttered.

"I was born in one of the poorest areas of Livingston Parish. Our house was small, and our furniture was old. My parents worked hard so we could have decent clothes and good food despite the hard times. There was a creek near the house, and my friends and I used to pretend it was a river. We'd fight battles over it, swim around the world, fish, throw rocks, whatever. I spent some of the best times of my boyhood playing there."

Daniel squeezed Sarah's hand and asked her father, "You've never gone back?"

"I haven't been to the house or the River in about twenty years." Tristan took Sarah's free hand and said, "It would be something different."

"Are you sure you want to do it?" Sarah asked apprehensively. "It's not going to trigger some new problem for you?"

"I think it's a good suggestion," Daniel volunteered.

"Me, too," Tristan agreed. "Let's do it. Dan, you want to come?"

"I think I'll pass on this trip," Daniel said, as he stood and slapped the dust off of his backside. "This is something you two should do alone. Call me later."

Chapter Nine: The River

As Daniel headed for his VW, Tristan and Sarah returned to the house to get ready for their excursion. Once Tristan was satisfied that his daughter had eaten something, even though it was only a piece of toast, they climbed into his Chevy Blazer and were on their way. Within twenty minutes, they'd arrived in Denham Springs.

"Everything's so different, yet still the same," Tristan muttered. "It's bigger than when I was a kid."

Tristan drove aimlessly for a while, as his daughter listened to his description of this place or that place. Finally, he made a right turn, and they made their way to the fringes of town.

"This is it," Tristan announced, as he parked the Blazer and shut off the engine.

Sarah stared at the neat, white wooden home. Its yard, like those around it, was well kept, and most of the houses looked as though they had been painted recently. Children were playing ball in the street, and the neighbor at the house next door was cutting the grass.

"It never looked this good twenty years ago when we moved to Baton Rouge," Tristan laughed. "It must have gone through some town fix-up plan or something. I'd like to get down, if you don't mind."

"I'm ready."

They stepped out of the truck and went to stand at the gate. After hesitating briefly, Tristan held it open for his daughter. The gravel path that led to the front porch had been freshly laid; the stones were still bright white. They knocked on the door and waited while shuffling sounds emanated from inside.

The locks clicked, and the door opened to reveal an old woman of perhaps ninety. From behind the woman, they heard "MawMaw Beth! You should know better than to open the door to strangers!" and saw a middle-aged woman come forward and glare suspiciously at the two of them.

"Excuse me," Tristan said hastily. "I'm Tristan Maes. I'm sorry to bother you, but I used to live here a long time ago, and I was wondering if my daughter and I might look around if it's not too much trouble."

The eyes of the younger of the two women roamed over first Tristan then Sarah.

"We won't be long. Believe me," he urged, certain that his stature was responsible for her hesitation. "We're not here to rob you or anything. Our truck's right here in front."

He gestured towards the street, and the woman squinted past him. The lines in her face softened a fraction.

"All right. But I'd be happier if you'd close the door behind you when you come in. I need to get MawMaw Beth back in her chair."

Tristan complied as he followed Sarah into the living room, which was a little bigger – but only just – than the largest bathroom in their present house. MawMaw Beth was sitting in a faded brown chair watching *The Lawrence Welk Show*. The other woman hurried to check on some sizzling noises coming from the kitchen. Tristan looked around the cramped little room and pointed to the doorframe next to him.

"Would you look at that?"

Sarah studied the wood then asked, "What is it?"

"It's where my mother used to mark how tall I'd grown. I can't believe that nobody's painted over it. The lines are still there. Too bad the years have faded off." He reached out to touch the top line. "This was the last one. She did it right before we left for Baton Rouge. It's about your height."

"I can't imagine that you were ever my height."

Sarah experienced a deep melancholia, as she stared at the line. The woman who had taken a pencil and made that mark had been going on to a new place, to what she hoped would be a better life for her family. Little did she know that within two weeks she and her husband wouldn't be alive at all and that her son's stable existence would disintegrate into a life of living on the streets, teenage marriage and fatherhood, and drug and alcohol abuse.

"Right here," Tristan was saying, "was where the sofa was, and there's where the piano was. There was a nice, rectangular coffee table that my father had found somewhere and refinished. That's where I used to do my homework."

"Didn't the TV distract you?"

221

Tristan smiled indulgently at her and said, "We didn't have a TV until I was eleven. It was a little black-and-white deal, and, no, I wasn't allowed to watch it while I did my homework. If my parents wanted to see the news, then I had to take my books to the kitchen table."

They ambled through the doorway to the kitchen, which was roughly the same size as the living room. A small, round table had been positioned on one side of the kitchen.

"That's where our table was, too. Another refinishing project of my dad's. I wonder what they did with all of that furniture after my folks died."

Sarah followed her father through a narrow hallway. To the left was a room no bigger than a large walk-in closet.

"That was my grandfather's place. After he died, that's where the boarders stayed." As they walked a few more steps, he announced, "This was my room."

It was marginally smaller than the boarders' room.

"My bed was here, next to the window. I had a chest of drawers near the door." He pivoted and added, "This is the bathroom, and this was my parents' room. It's a shame they didn't fix up the inside when they cleaned up the outside of this house." He walked over to a door on the far side of the master bedroom. "This one actually has a closet. Neither of the others has one. I kept all of my stuff in my chest of drawers."

Feeling like an intruder, Tristan turned the knob and pulled, flipping the light switch as he did so. The open door revealed a hodge-podge of clothing, footwear, and extra blankets. He was about to close the door when something caught his eye.

Behind Tristan, Sarah was peering through the sheers at the yard on the side of the house. Stepping into the closet, Tristan reached across the shelf on the left-hand side. A soft material teased his fingertips, as he closed his middle finger and index finger together and pulled gently at the neglected article. Of course no one else had seen it. The shelf was too high to reach without a tall stepstool. It didn't appear that the occupants had ever used it, since it was bare and dusty.

Well, not completely bare.

"I wonder how this got back there?" he muttered, bringing the white glove towards him. As he closed his eyes and brought it close to his face, the glove unfolded and a whiff of familiar floral scent wafted up into his nostrils.

"Daddy?"

He wanted to spin around and jam the glove under her nose. Of all the people in the world, he felt as if he was the only one left who remembered his mother and father – what they looked like, the timbre of their voices, the way they moved. It was an awful feeling not to have anyone to share those memories with.

There was moisture lacing his eyelashes as he turned deliberately towards his daughter. Mutely, he held out the glove as if it were an offering or a plea. She took it carefully and brought it to her face, taking in the scent of her father's mother. She began to cry, not great heaving sobs, just light tracks along the curve of her cheeks.

Never taking her eyes off of the glove, she said, "I want you to tell me about them. That way I'll know, too." As she handed the glove back to her father, who slipped it into his pocket, she said, "Maybe we shouldn't have come."

"No. I needed it. Them." He scanned the tiny master bedroom and remarked, "It's hard for me to imagine my father living here. The place is so small, and he was almost my current height."

"It's not much different from the house we rented when I was little, Daddy. Well, the rooms were slightly larger there. Maybe because we didn't have a third bedroom."

It was an accurate parallel, one that had never occurred to him.

They inquired of the two women whether they could exit through the side door in the kitchen. The middle-aged woman granted them permission and told them how to get back around without having to come through the house. Tristan thanked them both and headed for the door.

Sarah hurried down the steps. Tristan descended more slowly then turned back.

"Did you forget something?"

"No," he said. "I remembered something. My mother, she used to come out here when I was a boy, and she'd watch me and my friends horse around. I can picture her with a bowl of snap beans in her lap. We'd be showing off for her, and she'd be laughing at our antics, all the while snapping the beans and pulling out the strings." Tristan pushed his hands into his pockets and fingered the glove for a few seconds before saying, "It's time to go to The River."

As they walked down the slope behind the house, Tristan took his daughter's hand and swung it slightly as he had when she was a child. He watched her walk out of the corner of his eye. She wasn't a child anymore. She was a young woman. It was hard for him to believe that his little girl would be seventeen years old the following week.

The creek was still there. Unlike the house, it didn't look smaller than Tristan remembered. As Sarah sat on the bank, he crouched beside her and stuck his fingers in the water. Then he cupped his hand and drank from the creek.

"I wouldn't drink from there if I were you. Who knows where it's been?"

Sarah scrambled around, as her father rose quickly to see who was watching them. The light was blocked slightly because the figure was standing near a grove of trees where he couldn't easily be seen. His face was obscured by shadows. Sarah moved closer to Tristan.

"Thank you for the warning, Mister...?"

There was silence then a chuckle.

"You don't remember me, Little Buck?"

Tristan froze, then stalked forward and said angrily, "Who are you? How –"

"It is I," the man said, as he stepped out of the shadows.

The man standing before them was older, but not old. He was several inches shorter than Tristan and had ruddy cheeks and a leathery complexion. He wore boots, jeans, and a plaid shirt.

The younger man's mouth twitched, and a grin began to spread slowly across his face. Sarah was certain that she was missing something vital.

"Daddy? Who is this?"

He took her hand again and brought her across the grass to stand in front of the older man.

"This is John Lightfoot. He was my father's best friend from before the time they moved here. They grew up at the same place and came together to Denham from out West."

224

Lightfoot extended his right hand, and Sarah shook it firmly as Tristan said, "My daughter, Sarah."

"And what is your other name, child?"

Sarah shook her head and said, "I don't have any other name unless you mean my middle names."

Lightfoot looked severely at Tristan and said, "That's unwise."

Puzzled, Sarah turned and lifted her head in mute befuddlement.

Her father seemed reluctant to speak. Or maybe he was simply being respectful. Finally, he admitted, "She has another name."

This is getting weirder by the minute, Sarah thought.

The older man nodded and waited patiently. Tristan said a word in a language she didn't understand. When she looked confused, he translated, "Blossoms in Stone."

"I see." Lightfoot nodded gravely then asked, "Is she aptly named?"

"Very much so."

Sarah said nothing to either man. There were too many questions to ask, too many things she didn't understand. She would wait until she and her father were alone.

As they started up the grassy slope, Tristan asked, "How did you know I was here?"

"You saw the man cutting the grass next door? He is my son. Called me up to say that he'd seen the ghost of my friend walking up the steps at this house. He'd seen pictures."

Tristan came to an abrupt halt and stood rigid.

"You have pictures?" he asked in disbelief.

Lightfoot put a hand on Tristan's shoulder and said, "Yes, several pictures. Some of your father and me when we were boys. Some of all of us. One is even of your parents on their wedding day. And there are a few of you as a little one."

Tristan swallowed the lump in his throat and confided, "I have no pictures. Would you mind if I borrowed yours sometime to make copies? I'd like to see them and…my children…they don't know….I never…."

"That would be fine."

"I'd also like to talk with you, if that's all right."

They had reached the front sidewalk. Tristan took out a business card and scribbled his home phone number on the back.

"Here's where you can reach me."

"An architect," the older man said approvingly then pocketed the card. "You're a successful one, then?"

"Yes," Tristan agreed.

"And in your home are you successful, too?"

Tristan pondered how he should answer this particular question. His first impulse was to say that he had failed in his duties to his family. That wasn't completely true. He couldn't exactly say that he had done a stellar job either.

"I'm a man who always tries to do the right thing."

Lightfoot looked shrewdly at Tristan then said. "That's all one can ask of any man."

"Sometimes, I wonder."

"Sometimes, every man wonders," he declared. "I didn't find out about Tom and Anne's deaths until three weeks after the accident. I called the State people to try and find you. My wife and I would have taken you in, but they said that you had disappeared a week earlier. You ran away."

"Yes, I did."

"You found a good home and a good family to live with?"

"No."

"I'm sorry for that. You could have had a place with us."

"I'm sure I could have. I didn't want to burden you with another child. You already had seven of your own. You didn't need another mouth to feed."

"No, we didn't. We would have fed it anyway."

"Thank you."

"I'll call you tomorrow. Perhaps we can meet for a long lunch somewhere."

"The first of many lunches?"

"Yes. I would very much like to hear how you survived and did so well in life on your own." He touched Tristan on the shoulder and muttered, "My best friend's son."

They all shook hands, and Sarah and Tristan got into the truck, with Tristan apologizing for being so long.

"I didn't think we were that long. Did you find what you wanted to here?"

"I did. And you?"

"Yes and no. I have so many questions."

"Such as?"

"Don't you regret that you ran away? If you hadn't then maybe you could have had a normal life here. Maybe things would have been happier for you."

"Easier maybe. Happier? Without loving your mother? Without you? What about Vaughn, Will, and Katie? I'd never have known Helen and Jim. And Jamie, even though I could wring his neck today. Max, Lillian, Benjamin, Halley…everyone…all of the people I love, odds are that I never would have met them.

"Maybe I could have married Polly Gaudet, the girl next door. We could have had an unfulfilling marriage and five – no, six – screaming, ungrateful brats. I could have gotten a job doing construction like John and had my very own closet full of jeans, boots, and plaid shirts. And a cap. Don't forget the cap."

"Daddy!" she giggled.

"I'm only teasing, Honey. John is a good man, and I'm sure that he and Uma would have been good to me. But that doesn't mean that my life would have turned out any better. That part of my past is history. I can't look back and wonder about it; it's over and done with."

"What was all that about another name?"

"I gave you that name when you were small. It's Lakota tradition, although your Lakota name doesn't quite translate to the English the way I intended it to. I guess I felt strange about the whole thing. I never carried on any of the other traditions. So, I named you while you were asleep one night and filed it away."

"And just forgot to tell me?"

He shrugged, and they rode without speaking back to the house.

That night, when the house was quiet, Tristan slipped out of bed and went to his daughter's room. He sat on the edge of the bed and turned on the small lamp she kept on the nightstand.

"Daddy? Is something wrong? What time is it?"

He put a hand on her arm and said, "Shhh. Nothing's wrong. I wanted to talk with you about something, something nobody else knows except me and Jamie."

That got her attention. Interested, she sat up and leaned against the headboard.

"When I met your mother all those years ago, she was alone. She wasn't a runaway; she'd been kicked out by her dad."

Sarah didn't bat an eyelash. She'd come to expect the unexpected.

"When she was a child, she'd been the apple of her father's eye, her mother's pride and joy. She was smart; she was pretty; she was sweet. That lasted until her mother died, and her father remarried and had a son. Suddenly, Emma was dumb; she was messy; she was unmanageable. Nothing had changed, except her father's priorities. From the moment his son was born, Emma ceased to exist." He put his elbows on his knees and rested his chin in his hands before continuing, "She was...worthless to him. What a load of crap."

"What about her brother? What was he like?"

"She said that he became the spoiled brat the father had raised him to be. They were wealthy, and he had anything and everything he wanted. Emma had things, too." He ran his fingers through his hair and said angrily, "She never wanted things. She wanted her father's love. He didn't have enough love to give. The universe revolved around his work and his son."

"But, that still doesn't explain why she got kicked out of her own house."

"Your mother knew she was being treated unfairly, but what could she do? Emotional abuse is not as easy to prove as physical abuse. Who would believe that such a prominent man was mistreating his daughter?

"Eventually, she confronted him about how wrong it all was. He was furious. He told her she was an unworthy child and that he wanted her out of the house. Not only that, he never wanted to see her again. He would see to it that she never got a dime from him, that her brother would have it all, and she'd be living on the streets. Unbelievable, huh? He wouldn't even let her take a toothbrush. She had only the clothes on her back."

"How could anyone *do* something like that to anybody, much less his own child? Didn't it make her hate him?"

"She never told me that." He rubbed thoughtfully at his lower lip then said, "She wanted so much to do right by you and not be like him. And she did."

"Is her family still in town?"

"Her family?"

"They're not our family."

"Fair enough. They don't deserve to be involved in either of our lives."

"Are they still alive?"

"As far as I know. Her father lost his money through some bad business dealings. There was an article in the paper because of how well-known he was in the corporate world. Emma couldn't help but feel some satisfaction. What goes around comes around and all that."

They could hear Katie Belle stirring in the other room. Tristan stood and stretched.

"I'd better go get her before she wakes everyone up." He paused at the door and said, "If you have any questions, ask."

"Daddy? Why are you telling me this now?"

"Because I don't want you wandering around looking for your past when you're thirty-three years old like I am."

As he shut the door behind him, he thought he heard her say "Amen."

Chapter Ten: Perception

Sarah hurried through the Redemptorist High parking lot, hastily slid the key into the lock of the blue Corolla, and felt for the *click*. Hoisting her book sack onto the rear seat, she climbed in and reached over to unlock the passenger door for her friend, Victoria, who was jumping up and down in an attempt to keep from freezing in the November wind.

"It was really nice that your grandparents are letting you drive their car while they're here," Victoria remarked, tossing her blonde hair behind her shoulders as she got in and lowered her book sack next to Sarah's. She added wistfully, "It must be nice to be able to drive yourself to school."

As she started the engine, Sarah said, "Too bad it won't last forever."

"Thanks again for the lift," Victoria said, as she hunched forward and switched on the radio. "It'll give Mom a break. She's been going nuts trying to get everything done by herself with Dad out of town. It's really dense of the company to transfer Dad here then send him off for two weeks to the Anchorage plant. It's not fair to Mom. Having six kids can keep you hopping without trying to unpack boxes and handle all the business of running the house and working."

"If I had six kids and no husband for two weeks, I think I'd be pretty harried, too." Settling back into the driver's seat, Sarah ventured, "We've known each other for six weeks now, right?"

"Right-o."

"And ever since I introduced you to Robert Taylor, you two have been hot and heavy. Right?"

"Yeah," she grinned. "I guess we have."

"Well, you moan and groan all the time about sharing the house with your brothers and sisters."

"So?"

"So, how many kids are you and Robert going to have?"

"None! I've already spent too much time helping my parents raise the others."

"Oh, come on. Don't you want at least one?"

"Okay, maybe one. When you and Dan have six, then you tell me which one of us is saner."

Sarah concentrated on fighting the afternoon traffic and managed to get Victoria to her appointment on time.

"You sure you don't want me to stay? Or I could come back for you."

"Nah. Mom should be able to get me at 5:00. Who knows? I might still be waiting to see the dermatologist. See ya!"

As she approached the Interstate, Sarah's thoughts turned to the biology test she'd taken that morning. She merged with the I-10 traffic then veered right and merged onto I-12. As she did so, she experienced a moment of complete panic.

Maybe I'm finally cracking up, she thought. *No, that can't be it. It's that car in front of me. Something's wrong with the way it moved over.*

As she exited the interstate, Sarah paid closer attention to what she was seeing. Yes, something was amiss, but she couldn't isolate exactly what it was.

Once she reached her house, Sarah eased the Corolla into the driveway and noted that Max's car was parked at the curb. Getting out of the Toyota, she grabbed her book sack, slung it over her shoulder, and went across the grass towards the backdoor. She passed through the kitchen and went to the living room where Max, Lillian, Helen, Jim, and Vaughn were seated. Will was playing on the floor. Lillian cradled little Katie Belle in her arms.

"Sarah!" Max greeted her with a broad smile and declared, "We've come for a visit with your grandparents and now find ourselves invited to dinner."

"Are you *sure* you have enough?" Lillian asked. "Don't feel obligated."

"There's plenty of room and plenty of chicken noodle casserole," Vaughn assured her. "All we'll have to do is throw together a salad and warm some bread."

"I'll get the salad started," Helen offered.

"No, Grandma," Sarah protested. "I'll do it."

Will looked up from his coloring book and asked, "Can I help?"

Before Sarah could answer, Vaughn said quickly, "No, Will. You said you were going to finish that picture for Max and Lillian. You have to finish one thing before you can start another."

"But *Mom*!"

As Vaughn began to lecture her son about the value of following through, Sarah went to the kitchen and pulled out the colander, then gathered the lettuce, olives, tomatoes, and artichoke hearts. Removing the large salad bowl and herbs, oil, and vinegar, she moved to the sink and began to wash the lettuce.

When the backdoor opened and her father entered, she glanced back at him but continued to wash the greens. He looked happy and at ease after his workday, and she didn't want to burden him with her worries.

"Hey!" he sang out.

"Hey."

Tristan had been heading for the hallway. Suddenly, he stopped and walked over to stand next to her.

"What is it?"

"I just said 'Hey'."

"What's up? Give."

Sarah turned off the tap and started to transfer the lettuce from the colander to the bowl.

"It's probably nothing," she assured him, as she reached for a tomato. "I think I might need glasses or something."

He blinked at this unexpected comment and asked, "Are you having trouble seeing the blackboard at school? Are things blurry?"

"No. Just different."

They stared at each other in silence. It wasn't necessary for her to say aloud how bothered she was by whatever was happening with her eyes. Her father sensed that she was afraid that something more than corrective lenses were needed.

Sarah grabbed a small knife and went to work on slicing the tomato. Thinking about the way she had felt in the car was making her feel anxious and vulnerable.

Tristan checked his watch and said, "It's only 5:15. Maybe the eye doctor's still in the office."

"Daddy, I don't think they're going to see me today."

"Maybe not." He crossed the kitchen, lifted the phone book, and removed the receiver from the wall phone then told her, "They might make an appointment for tomorrow, though."

Sarah opened the jar of artichoke hearts and the can of black olives. By the time she'd unscrewed the top to the jar of green olives, Tristan had replaced the receiver.

"Tomorrow at 4:00. I'll meet you over there. Did you tell Vaughn about this?"

She withdrew the salad tongs from a drawer and declared, "I'd rather not say anything to anyone until I know what's really the matter."

He came up behind her and squeezed her shoulders.

"It's probably nothing."

"Probably."

The timer rang. Tristan squeezed his daughter's shoulders one more time then went to greet the others. Sarah wrapped the French bread in aluminum foil and slid it into the oven before removing the casserole. The adults and Will filed into the room, and Sarah actually relaxed and forgot for a time about her eyes.

The next afternoon, she pulled into the parking lot of the large ophthalmology clinic and saw that her father's truck was already there. He was sitting in the waiting room, filling out forms.

"I think I've put everything down that they need," he said, as she sat in the chair across from him. "Oh, except how many times you blinked in the last ten years."

She smiled and began to tell him about her day at school, but a woman came out from the back and called her name. They rose and followed the assistant to a room at the end of the corridor. Sarah climbed into the examination chair, while Tristan stood close to her and leaned against the wall. Dilation drops were administered to Sarah's eyes, and then the father and daughter were left alone to wait for the doctor.

Eventually, the door opened, and the ophthalmologist entered. As pleasantries were exchanged, he went about the business of examining Sarah. Periodically, he would insert a question.

He's good, Tristan thought. *It's like he's just passing the time of day, instead of performing an exam.*

As Tristan watched, the doctor took out a small, round magnifying lens. Sarah was asked to tilt her head back and look

233

this way and that, while the doctor shone a light through the glass. After some further questions, the man sat on the rolling stool next to the counter.

"Well, I do see some disturbance on your retinas, Sarah, especially the left one. I have an idea as to what it is, but I'd like to do a retinal angiogram and take some pictures to make sure. The angiogram's done down the hall. We're extremely fortunate to have the equipment to perform the test here. If you'd like, we could do it right now; then I can talk with you afterwards."

Sarah trailed after him to a small room that held a large machine resting atop a square table. A technician motioned for her to sit and proceeded to insert an intravenous lead into her hand.

"I'm going to inject a dye into the tube," he informed her. "Put your chin here so that I can get some good shots, okay? Here we go."

Sarah suddenly sat back and closed her eyes. Tristan took a step forward, but the tech shook his head.

"Here," he said, putting a trashcan next to Sarah's chair. "In case you need to throw up."

Sarah opened her eyes then said, "No, it's passed. Why did I feel like that?"

"The dye's cold. When it hits your stomach, it can make you feel sick." Resuming his position on the other side of the machine, he directed, "Let's get this show on the road. I have to get these shots while the dye's passing through your eyes."

Once several pictures had been taken, the technician took Sarah and Tristan back to the examination room. Forty minutes later, the ophthalmologist returned and sat facing them on the little stool.

"Well, the results confirmed what I suspected. I had another associate here at the clinic take a look as well to be sure. What you have is the early stages of juvenile macular degeneration. What this means is that your central vision is deteriorating, although your peripheral vision stays the same. If I hadn't worked on some similar cases when I was in Houston, I probably would have been at a loss. Diagnosis can be –"

"What are the treatments?" interrupted Tristan.

The man rotated towards him and said, "At this time, there are no treatments. However, researchers are always working on cures and treatments for eye disorders, so you never know."

"How long?" Sarah asked. "How long before my central vision is gone?"

"There's no pattern. It might be a year; it might be forty years. There's some evidence that certain vitamin supplements can help to slow the progression. The retina deteriorates because of a lack of oxygen to the pertinent cells. The vitamins make for healthier blood. Healthier blood should help to maintain a higher level of oxygen."

"How did she get it?" Tristan asked, as he paced from one wall to the other.

"It's a genetic disorder. A rare one at that." Addressing Sarah, he added, "You shouldn't worry about passing it on to any children you might have someday. The odds are low, although those children could be carriers of the gene. However, do you have siblings? They could be at risk."

"A half-brother and a half-sister."

The ophthalmologist shook his head again and said, "The odds are in their favor that they wouldn't have inherited the disorder. It's possible, but highly improbable. If the three of you had the same biological parents, then I'd have them monitored very closely." He closed the folder in his hands and said officiously, "Unless something changes, I don't need to see you back here for six months. I can't do anything about your condition, but I'd like to track the progression of the disorder for your information and mine."

The assistant escorted them to the front desk. Tristan paid the bill, and they stepped out into the darkness. When they reached the Corolla, Tristan pulled Sarah to him and tightly wrapped his arms around her. She didn't cry about the diagnosis or contest it. She simply stood and let him hold her. It was what they both needed.

"Are you all right, Sarah?"

She nodded against his chest.

"Can you see well enough to drive home? I mean with those dilating drops, not because –"

"I'll meet you there."

"Why don't you meet me at the Ground Pat'i instead?" he suggested. "I don't feel like going home right now. Do you?"

"Not really. What about the others? I know you said you told Vaughn that we had some stuff to take care of, but we're already late. She'll be worried."

"We'll call from the restaurant."

They managed to get a table near the fireplace. Neither of them said much as they waited for the food. Once it arrived, they lingered over their cheeseburgers, fries, and Cokes. It was 9:00 before they reached home.

"I don't believe it," Vaughn declared when they told her about the diagnosis. "It has to be something else. You need another opinion. There has to be a more qualified doctor."

"Two doctors looked at the test results!" Sarah snapped angrily. "You weren't even there!"

"They're wrong. I want you to go see a specialist, somebody in Chicago. Chloe's aunt went to him last year. He's supposed to be the best."

"No," Sarah said firmly. "This is ridiculous."

Jim stepped forward and said gently, "Another opinion might not hurt."

"No!" Sarah clenched her hands and stared out of one of the larger windows in the living room.

"Sweetheart –" Helen began.

"Do you know what it was like for me to have to sit still and let him touch my eyes? Do you know how many times he brushed his fingers across my nose during the exam? I wanted to scream. And now you want me to do it again? The doctor's right! I know he is!"

Pushing past Tristan, she ran up the stairs to her room and slammed the door. A thin wail came from the master bedroom where Katie Belle's cradle resided.

The four adults stood rooted to the floor. Vaughn broke away from the group and moved toward the stairs.

"I should go to her. Tristan, if you'll see to the baby –"

"No, I'll talk to her," Tristan announced. "You see to the baby."

He left the room before Vaughn could argue. Once upstairs, he rapped his knuckles on Sarah's door. When she didn't answer, he tried the knob. The door was unlocked.

She was lying on the bed, her face turned away from him. He sat on the mattress and stared at her back.

"I'm sorry, Honey."

"About what?" she mumbled.

"Everything."

She rolled over onto her back and looked questioningly up at him.

"It's my fault, as usual. They're my genes."

"Daddy, you didn't do it on purpose."

He fixed his eyes on the porcelain clock by her bed and muttered, "It doesn't matter. It's still my fault. And if I hadn't –" He broke off and looked sadly at her before saying quietly, "I'm sorry it was – it is – so hard for you to let people touch your nose."

He should be sorry, she thought. *He should never forget it.*

"And Vaughn's attitude? How is that your fault?"

"I don't know," he said wearily. "But I think you should go."

Sarah rolled away from him.

"I don't think it'll do any harm if you can stand the exam," he continued. "And she doesn't sound like she's going to accept the diagnosis until you go."

"Do you accept it?"

"Do you?"

"Yes."

"Just like that?"

Sarah covered her head with a pillow and groaned, "What good would it do to weep and wail? It's not terminal, for cryin' out loud."

"You're not scared?"

"I wish I could visualize what it'll be like not to be able to see in the center and to know how long it'll take. I only started driving two years ago. How long will I have a license? How will I get around?" With a sigh, she removed the pillow and pushed herself up onto her elbows then said, "It's kind of like when I was seven, and you and Max told me that someday I wouldn't be able to do certain things, but you didn't know when or really even what. I obsessed about it for a while but nothing terrible happened, so I relaxed. Then, one day, boom! That was it. It hit me that I was limited in ways other kids weren't. I had to adapt. I guess I wonder if it will be the same with this. I don't know what to expect."

"I think you should go to Chicago with Vaughn. Maybe you'll both get some answers."

Draping one arm over her face, Sarah said grudgingly, "I guess I could live through it. I don't want to tell anyone about my eyes right now, okay? I don't want them to be looking funny at me. I don't want them to pity me or anything.

"How am I going to tell Daniel? What if he doesn't want to be with me any more? I feel like I'll be damaged goods. He'll be limited, too. And what if we get married and have kids? Will I be able to take care of them without being able to see in the middle?"

"Damaged goods? I don't ever want to hear you use those words again, you understand?" Tristan commanded. "And by the way, you didn't see what Dan looked like underneath his clothes nine years ago. I don't think he'll consider you damaged goods because your retinas are scarred. Now, get some sleep, and we'll arrange things in the morning."

By Friday, Sarah and Vaughn were Chicago-bound.

"We could spend the night," Vaughn reminded her stepdaughter, as they stood waiting at the ticket counter. "Mom and Dad are very capable of taking care of Katie, Will, and Tristan for months, much less a couple of days."

"Daniel and I are supposed to go out tomorrow night. I don't want to have to explain to him about this trip."

"You'll have to explain it to him soon."

"One thing at a time."

At the retinal specialists' office, Sarah went through the motions. Her eyes were scrutinized by three different doctors. She was subjected to another retinal angiogram and a field of vision test, which left her with a massive headache. After all was said and done, the specialists confirmed her diagnosis and gave it an official name: Stargardt's.

As they left the office, Sarah wanted to shout, "You see, Vaughn? I was right!" Instead, she said, "I'm hungry, and I have a headache. Can we get something to eat?"

"Sure," Vaughn answered automatically. "There's a restaurant over there. Why don't we try it, then we can catch a cab back to the airport?"

The cuisine was Italian. Sarah was delighted and ordered eggplant parmigiana. Vaughn chose the manicotti, then excused herself to go to the restroom. When she didn't return to the table after several minutes, Sarah went in search of her and found her stepmother crying in one of the stalls.

"Vaughn, are you all right?"

"I don't want to see you suffer anymore," the woman cried. "You've had enough pain and disappointment in your life. It's not fair."

Whoever said life was fair? Sarah thought wryly.

"It could be worse."

Her stepmother emerged from the stall and grabbed some tissues from the box on the counter.

"I know. But it could be so much better."

"It is what it is. I'll survive. I always Have."

Part Three - 1994

Chapter One: A Door

"And then that big, strong man came over to me and asked, 'Do you need some help, ma'am? I wouldn't want you to hurt yourself trying to reach up there, being as you're so delicate-like.' Oh, he thought I was the cutest little thing in the world!"

Sarah looked dubiously at Evelyn Edwards, her boss's older sister. The woman was five foot seven, two hundred and fifty pounds, and had some of the most limp, thin brown hair that Sarah had ever seen. She had a penchant for stretch pants and short floral-print tops. Evelyn was not exactly what Sarah would consider "cute" or "little."

The woman continued, "I can hardly wait to tell my brother when he gets back from vacation tomorrow. You know how the men can't keep away from me." Smiling, she asked, "Did I tell you about Hans Inqvist? I saw him at Reeves and he said he couldn't believe how much more radiant I looked since I was Born Again."

Reaching up to rub at the bridge of her nose, Sarah braced herself. She knew what was coming.

"Tell me, Mrs. Nash, have you been Born Again?"

"No, Miss Edwards, "Sarah answered sweetly. "Once was enough."

Evelyn harrumphed but didn't get up and leave, as Sarah had hoped she might.

"I'd think you'd want to accept the true way of God."

"Miss Edwards, perhaps you've forgotten that I'm not a person who believes in blind devotion to any one denomination. I like to incorporate many different spiritual traditions in my life. I feel no compunction to be converted by you or anyone else. We should respect each other's choices."

"Even if they're wrong?"

Sarah slammed her desk drawer a little too forcefully and asked hotly, "You've been a member of how many different congregations since I've known you? Four? Five? More? I don't really need a lecture on sincerity from someone who socializes from one church to the next. I make no pretense that I'm the best believer in the world."

"Certainly not! And your husband is an atheist!"

"That's right. But my husband, atheist that he is, attends 10:30 Mass with me and Kris every Sunday so that we can give our son a spiritual foundation in hopes that he'll find his own path someday. There's a difference between searching for God and meaning in one's life and in ridiculous hypocrisy. I suspect that you've crossed that line."

"Mrs. Nash!" Evelyn exclaimed. She seemed confused but insisted, "That is totally untrue!"

"In what way? Please enlighten me." Sarah sat back, triumphant. "I'd be most interested in debating theology with you."

"I, um, that is. –"

Pushing back her beloved old chair, Sarah stood and went towards the door of her office.

"I'm expecting a book rep any moment. Maybe the next time you accost me, you'll have formed some sort of coherent argument."

Before the woman could say another word, Sarah pushed out through the door and stalked angrily across the landing. At the top step of the narrow staircase that led down to the bookshop, she paused to smooth out the folds in her dress.

Relax. It's your birthday. Don't let her ruin it for you.

Millie, the sprite-like blonde saleswoman at the counter, looked up and rolled her blue eyes emphatically. Sarah came slowly down the steps and walked over to stand next to her friend.

"You got away!" Millie whispered.

"Sadly, you may be the next victim," Sarah giggled. "I feel so bad for you when you're out here on the shop floor. You're so vulnerable. Evelyn's unfailingly persistent."

"Well, she won't get me today."

Millie picked up a handful of books and headed for the sliding ladder on the right side of the shop. Using her free hand to help hoist herself up each rung, she cradled the books in her other arm. Once she'd gotten to the top, she struggled to reach the highest shelf.

"Need a hand?" Sarah called up to her.

"No way, Jose. You know what they say about you tall people. Give them an inch, and they'll walk all over you."

"Get off your high horse. That is, if you can get on it," Sarah teased. "I know people like you, who're barely four feet eleven, are merely jealous of those of us who've attained the majestic height of five feet."

With a final shove and a grunt, Millie thrust the books into the appropriate slot on the shelf. She climbed down and came back over to the counter where Sarah was busy straightening a rack of bookmarks.

"Stop being such a perfectionist," Millie ordered.

"I can't help it. Evelyn's in my office, and I don't want to have to go back up there to wait for Horace."

"That woman is a menace. Somebody should tell her off."

"Done," Sarah smirked. "Your wish is my command. Isn't it amazing how I anticipated it?"

"You didn't!" Millie cried. "What did she do?"

"Stared at me while she tried to filter what I was saying through that tiny brain of hers." Sarah slapped herself on the arm and said, "Bad girl!"

"I'm proud of you. I wish I had the guts to really tell her what I think about her baloney."

The bell on the door chimed, and both women looked up expectantly. A teenaged boy and girl entered and began to wander through the bookstore.

"Dig those big, baggy pants he has on," Millie muttered. "And that oversized orange shirt. Oh, God. Look at that hat."

"I kinda like the girl's fuzzy pink sweater and those too-tight jeans. The platform shoes have to go, though." Sarah leaned on the counter and scrutinized the couple before announcing, "Romance and Science Fiction."

"I'd say Romance and Entertainment."

As they watched surreptitiously, the boy went to the science fiction section, while the girl went straight for the romance novel shelves.

"Ha!" Sarah crowed. "This round goes to me."

"The last round went to me, remember? You just got lucky because today's your birthday. Whoa! What do you make of that?"

The teenagers glanced furtively around then converged in one corner of the store.

"Great. Health and Family," Millie groaned. "Do you want to break it up, or should I?"

Sarah sighed and said, "You know the answer to that one. What's the harm? Maybe they're not getting any explanations at home."

"What's the big deal? You always get so touchy about this. Is that how you learned about sex?" With a mischievous gleam in her eyes, Millie added, "Or did Dan teach you everything you needed to know?"

"Neither. My dad told me the basic facts when I was seven. I got the whole scoop from my grandmother when I was seventeen. My stepmom was too uncomfortable to talk about sex with me. I don't know why."

"What did your grandmother tell you?"

"What sex was really like. My first experience wasn't the best, and I think she wanted me to know that it was supposed to be enjoyed by both partners." Sarah grinned then confided, "Daniel was an excellent teacher when it came to the real thing."

Millie shook her head and said, "I vaguely remember sex. It was before my divorce. There was no AIDS to worry about back when I was single the first time."

"There are other single men in the world besides your ex."

"All the men who are approximately my age are either priests, married, gay, or weird."

Sarah put an arm around Millie's shoulders and said encouragingly, "There are tons of people in their forties out there in the world. The right guy will come along."

"Thanks, but forgive me if I don't hold my breath. Now, are you gonna do your duty or not?"

"I'm going." Reaching over to the rolling cart filled with books, Sarah selected titles that would require shelving in various locations throughout the store before declaring, "I refuse to do this any more."

"Your obligation will have been fulfilled forever after today. How's that?"

Sarah took her time, shelving books and reorganizing. She had lost almost all of her central vision over the past sixteen years, but a small portion remained in each eye. She used this and her peripheral vision to the fullest extent possible and utilized special magnifying reading glasses when she needed to read regular print. Besides that and her inability to drive, Sarah felt that she did quite well despite her loss of vision. She didn't use a cane, although she'd had cane training in case she needed it in the future. Those who didn't know her well didn't even realize she was visually impaired, although she made no attempts to hide her condition and spoke freely about it when the subject came up.

Sarah's arms were becoming less and less full. Finally, there was only one book left in her hand. Taking a deep breath, she walked slowly over to Health & Family. The teenagers were huddled close together, heads bent low over the book they'd selected.

Clearing her throat, Sarah said, "Excuse me, but do you need some help?"

Startled, the boy and girl glanced up, panicked looks on their faces. The book clattered to the floor, and they dashed towards the front door of the shop. The bell clanked against the wood as they made their hasty retreat.

Their reaction was almost laughable, and, yet, Sarah couldn't even force a smile. She moped her way back to Millie and tossed the offending book onto the counter.

"*The Joy of Sex*. You know Tanner would freak if he found out that we were letting kids look at this stuff." She eyed Sarah suspiciously and asked, "What spooked you?"

"The expressions on their faces."

It was the same fear she'd seen in Daniel's eyes the first time they'd met. She wondered whether the boy and girl were subjected to parents who tyrannized them or worse.

"If Tanner has a problem, he can talk to me about it."

"I'll do it from now on," Millie said reassuringly. "Put it out of your head and stay down here with me for a little bit longer. It looks as though Evelyn's camping out in your office. Perhaps she's thought of something intelligent to say."

"That'll be the day. I wonder which one of them is adopted, Evelyn or Tanner?"

"I didn't know that either of them was adopted."

"One of them has to be. How could two people who are so totally different have come from the same parents?"

An elderly male customer touched Sarah on the sleeve.

"Excuse me. I've been enjoying your lovely nature section for the last hour, but I can't find a specific book on North American thrushes. Do you have any?"

"Let me see what I can find," Sarah offered. "Why don't you come with me over to the Pet section? You'd be surprised by some of the ways these books are classified."

As Sarah stepped away to assist the man, the door to the shop opened and in walked Horace, one of the local sales reps. He was a short, middle-aged man with black hair and a moustache and beard.

He's about forty-five, Sarah thought, as she walked across the store. *Just about Millie's age and definitely her type....*

"Millie! Good to see you!"

"You, too. Unfortunately, I don't think Sarah's having a very good morning."

The door to Sarah's office opened, and Evelyn Edwards huffed down the steps, hurried past Millie and Horace, and slammed the front door on her way out.

"I can see why," Horace remarked, shifting his briefcase from one hand to the other. "I'll have to see if I can brighten her day."

Sarah returned to the register with the customer. She nodded at Horace while continuing to talk to the older gentleman. Once the bright red book on North American thrushes had been paid for, the man thanked Sarah profusely and left.

"Sorry for the delay, Horace."

"Not a problem. Another satisfied customer, I'm sure."

"We do try."

"You do more than try," he said with a smile. "By the way, you both look lovely today." He nodded at Sarah's dress and commented, "Purple is definitely your color. And you, Millie...I always like you in that shirt and those pants."

From behind the counter, Sarah nudged Millie with her toe.

"Ah, thanks. I'd like you in them, too."

"What?"

"Um, I mean...."

Sarah let her friend flounder for only a few seconds before suggesting, "Horace, why don't we go upstairs so that you can show me the new releases."

Once they'd entered the office, Sarah took her seat and asked, "How long has it been since you and your wife split up?"

"Must be going on ten months."

"And have you been seeing anyone since then?"

"Sarah, I'm surprised at you. You're a married woman."

Covering her mouth with her hand to hide her smile, she said, "It's not for me, although if I weren't married, I'm sure I'd be tempted. It's Millie. She's been divorced since Christmas before last. Anyway, the two of you seem to get along really well, so I thought I'd ask."

"Oh. Well, then. No."

Sarah waved a hand in the air between them and said, "Forget I mentioned it. Please don't tell Millie. She'd be embarrassed."

"I didn't mean "no" like I'm not interested. I meant "no" like I haven't been seeing anyone. I went out with a couple of people before I moved from Crowley, but there wasn't a spark. But Millie...I like Millie a whole lot. I'd like to ask her to dinner sometime."

"Maggio's is her favorite restaurant."

"Thanks." He undid the clasp on his briefcase and withdrew some promotional literature. "By the way, here's the latest from Fines Publications. We've got plenty of good stuff from the local boys this month. I especially like this one." He passed her a flyer and added, "It's a nice nostalgic look at the Grand Isle of fifty years ago. Lots of local flavor."

Sarah nodded, put on her glasses, and slowly began to scan the material.

"There's something else I wanted to talk with you about," the rep said seriously. "Something personal."

Putting down the brochure, she rested her elbows on the desk and waited.

"A lady I know in the public relations department is leaving. Her last day is tomorrow. She's got to take care of her ailing mother. I think you'd be perfect for her job." He rummaged around in the briefcase and produced a job description then said, "Take a look."

"Horace, I'm not out to look for another job. I've been here for a long time."

"Too long. I'm not saying Tanner doesn't run a great place. I'm saying that you've got the brains to do more with your life than this. You should have been a lawyer or a doctor or something."

Sarah snorted derisively.

"I'm serious. Will you take a look before making any wisecracks?"

She took a look.

College degree required. Proficient in Microsoft Windows/Word/Works and Excel. Strong people skills. Excellent organizational skills. Previous experience in the book or publishing industry. Three + years of management experience.

"It does sound good but –"

"But nothing. You got a resume worked up? Give it to me, and I'll hand-deliver it to Calvin Couvier. He's the supervisor over the position."

"Horace –"

"I'm waiting."

"Why are you so insistent? You don't owe me anything."

"No, I don't. Will you quit being so suspicious and give me the resume? Does everybody have to have ulterior motives in this world?"

Reluctantly, Sarah opened her Documents file and printed her resume. Hesitantly, she handed it to the rep.

"See, that wasn't so hard, now was it? I'll put this in, and they'll call you. I'll be back Monday to see what you'd like to order for the shop from the materials I just gave you. Right now, I'm going to have a little chat with Millie." He left the room then leaned back in and said, "By the way, happy birthday."

Sarah sat staring around her cramped, cluttered, comfortable little office for the next fifteen minutes.

Maybe I shouldn't have given the resume to Horace. Why did I do that? Why am I so afraid? I've been bitching and moaning about how stagnant my professional life is for quite a while. I should be eager to move on. Why am I holding back?

There was no single answer to any of her questions. Her emotions and her reasons were intertwined with years of hard work and diligence on her part.

First and foremost, she was safe at Calico Bookshop, Inc. She had a stable job working with something she loved: books. But she had mastered her duties years before and found that she was withering intellectually at work.

She was reticent to accept another job because of her eye condition. Tanner didn't care about her visual impairment; he never had. However, she knew from experience that his attitude wasn't exactly the norm when it came to employers.

And that led to another reason she wanted to stay. Sarah and Tanner had been close since the day he'd hired her. He had never failed to be supportive and intuitive when it came to Sarah, who returned the favor with equal measure. Both of them were devoted to the business. Was she betraying him by applying for another job?

"I wouldn't call it betrayal at all," Millie said, once Sarah had sworn her to secrecy. "Are you going to stick around until retirement even though you're ready to push on with your career? I'd miss you like hell, but I'd understand. Wait and see if they call, then you can talk to him. Tanner only wants for you to be happy." Millie leaned even closer to her friend and confided, "Speaking of happy, guess what? Horace asked me out for dinner and a movie this weekend. You don't suppose you might know what prompted that, do you?"

"I have no earthly idea what you're talking about. Are you excited?"

"He told me I was stunning." She looked down at her khakis and brown and white cardigan. Both were dotted with little pieces of cardboard and styrofoam packing. "Yes, I'd say I'm pretty excited. He's such a gentleman. Not like the losers I've come across, lately."

"You'll have a great time."

The bell on the door rang. As Sarah turned, she automatically asked, "May I help you?"

"I certainly hope so," her husband said. "If not, I'm in trouble."

Chapter Two: A Night to Remember

"Daniel? What are you doing here? Aren't you supposed to be at work?"

"Well, that's a fine how-do-you-do!" Millie said with a laugh. "Your husband arranges to take off early so that he can surprise you on your birthday, and you're giving him a hard time. Some women don't know what they have."

"You took off to come get me? Mr. I-work-whether-I'm-running-one-hundred-and-four-degree-temperature-or-not? I'm impressed."

Daniel turned to Millie and said seriously, "You see why I married her."

"I'll get my coat."

They stepped out into the frigid air and hastened towards the shelter of their car. As Daniel started the engine and pulled out into the afternoon traffic, his wife told him of the exchange she'd had with Horace.

"If you don't like it, you don't accept the position," Daniel said matter-of-factly once Sarah had finished. "If it was meant to be, then it'll happen."

"I guess," she said uncertainly. "By the way, where are we going? What about Kris?"

"I wanted to do something special for your birthday. Kris is with your folks and his cool uncle and aunt. They agreed to babysit tonight. You know he's in for a good time."

"They'll spoil him mercilessly. He'll be in heaven." She settled back in her seat and asked, "So? Where are we going?"

"I'll never tell."

She knew that this was true. No matter how impatient she got, he would never give in. She resigned herself to momentary confusion and tried to relax. It was something she had been trying to do all day without success.

"How was work?" she inquired. "Anything exciting?"

"Lots of excitement. Would you like to hear about individual returns or how the market did today?"

"Neither at the moment. My day was full of stress, but I'd like another form of distraction."

"Later. What happened with your day that was stressful, except all the worrying about Fines?"

"Evelyn. God, the woman is irritating. I told her off big-time."

"Wow." Daniel grinned, then confided, "I wish I could have been a fly on the wall. How did she take it?"

"I'm not certain," Sarah grinned back. "I don't think she understood a lot of what I said."

"What a shame." As he turned off College Drive, he announced, "Here we are. I thought we could do dinner at Mansur's since we've never eaten there; then I have something I want to show you. I think you'll appreciate it."

"That sounds wonderful, but I want to call Kris when we get in. Then, we can eat, drink, and be merry."

By the time their desserts arrived, Sarah was feeling more at ease.

"Better?" Daniel asked, as he laid his napkin by his empty dessert plate.

"Mm-hm"

Daniel took a sip of his coffee and reached across the table to tuck one of his wife's loose curls behind her ear.

"Good. Are you ready?"

He led her back out into the cold evening air. Instead of returning to the car, Daniel guided her around the corner and down the path, pulling her gently until they were standing on the small wooden bridge that lay in between the shops. He silenced Sarah with a kiss before she could voice any objections or ask any questions.

Standing next to her husband in the chill of the night, Sarah was alternately warm and chilled. When she began to shiver, Daniel abruptly broke the contact and unbuttoned his coat. Pulling her closer, he wrapped the coat around his wife, as she slid her hands around his waist and rested her head against his chest.

"Remember the last time we stood here kissing on this bridge?" he asked quietly, as another couple walked past them on their way to the Coffee Call.

"Just because it's been fourteen years doesn't mean I could ever forget." She nuzzled against him, enjoying the little pocket of warmth he'd created for her and added, "It was freezing that day,

251

too. As I recall, it was also rainy and windy. A lovely day for my eighteenth birthday."

"*I* thought it was a lovely day."

"I didn't say it wasn't wonderful, but I was cold then like I am now until you took me back to your place."

"Allow me to take you back to my place, then." He turned, keeping her sheltered with his coat and continued, "I was going to tell you about your birthday present here, but I guess I'll have to wait now."

"Oh, come on! I haven't even asked all evening!"

"No, you haven't. I'm sure it's been torture."

"You have no idea."

"You only have to endure the agony for another ten minutes or so. Think you can make it? Your present's on the back porch."

When they arrived home, Sarah hurried through the kitchen and out the back door. Daniel smiled to himself. She was like a small child waking up on Christmas morning to see what Santa Claus had brought from the North Pole. He loved it.

"They're beautiful!" she cried from the backyard.

Daniel pushed open the storm door. Ralph bounded out, a slob-covered rope toy in his mouth. The dog raced over to his mistress and nudged her with the rope.

"In a minute, Ralph. I want to hear how they sound." She reached up to push at the heavy metal circle that hung in the center of the wind chimes. Before her fingers made contact, the breeze picked up, and the circlet clinked against the suspended pipes.

"Does it sound okay? I know you don't like the ones that just clank around. These sounded a lot nicer."

"I love them. Let's sit out here for a while and listen to them."

"You couldn't wait to get out of the cold, but now that it doesn't suit you to stay inside, you'll freeze to hear the wind chimes."

"We can go back inside in a minute. Ralph looks so pitiful. Come here, boy. I'll throw the rope."

As it turned out, Ralph only wanted to play tug-of-war. Within five minutes, Sarah tired of the impossible task of trying to wrench it away from him, so Daniel went out into the yard and threw a stick for the Lab to fetch.

Sarah watched her husband as he romped in the grass with the dog. Twenty-five years earlier, she would never have envisioned that the scrawny twelve-year-old with the bruised face would one day grow into this tall, sturdy man in the brown, pleated pants, dress shirt, and silk tie. Nor would she have dreamed that he would be her husband. The past, their childhood – all of it seemed so remote and blurred to Sarah. She thought it best to leave most of it behind them.

"Daniel, I think you've run Ralph into exhaustion. Why don't we go in?"

"Probably a good idea, since my arm feels like it's about to fall off." As he and Ralph followed her into the kitchen, he offered, "I'll feed the fish and lock up. You go on."

Sarah walked towards their room, automatically stopping at her son's door. Yawning, she went to the master bedroom and unlatched the door of her armoire. She pushed through into the back for the nightgown she saved for these nights when she and Daniel were alone. It was a deep golden brown negligee made almost entirely of lace. The nightgown conformed to her breasts and hips and downplayed her waist. It wasn't a very practical thing for a woman who had a small child who might call for her during the night. So, it hung in the back of the armoire and was pulled out six or seven times a year.

"I love that nightgown," Daniel murmured, coming up behind her. "When Kris goes off to college, will you wear it every night?"

He undid the clip that held her hair back from her face. The tangle of curls fell forward around his wife's cheeks. He slid both hands into her hair then squeezed the mass in his palms.

"And never cut your hair ever again."

She turned and hugged him, intoxicated by the feel of him through the thick material of his pants and the thin lace of her nightgown.

"Tell me what you want," he whispered, as he bent low to kiss her.

"I want you to make love to me the way you did fourteen years ago on my birthday." She laid a hand on the back of his neck, rubbing the stiff hair above his collar. "I want you to be totally in control."

"Anything else?"

"I want you to hold me all night long."

"You won't sleep."

"I don't care."

"Happy birthday to you, then."

Daniel slept afterwards, but Sarah lay wide-awake in his arms. She reflected that they had changed so much and so little over the years. She thought of how their life together had truly begun.

They had stumbled into Daniel's apartment with numb fingers and faces after their encounter on the bridge the day she'd turned eighteen. The place was deserted and deliciously warm, and they'd quickly moved to the bedroom. Once there, Daniel had lowered one hand from Sarah's collarbone and slipped his fingertips under the edge of her sweater. Then, he'd stepped back.

"What is it?" she'd asked, bewildered. "Did I do something wrong?"

"It's not you. It's me."

"You? But don't you want to...."

"Of course I want to!" He slid his hands into the back pockets of his jeans and muttered, "It's only that nobody except me and my doctors have seen my scars since I was twelve. What if they disgust you?"

"They won't disgust me. They might make me mad because I remember how you got them, but that won't change how much I want to be with you." As much as she didn't want to spoil the moment, Sarah had to ask, "What about the other girl?"

"I didn't take my shirt off when we had sex."

Sarah sat on the bed and said, "You can leave your shirt on if you want to, but it won't bother me if you take it off. I'd really prefer it."

He knelt on the bed, took her hands in his, and brought them up to the front of his shirt. She undid the buttons, catching a glimpse of what lay underneath as she did so. Once all of the buttons had been undone, she pushed back the shirt and viewed his chest and stomach.

It was like a roadmap of sorts, a roadmap drawn in white, pink, and red lines. Some of the lines were raised, and some were smooth. There were a few odd scars that dotted the landscape. Sarah imagined that those were the landmarks of abuse, the individual blows or burns that stood out from the tapestry of the other threads of cruelty.

She traced the lines and touched the scars with her fingers. Then, she took Daniel's hands and brought them to the top button of her sweater.

"Do it, Daniel."

He was forceful, passionate, and very focused. Later, Sarah marveled that it had been nothing like her encounter with Billy Baudoin. Whereas before there had been pain and a feeling of isolation, now there was only pleasure and a sensation of overwhelming completeness.

It was a memory that Sarah treasured. It wasn't only the remembered pleasure of her first sexual encounter with the man who would become her husband. It was mostly the fact that he'd trusted her enough to make himself completely vulnerable to her, allowing her, in turn, to relinquish her driving need to always be in control of herself.

Sarah smiled at the memory and nestled her head into the crook of his arm. Within moments, she was asleep.

A short time later, she woke with a start, as Daniel jerked his shoulder out from under her head. Sarah started to make a comment about rude awakenings, but the words died in her throat when she looked at him.

She had never seen him in the throes of a nightmare before. Since she was a relatively light sleeper, she'd always assumed that he never made any noise, except on those rare occasions when he'd wake up screaming and disoriented.

That night, something was terribly wrong. Daniel lay rigid, his jaw set in a horrible grimace. His fists were clenched so tightly that the muscles of his arms were taut with the tension. He moaned from somewhere deep in his throat.

I have to wake him up soon. This is bad. Tears came to her eyes as she thought, *This isn't bad; it's awful. How many nights does this happen and he doesn't tell me?*

Sarah reached out to touch Daniel's shoulder, but it was too late. His body wrenched convulsively into an upright position, and he began to cry out in hoarse, terrible screams that made his wife want to cover her ears.

"Daniel!" She scooted around in front of him and said more loudly, "Daniel!"

He opened his eyes. She watched as they slowly flooded with awareness then tears. This part of it was familiar to her. She took him in her arms before he began to sob and eased him back around, pulling him down on top of her until his head rested on her chest. He slid his arms around her hips, and she rubbed his back and spoke softly to him.

"Do you want to talk about it?"

Wordlessly, he rubbed against her: no.

"Do you want to talk about something else?"

Same reply.

"Do you want me to talk about something else?"

This time, there came a nod.

So, she talked about pleasant things – that first time they'd made love, Kris's preschool play, their family trip to Gulf Shores. As she rambled on, Daniel's shuddering subsided into shivering, then to trembling, then to stillness. Finally, sometime after 8:00, Daniel's breathing became slow and even.

Sarah's throat was dry. She needed to get up and call her work and Daniel's work. She needed the bathroom. She needed her father. Near 9:00, she decided that Daniel had been sleeping long enough for her to ease out from under him without waking him.

First, she dialed Calico Bookshop, Inc.

"Millie. Hey. Yeah, my evening was nice, but I'm not feeling well this morning. No. I didn't get much sleep. I wish that was all of it," she sighed and confided, "Daniel had one of those nightmares, and I've been up almost all night. I feel awful. When Tanner comes in, would you just tell him that I'm sick? I'll explain it to him later. Thanks. Yes, I'm sure it will be, too. Bye."

Next, she called Daniel's secretary.

"Penny? Hi, it's Sarah. Thank you. Yes, I was surprised. It was a wonderful dinner, and I loved my present. Wind chimes. He wouldn't tell you? Yes, I know. Listen, he's not feeling well this morning. No. No, I'm not doing so hot myself. I don't think he'll be in today. Thanks, Penny. I appreciate it. No, I'm sure he'll be in Monday. I will. Bye."

And, finally, she called her father at the office.

"What should I do?" she asked once she'd finished rehashing all of the details of the previous night's episode. "I know. Yes, it would. Okay, I will. I love you, too."

Sarah returned to bed and lay uneasily next to her sleeping husband. She wondered if she should take her father's advice to call Max or wait and see if things could work themselves out. She was still wondering when sleep reached up and grabbed her by surprise.

Chapter Three: Chance

Three days later, Sarah was still attempting to shed her feelings of worry about her husband. No matter how hard she tried, she couldn't escape the niggling sensation of uneasiness. It was like trying to shake water off a raincoat. Most of the rainwater would fall away, but there were always those tiny droplets that kept clinging to the coat itself.

By early Monday afternoon, she couldn't deny that she was also experiencing some measure of euphoria, although it was euphoria tempered by apprehension. She had been offered the position at Fines less than an hour earlier. She wondered how she was going to tell Tanner and what she should expect from her new job.

Sarah got up and walked halfway across the landing. Then, she turned and headed back for her office. From down below, Millie caught her eye and hissed, "Go on! You can do it!"

Tanner Edwards's head was bent over some papers on his desk. He was so intent on what he was writing that he didn't notice Sarah. She looked at him and smiled.

He was forty-four years old. His hair was thinning on top and turning gray on the sides. He was none too trim around the middle. There were thin creases spreading out from around his eyes. His affinity for patterned suspenders had led him to choose a maroon and blue paisley design that day. His wife must have gone overboard with the starch again, because his collar appeared to be so rigid that it would crack at the slightest touch. Sarah had never heard him complain about the starch or anything else.

If I don't do this soon, I'll never be able to go through with it.

"Hey, Tanner? May I talk with you?"

Without looking up from his work, he said, "Sure. What's up? Don't tell me my sister's come back. I really don't know what to do with her."

"No, it's not Evelyn," she assured him, as she sat in the chair in front of his desk. "Although to tell you the truth she was here quite a bit while you were on vacation."

"She was?" Tanner put down his pen and asked, "Is it interfering with people's work?"

Sarah squirmed in her seat and admitted, "She's been showing up a lot and kind of taking up work time."

"Dang it!" Tanner shook his head and confided, "She's always been like this. I love my sister. However, I was hoping that someday she'd find herself a man. I know that she wants one. Hell, she needs one. But she drives them away." He rotated his pen, watching the gold gleam as the light from the window shone through on it and added, "I promised my mother that I'd take care of Evelyn. Sometimes, it can be trying."

"I have a feeling that I'm about to be trying."

"Why?" He stretched back in the leather chair and asked, "Are you all right?"

"Yes. The problem is, I don't want to hurt you. You've been a good boss and a good friend."

The corners of his mouth turned down but only for an instant.

"Sounds like you're going away."

"I think I am."

"Where? Are you moving?"

"No-o-o," she answered slowly. "I've been offered a position at Fines. I got called this morning to be the first person interviewed. They were really impressed by my resume. Anyway, they asked if I could come for an interview during my lunch break. So, Daniel took me over, and they hired me on the spot."

"Are you unhappy here?"

"Not with you. It's…it's just a lot more money and new challenges. I have mixed feelings about this, but I guess it's an opportunity I can't pass up."

"Congratulations then. I'll be sorry to lose you. I wish that I could pay you more, but you know how that goes. These book warehouse stores are really hurting small businesses like mine." He picked up his pen and casually asked, "It's none of my business, but what about your eyes?"

"That was the strangest thing. We had the interview and discussed my job duties."

"Which are?"

"Mostly computer systems work and public relations. I'll be wooing new clients and fine tuning ways to improve customer satisfaction. Anyway, I explained in detail about the eye disorder, and the supervisor said he didn't care about that. Then, he offered me the job."

"Your skills and background are strong. Still, no one even called me for a reference. I figure I'm a reference?"

"You are. I was going to come back and tell you about the possibility of my leaving and that he might call. I didn't expect him to hire me right then and there, especially since I have the disability."

"Don't downplay yourself, with or without the disability. You'd be a terrific find for any boss. I think it's wonderful. We'll all go to lunch or dinner next week before you leave. Unless you'll be leaving sooner?"

"I told him I had to give two weeks' notice."

"Thanks. I guess I'd better get cracking. Oh, here, look at this," he said, passing her an invoice. "I can't figure this out. There's something missing in the second column." As she donned her glasses and slowly scanned the invoice, he asked, "How was your weekend? Did you have a nice birthday celebration?"

"Um, it was fine. Daniel took me out Thursday, then we had a party at my parents' place on Sunday." She continued to stare at the invoice and said again, "It was fine."

Tanner rose from his chair and walked around the desk. He snatched the paper out of Sarah's hand and demanded, "Okay, what's wrong?"

"Nothing," she said innocently.

"Yeah, sure. You just had another birthday, which always excites you. You got a new job that's more interesting and pays better. Yet, when I ask you about your weekend, you say it was 'fine.' " He pulled up another chair and sat facing her before saying, "That's not like you. What's up?"

She told him about Daniel, finishing with "I don't know what to do. Something's terribly wrong, but if I go over his head and talk to Max...."

"You might save his life, whether he likes it or not. You said your father told you to talk to Max. If there's anyone who should know when someone needs help, it's your dad. He's been through a lot himself, right?

"Remember that night we got caught up here when you were pregnant with Kris? I had fired that bimbo who misfiled all those papers I needed for the IRS. We were stuck at the shop, looking for them until 4:00 in the morning."

"Of course I remember. You got me to try jalapeno peppers on my pizza, and I loved them."

"As I recall, that wasn't all we did." Tanner grinned conspiratorially and admitted, "I've never talked so much about myself in one evening before or since. You either, I'd wager." He placed his palms on his knees and said earnestly, "You've been through this kind of stuff with your dad. I'm not saying that Dan's doing drugs. All I'm saying is that you said you should have told someone when it started with Tristan, that maybe you could have saved him and yourself some of the grief. What makes this any different? It works for your dad but not for your husband?"

Sarah mulled over his words as Tanner stood and returned the chair to its corner spot.

"You know that he's keeping something from you. Whatever it is, you think it's responsible for the increase in these episodes?"

"Yes."

"Talk to Max if Dan won't. With his past, who knows what's going on in his head? What if it's something horrible, and it puts you and Kris in jeopardy? Or even Dan himself?"

"You're scaring me," Sarah said, as she took the invoice out of his hand and made for the door.

"Good. Now, go do something about it."

She stared at the phone in her office for most of the afternoon, but she couldn't bring herself to call Max. Perhaps she could psyche herself up to make the call before it was time to go home.

"Well?" Millie looked hopeful as she asked, "Did you call?"

Sarah's head moved from side to side. Millie put an arm around her shoulders as they walked to the car.

"Listen to your best friend and to your boss. Go home and give Max a ring."

But she didn't. She watched Kris play on the swing set with the little boy from down the street. When they wanted to play baseball, she pitched to them, even though she couldn't follow the ball with her eyes and had to duck each time they swung for fear of being hit. Once, she wasn't quick enough and got knocked in the shoulder.

Later, Sarah helped her son with his homework and made his supper. They played Chutes 'N Ladders three times. She was willing to do anything to deflect the queries as to why Daddy wasn't home yet. Kris finally fell asleep, trying to stay awake so that he could kiss his father goodnight.

Sarah ended up sitting in the living room with an open book on her lap, wondering why her husband was late. It had never bothered her before; he had always phoned to let her know. That evening, he hadn't called, nor had he answered the phone when she'd tried to reach him at work.

When Daniel came in at 10:20, Sarah didn't rise to greet him in the kitchen. Instead, she stayed in her chair and waited for him to come to her. When he did, he bent low to kiss her. She shied away from him and said, "I want to talk."

"About what?"

"About why you were five hours late," she said angrily. "About why I couldn't answer our son when he asked me where you were and when you'd be home."

"What is there to talk about?" he replied defensively. "I was doing some market research, and I lost track of time. I apologize for not calling."

"What about not answering? I tried your office, and no one picked up."

"I shut the ringer off. I was pretty absorbed."

He headed for the pantry. Sarah got up and followed him.

"Absorbed in what? Statistics? Or was it something or someone else?"

He stopped and put one hand against the doorframe. His face contorted, the muscles struggling to settle on one expression. Exasperation won out over anger and fear.

"Sarah, what in the hell are you talking about?"

"Are you having an affair?"

"No! Why are you asking me this? I don't want anyone else. Besides, who would want *me*?"

She blinked back tears and said quietly, "I would. I do."

He slipped his hands into his pockets and said, "I am not having an affair. I never have and never will." He brought his right hand up and raked his fingers through his hair then asked,

"You want to know what's bothering me? I saw my father on the street last month."

Sarah's lips parted in a silent "oh" of surprise.

"I didn't think it was any big deal since it's been twenty-five years. He didn't recognize me, and I haven't seen him again. When I had the first bad nightmare that night, I just figured it was the usual semi-annual torment, but after last Thursday...."

"Why didn't you tell me? You should have said something."

"About seeing my father or about what I saw in the nightmares?"

"Both."

He stared out of the small kitchen window into the darkness of the yard. Ralph was barking at something, probably a cat or a raccoon.

"I don't know why I didn't tell you about my father. I think it was so unexpected and I was so shaken by it myself that I couldn't share it with anyone."

"What did he look like? Are you sure it was him?"

"He hadn't changed that much. Even if he had, I would have recognized him."

"How?"

"I saw his eyes. I'll never forget those eyes as long as I live."

Daniel had that furious look on his face that he always got when he was remembering something unpleasant from his boyhood. Sarah decided to press forward to an equally unpleasant topic.

"And the nightmares?" She took a step towards him and nervously asked, "What about them?"

"I can't tell you about those." He closed his eyes and added, "If only you knew the things I see in those dreams."

Sarah bridged the distance between them and put her arms around his waist. He laid his hands on top of her shoulders and squeezed gently and persuasively. She refused to relent.

"If you can't tell me, then you have to talk to Max or find another therapist if you don't feel like you can talk with him. I'm scared for you and us and Kris."

As she rested her head on his chest, Daniel said, "I'm sure it'll pass."

"I'm not." She was getting desperate and declared, "I'll leave you if you don't get help."

"I – you can't."

"I will. I swear I will."

"All right," he murmured, caressing the long auburn curls. "I'll get with someone as soon as I can."

"Tomorrow?"

"Tomorrow." He kissed the top of her head and assured her, "Whatever it takes."

They stood holding each other in the kitchen for a long time. Finally, Sarah asked tiredly, "Are you ready for bed?"

"Not really. I'm…afraid to sleep after that last nightmare."

"You can't stay awake forever. You've hardly slept for days."

"I know," he said with a sigh. "How about if I make love to you all night until I'm so exhausted that I don't have the energy left to dream?"

She put the back of her hand across her forehead and pretended to swoon.

"Why, Mr. Nash! You do say the most scandalous things!"

"And you love it." He pulled back and combed her hair away from her face with his fingers before asking, "Are you sure you want to? You haven't been sleeping well either. You look worn out."

"Anything for the cause."

There were no nightmares for Daniel that evening.

In the morning, he made some calls from his office and finagled his way into an afternoon appointment with a psychiatrist one co-worker had mentioned seeing during a rough period after his divorce. It was as good a recommendation as any.

Daniel couldn't talk to Max about his current situation; he didn't know why. Perhaps it was because Max was in his eighties now, and his son didn't want to cause him unnecessary stress. Or perhaps it was that Daniel wasn't a child anymore. Over the years, Max had ceased being his psychiatrist and had become his father, just as Lillian had become his mother. He didn't want to burden either of them with all this baggage from the past.

There was a knock on the door of his office, and Daniel called out, "Come in, Moneypenny."

Penny entered the room with a small smile. When Daniel Nash had chosen her to be his secretary, she'd been twenty-one, skittish, and shy. It was her first real job, and she'd been unsure of herself. Her self-confidence had been low since eighth grade, when she had grown to the dizzying height of five feet eleven inches. Her classmates had mercilessly teased her throughout high school, and her esteem level had plummeted.

Daniel had given her a chance to prove herself, but she'd remained timid. So, he and his wife had asked her over for lunch one Saturday. Away from the office, Penny was surprised to hear herself telling them about her love of cats, reading, and James Bond movies. From then on, Daniel had called her "Moneypenny" at the office. She loved the nickname, and she loved her job.

"Mr. Nash? I have those records you asked for."

"Thanks." As he reached across the desk and took the packet from her, he said casually, "By the way, I have some personal business to take care of this afternoon, so I'll be leaving at 2:00 instead of 5:00. The people in the leave department are going to love me this month. Leaving early on Thursday to pick up Sarah, off Friday, taking Sarah to her interview on Monday and then leaving early again today. I don't think they've had that many leave slips from me in a year, much less a week."

"I'm sure it'll knock them for a loop. What will they think once Mrs. Nash starts her new job? How is she going to get home from work every day? I mean, normally you take her in the morning, and she gets a ride with her friend from work most afternoons."

"We've already thought of that," Daniel said, as he opened the side of the packet and pulled out the papers. "She'll have to be there a little earlier and stay a little later if I'm going to take her and pick her up. Maybe once she's been there a while, she can get a ride home with someone from Fines who lives out our way."

"And your son?"

"Our next-door neighbor stays at home full-time. She said she'd watch him after school until we get home. She has a son who's a year younger than Kris, so he'll have someone to play with for an hour and a half or so."

"It must be so difficult with Mrs. Nash not being able to drive. I know when you have to go out of town on business she has to

265

arrange rides with her parents or friends to get to the store or to Cub Scout meetings or to the mall. It must be inconvenient."

"Things will work out somehow. They always do."

Chapter Four: Beginnings and Endings

The light blue scrawling script screamed at Sarah from the lime green index card she held in her hand. She stared at it, willing it to move, trying to make the lines conform to a discernible pattern. The ink didn't budge.

She couldn't believe this was happening. She'd only been at Fines for a day and a half. Nothing had gone smoothly except her tour of the company offices.

Her supervisor, Calvin, was saying, "There are about five thousand of these cards. The information on them is vital to our records. What I want you to do is to take the information on the cards and set up a database. If you have any questions, there are more details in those cabinets along the far wall." His watch alarm beeped, and he said hastily, "I've got a meeting. Let me know how it goes."

Without giving her a chance to ask anything further, much less to say what was on her mind, he rushed off through the door.

Sarah squinted at the illegible writing on the card she held. There were boxes and boxes filled with these cards. She went over to the rows of oblong, gray cabinets Calvin had indicated might be helpful. Randomly choosing a drawer, she tugged at the front handle and pulled it out. All of the files had headings typed on clear green tab dividers. There was hardly any contrast between the typed letters and the tabs. She took out a file and opened it. Some typed invoices had been inserted, along with a few handwritten notes and memos. Her vision blurred with tears.

"Mrs. Nash?"

Sarah busied herself with replacing the folder until she had her emotions under control. She shut the drawer and turned to face an eager young man, probably a college student who was trying to make a little extra money. She affected a smile.

"I'm the local gopher," the man told her. "Today, I'm distributing memos about the new procedure for distributing memos. Here you go."

"Thanks."

He started to leave, then stepped back.

"Is there something I can help you with?"

"No, thanks. I guess I'll get used to everything someday."

"Gave you a bunch of stuff that has nothing to do with your original job description?" he asked with a sympathetic smile. "Don't let it get you down. It happens every day around here. Nobody in the main office ever does what they were hired to do. Well, except the sales reps, but they're sort of separate from the office anyway." He shuffled towards the doorway and said, "I'd better finish handing these to the others. You have a good day now."

As he walked out, Sarah glanced down at the memo. It had been written hastily by someone who had obviously never had a penmanship lesson in his life. She took the paper to the window and tried to angle it in such a way that it was readable to her. It was hopeless.

Somehow, she made it through the first part of the afternoon. But she kept thinking that maybe she wouldn't be dealing with those materials in the boxes as much as Calvin had led her to believe, that the public relations and fundraising work they'd described to her in the interview would still be her primary concern.

"Nobody at Fines ever does what they were hired to do," kept echoing through Sarah's mind.

Sarah pulled out the database guides that Calvin had presented to her earlier that morning. If she applied herself to learning the system, then things might seem a little more promising.

But at 3:15, a female co-worker unknowingly dashed Sarah's hopes.

"Hi. I'm from the promotions department, remember? Calvin said you were a real good writer and that you'd be proofing our work from now on. Here." The woman waved several sheets of paper in Sarah's face. "I need this in five minutes."

"Five minutes?" Sarah echoed as she stared at the top page. "Try fifteen or twenty. These are a mess."

"Five," she snapped. "I'll be back."

Five minutes later, she was back.

"You're not done, yet?"

"I'm on page two. There are quite a few grammatical errors and typos on page one, and there's some information about the projected outcomes that's not even mentioned. I guess someone simply forgot to check on those figures, or maybe they're not important. After all, who needs to think about such minor details as earnings potential?"

Push me and I'll push you back, Sarah fumed.

"You can either take that page and get started or stand there and wait until I've finished."

"You'd better speed up." The woman glared at her and held out her hand for the paper before announcing, "You have to be quick around here."

"I'm going as fast as I can," Sarah said curtly. "I love proofing, and I'm good at it, but you have to give me time to clean things up."

Her co-worker growled and stomped off with the first page in her hands.

Things have to get better.

By 5:00, Sarah acknowledged that the situation was critical. The job they were asking her to do was not the job for which she'd been hired, and she would have a difficult time without some type of accommodations because of her visual impairment. She had never needed accommodations before and didn't know what to do. Intellectually, she was more than capable; physically, she would need help. But she hated asking for help.

Sarah was in a black mood when Daniel pulled up to the curb at 5:10.

"How was Day Two?" he asked when she opened the door.

"Horrible," she said morosely, as she buckled her seatbelt. "Frustrating. Aggravating. Deflating. Maddening. Let's see, are there any other adjectives that I left out? Oh, terrible and awful."

She recounted the incidents that had clouded her day. Daniel listened intently, asking questions and soliciting ideas as they came to him. They were the same questions and ideas she'd been going over in her head for the last six hours. She knew that Daniel was concerned and was only trying to help, but she was irritable and scared and, therefore, ultimately argumentative. They rode in silence for the last five minutes of their commute.

A sense of inadequacy began to wheedle its way into Sarah's psyche. It gnawed at her insides as she breaded redfish fillets and prepared mashed potatoes and salad for her family. She wished that Daniel could cook, but he was a complete disaster in the kitchen. He had suggested that they go out for dinner, but she had stubbornly refused. Now, she wished she'd given in and just let the redfish spoil. That night, cooking was a burden, not a pleasure.

Sarah didn't feel like going to the party at the library either, but the children's reading program Kris participated in held the celebration only once a year. The students received a certificate, played games, made balloon animals, and ate cookies together. She couldn't ask Kris to miss it, and he would expect both of his parents to be in attendance.

She wandered in a daze behind her son and wondered, *What am I going to do? How can this be fixed? What if I can't fix it?*

Sarah arrived at Fines half an hour early the next day. She knew that Calvin was always the first one from their division to arrive each morning. At least she could talk to him alone without having to worry about others interrupting them. She locked up her purse in the large drawer of her desk and proceeded to take out one of the manuals that she'd been reading the previous afternoon.

It wasn't long before she heard Calvin's footsteps echoing in the empty hallway. Sarah waited until she heard him hang up his coat and sit at his desk before steeling herself and going to his office.

"Calvin?"

He leaned back, pulled up the blinds, and said, "Good morning, Sarah. How are you today?"

"Actually, I'm having some problems." She started to cry, hating the fact that she couldn't stop the tears, and said, "I think we need to talk."

"Of course," he said seriously, as he handed her some tissues. "Please, take a seat."

"I'm having difficulty seeing some of the work that's passing across my desk. During the interview, I was under the impression that my job would involve mostly computer work and printouts, as well as dealing with clients over the phone and in person. Yesterday, I was given many things that were illegibly written or typed on surfaces where there was little or no contrast, and I found out that I'm to handle the majority of the documents…. Well, it's very hard for me to see with my eyesight the way it is."

"Would you consider going back to the bookstore if your job hasn't been filled?"

Sarah was speechless for a full minute.

"I – I guess it's a possibility, but I'd like to stay here and do the job that I was hired to do," she eventually managed to say.

"You told me you could see," the man said coldly.

Sarah's nails dug into the palms of her hands. She began to unravel emotionally, but she was determined to maintain some semblance of self-control in Calvin's presence.

"I *can* see. I'll always be able to see. You must understand that I'm coming from an almost all-print environment, one where people could print their own names without difficulty. It would never have occurred to me after that interview that I would basically be doing a completely different job than the one we discussed."

"I told you that there would be "other duties" occasionally."

Occasionally? Sarah thought in disbelief.

"I'll need to talk with the boss when he comes in. We'll figure something out."

"I understand. I'll see what I can figure out in the meantime. There's a State agency that helps people with disabilities to get services and technology to assist them. I've never really needed their help before, but I think it would be good to check them out at this point."

"Whatever you think," he said flatly.

As she rose, fuming at his attitude and the fact that she couldn't seem to stop crying, Calvin said kindly, "Don't worry about all this. Stressing out about it won't get anything accomplished. I'm sure it will all work out for the best."

She returned to her office, wondering how relaxed he would be if he were in her shoes – or could see through her eyes.

A quarter of an hour later, she got through to Vocational Rehabilitation and set up an appointment for the next morning. She went back to tell Calvin.

"Good," he said, as he headed towards her. "Mr. Fines wants to see us now."

Sarah followed Calvin down the corridor and rode the elevator with him up one floor to the spacious office of the owner of Fines Publishing. It was a huge room furnished with a massive desk and imposing chairs. Heavy, brown velvet drapes framed the windows. Paintings of ducks and hunting dogs dotted the walls. It looked like the smoking room of an exclusive men's club, not the corporate office of a local publisher.

Mr. Fines stood behind his desk when they entered and called out, "Hello! Come in. Come in. Have a seat, and tell me all about this!"

They sat, and Sarah told him. He asked more questions about the eye disorder, and she drew him a diagram detailing how and what she could see, just as she'd drawn for Calvin during their initial meeting. When she'd finished speaking, Mr. Fines leaned back in his chair and said congenially, "I have no doubt in my mind that you're quite capable of doing this job without your disability. What do you need?"

"I'm not sure. That's why I went to my supervisor immediately. I have an appointment with someone in the morning. Calvin suggested that I go back to my job at the bookstore, but I don't think...."

"Well, then," Fines said, as he stood again and cheerfully shook her hand. "Good luck!"

The intimation was impossible to miss.

Chapter Five: The Road to Nowhere

Shaken, Sarah returned to her desk and called her parents' house. When she got no answer, she dialed her father's office. She'd been successfully fighting the tears that had been welling up behind her eyelids, but when she heard Tristan's voice she couldn't speak for fear of unlocking the floodgates.

"Tristan Maes," he said automatically. After a few moments of silence, he said, "Hel-lo?"

"Daddy?"

Instantly, he sobered and said worriedly, "Honey? Is everything all right? Is it Dan?"

"No, it's not Daniel." She drew in a deep breath and wiped at her eyes with a tissue before asking, "Would you pick me up for lunch? I'm sorry to be such a pain, but –"

"How's 11:30? That should be plenty of time for me to get to your building."

"Okay. I'll meet you out front. You know where it is?"

"Yes. I'll see you then."

On her way out, Sarah leaned into Calvin's office and said, "I'm going to lunch. I need to take care of some business relating to our meeting this morning. I may be a few minutes late, but I'm not sure. I'll fill out a leave slip when I get back if need be."

"Don't bother."

Sarah reflected that this was not a very encouraging statement and insisted, "I'd rather fill out the slip."

"I called Mr. Edwards at Calico Books and explained the situation to him. He says he's already hired somebody else and that he doesn't have an open position available at this time. He said that he'd hire you back right away if he could. Too bad."

Sarah had known that her former position was not available and hadn't intended to call Tanner until things at Fines had been resolved. She felt humiliated and angry. With a quick nod to Calvin, she walked deliberately out of his office and down the corridor to the elevator.

"It figures," Tristan said at lunch. "You're honest with them about the disability, and you *still* get screwed. Didn't you say Calvin told you four times during the interview that by law you

273

weren't required to even divulge the fact that you had a disability?"

"Yes, but I insisted that it wouldn't be ethical for me not to tell him since I didn't know the duties of the job, yet." She took a small bite of her po-boy, then said angrily, "If he would have shown me a file or one of those boxes, I would've known instantly that it would be…difficult."

"What are you going to do now? Call a lawyer, I hope. This doesn't sound right."

"I know, and I will call my lawyer and at least tell him about the circumstances. I'll go to my appointment at Vocational Rehabilitation and call the agency that handles human resources for Fines. Then, we'll see."

Tristan nodded thoughtfully. He removed the black cord from his hair and then gathered the shoulder-length auburn curls and bound them back again at the base of his head. Although he was forty-eight years old, he refused to cut his hair any shorter and declared that he'd kept it long since he was fourteen and wasn't about to chop it off when he liked it that way. As a well-respected, sought-after architect, he didn't need to impress anyone by conforming any more than he already did by dressing and behaving appropriately at work and at home.

He reached across the table to wipe a crumb from the side of his daughter's mouth with his thumb. His hand lingered, and he cupped her cheek with his large palm.

"I'm sorry you're having to go through this."

"Thanks. Me, too. I feel like…like I've done something wrong, committed a crime or something, but I haven't."

"No," he said firmly. "You haven't. You keep that straight in your head no matter what happens."

Sarah returned to work. She wished she could call Daniel, but he was in meetings all day and couldn't be reached. Sarah went through the motions, attempting to concentrate on the tasks she was given. Her co-workers were alternately pleasant and unfriendly in their dealings with her. At 4:00, she was finally able to get through to the human resource agency and make an appointment for the next afternoon.

She picked up the phone and called Vaughn. She and her stepmother had remained close over the years, although they often had different outlooks on how to approach difficult situations. The woman had been there for her since she'd been seven, and Sarah continued to love and need her.

"Hi, Vaughn. It's me. Yes, I know. When did Daddy call you? You weren't home at 11:00. Oh. Yes, it is a mess. Look, I need to ask you a favor. Are you busy tomorrow? I need transportation to two appointments. It's so ridiculous that we live in the capitol city of Louisiana and that our bus system is so…awkward. You know there's not even a bus route anywhere near our home or a lot of the places I need to go. You can? Is 7:30 too early? Thanks. Love you, too. Bye."

The following morning, Vaughn picked Sarah up on time. She had put on a little weight during the past twenty-five years but wasn't what Sarah would consider overweight by any means. Her dark red hair hung past her shoulders. Sarah suspected that she dyed it now that she was in her mid-forties but had never asked.

Sarah and Vaughn arrived at the Voc Rehab office at 8:00. Thankfully, the counselor was on time. Vaughn waited in the reception area, while Sarah filled out forms, described her disability, rehashed the previous day's incidents at Fines, and talked with the counselor about available resources. The woman gave her some numbers to call regarding technological assistance and told Sarah to keep her updated. Sarah thanked her and promised to phone soon.

She rode with Vaughn to the house and started making calls. She'd never needed technological assistance before, and there were many numbers to try. Most of them gave her voicemail messages. Hopefully, the persons at these offices would answer her inquiries soon.

Sarah also phoned Calvin to tell him about her meeting and the calls, and would he please turn in a leave slip for eight hours, since it looked like this would take all day? He insisted that it wasn't necessary to take leave. She insisted that it was. He refused again. She insisted again, making a mental note to check and see if he had submitted a form for her.

Calvin cleared his throat and said uneasily, "Uh, Mr. Fines says he needs your answer by today."

Sarah's heart sank.

"What answer? I'm trying to work this out. It hasn't even been twenty-four hours, yet."

"We can't wait forever."

"I'll plan on coming to talk with you right after my 1:30 appointment with Human Resources," Sarah said firmly.

"You do that."

The human resource office was not large and was decorated in Early Office Boring. Sarah and Vaughn sat in the mustard-colored vinyl chairs in the reception area and waited. At 2:15, the receptionist finally called Sarah's name.

Sarah turned to Vaughn and said, "I have a bad feeling about this. Would you come in with me?"

The human resource counselor gestured to the two chairs in front of his desk and took his place behind it. Sarah was tired of explaining the situation over and over, although she knew it was necessary. As she reviewed the pertinent details, the man listened without making any comments or taking any notes. Then he folded his hands on his desk blotter and asked, "So, can we do anything here?"

"I don't know. That's why I went directly to my employer, to this counselor, and to your agency. I've made some calls –"

"You're having trouble with almost every aspect of the job. Correct?"

"Pretty much, but –"

"Well, if you can't do your job, then you can either resign or be terminated."

Vaughn and Sarah sat in stunned silence. Eventually, Sarah said, "I have no intention of resigning. I'm trying to find a solution. I haven't had time to get all the answers. I've had little more than twenty-four hours to sort all this out – by myself, I might add."

The man removed a piece of paper from his desk and said officiously, "You'll have fourteen days severance, so there's no need for you to go back to work. Where would you like the termination letter sent?"

"To my employer. I'm going back to work right now."

"As I said, there's no reason for you to return to Fines."

Sarah stood and declared, "As *I* said, I'm going back to work. You can contact me there."

She and Vaughn left the office and walked without speaking to the car.

"He had his mind made up before you started talking," Vaughn said grimly before unlocking the doors.

"Yes, I think he did. I think Calvin and Mr. Fines did, too."

Vaughn drove directly to Fines. Once Sarah had retrieved her purse from the floor, Vaughn leaned across the seat and gave her a brief hug.

"Everything happens for a reason," she said, giving her a little squeeze.

"I'd love to know what the reason for this is supposed to be."

Sarah went immediately to talk with Calvin. He had not put through a leave slip, so she filled one out herself. Within the hour, he handed her the letter, stating that she was terminated as of two weeks from that date, but he stressed that she need not come back to work after that day. As he asked for her keys, she had that feeling again, as if she were a criminal of some sort. It was a terrible feeling.

To add insult to injury, Calvin had commanded the gopher to go around and ask everyone if they had spare bags or boxes for Sarah so that she could take her personal items home with her. She came back from a trip to the bathroom to find two small boxes and a Walmart bag in her chair. Her cheeks burned with embarrassment and rage.

The first thing Sarah did when she arrived home was phone her lawyer. The man had drawn up wills for her and Daniel after Kris had been born. He didn't deal with disability law, but he assured her that he would find out who the best person was and get back to her as soon as possible with the information. He commiserated with her before ringing off to make his calls.

Sarah tried to act normally in front of Kris. She didn't want him to see how tense and upset she really was. She made his favorite meal, which consisted of fried chicken, macaroni and cheese, and carrots. They played a game of Chutes 'N Ladders. It was Daniel's night to bathe Kris and Sarah's to read him a story. By 8:30, their son was asleep.

Neither of Kris's parents felt like doing anything. Neither of them knew *what* to do. Finally, Daniel turned on ESPN, while Sarah sorted through the mail.

At 9:00, Millie called.

"Hey, girl. What's going on with you?"

"Oh, you wouldn't believe. I was going to call you, but things have been terrible over here."

"So I gathered. I called your new office this afternoon, and they told me you no longer worked there."

Sarah felt as though she couldn't breathe.

"When did you call?" she asked quietly.

"2:00. I was on my break. Some woman answered the phone and said you were no longer employed by Fines."

Daniel got up from the sofa and went to sit next to Sarah, resting his hand on her shoulder.

"Are you sure about the time?" Sarah asked her friend. "And that it was a woman you spoke with?"

"We've been best friends for eight years. We always used to take our break in the afternoon at 2:00. I haven't changed that, even though it's dull going on break without you. This new girl is no fun. And, yes, it was definitely a woman. Why do you ask?"

"I was fired today because of my eye condition. At the time you called, I was with the human resource management agency telling them my story. I didn't leave there until 2:30. Yet, someone other than my very *male* boss told you that I was no longer working at Fines when supposedly that decision hadn't been made, yet."

Sarah went on to explain everything again. By the time she'd reached the conclusion of her tale, Millie was outraged. She rang off after eliciting a promise from Sarah to contact her the next day.

"They knew," Daniel said furiously. "Those fucking bastards! They knew."

"I think they knew yesterday. I think I was fired then and there in Mr. Fines's office, but they had to make it look like they were following proper procedure."

"They gave you one day to find a solution. They didn't offer any help other than asking you what could be done. How could you know? You've never needed any help before."

In the course of Sarah's conversation with Millie, he'd moved to stand by the window. Now, Daniel came back to his wife and knelt in front of her. She gently stroked his cheek with the tips of her fingers, but when she spoke, her voice was hard.

"I guess I'll have to give up the notion that people should be nice and do the right thing. That helping others is a natural desire of man. That being ethical is something one should expect from other human beings."

"Don't." He took her face in his hands and insisted, "People *should* act like that. If no one expects human beings to have morals, then I don't think some would even have a reason to try and be civilized. You know there are lots of good people out there. It's just that there are some monsters out there, too."

"Like your father?"

"Like my father. Like these men. Imagine how indignant they'd be if you were their child or if it was happening to them. Someday, they'll get theirs. No one can run from his sins forever."

"Maybe not, but we all do try, don't we?" she asked, as she put her forehead against his. "Why can't I just trust that some greater power is watching over me? Us?"

"*If* He's even there."

"What if we're just not paying attention? What if we're too lazy or arrogant to put in the effort?"

"I'm as lost as you are on that one. More so. Maybe we should just say that we'll believe and let it go."

"We've tried that before. I can't change the way I feel. I can't trust anyone to take care of me but me."

"Not even your husband?"

"You're telling me that you wouldn't say the same thing?" When he didn't respond, she continued more tenderly, "There has to be a reason for what's happening to us. Maybe we'll find our faith through this. Maybe that's why it's happening in the first place."

"Maybe."

Neither of them truly believed it, and therein lay the problem of their lack of faith.

As Daniel checked the locks and fed the fish, Sarah remembered something she'd been waiting to ask him about since he'd picked her up from work.

"How was your therapy session Wednesday? With everything going on this week, I forgot completely about it. Was it as hard as the first two?"

"It was." Daniel studied the fish and said, "There's so much background I still have to tell this guy, even while I'm working with him on what's happening in the present. There are so many things I don't even remember. This week wasn't the time to talk with you about that."

He expected her to argue, but she merely nodded and said, "Are you coming to bed?"

"In a minute."

Both of them tossed and turned all night until the sound of Kris's cartoons penetrated the quiet of the house the next morning.

They got up.

Chapter Six: Direction

"Give me a break," Jamie groaned. "You have got to be kidding me. What did you do?"

"I went with Daniel to see a lawyer." Sarah flipped the quesadilla and said, "The upshot of it all is that she's going to write a letter to Fines because there were several accommodations that could have easily been made if I'd been given time to figure out what they were.

"There's so much available for people with visual impairments. I had no idea. There's adaptive software that magnifies the text on the computer screen and speaks whatever you're doing as you're typing. There are talking clocks and electronic magnifiers and these little raised dots you can stick on things like appliances so you don't have to struggle to see numbers on dials or whatever. I wasn't aware of any of it and am looking forward to exploring what's out there that works for me. There's still so much I don't know, but I'm finding out more every day."

"That's fantastic. What's the ultimatum for Fines? Lawyers are hired to give people ultimatums, aren't they?"

"The management of Fines either needs to comply and return me to my former position or give me a comparable position someplace else within the company. If they don't do that within thirty days, I can sue them." She flipped the quesadilla again and removed the skillet from the heat then asked, "Would you hand me your plate?"

As he held out the dish, Jamie said, "I thought you didn't want to go back there."

"I don't," she admitted, as she laid another tortilla in the skillet and topped it with chicken, onions, peppers, and cheese. "I think it would be unbearable, but the lawyer says that it's the best avenue to take legally."

As she spoke, Jamie mashed together avocados, lemon juice, salt, and pepper. He put some of the mixture on each plate and added a spoonful of sour cream and some salsa. When Sarah's quesadilla was ready, they moved to the table.

"It's strange to be at home all day," she told him. Unfolding her napkin and placing it into her lap, Sarah picked up her fork and knife and proceeded to cut her tortilla into long, thin strips. "Usually, the only time I'm ever home like this is when Kris is sick or has a holiday from school. I guess I might enjoy it more if I could drive. If I could get around and we had the extra money, then maybe I'd like to play housewife for a change. I could run errands, attend field trips, and volunteer more. As it is, I'm sort of trapped. At least I've been able to make good use of my time by doing some serious information-gathering. I've been on the phone from the time Kris gets on the bus until the moment he comes home. I've called State agencies about technology, Federal agencies about my rights under the ADA, private groups who promote disabled workers, and just about anyone else I can think of."

"What about Fines? Have you been in contact with anyone there since it happened?"

"The person who handles the leave slips. I didn't want anybody accusing me of not following proper procedures or of abandoning my position. Vaughn took me downtown to Fines so that I could sign the leave form."

"That must have been a bitch."

"I got onto the elevator with my supervisor and a group of his cronies on the way down."

"Did you punch the jerk?"

"I wanted to. It was a really tense sixty seconds."

What Sarah didn't say was that her entire week had been dominated by insomnia, stomach upset, and headaches depending on the time of day or night. Physically, she was vacillating between short bursts of energy and long bouts of lethargy. She was tired all the time.

Sarah had also been riding an emotional roller coaster. In the mornings, she would be calm for a time and feel confident that things would work out in her favor. Then, as the day wore on, she would become panicked about the uncertainty of her predicament. Anxiety would strike hard if she happened to wake during the night. On these occasions, Sarah wished that Daniel could hold her and provide her with some assurances that things would be all right. Sometimes, she would softly say his name, but she never actually had any intention of waking him. He'd seemed more exhausted than she was.

"Earth to Sarah," Jamie said, interrupting her thoughts. "How's Dan doing with this crap?"

"He worries about me, and he's angry with the men at Fines."

"No shit. What about his shrink?"

"Daniel's not sure. He likes him but doesn't really feel as though it's helping."

"Too bad. It'd be good to have a therapist he could open up to, especially with all this happening," Jamie said, as he polished off his last bite of guacamole. "I'm sure he's worried about money, just like you are."

"He makes a good salary, but we need my income, too. We've got the big student loans to repay and the credit card debt from when he got his M.B.A. a few years ago. So far, we're doing all right paying our bills, but it's going to be rough if I don't get a job in the next few weeks."

"You two know how to manage your money."

"There has to be money to manage."

Jamie smiled encouragingly at his goddaughter. He felt as though he'd been talking nonsense to her, killing time, knowing all the while that she was lost in her own thoughts. It didn't matter. That was the point of his visit, and he intended to make the most of it.

"We need to do this more often," he suggested cheerfully. "Maybe we can make it a weekly thing. When I'm in town, I can drop by for lunch or take you out somewhere. When you go back to work, we can still have lunch dates. That way, we'd see each other one-on-one regularly."

From out of the blue, the thought came to Sarah: *Jamie's going to be fifty in a couple of years.* It was incomprehensible. His short hair was still blonde, and he hadn't gained any extra weight over the years. The shape of his face was slightly different, but she couldn't say exactly how, not without a picture for comparison.

"How is Kris taking all this?" Jamie asked casually.

"We haven't really told him. All he knows is that the people at my new job weren't very nice. He doesn't know I'm unemployed. I told him I was working with a lawyer, which is true."

"That's for the best. He doesn't need to be worrying."

"Exactly," Sarah agreed, as she moved some avocado around with her fork. "If this goes on, we'll have to say something, but I don't want to jump the gun. We have enough to deal with ourselves."

After lunch, Sarah put the dishes in the sink and accepted a compliment on her cooking from Jamie as they went to sit on the backyard porch swing. Ralph was overwhelmed by the excitement at seeing roofers next door, so he ran himself into exhaustion, collapsing near the swing to rest as the workmen packed up and left.

"Jamie?"

"Yeah?"

"There's something I've been wanting to ask you since I was a child. Do you ever wonder about your parents and your sisters?"

He bent down to scratch Ralph behind the ears and admitted, "I can't help but wonder, especially about my sisters."

"So, what do you imagine?"

He got up and walked to the edge of the porch. He folded his hands under his arms, trying to keep them warm in the folds of his sweater. His eyes searched the yard as if he were searching for his lost family.

"My parents stayed together and drank themselves to death, and no one cared. My personal version of revenge, I guess." He lifted his face towards the sky and supposed, "The younger girl got adopted by a really nice family, had a normal life, and is now a happy, slightly overweight, middle-aged housewife with a couple of kids and a mini-van. My other sister…. I don't see her as happy. I wish I could have taken care of her, made it all right."

He walked back to the swing and stood over Sarah. She looked chilled and miserable in the dull gray light of the afternoon.

"Any particular reason you're asking this? Not that I mind talking with you about it. I could never stand to tell all that junk to strangers. It's probably why I didn't get around to therapy."

"No reason," she said quickly, as she rose and went down the steps into the yard. "I can't explain it. It's nothing."

Jamie jogged up behind her and put out a hand to grasp her shoulder.

"If it was nothing, then you could talk to me about it."

Sarah wrenched her shoulder away, headed for the swing set, and sat on one of the old wooden swings. Jamie took a seat on the swing beside her. He watched her as she moved slightly back and forth. She sensed it and looked up at him.

"You've got that wicked look in your eyes," she remarked. "Actually, it's good to see it there. I've missed it. I've missed you."

He covered her hand with his and said truthfully, "I've missed you, too. Lately, we haven't seen each other a lot, have we?" He breathed in the cold November air, exhaled it in a puff of steam, then added, "Not at all, unfortunately."

"You've been traveling so much for work that it's pretty understandable. Your kids have been keeping me informed."

"I'm sure they have." As he started to swing, he asked, "Did they tell you that Chloe and I have been seeing each other again? I spent years with Winter. Hell, we had two kids. Then I moved on and then moved back with Chloe. Then I struck out by myself. Do you realize that I've been on my own for more than four years? No serious relationships, just trying to – what do they call it? – find myself."

"And?" Sarah expectantly raised her eyebrows and asked, "Did you?"

"Me?" he called back as he went forward. "The truth is that I've always known who I was. It's been difficult coming to terms with it, but I think I have at last."

As he went past her, Sarah cried, "So, go home! With Chloe you can run away as many times as you like, and she'll take you back. She's always loved you, no matter how much you screwed up!"

Jamie let himself slow naturally until both swings were virtually motionless again. He loosened his grip on the chains and said, "I'll go back, if you'll go ahead."

"What's that supposed to mean?"

He went to stand behind her, and she had to twist around to see him.

"It means that you don't have any fun. I've always had too much, and you've never really had any."

He pulled on the chains of her swing, and she had to turn around quickly before he let go.

285

"What are you talking about? I have fun!" she insisted, as she went forward. When the swing returned to him, she felt his hands on her back and cried, "I'm having fun right now!"

"Good!" he said into the air between them.

Sarah closed her eyes. Fast motion always made her a little dizzy because of her missing central area of vision. The cold wind blew her hair out behind her, then caressed her face as she went back. Suddenly, the urge to vomit hit her, and she dug her toes into the ground and jerked to a stop. Jamie stomped around to stand in front of her.

"Why'd you do that?" He glowered at her and growled, "I thought you were having a good time!"

"I was." Her lungs were cold, but her blood was boiling and she snapped, "I get dizzy when I swing or go on rides. Remember that?"

"How could I fucking forget it? It's things like that which keep you from taking a chance on enjoying life ninety-nine percent of the time!"

Sarah jumped to her feet and cried, "I'd love to go on all the rides at the State Fair, but I have to stand and watch because I get disoriented and sick to my stomach when I ride them. I'd love to get in the car and drive *anywhere*, but I don't want to crash into anybody. I'd love to go to a movie alone sometimes and be able to see everything that's happening on the screen throughout the entire show without having to ask someone else who's doing what, but I can't." She glared at him and hissed, "Do you want me to go on? I don't see the point. Obsessing about it isn't going to change anything. There are just some things I *can't* do."

She began to stride towards the house, but Jamie grabbed her arm and demanded, "You think I can't imagine what it must be like with your eyes? To be limited? But that's not all there is to it. It goes back to the day your mother died. You haven't let yourself truly have fun since you were six or seven years old."

The back door swung open, and they turned their heads in that direction. Tristan was standing on the porch. Jamie's hand remained on Sarah's arm as they watched Tristan come down the steps and walk across the yard. When he stood only a few feet from them, he said, "I didn't mean to interrupt. Just thought I'd stop by on my way to a site."

286

The look in his daughter's eyes reminded him of the day he'd headed for the phone to call the police, and she'd begged him not to. He turned to Jamie and waited.

Trust it to Jamie to bring any situation to a head, he thought.

"We were discussing Sarah's inability to be happy," Jamie remarked to his friend. He returned his attention to Sarah and asked, "When have you had fun with *life,* with yourself? You know, just blown things off and had a good time with it?"

Sarah pulled her arm back. This time, Jamie let it go.

"So, I should throw caution to the wind? Do you do that? What has it gotten you?"

"My life. It's given me grief, but I can honestly say that I have a great time being alive. I have problems, but everyone does. I simply believe there's a purpose for everything. What do you believe? Are you at peace with yourself any more than I am? Is that what responsibility's done for you? "It doesn't matter what you do to relax, but you've got to let go sometime. Have you ever done anything wild like gotten rip-roaring drunk in your whole life?"

"I don't like not being in control," she admitted.

"What good is control without happiness?" Tristan interrupted.

"Daddy!" she cried in exasperation.

"I speak from experience, Honey. What do you do just for yourself?"

"Well, I didn't expect the Spanish Inquisition." She sounded defiant in her attempt at sarcasm, but there was a quavering undertone in her voice. "If you must know, I haven't really let go too many times in my life, but I couldn't. I don't think I know how."

Sarah realized that this conversation was hurting her father. A part of her was glad of it. Another part of her was ashamed of herself for being glad.

"Honey, if only you could've simply let go and –"

"And what?" she asked with a bitter laugh. "How? You were so messed up at the beginning. I had to keep things together or who knows what might have happened? If I didn't take care of you, who would have? Who would have taken care of me? I took care of both of us as best I could. I think I did better than most kids in similar predicaments." She wiped at the corners of her eyes with her knuckles and whispered, "And it still wasn't enough." Sarah focused on Jamie again and continued, "I have to take care of everything to stay sane. When I'm in control, I'm very good at reading people and at manipulating them to get what I need." She looked away and murmured, "That sounds pretty cold, I guess. I'm only trying to keep myself safe."

As she stalked off towards the house, Jamie called out, "So, are you happy playing it safe?"

Ralph scooted in as she went through the door, leaving the two men together in the center of the yard. They heard pots and pans clattering in the kitchen. Sarah had always been one to slam things around when she was angry, although she never actually threw anything. Wordlessly, the men began to walk towards the house. Then, they heard the crash.

Tristan rushed for the kitchen with Jamie close behind. As Tristan pulled open the door, Ralph made a break for the yard.

Sarah was calmly picking up pieces of porcelain. From the number of white chips that were visible, Tristan surmised that she'd dropped a platter or a large bowl. About three inches above her left wrist her arm was bleeding freely from a jagged, zigzagging wound.

"Jamie, get the broom!" Tristan ordered, as he crunched his way across the kitchen. Crouching in front of his daughter, he took her left wrist, rotated her arm, and examined the gash. It would definitely require stitches. Sarah tried to pull her wrist from his grasp so that she could resume her retrieval of the broken porcelain.

"Sarah, leave it. We'll clean up."

She stopped but continued to stare at the pieces in her hand. The white was streaked red with blood. Finally, she said, "I tried to catch it, but I wasn't fast enough. It hit the edge of the counter."

Jamie had returned with the broom and a dustpan, but he remained at the edge of the room. Tristan stood and carefully made his way to the sink. He pulled down the tea towel from its hook and brought it back to Sarah. Wrapping it around her arm, he pressed down firmly. She winced and looked up at her father, simultaneously letting loose a flood of words.

"I can't be something that I'm not. I don't know any other way. I'm not unhappy all the time. Really, I'm not. Daniel makes me happy. Kris makes me happy. *You* make me happy...."

"Princess, we'll take care of it," Jamie said reassuringly.

"What if I can't let you? I've always been the glue that holds everything together. You don't know how I do things. Things might not get done."

At that point, she felt as though she wasn't making any sense, so she stopped talking. Her eyes were shining with tears as she looked again at the broken bits in her hand. She started to cry quietly.

"Why do I have to defend my whole life to you, both of you? I need your help, not some sort of condemnation."

"Nobody's condemning you," Tristan said, as he continued to apply pressure to her injured arm. "And you know you have our support."

"I didn't mean to make you feel worse than you already do," Jamie began. "I only wanted to talk. No one can get away from every problem, but you can free yourself of some of your burdens. Sometimes, I sense that you cut yourself off emotionally."

"How else do you think I can keep putting one foot in front of the other? What else should I do, turn to drugs and alcohol to make it better?"

Tristan sighed and looked away.

"Sarah, that was low," Jamie flashed accusingly.

"I wasn't trying...I was...I meant it for me, not to...not as a reminder for him."

"It's okay, Honey."

She closed her eyes and let the pieces of the dish clatter to the floor, muttering, "But it's not. It never was, was it?"

"You're tired," her father said quietly. "C'mon, Honey. Let's go sit while Jamie sweeps this up."

Her father helped her to stand then led her to the couch. As Jamie swept the debris, Tristan wrapped his arms around his child and stroked her hair. A feeling of hopelessness tugged at Sarah's heart, and her crying intensified slightly then tapered off. The blood was pounding through her temples and almost drowned out her father's next words.

"You say you're like me, and it's true. You say you can't throw away your responsibilities or others might suffer, and that's true as well. The problem is, if you don't let go a little, then you're going to end up more like me than you can imagine."

Without moving in his arms, she said, "You know I would never drink or do drugs. I could never hurt anyone like that and –"

Sarah broke off abruptly and was still. For a moment, Tristan sat very still as well. They listened as Jamie made one trip to the garbage can in the garage, then another.

Eventually, Tristan said, "You have to listen to me and learn from me. My whole life I felt compelled to take care of everybody. I took care of everyone but myself, and we both paid the price." He rested his cheek against her forehead and whispered, "You knew that the only reason I didn't end it all was because of you. I gave you your first lesson in responsibility then, didn't I?"

Sarah brought up her knees and burrowed into her father's embrace. Jamie watched them from the doorway. Behind him stood Daniel, who had driven up as Jamie was dumping a final load of white fragments into the trash can.

"What do you think we should do?" Tristan asked.

"I can't *do* anything."

"What do you *want*, then?"

She shut her eyes and mumbled, "I miss my family. We see you, Vaughn, Will, and Katie off and on all the time. Same with Max and Lillian. We talk to Grandma and Grandpa on the phone but only see them once or twice a year. We never see Jamie or Chloe or the kids anymore, not really. Cancer got Benjamin, and Halley's moved away. We never had any blood relatives around, but I knew I had a huge extended family I could count on. My son doesn't have that. *I* don't have that anymore. I want it back." She shifted her position and added, "Plus, I want a doctor to look at my arm."

"We'll take care of that and get our family life back on track," Tristan assured her. "You keep working on this discrimination thing and see where it leads."

Sarah watched as her husband came across the room to sit next to her. He gently lifted her arm, carefully unwrapped the now-red tea towel, and raised it away from the wound. He shook his head and asked Jamie for another towel.

"Are you okay?"

"No, I don't think I am."

Sarah moved away from her father and nestled against her husband. The two men looked knowingly at each other over her head.

From across the room, Jamie said, "Why don't you try this, Princess? Let *us* take care of *you* for a while. You don't worry about us, not even Dan. You focus on yourself and what you need."

"Just like that?"

"Old habits are hard to break. So, relax a little bit and let some other people pick up the slack. Aim for a different perspective."

She nodded and declared, "All right. I'll try." Her shoulders sagged marginally, as she repeated with less confidence, "I'll try."

Chapter Seven: A Stitch in Time

"The doctor will be with you shortly," the nurse said mechanically, as she pulled the curtain on the left side of the gurney.

"Whatever you say," Daniel muttered under his breath.

Sarah stared at the white ceiling tile directly above her head. There were tiny holes in it.

If only I could see well enough to count the holes, then maybe the time would pass more quickly, she thought.

"Where are Daddy and Jamie?"

"I think they went to find a phone to call Vaughn and Chloe."

"Jamie called you?" she asked suddenly. "Is that why you came home early from work?"

"No, I just wanted to check on you. I was worried."

"Oh."

"How's your arm?"

"It hurts. What time is it?"

Daniel glanced at his watch and said, "2:12."

"What about Kris?"

He leaned on the rail of the bed and said, "We still have almost two hours before he gets off the bus. We might make it." When she appeared skeptical, he smiled and said, "You're right. I'll go call and make sure someone will be home next door, just in case."

Once he'd gone, Sarah went back to staring at the ceiling. She prayed for a diversion, and it wasn't long before there was activity in the area to her right. The curtain was drawn back slightly near the head of the bed, and Sarah could see a young woman whose hair was soaked with blood being helped onto the gurney.

Once the patient was lying prone and the guardrail pulled up, the hospital people filed out to attend to some other emergency. The girl pressed her cheek to the pillow and saw Sarah watching her.

"Sorry. I didn't mean to stare. Just bored, I guess."

The girl reached up to touch her head and winced as she did so.

"S'okay. I'm kind of scared. I've never been to the hospital before, and I'm afraid of needles."

Indicating the bloody hair, Sarah asked, "What happened?"

"It's stupid. I was putting on my earrings, and I dropped one. I bent down to pick it up, and when I stood up again I hit my head on the corner of the medicine cabinet. Nobody was around, and I couldn't stop the bleeding, so I drove myself to the hospital." She squinted at Sarah and asked, "What's wrong with you?"

"I broke a dish and cut my arm in the process. I know it needs stitches."

The younger woman paled and said weakly, "Are you scared?"

"Not really. It just needs to be cleaned and sewn up." She sighed and then said, "We may be here for a while. Why don't you try to think about something else?"

"I've tried. There's nothing scarier than getting stitches in my head."

Sarah attempted to stifle a bitter smile.

"What? You think it's funny?" the stranger asked belligerently. "You can think of worse?"

Rolling over on her side, Sarah gingerly placed her left arm on top of her right and said, "Much worse."

"Wow. What's the scariest thing that ever happened to you?" Maybe it will make me not be so terrified of this."

Sarah doubted that but merely said, "I can think of several things."

"Like what?"

"Hm. A few years ago, I went to see a friend who was going to college in Lafayette. I took my two-year-old son with me. Anyway, my husband was going back to school at the time and had this huge paper to write, so he stayed home to take advantage of the peace and quiet.

"My son and I left Lafayette about 8:00 p.m. I suppose normally that wouldn't have been a problem, but that time it was. I don't see too well, and my vision had gotten worse. I didn't realize how much worse until we were on the bridge over the Atchafalaya Basin. My night vision was terrible. Each time I reached an overpass or a hump in the highway, the lights from oncoming cars temporarily blinded me. I literally *couldn't see*. As

I'm sure you know, there's no place to pull over once you're on the Basin." When the woman nodded, Sarah said, "By the time I got off that section of the highway, I was shaking. I hadn't been sure that we were going to make it across without crashing into a guardrail or another car. I never drove again. I didn't want to get my child or myself or anyone else killed. I was scared to death."

"I would be, like, petrified! But isn't it a hassle not to drive?"

"A major hassle."

"That would be awful." Looking slightly less fearful, she prodded, "Tell me another time, something from when you were a kid."

Closing her eyes, Sarah said softly, "I was very small when it happened."

"How small?"

"Seven." Sarah wrapped her right hand around one cold aluminum bar and shivered before continuing, "My father was…sick. My mother had died, and he was very young and alone and all that I had in the world. I got a bad cold, but he didn't realize how serious it was.

"One night, I woke up, and I was really hot. My nose was running, and I kept coughing and coughing. I went to my father's room, but he was too sick to do anything. I don't remember everything else that happened. I think I opened a window because it was cold outside, and I thought it would make me feel not quite so warm. My ribs hurt from all of the coughing, so I went into the kitchen and tried to reach the cough medicine in the cabinet. I guess the bottle slipped and shattered on the floor. Some of the glass flew up and cut me on the legs. I think I fell, too. That's probably how I got cut so badly."

"What did you do?" asked the young woman, her eyes wide.

"I knew I was sick, and he was sick. They tell me that I called my godfather. I don't really remember doing that, but I'm sure it must have happened. Looking back, I'm certain that I was in and out of delirium for who knows how long. I do remember that I thought I was in a field with some horses. I went deaf for a while." She smiled sadly and shook her head before admitting, "I'd forgotten about that. I wonder if I told anyone when I came to."

"What was it like to be delirious? Was it like in the movies?"

"Pretty much. I was floating above myself. I saw my godfather pick me up, then I remember him putting me in the shower. The water felt so good.

"But then the paramedics and the police arrived. I wanted so badly to run and drag my father out of the house. I couldn't even move. I was trapped inside my own body. I came out of it, but I never forgot that feeling of being completely helpless and at their mercy. I was terrified, not by the medical part of it but by the emotional part, the fact that I had no control.

"And here I am at the hospital twenty-five years later..."

A male nurse entered the young woman's cubicle and announced, "Time for some pictures of your head. We need to make sure you don't have a concussion. We don't want to put it off too long, do we?"

"No," she agreed. Looking across at Sarah, she said, "Thanks for talking. It really helped."

Sarah surprised herself by answering, "It helped me, too."

As the girl was taken for her x-rays, Sarah went back to staring at the ceiling. She was past ready to be home and wondered how much longer it would be.

She was pleasantly surprised when Daniel, Tristan, and Jamie returned shortly with an E.R. doctor. He was young, personable, and efficient. The male nurse joined him as he began to examine and treat Sarah's wounded arm.

Eleven stitches were required to close the gash. The doctor asked her more than once if the injury had been intentional. She assured him that it was not, but she sensed that he didn't quite believe her.

On his way out, the doctor offered Sarah a prescription for painkillers, which she refused to accept. Daniel pocketed the slip and assured Tristan that he would fill it and get her to take one of the pills before she went to bed. He went to sign the remaining paperwork then set off for the parking garage.

"C'mon, Princess," Jamie coaxed. "Let me help you get down from there."

"No thanks." She waved him away and insisted, "I've got it."

"Honey, will you stop for a minute?" Tristan felt the sudden urge to shake some sense into his daughter. "What were we talking about at the house? For God's sake, will you let somebody do something for you for once?"

The tone in his voice made her hesitate, and she grudgingly allowed him and Jamie to assist her in climbing down from the gurney. They walked slowly with her to the exit. When Daniel drove up, Jamie opened the car door so that Tristan could help her into the passenger seat. Daniel leaned across his wife and hooked her seatbelt, nodded to the two men, and then waited for Jamie to shut the door before driving off.

Tristan watched their car pull out into the evening traffic.

"You want me to drop you off somewhere?" Tristan asked Jamie, who was actually standing behind him.

"If you don't mind. My car's still in the shop. I can take another cab today if you can't spare the time."

Tristan looked over his shoulder and groaned, "When can I not spare the time for my best friend?"

He tried to sound casual, but he couldn't hide the strain from Jamie, and he knew it.

"Do you mind if we take a detour?"

"Course not."

As Jamie set off back towards the E.R., Tristan called, "Ah, Jamie?"

"Yeah?"

"The garage is this way. You have a bad habit of wandering off in the wrong direction."

"Sorry," Jamie said sheepishly. "I guess I was thinking about that pretty nurse I saw and –"

"You never learn," Tristan said with half-serious, half-mock disapproval. "It's time to go, Man."

Twenty minutes later, they were standing on the small bridge at City Park. Jamie strolled back and forth across the wooden planks, as Tristan leaned against the railing and gazed down into the dark water below. Sleet was beginning to fall.

Jamie asked soberly, "Not that you're a lousy date or anything, but can you tell me why we're standing here in the freezing rain?"

His friend sighed and shook his head, his ponytail moving back and forth like a wave across the nape of his neck.

"Sarah's in trouble. Maybe I thought her mother's ghost would be hanging out here and would tell me what to do. If her spirit were anywhere, then it would be here. You know that this is where we met. It's even close to LSU where she died."

"Yeah. I wonder what the punk who killed her is doing right at this moment. He's probably safe in his little house with his wife and kids."

"I hope so. I forgave him for being young and stupid a long time ago."

"You're too fucking nice, Tris."

"Being bitter was causing me a lot of problems. You know my dad used to say that a bridge is like a solution to a problem. Sometimes, you have to be creative to make it to the other side of the river. You have to find a way."

Jamie finished for him by saying, "Go over, under, across, or through. You told me before."

"It's a nice analogy. But what do you do if the bridge is out and the waters are rough?"

Jamie placed one hand on his friend's shoulder and the other on the slick rail of the bridge. It bothered him when Tristan became even the slightest bit anxious or depressed. He recognized the futility of trying to anticipate what his best friend might or might not do and attempted to offer Tristan what comfort he could.

"There's always a way to get to where we need to go. It may not be the way we'd hoped for, but we get there one way or another."

"At what cost?"

"She'll be all right, Tris."

"Will she?" Tristan asked then looked up to the sky, half shutting his eyes against the sleet. "We'd better go. I don't think I'm going to get anything out of standing here in the rain tonight, except maybe a cold."

As they walked carefully back to the car, Tristan felt a pang of…what? He realized it was a deep feeling of sadness. It wasn't only about Sarah. It was also about his second family.

Things had never been quite right between him and Vaughn since Katie Belle's conception and the turmoil that had followed. Will would be out of college in a couple of years. Would he take a job somewhere else? And Katie, she would be graduating from high school in the not-so-distant future. Would she want to go away to school? What about after that? Would he and Vaughn stay together once their children had flown the nest?

As chaotic thoughts danced in his head, Tristan drove Jamie to Chloe's house. At least one of them had made it across the bridge.

Chapter Eight: Safe as Houses

"Absolutely not."

"Sarah, you have to take one. I can tell that you're hurting, and you're upset. You need to take the painkiller."

"Daniel, you know I hate those things. I'll take an Advil instead."

"No. You'll take a Percocet. I'll hound you until you take it. You know I will."

They were standing in the laundry room, speaking in low tones so that their son wouldn't overhear their disagreement. However, they were so deeply absorbed in this debate that they didn't notice that Kris had already wandered into the kitchen. Although he had been hanging back, he could hear every word.

"Mommy, how come you don't want to take your medicine? When I don't feel good, you tell me that I have to take the medicine the doctor gives me so I can get better."

Daniel could see that Sarah was thinking furiously in an attempt to come up with a reasonable answer to Kristopher's question, but she was in pain, and she was shaken. It was futile to try and argue with the logic of a five-year-old, especially when she knew he was right.

"I guess that's true," she finally admitted. "I should do what the doctor said."

She accepted the tablet and a glass of water from Daniel. He watched her closely to make sure that she actually swallowed the pill. Satisfied, he said, "Good. Now, it's time for you to get to bed."

"But it's only 6:30!"

"Okay, Miss Priss," he drawled with Kris giggling beside him. "Ten more minutes."

"You're not going to bend on this, are you?"

"Nope."

"Fine. Kris, will *you* read *me* a bedtime story?"

Her son darted off towards his room, emerging moments later with a worn copy of *Goodnight, Moon*. Sarah lowered herself into the recliner and opened her arms to welcome Kris into her lap. He leaned against her right shoulder and opened the book.

Once the story had been read, Daniel said, "Kris, why don't you play with your K'nex or Legos while I help Mom? Then, I'll help you. You can come back in the room and kiss Mom when she's in bed."

"Can you and me play Hot Wheels?"

"Sure. I'll try not to be too long."

Daniel led Sarah into their bedroom then into the master bath.

"You get undressed," he ordered. "I'll get your nightgown."

The painkiller was beginning to take effect. Try as she might, Sarah couldn't undo the button at the top of her jeans. She decided to take off her tennis shoes first, then attempt the button a second time. As she bent to untie the laces of her shoes, the room tilted, and Sarah put out her right arm and steadied herself on the doorframe. Twisting, she pressed her back against the wall and began to slide down into a sitting position.

Daniel suddenly grasped her shoulders and the vertigo subsided slightly but not completely. Sarah lifted her good arm and brought her fingers up to touch his face. It took her three tries before she succeeded.

Is this what it's like to be drunk? She wondered.

"I can't make my hands work right. I can't get undressed. Maybe I should go to bed in my clothes."

Daniel knelt to untie her shoelaces and insisted, "I've undressed you before, although it was usually for another reason. I think I can handle it now." As he slipped off her Keds and her socks, he said, "I'll help you to stand. Then you can hold on to me."

Once she was vertical, he took her hands and placed them on his upper arms.

"See? Just give me some warning if you're going to pass out."

"At least Kris doesn't seem alarmed by all of this. I guess he thinks it's exciting."

Her tongue felt thick, and she was finding it difficult to form words.

"Something different," he agreed.

"He wants to see my stitches."

Daniel bent over, and Sarah leaned across him, resting her head on his back.

"I'm comfortable like this," she mumbled. "Can't we stay this way until morning?"

"Kris would love that. Hot Wheels and Legos all night."

She felt his fingers at her waist, and the button of her pants was deftly undone. Once the zipper had been lowered, Daniel eased off her jeans. He slowly straightened, and Sarah allowed herself to be pushed upward until she was standing once more. Soon, her sweater and bra were added to the pile on the floor.

"Daniel?"

"Hm?"

"How come people in the movies never get up to go to the bathroom after they have sex? Why isn't their hair mussed up? Their make-up is always perfect, and they fall right to sleep in each other's arms afterwards."

Daniel burst out laughing. His wife bit her lip and looked as though she was going to cry.

"Sarah, I'm sorry. I don't know. Are there any other questions you want to ask while you're –"

He was going to say "high," but he caught himself just in time. That had never been a good word to use around her. It was fortunate that the Percocet was affecting her brain or else Sarah would have picked up on it. Daniel didn't want to cause her any further unrest. She was in a precarious emotional state as it was.

"I've been…I want to ask you something. Tell me the truth." Her face was shadowed with fear as she asked, "Are you all right? I mean, with everything that's happening? I mean, I know that you're seeing that therapist, but what if –?"

"I can handle it," he interrupted.

"Will you tell me if you can't?"

He nodded then slipped the nightgown over her head. Getting her arms through the sleeves was tricky, but he managed without causing further trauma to her injury. That task accomplished, he took her to the bed. Once she'd been tucked in, he said, "Don't go anywhere. I'll be back."

Sarah lay warm and drowsy under the covers. She could hear Daniel playing Hot Wheels with Kris, bathing him, helping him with his homework, and reading him a bedtime story.

I should be in there with them. If only the medication weren't making me loopy.

Kris came into the bedroom bringing her his favorite stuffed toy, a dog he called Elliot.

"Here, Mommy. I know you don't feel good. I thought maybe you'd like to sleep with Elliot tonight."

"Thanks, Sweet Pea. Are you sure Elliot won't miss you too much?"

He shook his head, as Daniel said, "I'll leave the door open a crack so you can call for me if you need to. I shouldn't be long. Once Kris is asleep, I'll let Ralph in, lock up, and come to bed."

Sarah shut her eyes and listened as her son and her husband went through the nighttime routine. She had the oddest sensation that there was sunlight shining on her face. That was impossible, of course. It had been dark before they'd arrived home. Still….

She opened her eyes and was sixteen-years-old. Her friend, Victoria, was grinning down at her, as light streamed in through the blinds.

"What – or should I say *whom* – were you thinking about? You had this look on your face…."

"None of your business. And put the homework away! It's time for *Little House on the Prairie*."

Victoria waded through the textbooks, magazines, and papers that covered the bed. She flicked the metal knob of the little television set that rested atop the dresser. True, it only caught three channels, but Victoria didn't watch much TV anyway. The only program she and Sarah made time for was *Little House on the Prairie*, their favorite "fairy tale."

As the program began, the television went awry. The screen flashed black, and the actors were momentarily highlighted in brilliant white light. The friends blinked in surprise then looked at each other and said simultaneously, "*Nuclear Warfare on the Prairie!*"

It wasn't just funny; it was hysterical. Several minutes later, they sat wiping their eyes. Exhausted from the convulsive laughing fit, the girls leaned back against the headboard to watch the rest of the show. Sarah closed her eyes during the commercial…

…and woke in Interior Decorator Hell.
What am I doing in Benjamin's apartment?

She managed to get out of the papasan chair she'd been sleeping in and struggled through the barrage of bric-a-brac to the kitchen. Benjamin and Halley were playing cards at the table.

"How'd I get here?" Sarah asked.

"You got caught in the rain, Darling," Benjamin remarked. "Don't you remember? You came in to get out of the storm."

Sarah went into the half-bath on the other side of the kitchen. The face of the girl in the mirror could be no older than nine.

She returned to the kitchen table and sat.

"I don't understand."

"Why don't you rest again?" Halley suggested.

"Yes," agreed Benjamin. "Maybe you can clear your head."

Sarah folded her arms on the table and laid her head on top of them. She pressed her forehead into the hollow made by the crook of her elbow, closed her eyes...

...and woke in a room filled with chrome, steel, and glass. Sarah lifted her head from the sleek dining room table and pushed back the chair. She caught a glimpse of her reflection in the door of a stainless steel hutch. She was seven years old.

Sarah crept over to the only door in the room and took a tentative step across the threshold. This other room had no furniture, just one light hanging from the ceiling. In the darkness of the room, it made a wide, glaring circle. Sarah took another step forward then stumbled back as a shadowy figure stepped into the light.

"We shouldn't be here," her mother whispered. "It isn't safe."

When she could breathe again, Sarah took in the sight of her mother. Emma wore a white dress with bell sleeves, a scooped neck, and a short skirt. She took another step towards her daughter, who reflexively took another step backward.

"You have to get out of this place. I almost got trapped here once when I was younger. Please! Run!" she urged. "Run! Run!"

"Mama, I –"

"Go, Sarah! Please!"

Emma began to cry, but there were no tears, only rivulets of dirt.

The dirt from her grave, Sarah thought, as terror seized her.

She ran. Sarah threw herself down shiny corridors at breakneck speed. There was no way out. Blackness began to seep into the edges of her vision, swirls of it sweeping across her eyes and then she was falling and falling....

"Sarah?" A pause. "Sarah?"

The voice was soft, but persistent.

"Sarah."

She opened her eyes and stared at her tennis shoes. The uneven surface of the carpet pushed against her cheek. Daniel's hand was making a gentle up-and-down motion across her back. Her injured arm burned slightly. She had a headache.

"Daniel?" Very slowly, she turned over and said incredulously, "I had a bad dream."

"I know. I was getting ready for bed, and there was this little cry. I heard you tumbling off the mattress. I think you hit your head on the wood here on the side of the sleigh bed. I was worried that you'd knocked yourself out."

Sarah reached up with her right hand and gingerly touched the tender spot on her forehead.

"No wonder I have a headache. I guess I needed something to off-set the pain in my arm."

Daniel smiled and helped his wife to her feet. She swayed slightly and held onto her husband in order to steady herself. Once he had returned Sarah to bed, Daniel climbed in beside her and cradled her against him.

"Daniel?"

"Yeah?"

"I'm...afraid."

"You're not used to having nightmares. I can't ever remember your having one."

Sarah pressed her face against his chest and drew in a breath through her nose. The smell of him, so familiar to her, was reassuring, and she relaxed a little.

"It scares me what you must go through and the nightmares you have. No wonder you don't want to go to sleep." She asked in a small voice, "What if I have another nightmare?"

Daniel shushed her and stroked her hair. He tried to recall the things she did for him when their roles were reversed.

"Do you want to talk about it? Or something else? That's what you always ask me. I may be a stubborn fool, but you could try it."

Sarah pressed herself against him, as if she could draw some strength from his body if she could only get close enough. She lifted her head, and he angled his down towards her.

"Will you take care of me, Daniel?"

"You're safe with me; you know that. I love you, Sarah. Now, get some rest."

She fell asleep as he held her. Daniel stayed awake all night and watched over her, but there were no more surprises, only Sarah's steady breathing and the all-encompassing love Daniel felt for his wife.

Chapter Nine: Wonder

At 10:30 the following morning, it occurred to Daniel that he should talk with his parents. He had been concerned about upsetting them in regards to his own problems. However, the recent incident involving his wife had made him realize that he could no longer avoid a serious discussion with Max and Lillian. They would be hurt if he did and rightly so.

"Admit it," he muttered. "You *need* to talk to them."

He dialed his parents' number and waited for what seemed like an eternity.

"Hello?"

"Hi, Lillian."

"Daniel? What's wrong?"

He stiffened and asked, "Why does something have to be wrong for me to call?"

"You stop that," she chided. "You can call anytime. We just haven't seen you much, and I've missed you. I thought maybe something was wrong."

"You should have called."

"Excuse me?"

"I'm sorry. *I* should have called. You're right. I haven't been very good about phoning or coming by. And something *is* wrong. But I didn't want to worry either of you."

Or watch Max decline any further, he added silently.

"Mind if I drop by for lunch? Or I could take you and Max to Mike Anderson's or The Chimes."

"No, indeed!"

Daniel could picture her standing in the kitchen with one hand on her hip and the other holding the phone. Now sixty, she had gray hair but no wrinkles. She would be wearing her favorite apron and an indignant expression. He smiled to himself and wondered when she would inform him what was on the menu for lunch.

"I've already started making some soup. There's plenty."

"My mouth is watering. I'll be there around noon if that's okay."

"Of course it's okay. Sometimes I think you could drive a saint crazy! Who else would put up with your tomfoolery?"

"That must be why I ended up with you, Saint Lillian. I'll see you at noon."

It was a blustery day, and Daniel felt chilled to the core as he ran from his car to the back door of the old Nash home. Lillian shook her head as she hustled him inside.

"Where is your coat?" she asked disapprovingly.

"I forgot it at the office."

She frowned, and he was twelve years old again.

"My car's always parked in the garage that's attached to the building. I didn't think I'd get that cold running from the car to the house."

"Ah, that explains it then."

They turned and saw Max standing on the far end of the kitchen. Daniel's heart pained him for a moment, as it always did when he saw his father like this. He hoped his feelings weren't reflected on his face or in his eyes.

With difficulty, Max slowly made his way across the room to the table. He'd lost more weight since the last time Daniel had seen him. Because he'd been portly since Daniel had known him, one would assume that this would have been an improvement, but it wasn't. The skin sagged on his bones as he withered away. The sharp mind was still intact, but, in a way, *that* made it worse. He knew.

"I don't know about you, but I could use something nice and hot right about now," Max told them. He raised his eyebrows expectantly. "Lillian?"

"Maxwell Nash!"

Daniel tried hard not to smile. He wondered if Lillian would say, "Not in front of the child!" Mainly, he was relieved to hear that Max was still capable of joking. The longer Daniel had stayed away, the more certain he'd become that the man who'd been his father for so long would no longer be there if he returned home for more than a cursory visit.

"What?" Max said innocently. "I didn't think you'd mind getting me a bowl of soup." He winked at Daniel and added, "What kind of soup are we having today?"

"Cream of asparagus and bacon."

307

"One of Daniel's favorites. How appropriate."

Once they were seated, Max and Lillian said a blessing, while Daniel stared at his soup. Following the prayer, Lillian passed Max the breadbasket, which was filled with buttered rolls.

With the sort of food Lillian cooks, it's a wonder that Max has lived to see eighty-two, Daniel thought. *It's probably why I love to eat the things I do. I should eat healthier if I don't want to have an early coronary.*

"I do wish you'd say Grace," Lillian remarked, as she passed Daniel the basket. "I'd sleep easier."

Daniel ate his soup and refused to comment.

Max noisily put down his spoon and said, "Oh, do leave the boy alone. We did a good job of not harping on him about that. Why start now? He's almost forty years old!"

Lillian pursed her lips.

"Tell me, my boy," Max began. "What's been going on with you? How is Sarah's new job? What is Kristopher doing in kindergarten? How is your work?"

He watched his son sit back and drag his spoon around in the creamy liquid for a moment. Daniel slouched and tugged at one corner of his placemat.

"Things have been better."

Lillian lowered her water glass onto the table and asked anxiously, "Something's very wrong, isn't it?"

"Where should I begin?" Daniel asked, as he straightened in his chair and propped both elbows on the table. "Kris is fine and doing well in school. That's the good news."

"And the bad news?" Max prompted soberly.

"Sarah was fired because of her eyes and is now unemployed. She's been talking to agencies, a lawyer, and anyone else who might be able to give her ideas on how to proceed. The entire dismissal thing was totally bogus, and she's an emotional wreck.

"Yesterday, she got mad because Jamie and Tristan were trying to talk to her about stuff from the past and her refusal to deal with things. She was washing dishes in the sink and…well, you know how she gets when she's really angry. She dropped that oval platter that goes with our plates. She needed eleven stitches in her arm."

"Eleven?" Lillian gasped.

"How is she coping today?" Max asked in that professional psychiatrist's tone of voice that Daniel hadn't heard in years. "And I don't simply mean the physical pain. She's always been a very independent person and has prided herself on her capable nature. This situation with her job must be quite devastating to her."

"I think she feels like somebody's pulled the rug out from under her."

"That's totally understandable."

"Jesus H. Christ, it was so hard for her to ask me for help last night, and I'm her husband!"

Lillian blanched and said, "Don't you dare take the Lord's name in vain at this table or anywhere else!"

"How do you know that I was taking it in vain and not using it in supplication?" he snapped.

"Don't you sass me either or mock your Lord," she said hotly.

"He's not my Lord."

Lillian clutched at the napkin in her lap and exclaimed, "Don't say that!"

"Calm yourself, my dear," said Max, as he took another roll out of the basket. "Although I don't disagree with anything you've said, let's please save the shouting matches for another time." He turned to his son and said evenly, "I don't think that you took the Lord's name in vain for that purpose. However, I am disappointed in your continued attempts to denigrate our religion. Is the name of Christ truly that meaningless to you that it's only to be used as part of an oath or as a tool to bait your mother into a diversionary argument?"

Max immediately saw the stricken look on Daniel's face. Forcing his own features to remain impassive, he asked kindly, "What is it, Son?"

In that brief instant, Daniel recovered himself enough to mask his own emotions. He ate another spoonful of his cream of asparagus and found that it didn't taste like much of anything to him now.

"Nothing," he said tightly. "I'm sorry if I offended either of you."

"Baby?" Lillian prodded, "What's the matter?"

309

Daniel shook his head. He was remembering, thinking back to something he had buried deep within himself when he'd been a child: His biological father towering over him with the belt in hand.

"I am disappointed in you, Danny."

Would it serve any purpose if I told Max how what he said affected me? Daniel thought. *No. It'd only make him feel guilty.*

He reflected that Max was correct in his observation that his son had been using religion as a diversionary tactic. The question of the existence of God was a convenient theoretical argument, one that he had used frequently to channel Lillian's attention away from other unpleasant subjects.

"I'm sorry," Daniel said more easily. "I've just been under so much stress, lately."

He could hear his conscience saying, *Take responsibility.*

"But that's really no excuse. I know it gets to you, the religion part. I'll try not to be so difficult."

"Thank you," Max said with an appreciative nod. "Now, who are you, and what have you done with my son?"

Daniel grinned sheepishly at him and reached for a roll.

"Seriously, what is going on with you?" Max took a sip from his still-full water glass and went on, "We'd rather not be in the dark."

"I – I began going to a therapist recently."

"Because of Sarah?" Lillian asked.

"No, because I saw Zachary Samuels walking down St. Ferdinand, and I guess it kind of triggered some old memories." He looked at the only father who had ever shown him any kindness and compassion and confided, "I didn't want to burden you or Lillian with all this."

Max settled back in his chair and said, "In the first place, don't worry about that. Sometimes an objective opinion is the best thing. However, as your father, I'm concerned about you and Sarah. Do you like your doctor? Do you think she should see him, too?" Lillian opened her mouth to speak, but Max cut her off. "Don't you go asking him why he didn't come to us sooner. The fact that he didn't goes to show how much he cares for us, my dear. We're not as young as we used to be, although that goes without saying, I suppose."

Lillian stayed quiet and took a bite from her roll.

"I like the therapist okay. I haven't seen him enough to know if he's the right person for me, but at least I haven't had any more of the bad nightmares."

He shuddered involuntarily, then cursed himself for letting them see it. They hadn't even known that he'd been having nightmares. Now, they would be stewing over his well-being with even greater intensity. He plunged on, hoping that they wouldn't press him for more information on that topic.

"I don't think Sarah should necessarily see him at this point. I don't know if she'd feel comfortable seeing the same therapist as me. She might want to talk to someone else. She had sort of a crisis yesterday, and I think she needs to take a break from everything. If she needs to go to someone, she will though. I'll see to it, just like she did with me."

Max nodded approvingly and gestured for him to continue.

"As for me, I'm taking it day by day. The lawyer we retained seems to be doing all the appropriate things. Sarah needs a job, but good jobs are hard to come by, especially when you have a disability. That's why we were so excited by the job at the publishing house. They didn't seem to care about her eyes at all."

"Sometimes people have their own agendas," Max reminded him. "Sometimes, they simply don't think beyond the next sixty seconds."

"So, the sons of bitches built up her hopes of a great career with them then crushed her dreams in the blink of an eye. You can't imagine how I'd like to –"

Damn it!

He had done it again. He let the handle of his spoon fall back onto the rim of his bowl. Lillian reached across the table and touched his arm.

"Will you stop worrying about how everything you say will affect us? Why do you look so surprised? I've been your mother for over twenty-four years; I think I know you well enough by now. We're adults. We don't need for you to shield us from unpleasantness."

"Hear, hear!" cried Max.

Daniel looked from one to the other and declared, "Well, I don't need your protection either."

Max pulled the napkin from his lap and put it next to his empty bowl. He sighed deeply then admitted, "No, you don't. However, parents want to protect their children, and everyone can use support during troubled times."

The telephone rang, and Daniel rose to answer it. He picked up the receiver from the wall phone, but the ringing continued.

"Oh!" Lillian cried. "I forgot to tell you that that phone's broken. Can you catch it in the living room?"

When he re-entered the kitchen several minutes later, Lillian had cleared the table and was in the process of making coffee.

"I don't know if you have time for coffee, Baby. You don't work too far from here, but I'm sure you have to get back."

"Actually, I don't. That was my secretary. All the electricity in the building went off due to the demise of some major piece of equipment. It doesn't appear that they'll be able to fix it within the next few hours, so they told everyone to go home early because of the upcoming Thanksgiving holiday. I bet the directors are having fits. It won't be good for business. Anyway, they're trying to get the word out to all those who were at lunch." He went over to Lillian and hugged her, then asked, "You mind if I stay for a little while?"

She held him tightly as if he was a boy again and said, "I'd like that." Peering around his shoulder, she asked, "Wouldn't you?"

"Very much," Max agreed. "Very much."

"Shouldn't you call Sarah and tell her you're here?" Lillian asked. "She would've been welcome to come for lunch, too."

"Vaughn told me she was taking her shopping to get her out of the house."

"You should tell her where you are," Max advised. "What if she calls your office and gets no answer? In her present state –"

"I intend to call. Give me a minute."

So, Daniel dialed their cell phone number and told his wife about work and his plan to spend the afternoon with his parents.

"Are you and Vaughn having fun?"

"We've been window-shopping, and we ate lunch at this little coffee and pastry shop. They make sandwiches, too. You're going to have to go there with me. It reminds me of that place we ate at on our first anniversary, and the food is delicious." She lowered her voice and added, "We'd better come back soon, though. These little places never last long."

He smiled as she continued talking. That was his wife, still a curious mixture of positive and negative. However, his feelings of unease lingered. She was in control again. Was that good or bad?

As if she'd heard his thoughts, Sarah asked suddenly, "Will you hold me again while I sleep tonight? I seem to be able to let you do that when I take the painkiller."

"You know I will."

"Good. I'll see you at home. I love you."

"Love you, too."

He stood by the phone for a moment, as an idea began to take shape in his head. Then Daniel went to explain his plan to Max and Lillian. Buoyed by their enthusiasm, he retreated to Max's office and got busy. Four phone calls and one half hour later, he was finished. As he leaned forward to shut off the desk lamp, the phone rang. He hadn't expected it, and he jumped involuntarily before answering.

It was Sarah.

"Hey. What's up? Where are you and Vaughn?"

"Standing in front of the Golden Swan. Vaughn and I were browsing in the china area when the lawyer called."

"The lawyer? She called you on the cellphone?"

"I told her she was lucky to reach me on it since we usually only have it around for emergency calls. You know, I'm starting to see more and more people using cell phones all the time now though...."

"Sarah, what'd the lawyer say?"

"She said a letter arrived at her office from Fines stating that I wasn't a disabled person and that I had been aware of everything about the job including the handwritten material before I'd accepted the position."

"So, they out and out lied?"

"Looks like it." His wife sounded angry but also...pleased. "The lawyer said we should file a complaint with the Equal Employment Opportunity Commission and the State Commission on Human Rights. Vaughn and I will pick up the forms from her office on our way back to the house. I'll fill them out and return them to the lawyer so that she can look them over and get it all filed."

"Are you okay?"

"It's not the resolution I wanted, but they're being so asinine about everything that I guess I shouldn't be shocked about anything they do. At least I know where I stand. I *will* be vindicated, Daniel."

Chapter Ten: Quicksand

When Max came into the office ten minutes later, he found Daniel standing near the window, staring out at the garden.

"Your plan didn't meet with approval from the others?"

"What? Oh. No, everybody I called was excited about that. It was the news I got from Sarah that pissed me off."

Max sat in the leather chair in front of the desk and said, "I know I'm not your official therapist, but would you like to talk about this man to man?"

Daniel fingered a loose thread in his pocket and nodded.

"I'm afraid that I'll lose her, Max. Every little thing sets her off, and her emotions fluctuate back and forth between optimism and despair."

"That's all perfectly normal for a person who's going through such unsettling circumstances. Tell me more about what happened when she was dismissed and what she did afterwards. How is *your* emotional health at the moment?"

They discussed Sarah's situation at length, but Daniel found that he was reticent to talk about his own current mental state and the events that had preceded it. Max accepted the information he was given and offered his son advice on the optimal way to approach both his and Sarah's problems.

Finally, Max said, "I think I'll lie down for a bit. Why don't you take a break and lie down in your old room? You look rather tired."

And he was. Daniel hadn't slept at all the previous night. He felt uneasy about Sarah and was furious about this latest development with Fines. He wondered what would happen if Sarah couldn't return to work. He was saddened by Max's declining health. Plus, he was still in the throes of dealing with his own emotional maelstrom.

Daniel followed Max's slow progression up the stairs. Lillian, who held an open book in her hands, was already asleep in the master bedroom. Max carefully took the book, laid it on the nightstand, and turned off the lamp. Then he shooed Daniel out of the room, telling him that he would wake him when they got up.

Daniel sat on the edge of his old bed for a while. Being back in his room like this was strange. He hadn't slept there in years. He slipped off his shoes, stretched out on top of the bedspread, and was quickly asleep himself. The house was quiet and serene for a time.

"Help me! Somebody, please!"

Daniel sat up in the bed when he heard the shrill cry. He sprang from the mattress and rushed for the stairs, but Zachary Samuels came up behind him and held him fast. Daniel struggled to free himself, but his biological father refused to release him. The blue runner on the steps turned red, as blood seeped *upwards* through the fibers. Where was it coming from?

"Help me!"

Daniel made one last valiant attempt to break away. Samuels abruptly let go, and his son tumbled head over heels and landed, bruised and stunned on the bottom step. His left wrist sang with pain when he moved it. He held it with his right hand as he staggered to his feet.

The blood was making its way across the hardwood floor towards him.

All of this is physically impossible, Daniel thought. *None of it makes any sense. How could the blood be going up the stairs? How can it not be at the bottom?*

"Please!"

Propelling himself towards the living room, Daniel took five steps before he slipped on the blood and crashed to the floor. He cried out as pain jolted his injured wrist. Pushing himself up with his good hand, he crawled on his elbows and knees in the right direction until he found his mother.

No one else would have been able to recognize Assumpta Samuels. The damage she'd sustained had twisted her features, but Daniel knew her immediately. He came to a halt near the coffee table and sidled up next to her shoulder.

"Help me!" she rasped. "Why didn't you help me?"

The fear was building in him, but he pushed it down and asked, "How could I help you? Why didn't you leave him and save both of us?"

She didn't answer. Daniel lifted her from the rug, clutched her to him, and wept for her and for himself. Then, he heard the

316

scream. Lowering his mother onto the floor, he pulled himself up by the edge of the table and staggered back towards the stairs. He stood frozen in horror at the bottom. Every step had someone he cared about lying dead across it. He had to step over them on his way up – Max, Lillian, Tristan, Vaughn, Jamie, Chloe, Benjamin, Halley, Will, Katie, Jim, Helen....

He lurched his way to the top where Sarah stood silently waiting for him. Her dress was long and white, all cotton and lace. If her hair hadn't been loose and so curly, she could have passed for a proper lady of the early nineteen hundreds. He could almost imagine her out for a stroll by the lake, a parasol in her hand.

There were no red stains on the material or on her flesh, and, for a moment, Daniel relaxed. She wasn't dead like the others. She looked like an angel.

Despair seized him when he saw the faint outline of the wings. She was an angel. She was gone, too. There was a God. There was a Heaven. She was there, and he was here. He was in Hell.

The scream came again. With dread, Daniel ran past the shimmering form of his wife, heading for the pull-down steps that led to the attic. He knew what was going to happen, what happened every time he had this particular nightmare. No matter what changed during the first part of the dream, the ending never varied. But he had to go there, had to try to stop it, just as he did each time. He always failed, but he couldn't stop trying.

"Daddy!"

The walls were going red now as Daniel yanked the cord with his good hand and pulled down the steps. He could see Samuels up in the rafters holding Kristopher with one arm. In his free hand, he held a sword. Daniel began to climb, but it felt as if he was wading through quicksand. He wouldn't get there in time, and Kris would die because of it.

"I'm disappointed, Danny."

"No!" Daniel roared. "You will not do this!"

Even as the words flew from his lips, he knew it was hopeless. The sword was raised. He could hear himself howl, the sound reverberating around the empty attic.

"Daniel!"

With one convulsive spasm, Daniel drew in a great, gasping breath and opened his eyes. He had no idea where he was, but

317

Sarah was there and that was all that mattered. She was stroking the hair near his right temple and saying something soothing. He held onto the sound of her voice.

He was shaking violently, and his clothing was drenched with sweat. If only he weren't so cold. From somewhere beside him, Sarah continued to talk and to caress, and the shaking diminished to shivering. She gently guided him until the backs of his legs touched the mattress. Only then did he understand that he'd gotten out of bed.

The covers were pulled down, and Sarah was speaking once more but not to him. There was a *click!* as the door was closed. His wife proceeded to undress him, only stopping when he'd been stripped of all his garments. Daniel automatically slid under the covers, as he became vaguely aware of his surroundings. He watched his wife strip off her clothing and crawl in beside him. Reflexively, he reached out for her and felt the warmth and comfort of her nearness. Within half an hour, he was sleeping once more.

Sarah eased out of bed and dressed as quietly as she could. It was unusual that Daniel had fallen asleep so quickly. She was thankful for small miracles.

She went silently out of the room, leaving the door open in case he woke soon. She crept down the stairs and went to the kitchen. She could hear the hushed voices of Max, Lillian, and Vaughn. The conversation ceased abruptly as they heard the approaching footsteps.

"He's asleep," she announced. "He should sleep for a while. It wears him out."

"When did these nightmares begin?" Lillian asked, making a feeble attempt to conceal her apprehension. "He had nightmares as a child, but not…like this. Does he have these often?"

"Usually once or twice a year. Lately, he's been averaging one a month." She rubbed at the bridge of her nose then muttered, "He never had these bad ones when we were first married."

"When did this start?" Max reiterated Lillian's question.

"When Kris was born."

"Can you remember what happened around that time when he had the first one?" Max asked. "Be a little more specific perhaps?"

"Max, it was the day I had the baby!" she said angrily. "What is there to remember? Would you like for me to talk about the weather that particular afternoon?"

"I'm well aware that this is an unpleasant subject for you. You both asked us not to press you for details about the birth, and we've honored that request. I think now we must hear them. The episode he had earlier was more severe than any I've ever witnessed with him. I must admit that I'm alarmed. Will you tell me?"

"How about a run-down of our entire day? Would that be enough?"

He nodded and gestured for her to proceed.

"It was Saturday, so we slept until 9:00 or so. Then we got up, ate breakfast, showered, and dressed."

Max could tell that she was holding something back, even this early on in her narrative.

"Nothing out of the ordinary until then?" he prompted.

Acknowledging that she'd been caught in her attempt at circumventing his inquiries, Sarah smiled and said, "You're an excellent doctor, Max."

"Don't try to change the subject by flattering the therapist. There's something else you're not saying here, Sarah. It may be relevant."

"All right. I woke up with a bad backache that morning. We decided that I must have slept the wrong way and dismissed it. The pain decreased after I took a shower. When we thought about it afterwards, it was probably the first indication of trouble. If we had known, then we probably would've called the doctor right away."

"Do you have to ask about these things?" Vaughn queried with a frown.

"I'm trying to help my son, her husband. I'll ask whatever questions I deem necessary." Max turned to Sarah and said, "I apologize for making you relive what I know was a difficult time for both of you."

"I know you have to ask. After we got dressed, we left to do some shopping for baby things. We had all of Katie's old baby furniture, but we wanted to pick out a stroller and some of the other items we needed.

"We were having so much fun. It was a really great afternoon until about 5:00. We had been talking about getting something to eat, but we couldn't decide between these two high chairs. We kept going back and forth, comparing their features and trying to picture how they'd look in the kitchen."

"And?"

"And that's when it happened."

Max rested a hand on his daughter-in-law's back. Sarah and Daniel had been too distraught to talk with them about any of these events at the time. As the days had passed, they had declined to confide in anyone. Typical of both of them, Max had thought. Now, he wished he had been more insistent on getting Sarah to share information with him or Tristan.

"One minute, we're shopping for a high chair. The next thing I know, there's this terrible pain, and it seems like I'm bleeding to death. Daniel got me to the hospital, and they rushed me to the delivery room, but they wouldn't let him in with me." Drawing in a shaky breath, she said, "I think they believed that the baby was already dead and that I might...." She broke off and looked towards the small kitchen window. "I remember calling out for Daniel, and then he was there. I don't know what happened, if he pushed his way through or if he talked his way into the room. The next thing I knew, the baby was born, and they took him away. I didn't even get to hold him. I wasn't sure where they were taking him until Daniel told me they were moving the baby to the NICU. Then, we were on tenterhooks for two days, not knowing if Kris's lungs were strong enough for him to survive."

"Is there anything else you think might be important?" her father-in-law prompted.

"You asked me for specifics," Sarah said to Max. "Well, I don't remember much else. I was a little preoccupied."

"Sarah, that's enough," Vaughn interjected. "You know that we're only trying to get to the bottom of things."

Her stepdaughter looked hurt, but said, "Sorry, Max. I'm just so worn out. I'm scared, and my arm's really hurting."

"And I'm sorry for having to press you further. Tell me about the first time Dan had one of these dreadful nightmares."

She rubbed at the bridge of her nose and said, "It was the night after Kris arrived. Daniel was sleeping on the fold-out couch in my hospital room. He'd been trying to get in touch with you and Lillian at whatever conference it was you were at, but the hotel desk clerk said you were out and would only take a message. Eventually, Daniel quit trying for the night and curled up under a blanket. I was in pain, and we were both terrified about Kris. We slept fitfully. Daniel woke me with his screaming at 2:00. I think he scared the daylights out of the doctors and nurses and the other patients. Those walls were so thin."

"Why didn't you say anything about the nightmare?" Vaughn prodded.

"It didn't happen again for about a year."

"But weren't you worried?" asked Lillian.

"Of course I was, but those nightmares were never like these last few. I swear he never used to make any noise until he'd wake up, and he's never, ever gotten out of bed before today." She looked across the table at her mother-in-law and said, "I was going to apologize for dropping in unannounced, but, thank God, we did."

"Amen to that," Lillian agreed.

"I just don't understand!" Sarah cried in frustration. "He hasn't had one like this since he started seeing the therapist." Then, realizing what she'd said, Sarah stammered, "Oh – I – um –"

"It's all right, my dear." Max patted her on the arm and said reassuringly, "He told us about his recent therapy."

The clock in the dining room chimed 3:00. Sarah turned to Vaughn and said, "I hate to ask you this, but could you pick up Kris for me? Even if I could drive, I can't leave Daniel when he's like this. After all these years, I sort of know what to do with him when it happens. I don't really want Kris going to my neighbor's since he was over there yesterday. He might start wondering about what's going to happen every afternoon while he's at school."

"No," Vaughn protested. "I think you need me here. Will's home and Katie should be walking in the door any minute. I'll tell them to meet Kris at the bus stop and go back to the house and order pizza."

As Vaughn went to make the call, Sarah asked, "What can I tell Kris today?"

"Tell him that his grandmother and I needed some help and that you'll be home soon," Max suggested.

"I don't know that we'll be able to go home tonight."

The old man looked aghast and asked, "How long does it take for him to recover from these episodes?"

Sarah watched through the window as the leaves of an oak tree rustled in the wind. She wished she could take a walk outside. It might help to clear her mind.

"How long, Sarah?"

"He'll sleep for a few hours. When he wakes, he'll be coherent but still badly affected. Sometimes it takes days for that to fade. I don't know what else to do to help him."

Max smiled indulgently at Sarah, and she was acutely aware of his age. She wanted to leap out of her chair and throw her arms around him before it was too late. She wondered sadly how much longer he had left.

"You're doing exactly what you should be doing." When she rolled her eyes, Max insisted, "I'm quite serious. No one can erase the scars left by years of trauma. Those scars can fade with time and good counsel, but they'll remain nonetheless. My son has done an extraordinary job of dealing with his pain, but suppressed feelings can only stay in check for so long. Dreams can be highly indicative of many things – a subconscious need for release, a reflection of our innermost thoughts and fears, or a warning signal. In this case, I'd suspect all three."

"What do you mean, a warning signal?" Lillian asked, as Vaughn returned to the room.

"The threat to Sarah and Kristopher at the time of the birth, combined with Daniel's futile efforts to contact us when he desperately needed our support, obviously triggered some overwhelming feelings concerning loss, lack of security, and guilt over his inability to make things right. This recent sighting of his father has most likely exacerbated the emotional weak links that Dan has successfully dealt with in the past," Max offered.

"Weak links?" Vaughn said in confusion.

"Feelings that he suppressed in order to function. Issues that he couldn't control or come to terms with as a child. His subconscious is providing a safety valve through the dreams, but the nightmares are also alerting him to resolve the conflicts within. If he doesn't, his conscious mind could be more affected than he may be able to handle." He looked to Sarah and said, "He's

322

getting help. That's a good sign. Do you know who his doctor is? I'll have to give him a call."

"Max, no! You can't do that. Daniel will resent it, and –"

"And I don't bloody well care if he does. This is his *life* I'm worried about. Don't panic. I won't tell Dan and neither will the doctor. Privacy rules be damned. I'll call to confer, to tell the man Daniel's background from a psychiatric point of view. Daniel was a victim of severe child abuse for an extended period during his formative years. It's time he healed those emotional wounds so he can get on with his life."

"That would be a huge relief," Sarah agreed.

"It wouldn't hurt for you to get some therapy with this man as well."

"I'd rather talk with you."

"Well, you know I am retired so...any time is fine. We'll work all of this out. You'll see. You both need some time and a little boost. You'll get through this."

"Maybe," Sarah said doubtfully. "If we're lucky."

"Luck has nothing to do with it," Lillian assured her. "Put your faith in God."

"Please, don't," Sarah asked, as she rose from her seat. "It would be nice and convenient to hand everything over to someone else and say that it was meant to be this way for some unknown Divine reason. I don't see any reason for any of these things in our lives that have brought us to where we are here and now."

"We can't always fathom why," Vaughn began.

"There has to be a purpose to our lives, or why go on?" Lillian added.

Max gave a mental groan. This was not a remark that he would ever make to someone who was suffering from depression and anxiety. He said quickly, "If we knew the purpose of every joy and tragedy that befalls us, then we, the human race, would be all-powerful and that would leave nothing to chance. We must trust that there is a reason for our triumphs *and* our suffering."

"Can you please explain to me any possible reason behind Daniel's abuse? How about if I go through every scar on his body, and you explain each one to me?"

Vaughn stood and stepped towards her, but Sarah glared furiously at her and shook her head.

"Well, Max?" she goaded. "Can you reason it away?"

"My dear child –"

"Give me a reason!" she shouted. "I need a reason for the burn marks and the knife marks and the bruises that we never even saw! Let me know why nobody tried to rescue him before Daddy! Why did his mother stay with that monster and allow herself to be slowly and systematically beaten to death? She knew Samuels would beat her son once she was gone. Why didn't she take her child and leave? Didn't she love Daniel?"

"I wish I knew," Max said with great sorrow in his voice. "I wish that many things had been different for my son. I'd like an explanation myself. However, no one has given me any reasons, so I must believe that there's a higher purpose to it all."

"You can believe whatever you want," Sarah said with a sigh. "I'm going up to take care of my husband."

"And I thank God for that," Max muttered once she had left the room. "Whether you believe in God or not."

Chapter Eleven: Truth

"Daniel, may I please take this thing off my head?"

"No, you may not. I told you I had a surprise for you today, and I also know that if you weren't blindfolded you'd peek."

"Kris?" Sarah spoke in what she hoped was the direction of her son. "Kris, do you know where we're going?"

"I can't tell you." He leaned forward as far as the seatbelt would allow and said in a conspiratorial tone, "It's a secret."

"Oh, all right."

She settled back and listened to the noises of the city, which were few on that Thanksgiving morning. The interior of the Mazda was finally getting warm, which translated to her that they would probably arrive at their destination soon. Sure enough, Daniel made a right turn, and the car slowed to a halt.

"Watch your step, Sarah."

As she climbed out, she held onto the sleeve of Daniel's coat. Well, actually, it was Max's coat. Daniel's was still locked up at his office, so Max had lent him one of the two he owned.

Sarah visualized her husband in his father's gray wool coat. It had always been slightly too long for Max, so the length was perfect for Daniel. However, Max had been heavier in the past, and the coat hung in folds around his son. Huge or not, she thought that Daniel rather liked wearing it. Maybe Max would let him keep it. She'd have to talk with him about that.

"Here come some steps. Kris, take Mom's hand on that side."

The small hand of her son slipped into Sarah's palm, and she was reminded of those Saturdays when she and her father would wander for hours enjoying being together while taking in the sights and sounds of their city. A lifetime ago when the world had been so different, there had been more time for wandering.

"Okay, that's it," her husband said and stopped.

She waited for Daniel to tell her what to do next. He knocked on a door, and the voices coming from inside wherever they were went suddenly quiet. The door creaked open, and warmth enveloped them as they went through into…. Where?

Daniel reached up and removed the blindfold. Sarah blinked at the sparkles in her eyes and tried to adjust to the lighting of the room. Then she blinked again.

They were at her in-laws' house, and the place was crammed with people. Will, Katie, her father, Vaughn, Jim, Helen, Max, Lillian, Jamie, Chloe, Abby, Abraham, and Allison were standing in close quarters in the living room. Lillian's sister, Carrie, and her husband and their children hurried in from the dining room. Isabelle, who looked as dignified as ever, smiled at Sarah from where she sat on the ottoman. Off to one side stood Halley.

"What is this?" Sarah asked incredulously. "I can't believe you did this."

"You'd better thank your dad," Daniel told her. "Remember he suggested getting together when we were at the house? It came to me later that this would be the perfect place to have everybody come for the holiday. Max and Lillian were amenable to playing host and hostess, so we decided to have a Thanksgiving potluck reunion of sorts."

Sarah cast about for something to say and finally settled on, "But we didn't bring anything for the potluck."

"We did, Mommy!" Kris announced. "I helped Grandma Lillian make a cake when you and Dad brought me over here to play yesterday. Why do you think I wanted to come so bad? Daddy paid for the cake and frosting and stuff. It's chocolate!"

Sarah was beginning to feel elated but anxious, and the odd combination of emotions was scaring her. Forcing herself to smile, she bent to hug her son and said, "That sounds great. Can I have a piece now?"

"Not before lunch! You can't eat dessert first. Right?"

"I guess not. I can't wait to taste it!" She tousled his hair, and he ran off to play with the other children as she said, "Thanks, Daddy."

"I think we all needed this," Tristan remarked. "We've drifted apart. It's nobody's fault, and it's everybody's fault. It's time we remember how much we need each other."

"Well spoken!" cried Max from his chair. "We're here to enjoy ourselves. I say that we get to it!"

Everyone mingled before lunch, talking, laughing and hugging each other. Jim and Helen were speculating on whether they should sell the farm and move to Baton Rouge. Isabelle and Max were deep in conversation about some journal article they had both read recently. Will and Abe were comparing college professors, while Katie and Allison were absorbed in a discussion regarding a movie they had seen the previous week. The children played on the floor, as the adults chatted on.

Sarah eventually found Halley alone in the dining room. Despite being in her early forties, the woman looked much the same as she had in her twenties. Admittedly, she appeared somewhat older, but the only major difference to her appearance was that her straight blonde hair had been permed.

It was awkward and unfortunate that Sarah and Halley hadn't seen each other in the ten years since Benjamin's death. His and Halley's romance had ended long before his passing, but, even so, his death from cancer had shattered his former partner. It had been as if she could no longer bear to be around the others. Everyone and everything in Baton Rouge became a painful reminder of him and their past together. She had escaped by marrying Xavier, and they'd moved far away.

Sarah and Halley exchanged pleasantries as they returned to the living room. Finally, Halley said, "Tris told me about what happened with your job. I'm so sorry."

"Thanks. Unfortunately, it hasn't gotten any better. I filed for unemployment, but Fines is trying to deny my claim. I don't want to litigate until the EEOC does whatever they need to do, and finding a job is proving difficult. There's not a lot out there right now, and I have some serious transportation issues. It's not the happy ending I'd imagined when I accepted the position."

Halley studied her cup of cider and said, "Certainly not."

Sarah reached over and squeezed Halley's hand then said, "I'm so glad to see you. Who called you?"

"Vaughn. From what I understand, Daniel contacted your father and Jamie when he was here with Max and Lillian the other day. He tried finding me himself but got nowhere, so Vaughn volunteered to conduct the search. She called Tuesday night."

"And you flew back just for me?"

"For you and for everyone, I suppose. For me." She scanned the room and said, "I needed to come back home. I've been so busy for the last few years with my work that I've forgotten about myself."

"Did you ever patch things up with your folks?"

"No. I was close to Xavier's parents, but that all changed when he and I got divorced five years ago."

"I didn't know. That's too bad." She saw Kris trying to help Carrie's three-year-old daughter build a tower out of some wooden blocks and asked, "Any kids?"

"Xavier and I never had any children together."

"The turkey's ready!" Lillian exclaimed. "Who wants to help me uncover all of this food?"

Later that afternoon, Sarah walked out into the garden. It had been a wonderful Thanksgiving, but the house was getting too stuffy for her. The cold air invigorated her as she headed for the bench.

She noted how forlorn the plants appeared in the November sun. Of course, they probably would have appeared forlorn no matter what the season. Their caretaker was too frail to maintain the garden any longer. She would discuss the situation with Daniel. Perhaps they could come out with Kris and put things in order.

"Needs some work, doesn't it?"

Sarah's heart skipped a beat as she yelped, "Daddy!" She put a hand to her chest dramatically and added, "You'll give me heart failure by sneaking up on me like that."

"My apologies."

He sat next to her and put an arm around her shoulders. That was fine with Sarah. It had been too long since they'd sat together in companionable silence for any length of time. Tristan was the first to speak.

"I wish Benjamin were here today. He always did enjoy a party. It's too bad things didn't work out for him and Halley. They loved each other till the end."

His daughter slid her arm around his waist and said, "She still loves him."

"I'm sure he still loves her."

"Do you really believe that?" Sarah asked, as she gazed at the clouds. "I'd like to think that he's out there somewhere."

"I do." He gave her a sideways glance and asked, "You're not so certain?"

"I'm not certain of anything. I'm unemployed. I'm disabled. I've got to consider legal action against Fines, which could take several years. And then there's Daniel.

"Sometimes I think I'm okay, and other times I get overwhelmed by all of it. Even when I'm feeling good, I get scared because I know that it won't last."

"What are you sure of?"

"That I love you, Daniel, Kris, and all of the other people who are in that house. That's the only thing that keeps me going."

Tristan pulled her closer to him and reflected on how boundless his love for her truly was.

"The people we care about make life worth living. We go on. We have good days and bad days. Sometimes it may seem like there's no point, but we do make a difference day in and day out."

"Everything happens for a reason?"

"That's what I've come to accept over the last half a century. It doesn't mean I don't still have questions. Nobody said life was easy."

Sarah leaned against her father's chest and said in a whisper, "I want to make a change."

"So, make a change. You don't have to change everything overnight. It took me a long time to understand that. We only have one life. We should try to make the most of it."

"You should have written greeting cards instead of being an architect," she told him, as she raised her head up to his shoulder and felt the leather under her temple. "I guess I should be more willing to give new things a try."

They listened to the birds and the rustling of the leaves in the trees before eventually rising from the bench. Sarah slipped her hand into his as they walked back to the house.

"Daddy?"

"Hm?"

"You think you and I can take a walk downtown this Saturday? Maybe if I wander aimlessly for a while I'll find some direction."

He held the door open for her and said, "You could ask me for a lot more than a stroll downtown."

"That's all I need for now."

"Then Saturday's fine."

As evening approached, Sarah, Vaughn, Halley, and Katie volunteered to help Lillian clean the kitchen, while the others played football in the backyard or enjoyed the replay of the parades on the television in the living room. After a while, Will took a break from the football game and offered to help his sisters carry some large bags of garbage to the side of the house.

Sarah put down her bag and removed the lid from one of the garbage cans, as Katie and Will opened two others and began lowering their sacks inside. When Sarah lifted her bag, she felt a series of pops. A burning sensation spread across the bandaged part of her arm, and she dropped the bag, which burst and spilled its contents onto the ground.

Will rushed forward and asked, "What is it?" while Katie cried simultaneously, "Are you okay, Sissy?"

Carefully, Sarah peeled back the tape on one side of the bandage. When the wound was exposed, she could tell that some of the stitches had come undone. She tried to determine how many, but it was too dim for her to see properly. All she could make out was a thin trickle of blood.

"You're bleeding!" Katie exclaimed. "I'll go get help!"

"I'm not dying."

As she spoke, Sarah attempted to feel how badly the wound had opened. Her stomach performed a nauseating flip-flop as she made contact with the torn part of the wound, and she began to feel faint.

Will steadied her and said to his younger sister, "Go ahead and get Dan. I'll stay with her."

Blackness was teasing the edges of Sarah's vision. Will helped her to lower herself to the grass.

"I don't know why I feel faint," she offered. "I never faint."

"You don't usually stick your fingers into your arm either." He pushed her head forward between her knees and said, "Jeez, it even made me want to pass out."

"Oh, *that* makes me feel a lot better."

She was getting light-headed, and the familiar fear was creeping through her muddled brain. Sarah lifted her head and instantly wished that she hadn't. Dizziness overtook her, but Will quickly caught his sister and laid her back onto the ground. As she closed her eyes, Sarah could hear the sound of running feet. She placed her palms flat against the grass, as if that would stop the swaying motion she was experiencing. There were two more pops and then a pool of wetness on her skin.

Tears welled up behind her eyelids as she wondered, *What else can happen? How much more can I take?*

The feet skidded to a halt. Sarah opened her eyes and looked up at the looming figures of Daniel, Jamie, and Tristan. When they began to tilt, she closed her eyes again.

"So, the cavalry's here. Where's the rest of the crew?"

"Around." Daniel knelt beside her and said, "We didn't want to scare the kids."

Jamie crouched next to her and lifted her wrist. As his fingers probed her arm, Sarah was hit by another wave of nausea.

"It needs to be restitched," he said unnecessarily. "What were you thinking?"

"I wasn't," she admitted. "It didn't even occur to me not to lift the bag. I've never had stitches before."

"You had a few when…you were little," Jamie offered.

"Did I? I don't remember."

Tristan touched her shoulder and asked, "Can you sit up?"

"In a minute."

Daniel took her hand and declared, "There's no need for everyone to come to the hospital. You know how emergency rooms are. It's a holiday. We'll be there a while."

Jamie gently wrapped a clean handkerchief around Sarah's arm and applied pressure. The tears threatened again, and she stayed motionless until she regained control.

"Okay, I'm ready."

When he saw his mother come in through the back door, Kris immediately rushed forward for a hug. Unfortunately, he knocked into her arm in the process. When Sarah gasped at the pain, her son jumped back in alarm.

"I didn't mean it, Mommy!" He came forward and gave her a tentative hug then said, "I didn't mean whatever I did."

"I know you didn't, Sweet Pea. It's just that I hurt my arm again, and now I have to go back to the hospital."

"Can I come? I want to see them sewing your arm."

"No," Daniel said firmly. "We may be there for a few hours. You'd be bored. Why don't you stay here and play until we get back?"

Daniel gathered their coats, as Sarah stood wrapped in a cocoon of weariness. She was outwardly at ease and inwardly numb. The anxious feeling she'd been fighting for days was swallowing her, and it was taking all of her strength to keep it at bay.

"Sarah?"

Startled, she turned. Halley stood beside her.

"Max asked if he could talk with you alone for a minute before you left for the hospital. He's in the office."

Sarah looked across the room at Daniel, who shrugged and said, "I'll wait."

She went to the office door and softly called out "Max?"

"Come in, close the door, and come here."

She obediently did as she was told, shutting the door and walking over to where he sat on the loveseat against the wall. He stretched out his bony hands and gestured towards her injured arm.

"May I?"

She stiffly offered him her wrist. He unwrapped the bloody handkerchief and examined her wound. Sarah looked away and fought a recurrence of nausea. He replaced the crude bandage then sat back and studied her appraisingly.

"You *are* in a bad way, aren't you?"

"It burns, but I'm sure they'll just stitch it up again and send me home with more antibiotics and painkillers. I'll have to be more careful, I guess."

"I wasn't talking about your arm."

Sarah stared down at him in surprise. He was gazing up at her out of those sunken eye sockets of his. His face was a crude reflection of the man she'd known for most of her life. Physically, he was almost unrecognizable as Maxwell Nash, but the wisdom, patience, and kindness emanating from his eyes could not be dimmed by the ravages of time and disease. His soul shone brightly in the husk of his physical form.

We're going to lose him now, she thought suddenly.

Without warning Sarah began to cry. She covered her mouth with her right hand and tried to stifle the noise and stop the tears. That the others should hear her was unimaginable to Sarah.

Chapter Twelve: Pivotal

"Come here, Child. Come here."

Max put an arm around Sarah's shoulders and pulled her close. He tenderly reached over and pushed the hand away from her mouth, guiding her so that she could muffle her sobs by pressing herself against his chest.

"There's a girl. Lean on me now. It will be all right."

All of the hopelessness and anxiety that had been building in Sarah surged forth in the form of long, shuddering sobs. A tangled skein of emotions was being unwound and rewound in her mind and body. It was all very irrational and all too human.

"I'll take her, Max."

Sarah was faintly aware of Daniel's presence in the room. She was seized by panic. Had he left the door open? Was everyone watching her crumble into a million pieces?

"No," Max was saying. "Let her be. You have the rest of your life to hold her like this. I haven't had a chance in twenty-five years."

Finally, Sarah quieted and opened her eyes. Daniel was leaning back against the desk, his hands jammed deep into his pockets and his face filled with concern. Max was still holding her. The front of his shirt was drenched with her tears and clammy perspiration.

"You...you won't tell anyone, will you, Max?" She accepted the proffered box of tissues that her husband handed to her and asked, "You either, Daniel?"

"No," Max assured her. "I won't tell anyone if that's what you wish."

"Daniel?"

Daniel ran his fingers through his hair, then shook his head and looked pleadingly at his father, whose nod to his son was so slight that Sarah missed it completely.

"It's your choice," Max declared. "Although why you feel you must be ashamed of crying is beyond me."

She pulled away and stood then escaped to the other side of the room.

"I'm not ashamed."

"Aren't you, then?" asked Max politely. "I believe we worked on this several years ago. Am I correct, or is my old brain already so addle-pated?"

Sarah stared into the empty yard.

"Let me guess. You haven't cried like this in sixteen years."

Daniel came up behind her and slipped his arms around her waist.

"That's not true," he said, hugging her to him. "She was crying worse than that right before Kris was born."

Startled, Sarah brought her head up and twisted around so that she could see her husband's face.

"I – I was? I…don't remember that."

"No, I didn't suppose you would."

"Perhaps Sarah would like to hear what happened from your point of view. I was under the impression that she subconsciously suppressed her memories of that time period." In response to Sarah's questioning glance, he explained, "You told me that everything was a bit hazy and that you couldn't recall anything specific about the birth. You weren't even certain as to how Daniel got into the delivery room."

Now, it was Daniel's turn to look startled.

"You really don't remember any of it?" Laying his cheek across the top of her head, he said, "I'll never forget."

"Please," Max prodded. "Would you like for me to leave?"

"I want you to stay," Sarah whispered, holding on tightly to her husband's arms.

"Then, of course I'll stay. Son?"

"Everything was going okay that day until we were about ready to leave the baby store. Sarah bent down to see something on a high chair, then she doubled over and called my name. I caught her before she fell and tried to help her to stand, but she couldn't straighten up. One of the clerks hurried over and asked if she should call 911, but, by then, I'd seen the blood. We were so close to Woman's Hospital that I figured it would be quicker to put Sarah in the car and drive her there instead of waiting for an ambulance. I told the clerk to call ahead and tell them we were on our way. I brought Sarah to the car and laid her in the backseat. It took us two or three minutes to get to the emergency room."

"And what did Sarah do during the drive?"

"She lay on her side with her eyes shut tight. I could tell that she was in pain, but she didn't make a sound until we got to the emergency room." He kissed his wife on the temple and said, "This doctor told me that I had to wait in the hall when they took her in. I started arguing with him, but he kept telling me that I should stay outside. That's when she called for me and started to cry. I told the doctor to get Security if he wanted and pushed through the door."

"And how was Sarah when you went in?"

Daniel moved his right arm protectively up around Sarah's chest and said, "Hysterical. I took her face in my hands, and she looked at me like she thought she'd never see me again. One of the nurses tried to order me out of the room, but the doctor in charge told her to get back to work."

From the darkened area of the office where he was trying to remain as unobtrusive as possible, Max asked, "Was there anything else that struck you as you surveyed the room?"

"There was blood everywhere. I understood why they were so unwilling to let me in. I wondered how much blood Sarah had lost and if the baby would...would drown in it."

"Right after Kris was born they rushed him off to NICU. Sarah was still bleeding too much, and the pain didn't stop. They finally got it under control, but you could tell they were worried."

Max asked grimly, "How much blood volume did she lose?"

"A ton. They gave her five pints of blood before it was all over."

"Good Lord. And neither of you thought that sharing what happened would be beneficial? Birth can be a harrowing enough experience under the best of circumstances." He struggled to his feet and said authoritatively, "Now, you two listen to me. You have got to stop pushing other people away. Asking for help is not synonymous with weakness or losing control.

"Daniel, you must discuss this with your therapist. Sarah, you could work with me, but I think that talking with another woman might be even better. I actually know a young doctor I'd highly recommend."

"Do you...not want to talk with me?"

"Quite the contrary. But this might be best for you." He patted her hand and suggested, "Think about it. Perhaps you could

336

meet with her and if you don't like her or don't get the right feeling about her, then fine."

"I can call."

"Good. I think we've spent enough time here. That arm needs to be attended to."

Sarah blew her nose several times and tucked her hair behind her ears.

"Do I look too bad?"

"No," Daniel assured her with a smile. "You just look tired. Why don't you go get your dad or Vaughn to help you with your coat? I'll be right there."

She nodded and went out of the office into the noise of the house. Daniel stood studying his father.

"Why did you tell her to go see that doctor woman? I'm not saying she's incompetent; I don't know anything about her. But why not talk to Sarah yourself?"

"I have my reasons. For one, I'm the child's father-in-law, and, as you know, there are some things one doesn't feel comfortable talking about with relatives. There's a question of objectivity. There's also the fact that I'm an old man."

"Not so old," Daniel said hoarsely.

"Old enough. She needs someone who will be around for a while, a good therapist who can help her for as long as it takes. I'd hate to start something I can't finish."

Daniel's eyes misted over. He faced the bookshelves and said, "How long will it take for both of us?"

He heard Max lower himself into the leather chair. He waited patiently for his answer and tried to blink the tears from his eyes.

"You know I don't like to make projections. It takes as long as is necessary. I worked with you for many years. We could have continued on for many more, I'm sure. However, you have to *want* to continue with therapy if it's going to be effective. I pray that you'll stay with a good therapist until you're sufficiently done this time. It may take a year or it may take many years."

"I may never be done."

"That's a possibility."

"You mean it's a certainty."

The leather protested as Max rose from the chair. He began to walk slowly towards the office door and said, "Promise me that

337

you'll see it through to the end this time and that, even if you are done and some other seemingly insurmountable obstacle presents itself, you'll always seek help."

Still facing the bookcase, Daniel muttered, "I promise."

"And that you'll take care of your mother after I'm gone."

Daniel nodded and wiped at his wet cheeks with the backs of his hands.

"Good. Now, you should see to your wife."

"Dad, wait."

Max stopped with one hand on the doorknob and said gravely, "Thank you."

"For what?"

"Lillian and I have been your parents for quite some time. We've loved and cared for you as if we'd raised you from birth. Although things have been understandably difficult at times, your feelings for us have never been in question. Still, you've never used anything but our given names when you spoke to us. I'm grateful to hear you call me 'Dad' at least once before I die."

"Please don't go, yet."

It was a heartfelt plea. Max shuffled towards the bookcases and raised his hands until they rested on his son's shoulders.

"You know that I love you," he said sincerely. "But have I ever told you how proud I am that you're my son? You're a bright, loving, handsome, successful man. You have a knack for perseverance against all odds. You're a good husband, father, and child. You're a good man, Daniel Warren Nash."

Daniel was composed when he emerged from the office. He slipped on his father's coat then held the door for his wife. Neither of them said much on the way to the hospital.

It was a busy evening at Our Lady of the Lake. Over the next two hours, Sarah and Daniel spoke little as they listened to the sounds of coughing and crying and voices in various stages of anxiety and relief.

By the time a doctor came in to examine her, Sarah was drowsy. She half-listened as Daniel explained about the gash and the incident that had torn her stitches. She held Daniel's hand but said nothing as the injections were given, the wound cleaned, and the injury sewn shut for the second time in four days. After receiving a stern warning from the doctor regarding proper care of a healing wound, Sarah roused herself enough to carefully slip off the hospital gown and pull on her sweater.

She waited at the Emergency entrance for Daniel, who had disappeared into the darkness to get the car. A child wailed somewhere behind her, and the sound of turning rotors heralded the arrival of a helicopter. A couple chatted amiably as they passed her on their way into the building.

Daniel pulled the car up in front of Sarah, then hurried around to open her door. She allowed him to fasten her seatbelt and close the door; then she sat dully as he drove around the paved circle and down the ramp.

"Do you hurt?"

"Not yet. It's still numb."

When they came to Perkins Road, Daniel said, "I want you to take another one of those painkillers when we get home."

"Whatever. It doesn't matter. I can't go back, and I can't go on like this."

Silence.

"Why can't we have a little peace for a change?"

Silence.

"Daniel, will you say something?"

"I don't know what to say."

"Say anything."

"What do you want to hear?"

"Never mind."

I am so profoundly unhappy, Sarah thought, as she stared down at her arm. *If only the gash had been a little lower....*

Suddenly, Daniel veered into a nearby parking lot and slammed on the brakes. The tires skidded on the icy surface as he threw the car in gear and grabbed his wife by the shoulders.

"Stop it!" he shouted. "Don't you dare think about that!"

"Daniel, what are you –"

"I saw! I know!" His voice became more measured, but there was no mistaking the emotion behind his next words. "I know what it feels like to be that close to giving up, to feel that trapped with no way out." His hands dropped from her shoulders, and he turned towards the window beside him. In a voice heavy with despair, he said, "Don't leave me, Sarah. Promise me."

She unhooked her seatbelt and cried, "You can't just ask me that! I need you to help me!"

Daniel stretched out his arms and cupped her cheeks in his hands. He gently pulled her towards him then kissed her until they both stopped shaking. Lowering herself down until her head rested on his leg, Sarah curled up slightly and sighed. Daniel covered her head with his palm and stroked her hair.

"I'm so afraid," she confided. "I'm living from minute to minute. I'm not even living; I'm existing."

He hunched over and twisted his torso as if he were shielding her from some kind of impact. The tension in her face began to ease visibly, which greatly relieved him. He continued to stroke her hair and murmured, "I'm here."

She nodded against his leg and asked, "Will you take me home?"

"Mm-hm."

"Hold me all night?"

"Mm-hm."

In the cooling air of the car, Daniel wove his fingers through Sarah's hair and debated on whether or not he should drive straight back to their house. Before he could broach his suggestion to his wife, the cellphone rang. Sarah jerked up and knocked into the bottom of the steering wheel.

"Ouch!"

Daniel put his hand on the back of her head and drew her forward until he was cradling her against his chest. He held her to him as if she were a small child or a wounded animal. The phone continued to ring shrilly from his pocket.

"Don't you think we should answer that?"

"Are you going to let me take care of you or not?"

She smiled softly up at him and nodded.

"Thank you. Now, let me stop the damned ringing before I throw this thing onto the pavement."

Sarah watched him as he listened to whoever was on the other end, and coldness began to seep through her veins. He finished with "I see" and hung up. His eyes remained fixed on the Circle K sign in front of the car.

"Max?" she asked.

"Max," he said flatly.

Chapter Thirteen: Golden

It was a miserable day. The torrential rain that had started during the night continued to blanket the city. The temperature seemed to be holding steady at thirty-five degrees. Strong, gusty winds rose and fell, lifting sheets of rain and bending small trees.

Two months earlier, Max had sat in the sunshine with Lillian on the bench in his garden and told her about the funeral arrangements he had made. The wake was to be at Rabenhorst Funeral Home. The funeral Mass would be held at St. Joseph's Cathedral. He wished for the burial to take place as soon as possible after his death.

"It amazes me how quickly a person can be buried," Tristan remarked to the Asian priest who was to preside over the funeral.

"Certainly in some cases services can be postponed for days until distant relatives are located or elderly and ailing family members can rally long enough to be in attendance. In this instance, the expediency is due in part to Max's forethought and in part to the Thanksgiving holiday weekend."

He knew this was coming, Tristan mused. *He was prepared for it. Why weren't we?*

"Could you tell me exactly how it happened?" asked the priest. "It helps to know the circumstances. I don't want to cause anyone undue pain during my sermon by not being prepared. Lillian has been quite resilient, but I'd rather not press her for the details."

Tristan agreed reluctantly and explained, "Max decided to lie down and take a rest about 6:00 last night. Later, when Lillian went to check on him, he was gone, just like that. I saw her come down the stairs and saw the look on her face. Lillian nodded to me, turned, and went back upstairs. I took Jamie – that's him near the table – aside and told him the news. He went up to join Lillian, and I went to the office and called my son-in-law to tell him that his father was…that Max was dead."

"And the arrangements?"

"Made in advance. One of Max's friends, a fellow member of the Knights of Columbus, works for the *Daily Advocate*. Lillian contacted him at midnight with the particulars. Somehow, he managed to get all of the information in the morning paper, and here we are."

"Thank you, Mr. Maes. I wish I'd known Max longer. With our head pastor temporarily out of the parish, we've all been working hard to cover the needs of the church. I'd spoken with Max at a few church functions over the past month. He seemed to be a genuinely nice person. Very intelligent as well. He was extremely interested in my Chinese homeland and its medical practices, but he was also interested in my own experiences as an immigrant to this country. I understand he was an immigrant from Great Britain."

"Yes."

"Is there any further assistance other than spiritual that you think Lillian might require at this time? I'd like to offer my help to her."

"You can ask. She'll tell you one way or the other. Her sister's husband had someone come take away the mattress and bring a new one this morning. I can't think of anything else that could be done, but, like I said, you can ask."

"Thank you."

"Thank *you*, Father."

Will Maes nodded to the priest as they passed in the doorway of the parlor where Max's body had been laid out. He then approached his father and stood beside him, looking uncomfortable in his suit and tie.

Thank God he wants to be a veterinarian, Tristan thought. *He'd never be able to take the dress code on Wall Street.*

"Yes, Will?"

"I think they're almost ready to close the casket. I'm going to take one last look. Just thought I'd let you know in case you wanted to see him up close again."

"You go ahead. I'll wait a minute."

Will nodded and went forward, sidling up next to his younger sister, who was already by the casket. Tristan watched them pay their last respects to Max.

"Your son resembles you quite a bit, does he not?"

Startled, Tristan looked down at Isabelle Elenstraub.

"I suppose he does. He has brown hair and brown eyes, and he'll never be as tall as me, but otherwise we're pretty identical physically."

"Even the timbre of your voices is the same. And, yet, he is very different."

"More stable, thank God for that."

Isabelle smiled and took his arm.

"What does he do? I must confess I saw him last night, but I was rather preoccupied and involved in other conversations. Does he work? Is he in school?"

"He wants to be a veterinarian. He's at LSU and works as a runner for my firm to make extra money." He placed his right hand over hers and said seriously, "He lives at home and is either busy with school, work, or his friends and girlfriends all the time."

"A far cry from your life at that age."

He tried to imagine his son married, in college, working, and the father of a four-year-old child. He shook his head. How had he done it?

"Your daughter, Katie, looks so very much like Vaughn, except for the strawberry blonde hair. Those curls of hers are beautiful. She must have gotten that trait from you. Her temperament, however, seems to be in complete contrast to everyone else's in the family. Katie appears to be high-strung and very easily frustrated."

"Vaughn isn't always so calm. And how do you know about Katie's temperament?"

"One of the conversations I was engaged in yesterday was with her. I imagine that she was quite a handful in her younger days."

"She can still be quite a handful. Vaughn and I sort of wrote it off as a response to a perpetually deficient immune system. She's battled one illness after another since birth. For the last two years, her counts have been much better. And she seems to be mellowing somewhat."

"Then I would say that your assessment of her personality is accurate."

"Thank you, Dr. Elenstraub," he said with exaggerated formality. "It's a shame that we haven't seen you more over the last few years. I know that Dan and Lillian came into contact with you more than the rest of us...."

"Max and I were good friends and colleagues for over half a century. We all had our own lives to lead. As it is, I have not seen Daniel frequently for some time now. Max had...discussed things with me two days ago and again last night. He was concerned about Daniel and Sarah. I must admit, I can see why. They both look extremely unwell."

Following her gaze, Tristan saw Sarah and her husband standing across the room with Jamie and Halley. Dark circles shadowed Daniel's eyes, and his expression was clouded with sorrow and exhaustion. He held Sarah beside him as if he were the only thing keeping her on her feet. Perhaps he was.

"I should go to them," muttered Tristan. "They –"

"Excuse me." Those gathered in the room turned their attention to the funeral director. "I'd like to ask everyone but the immediate family to head to the church at this time. This way, please."

The crowd filed out through the doorway. Will nodded to his father and guided his crying younger sister into the hall. As they passed Kris, who had been nestled in Vaughn's arms, Will held out a hand, and the little boy wriggled down and trotted off with his aunt and uncle.

Within sixty seconds, the room had been cleared of everyone, except for the funeral director, Lillian, Daniel, Sarah, Tristan, Vaughn, Jamie, Chloe, Halley, and Isabelle. The director went over to Lillian, spoke with her briefly, and then left, closing the door behind him. The nine of them stood awkwardly. No one wanted to be the first or last to say goodbye.

Halley was the first to step forward. She knelt in front of the casket, brought her hands together, and shut her eyes to pray. Then she rose and left the room without a word to the others.

Once she'd gone, Isabelle came up and laid a hand on Max's shoulder.

"You keep Jacob company until I get there, my friend."

As Jamie and Chloe stood in front of the body of Maxwell Nash, Jamie reached up to the spray of flowers that had been arranged on top of the casket. Breaking off a large, red rose, he laid it on the satin pillow next to Max's head.

Sarah quietly started to cry. Nobody noticed; everyone was too intent on the procession that was taking place.

Tristan and Vaughn did not linger long when their turn came. However, although Vaughn went off to find her children and grandson in the hall, something made Tristan hesitate, and he remained in the room.

It was only as Sarah approached the coffin that Tristan realized she was crying. Lillian took a step towards her, then stopped. Daniel drew himself up, as if he'd been called to attention. Evidently, he'd been unaware of her tears as well.

Standing in front of the casket, Sarah dug into the pocket of her black velvet dress and pulled out the small stone she'd retrieved from Max's garden path earlier that morning. She stretched out her hand and slipped the rock into the breast pocket of his jacket, being mindful not to rumple the handkerchief that had been folded so neatly into it. She knelt, as if she intended to pray. Instead, she rested her forehead against the cool wood, and her whole frame trembled as she wept.

Daniel came forward and lifted his wife up until she stood next to him. Her small body pressed against him, and he stroked her hair then tilted her face upwards and wiped at her wet cheeks with a handkerchief.

"I – I want to go out of here," she cried. "I n-need to go now."

Tristan took her then. She folded into his capacious embrace and allowed herself to be led through the double doors into the hall. Lillian went to the coffin and bent low to brush her lips across Max's white hair, then followed them, leaving Daniel alone with his father.

He stood in the stillness of the room and averted his eyes from the shriveled remains in the box. That wasn't how he wanted to think of Max.

"I wish I could be certain that there was an afterlife, but I'm not." Pacing the carpet in front of the casket, he added, "It feels strange for me to be talking to you when you're not really here. I just…." He stopped and placed a hand on the foot of the casket. "I want to…to believe that I'll see you again." He spread his hand across his face and wiped at the corners of his eyes with his thumb and middle finger then announced, "I'm glad you were proud of me, Max. I was proud to be your son."

Suddenly, he was seized by panic. He raced across the room then forced himself to slow to a stop and calmly pull open the door. His heart continued to pound as he headed for the limousine.

The grandeur of the enormous stained-glass windows at St. Joseph's Cathedral seemed unimpressive that afternoon. The gothic design of the building was a perfect echo of the morbid atmosphere of the day and the reason for the presence of those gathered for the funeral. Despite the inclement weather and short notice, the church was nearly filled to capacity by former patients, professional associates, friends, and fellow parishioners.

Daniel, Tristan, Jamie, and Carrie's husband were joined by one of Max's psychiatric colleagues and a friend from the Knights of Columbus as pallbearers. When the service had ended, they walked next to the casket and helped to load it into the hearse. The other mourners milled about the Cathedral, murmuring amongst each other as they donned their coats and prepared their umbrellas.

Through a haze of tears, Sarah saw Max's neighbor, CoCo Genevieve, sitting several pews back, wearing a simple black dress and a string of pearls. Shocked by the conventionality of the woman's clothing, Sarah's steps faltered. CoCo lurched across the others in the bench. Her husband, Jean-Paul, was close behind her.

"I'm so sorry about Max. It's a terrible thing. He was a great man and a great doctor."

"Thank you." Sarah hugged her and said truthfully, "You look…wonderful."

"I thought I owed it to Max, a tribute of sorts. I feel so drab wearing one color. So, I spiced it up a little. Do you like them?"

Glancing down at the woman's shoes, Sarah smiled. They looked like Dorothy's ruby slippers from *The Wizard of Oz*.

"I don't think you could have given Max a better tribute."

"We be goin' to de graveside service wit you," Jean-Paul informed her in his heavy Cajun accent. "But we won' be goin' back to de house. I don' think CoCo should be dere right now."

"Perhaps not," Sarah said without conviction. "Maybe we can get together at your house soon."

"Dat would be jus' fine," the Cajun agreed. "I know she'd be happy of de company."

By 10:00 that evening, the old Nash home was nearly empty. Tristan sat in the living room with his eyes closed and listened to the silence. He was struck by how the whole house smelled of coffee. It wasn't surprising; there had been a fresh pot of Community Coffee brewing about once every twenty minutes since they'd arrived at 4:00 that afternoon. Tristan was on his fifth cup, but he continued to feel chilled to the bone.

Only twenty-eight hours before, he had been sitting in that very chair, having a conversation with Max about the progress of the downtown redevelopment plan. They had discussed the architectural and financial aspects involved, and Max had been interested in the possibility of renovations to the old building downtown where his office had been located. He'd appeared so animated and alive.

"Tristan?"

"Yeah, Chloe?"

"Jamie and I are heading out." When he didn't respond, she came over to the chair and laid a hand on his back then asked, "Are you okay?"

Tristan glanced up at Chloe. At forty-three, she looked very much like what he thought of when he heard the term "earth mother." Her even temperament, long hair, casual style, and full figure made people feel secure when they were around her. He wondered how she had managed to deal with and continue to love Jamie Nesser as passionately as she had for more than two decades.

"Tristan?"

"It's just hard to accept."

It was all he could think of to say. It was the truth.

"I know," she commiserated. "I don't feel like he's really gone for good."

"Max may have been Daniel's legal father, but for so many years he was the closest thing to a father that Jamie, Benjamin, and I had as well. I hope I never have to be a pallbearer again."

"Me neither," came Jamie's voice from behind them. "That was awful. Knowing that he was in there like that was terrible."

He held out a hand to Chloe, who took it and began to walk towards the kitchen. Jamie let go and moved to stand next to Tristan. Chloe left them alone.

"So, where've you been?" Tristan asked, as he rose and went to the window.

"Upstairs with Lillian. Is everybody else gone?"

"Vaughn's parents rode home with Will and Katie. Halley took Isabelle to her apartment, then went back to the Hilton. Carrie and her family are staying at the Sheraton. I think you were down here when the rest cleared out."

"Are Sarah and Dan still around?"

"Yeah. Chloe said y'all were leaving."

"In a minute. I wanted to talk some with you about Max. I wanted to tell you what he said to me on the phone a few days ago about us and what we meant to him. You up for that?"

"No, but I think I need to hear it. Go ahead."

Chapter Fourteen: Down to Business

When Jamie passed through the kitchen twenty minutes later, his eyes were red and his face was puffy. Chloe took him home.

Vaughn padded down the hall to the living room and joined Tristan at the window. He automatically slipped an arm around her shoulders as she slid hers around his waist.

"Tristan, let's go. There's nothing more we can do here. It's making me so sad to stay. The house seems so empty without him. I wonder how Lillian will be able to stand it."

"Yeah, I know. As long as Max was here, I felt as though I could handle things. I figured he'd always be there to fall back on, just in case. I guess my safety net's gone." He turned away from her and said, "My friend is gone."

Vaughn encircled his waist from behind and said, "Let's go home. Mom, Dad, and the kids are waiting for us. Sarah will call if they need for us to come back before they leave."

"I suppose. Why don't you go talk to Lillian? I'll find Sarah."

His daughter was in Daniel's old room. Her son lay asleep on top of the bedspread. She was in the process of removing his shoes and covering him with a blanket. In the darkness, only her face, her hands, and the short string of pearls she wore were visible. Tristan leaned against the doorframe and watched her move quietly around the room.

"I don't want to wake Kris until we're ready to leave," she whispered, as she stepped towards the doorway.

Tristan whispered back, "I think we're going to be leaving in a few minutes, unless you need for us to stay."

"No. I'll call you in the morning. God knows how long we'll be here. Daniel's been holed up in the office for hours. I'm going to go check on him now that Kris is out for a while."

There was a rustling sound in the hallway. Vaughn motioned for them to join her.

"Lillian's asleep," she said softly. "It looks like she was going through some old photos, and she drifted off."

"I'll wake her when we leave," Sarah assured her. "You two go on and get some rest."

"Us? What about you?" Tristan asked. "You're barely able to stand, Honey. I know that your arm must hurt like hell. You need sleep, too."

"I'm tired, but I'll be all right. I'll go to bed soon."

Sarah knew her father was well aware that she was more than a little tired. She *was* exhausted. Between the stress, the lack of sleep, and the pain in her arm, she'd been near to collapse since the alarm had awakened her at 6:00 a.m. She'd fought nausea all day and, unbeknownst to the others, had vomited twice at the funeral home and once at the house. She desperately needed to lie down.

When the taillights of her father's Grand Cherokee dwindled into nothingness, Sarah turned and went towards the office. She tapped lightly on the door then went in.

Daniel was sitting on the floor, surrounded by papers of all shapes and sizes. When he saw Sarah, he stopped reading the document in his hand and propped his left elbow on his knee, letting the paper dangle in front of him. His hair was mussed up as if he'd been raking it with his fingers, which he probably had. His coat and tie lay across the rocker, and his shirt was unbuttoned at the neck. The dark circles under his eyes had changed from light gray to deep purple.

"How much sleep did you get last night? Three hours?" she ventured. "That painkiller really knocked me out. I didn't even hear you come in to bed."

"We were taking care of the arrangements until about 1:45. I guess I got to bed about 4:00."

She crossed her arms over her chest and said, "No wonder."

"What's that supposed to mean?"

"It means you look as wiped out as I feel. Please, stop," Sarah pleaded, as she stepped carefully over several piles of paper and bent to pick up a crumpled envelope that had missed the waste bin. "This will take days to sort."

When he said nothing, she lowered herself next to him and put her arms around his neck. Once she was certain that her injured arm had not been compromised, she squinted at the paper in Daniel's hand. It appeared to be a bank statement, although she couldn't be sure without her glasses.

"Is it all in order?"

"What? Oh, yeah. Max kept good records. His filing system is a little…different, but everything's here." He passed his right hand over his face and admitted, "You're right, though. There's a lot to sort through. I don't want Lillian to have to be bothered by all of this. As it is, I'll have to sit down and explain everything to her so that she'll know the lay of the land. Max had some savings and enough life insurance to pay for the funeral. The house is paid for, so she should be all right. We won't know all the details of his estate until the will's read. Since Milo died last year, there are no other living relatives who stand to inherit, except for Lillian and me. That should simplify things." He wrapped his hand around her right wrist and tightened his grip briefly before letting go and assuring her, "I won't be much longer."

"Let me help you," she suggested, releasing her hold on him. "We can put all of this away together."

Daniel replaced the paper he'd been studying on top of a stack to his left and said, "You're not going to quit until I call it a night, are you?"

"No. It's payback time for nagging me about taking those painkillers."

"But they were for your own good!"

"And this isn't for your own good?"

Daniel gave her a tired smile, which she returned.

"I need to come back to sift through these tomorrow."

"I think it might be better for Lillian if we were here with her anyway."

They stacked the papers neatly on the desk. When they'd finished, Daniel threw a glance around the office, making sure that they hadn't overlooked anything. He sat in the desk chair and rubbed his eyes, yawning and stretching his legs out underneath the opening in front of him. His entire body hurt. Although he exercised every day when possible in order to keep his previously battered body in acceptable shape, it was affected by the weather and by certain physical activities. That day, the weather had been terrible; he hadn't been able to exercise at all; he'd helped to carry his father's casket; and he'd been sitting on the floor sorting through documents for hours. He didn't want to put forth the effort to get up again. Sarah was going to have to keep him awake on the way home.

She walked around the desk and eased herself onto his lap. He put his arms around her hips, and she put hers around his neck once more. Resting her head against his shoulder, she closed her eyes. Daniel nudged her with his cheek. The old clock chimed 11:00.

They stayed in the chair until the clock chimed the quarter hour.

"I *really* wish we were home already," Daniel muttered, as he pulled the office door behind them. "I'm not excited about the prospect of going out into the cold rain."

Sarah hesitated with one hand on the banister and said, "We could always spend the night here. We could sleep in the guestroom. The weather's horrible. Do you really want to take Kris back out in it? You know how easily he gets congested, and he's been so well, lately. And besides, can you drive us home without nodding off?"

Daniel paused to consider the suggestion. He was reluctant to spend the night. So far, he'd managed to cope with Max's death and had kept his grief in check. He'd had no choice. If he stayed in the old house, could he maintain his resolve?

He thought of his son. The prospect of another trip to the pulmonologist decided the issue for him.

"I'll lock up and go tell Lillian that we'll be spending the night. I'm glad that Will went to feed Ralph and let him out. You know he pulled that rope toy, too. At least we know the dog will be fine until tomorrow morning."

Daniel watched Sarah climb the stairs before making his rounds of the house. Now that Max was gone, he should talk with Lillian about putting in a security system.

As if Max could have handled an intruder in his condition, he thought wryly.

When he entered the master bedroom, Daniel saw Lillian lying on top of the bedspread still wearing her woolen blue dress. There were pictures spread out in front of her. Daniel moved closer in order to get a better look. He sat down gingerly on the mattress and picked up the photo closest to him.

It was an old picture, yellowing with age. Two boys and a man and woman stared back at Daniel. They were not smiling and not frowning, and they were posed in what appeared to be a most uncomfortable and artificial manner. He flipped the photo over and read the back, which was inscribed in a florid script: *Warnie, Edith, Maxwell, and Milo, 1918.*

Daniel put that picture down and scanned the others on the bed. Sarah with him at the prom. A picture from Max and Lillian's wedding. Carrie's kids playing in the sprinkler. A photo from his wedding reception. Baby pictures of Kris. A snapshot of all of them at a barbecue.

Out of the corner of his eye, Daniel spotted one he didn't recognize. In it, a little black girl stood in front of a Christmas tree. She was grinning madly and holding up a small, painted wooden horse that had a fluffy tail and mane. Daniel looked at the back.

Bethany, Christmas, 1954.

The handwriting was unmistakably Lillian's. He squinted at the toddler's face a second time. A cousin, maybe? One could certainly see a strong family resemblance.

"She was pretty, wasn't she?" Lillian asked softly.

"I didn't know you were awake. And, yes, she was. How come you never showed me this before? Who is she?"

Lillian reached out and gently took the picture from him. She smiled at the image of the happy child and ran her fingertip over the surface of the photo.

"She was my baby girl."

Daniel's jaw literally dropped.

"What happened? Did Max know about her?"

He shut his mouth. It was none of his business.

"Don't worry," Lillian said, shaking her head. "I don't mind. It was a long time ago."

"You don't have to tell me."

"I want to. There are already too many things you never knew about me and about Max."

"I know you had lives before the day I came here. You don't have to tell me any of it if it's too painful."

"It's a good thing to remember those early years, even if it hurts to think on them. My life was very different then. Like Tristan, I married young and had a daughter. My husband and I, we were both children ourselves. He was a good boy who worked hard and was good to me and the baby. I have no pictures of him, unfortunately." Lillian looked back at the photograph and said, "I lost them both in 1959. I thought my life was over. I walked around in a fog for years. I was going through the motions of life until I came to work for Max. Life was easier somehow here with him, even before we were…together. My world began to have meaning again, but I still wasn't sure what God had planned for me. Was I where I was supposed to be?" She paused and lowered the picture into the pile. "Then, Tristan Maes came into my life. A boy who had lost his wife and his hope, just like I had lost my family and my hope years before. Also, of course, there was Sarah, motherless child that she was. And me without my little daughter." She surveyed the pictures covering the bedspread and smiled. "They all became my children – Tristan, Sarah, Jamie, Chloe, Benjamin, Halley. I knew that God was giving me a chance to make things better for them and for me, but I still felt like something was missing." She stretched out her arm and stroked the hair near his left temple before saying, "And then there was you. The first time I saw you lying there at the hospital I knew what God had done. You saved me, Daniel."

"No, you've got it all wrong. *You* saved *me*."

"I'm glad you feel that way, but don't you ever minimize how important you were – are – in my life. I do believe you'd argue with the Good Lord Himself." Sifting through some of the other photos, she added, "And, yes, Max knew about my husband and daughter. There was a terrible storm here in Baton Rouge not too long after I'd been hired. The storm caused a power outage. We sat in the dark with the candles burning and talked all night. That was when I explained to him about my husband and my child. That's when he told me about Gwen."

"Gwen? Who's Gwen?"

"Gwen was Max's first wife, Baby."

"So, you had both been widowed before you got married to each other? And you had lost a child. What, did he lose one, too?"

He had meant for it to be an empty attempt at sarcasm. Instead of the flat denial he'd expected, Lillian turned her head and stared through the window into the gloom of the night. A sick feeling began to creep into Daniel's intestines.

He swallowed the bitter taste in his mouth and pressed on by prompting, "What is it?"

Lillian shook her head and swore, "God forgive me, but I can't. I can't break a confidence, especially one with Max. I promised him."

"But I need to know!" he cried desperately. He could sense that whatever she wasn't telling him was of the utmost importance. "Maybe I should talk to Isabelle. Maybe she would know."

"Not even Isabelle knew about this."

"He's gone. Please, Lillian," he pleaded. "Why won't you tell me?"

"Because I want you to be whole, to move on, to live. Your life has been so hard already. I want to spare you from any more hurt. Can you understand that?"

"Can you understand that I know you're keeping something from me and that it's hurting me even more?"

"It's not my place," she said quietly. "Max insisted that he wanted to be the one to tell you. He wanted to explain things in his own way. He said that if he didn't before...before he died, then it would all become clear after the reading of the will. Please respect his wishes and trust that it's for the best."

"Do you know what you're asking of me, especially right now at this point in my life?"

She debated for several minutes. With great effort, Daniel refrained from speaking and focused all of his energy on remaining calm.

She finally said, "If I tell you, you may hate us both for not saying anything to you sooner. We had our reasons. Will you listen to those reasons and try to accept them?"

He nodded, afraid that if he uttered a word or made any sound before she began that she might change her mind.

Chapter Fifteen: An Epic Tragedy

"Max loved his first wife very dearly," Lillian said. "They wanted to have children, but Gwen was plagued by one illness after another."

"What was wrong with her?"

"None of the doctors were certain. Looking back on things, she most likely suffered from some immune disorder like Katie. Regardless, at the time it was a mystery. It weighed heavily upon her, Max said, knowing that she could never successfully bear him a child. They tried, but she couldn't carry a baby to term."

"But they could have adopted."

"Now, Daniel. Imagine that Sarah suffered from an unknown debilitating health condition that rendered her weak day after day, year after year. Would you consider adopting a child and bringing him into that household, especially when the physicians were telling you that your wife might just up and die at any time?"

"No. No, of course not."

"The week after their eleventh anniversary, Gwen did pass away. That was in December of 1955. Max told himself that he could handle her death and quickly returned to work. Or, should I say, he threw himself into his work? In the Fall of 1956, he even accepted an offer to teach some classes at the university."

Daniel was paralyzed with dread. He waited nervously for Lillian to go on.

"He liked the teaching, but his class load was a heavy one for someone who also had a full-time private practice. In the spring, the department head assigned him a student assistant, a girl named Tessa Downey. Your mother." She paused, giving Daniel a moment to absorb this miniscule yet monumental piece of information. "Max was drawn to her. She was exceedingly bright and had a youthful stamina, a lust for life that Gwen had never been able to enjoy.

"Tessa was equally drawn to Max, although for her own reasons, I'm sure. His intellect? His personality? His status? All of the above? Regardless, he should have known better. I don't know what he was thinking. He was forty-five; she was barely twenty-two."

"So, Max and my mother met in 1957 and developed a personal relationship."

"Yes."

"And they ended up in bed together."

"Yes, they did."

"And she got pregnant."

"Eventually, yes. She told him that she didn't want to ruin him with the scandal. A prominent psychiatrist involved with a college student? An illegitimate child? Remember, this was 1957. People today may be too accepting of some things, but back then they weren't accepting enough. So, she left."

Daniel was beginning to feel light-headed.

"Max tried frantically to find her. In the months that followed, he checked the hospitals every day to see if Tessa Downey had come in to deliver a child. Nothing ever came of it. After two years, he resigned himself to the fact that he would probably never locate her or the baby."

"When?" Daniel whispered. "How did he figure it out?"

"It was when he looked into your mother's death after you came to live with us. His friend at the medical examiner's office happened to mention your mother's full name: Assumpta Tessa Downey Samuels. It all fell into place.

"Your birthdate of March 12, 1958 coincided with what would have been Tessa Downey's ninth month of pregnancy. Max checked the records at City Hall and found that Assumpta Tessa Downey had married Zachary Travis Samuels in August of 1957. That was a month after she disappeared." A tear slid down her nose, as she told Daniel, "If only you could have heard him talk about what he went through when he realized…. To know that your mother had stayed in Baton Rouge and that he'd been unable to find her and you and that both of you had suffered at the hands of that…that man," she spat. "It almost killed Max. He felt like he should have been able to prevent it somehow. He felt he should have been able to save her life. There was no way he could have known she'd changed her name or that she'd married."

"She always told me she hated the name *Assumpta*," Daniel volunteered. "I used to wonder why she used it if she disliked it so much. That's probably why she went by her middle name when she came to college."

Suddenly, Daniel was swept away by grief and longing. For what exactly, or for whom, he wasn't sure. His *mother*? Those horrible years he'd watched Assumpta – Tessa? – take beatings and worse on a regular basis from the man he'd thought was his father? Being beaten himself after her death? The time he'd missed with Max? Tears welled up behind his eyelids; large droplets fell onto the bedspread.

Lillian pushed the photos between them to one side and scooted across the bed closer to him. She put her arms around his shoulders and held him, rocking slightly back and forth, back and forth. Daniel wanted to pull away but allowed it. He needed it. They both needed it.

"Why didn't he tell me? You could have told me."

"I didn't know myself until much later. As to why he didn't tell you, he had his reasons."

"What possible reasons could he have had for keeping such a thing secret?"

"At first, he was worried about whether or not you'd ever be able to function normally. You were struggling so hard just to stay alive in the beginning. You could barely get through each day. How do you think you would have reacted if Max had told you that *he* was your real father and that the man who'd caused your mother's death, the man who'd almost killed you, wasn't even a biological relative? That if your mother had stayed with Max you could have had a happy, secure childhood here in this house? You would have blamed her for marrying Zachary Samuels, and you would have blamed Max for not finding you somehow."

"But when I got older –"

"When you got older, you got better. We were so relieved that you were doing well in school and that you had lots of friends. Against all obstacles, you succeeded. Max was so afraid of setting you back and of losing your love and your faith in him. He was worried that you wouldn't understand his motives." She squeezed him tightly and added, "He loved you so. He wanted to tell you I don't know how many times. He came very close that first time we saw Kris in the incubator after the birth, but he couldn't bring himself to do it."

From somewhere around her neck, he said, "Mom, why didn't you have any kids with Max?"

She placed her hand on the back of his head and whispered, "You called me 'Mom.'"

"Is that okay?"

"God, yes. It's music to my ears. I've always wished for that, but I didn't want to push it on you."

"I – I didn't know how to say it, if that makes any sense."

"It does. As for Max and I having children, it just didn't happen. All things considered, it was probably for the best. People aren't so kind about mixed-race children sometimes, and you needed our full attention. Other children would have complicated things. Not that we wouldn't have welcomed them. It just wasn't part of His plan."

This time, Daniel did pull away. He got up and walked to the window, turning his back to her. Rain continued to pound the panes in gusty waves.

"At least everyone was here the day your father died. He got to see them all one last time."

Wordlessly, Daniel moved across the room towards her. He bent to kiss her temple.

"Don't tell me that was part of His plan, too."

"All right. I won't."

"We're going to sleep in the guest room tonight. Kris is already in bed. Maybe tomorrow we can talk some more. Goodnight, Mom."

As she collected the photos and replaced them in the box, she called out softly, "Sleep well, Baby."

Sarah was already in bed and asleep. Daniel removed his clothing and placed it on the chair. Clad in his briefs and T-shirt, he hastily climbed in next to his wife. She looked cold, despite the fact that she had on an old flannel nightshirt she must have found in the dresser. No doubt she'd wake up hot in an hour. Nevertheless, he went to get another blanket and draped it over her.

He lay next to her and carefully slipped his fingers into the curls that had broken free in his direction. They were so soft and so perfect.

The storm did not abate, and Daniel listened as the wind howled and the rainwater gushed through the gutters. He pulled his wife closer to him. Sarah stirred and half-opened her eyes.

"Daniel?"

Brushing some hair from her forehead, he murmured, "Shhhh. I'm keeping you safe."

She stared sleepily at him then turned on her right side and pressed against him, slipping her left knee between his legs. She placed her right hand against his chest and haltingly moved her injured arm around his waist.

"Good," she whispered. "Keep me safe."

In a moment of illumination, he understood the reciprocity of the giving and the taking of salvation. He held Sarah gently yet firmly, and they slept soundly through the remainder of the gale.

Chapter Sixteen: Calm

"Hey!" Daniel called out, as he hurried across the gravel path and grabbed his wife's wrist. "Sarah, stop!"

"What?" she asked with a hint of irritation in her voice.

"You have to ask?" He shook his head in disapproval and released her before demanding, "What do you think you're doing?"

"I was restless." She straightened, rubbing her hands down the front of the overalls she wore and explained, "When I came down to breakfast, Lillian said you went back to our house for some clothes. She gave me these and the thermal shirt. They sort of fit. I thought I'd get a head start on the clean-up in the garden. I was only going to pull a few vines."

"And take another trip to the hospital?"

"It didn't hurt," she protested. Her face flushed, she admitted, "Okay, so I forgot all about my arm."

"Just like you did when you picked up the garbage bag? Don't look at me that way. Why don't you keep me company while I start clearing some of this out?"

"Because I'm bored. I have to do *something*. I'll pull some weeds with my right hand. Happy?

"Ecstatic."

Daniel was still reeling from his conversation with Lillian the previous night. He was hurt, angry, and grateful – all at the same time. Deciding that he couldn't deal with his newfound knowledge regarding the truth of his paternity, Daniel studied the tangled mess that had once been his father's beautiful garden. He looked down at his worn Levis, faded sweatshirt, and old pair of Nikes and wondered if he had overdressed.

"I think I'll start by taking down all this dead Carolina jasmine."

"Can I help, too?" Kris asked as he came through the gate.

"Woof!"

Sarah raised an eyebrow at Daniel and asked, "You brought Ralph?"

"I didn't have the heart to leave him. We were gone all day yesterday."

"I don't have a problem with it, but *you're* the one who gets to wash him off before we go home." She motioned for Kris to enter the garden and said, "Of course you can help, Sweet Pea. Come, Ralph."

Boy and dog romped in the wet garden as the adults worked. By late morning, Daniel's arms, shoulders, and back ached, but all of the jasmine lay in a pile outside the gate. Sarah was surrounded by mounds of weeds.

"It hardly looks like we've made any headway," she groaned. "There's still so much to do."

"Rome wasn't built in a day."

"What was that, Kris?" Daniel asked absently.

"That's what Grandpa Max always says." His lower lip stuck out slightly, as he added, "I miss Grandpa."

"We all miss him," Sarah said gently.

Daniel squatted in front of the child and asked, "Wanna take a walk with me? Maybe talk about things man to man?"

Sarah listened to their voices fade as they headed for the wooded area behind the house. She rose stiffly from the ground and went to sit on the bench. Ralph, who was fairly filthy, came to sit next to her and affectionately threw his muddy head across her leg. As she scratched behind his ears and stroked his fur, Sarah took a moment to relax.

The birds were singing and twittering above in the trees. From somewhere in the woods, an owl hooted soothingly. The sky was a brilliant cobalt blue.

When was the last time I've seen it so bright? she wondered. *When's the last time I paid attention?*

She heard the back door to the house creak open. The sound of voices floated across the garden. The moment she saw her father, Halley, and Lillian, Sarah knew what was about to happen, but she was powerless to prevent it. Still, she had to try.

"Ralph, stay!" she commanded.

It was too late. He was off and running, his tongue flapping in the wind, heading straight for Lillian. Tristan moved in front of her as Ralph's paws were about to make contact with her waist. They hit Tristan's thighs instead.

"Ralph," Tristan said seriously. "I think you're in BIG trouble, boy." He proceeded to take the dog's head in both hands and playfully grapple with him, saying, "I'm gonna get you!"

Lillian came around to stand in front of him and exclaimed, "Don't you dare play with that dog!"

Grinning, Tristan said, "Down, Boy."

"Ralph, come here!" Lillian ordered sternly.

Head lowered, he went reluctantly towards her.

"Bad dog! You could have knocked me down! What if I had broken a hip?" When the dog raised his eyes and looked soulfully up at her, she said, "Well, don't let it happen again. You hear me?"

His entire hindquarters began to wag furiously as she patted his head.

"Sorry about your clothes, Daddy."

Tristan surveyed the damage, then said, "It'll wash off. Since you and I are both dirty, I might as well get a hug."

"I'd hug you Halley…." Sarah began.

"Another time. I came over to see how things were going. Tristan's been showing me what's changed in town over the last few years. I'd love to take a trip to Grand Coteau tomorrow to see the town and my old school. Would you, Dan, and Kris like to come? And you too, Lillian?"

"We'd love to, but I'm thinking we should stay here," Sarah said quickly.

"Go," Lillian urged. "I appreciate you being here last night and today, but I don't need babysitting. I have some things to take care of tomorrow anyway. Thank you for the offer, Halley."

"What about you, Daddy?"

"We have to take Jim and Helen to the airport."

"Want to tag along to Chloe and Jamie's?" Halley asked expectantly.

"When Daniel and Kris return from their walk, we'll probably grab a bite and get back to work. It's too gorgeous out here."

"Just be careful of your arm," Tristan advised as he leaned down to kiss her cheek.

"Yes, Daniel," she replied in a playfully sarcastic tone. "What time do you want us to pick you up, Halley? How about if I pack lunch, and we can eat out in Grand Coteau somewhere if the weather's good?"

"There are certainly enough wide open spaces. How about 10:00?"

Sarah, Lillian, and Ralph watched Tristan's Grand Cherokee rumble down the driveway and turn left onto Highland Road.

"I'm making some round steak for lunch. When do you think the boys will be back from their walk?" Lillian asked.

"I'm not sure." Sarah squatted to pick up a spade that was lying in a mound of Monkey grass and confided, "I think they were having a heart-to-heart about Max." She glanced uneasily at the older woman and asked, "Do you want to talk?"

"Not yet." Lillian looked towards the old house and said, "Soon. Some of my friends from church have lost their husbands within the last few months. They've asked me to go to lunch with them after Mass. I don't really feel up to going, but I will." Still looking in the direction of the house, she added, "I'd appreciate it if you and I could talk later. My friends knew Max but not in the same way you did. And Isabelle…I find it difficult to talk to her about Max right at this time. They'd been friends for so long."

They heard the sound of feet crunching leaves and then two voices, one low and one high. Ralph sprinted in that direction, as Daniel and Kris emerged from the foliage.

"You two look awfully cold." Lillian held out her hand to her grandson and suggested, "Why don't you come inside and help me get out the plates?"

Hand in hand, they went in through the back door. Sarah locked her arm around Daniel's waist then asked, "How did it go?"

"It was hard." Daniel put an arm around her shoulder as they ambled toward the house and asked, "How 'bout with you?"

"We talked a little. Perhaps next week she'll be ready. Perhaps by then you'll be ready to talk with me, too. Something else is wrong, isn't it?"

He nodded but said nothing. After several steps he asked, "What have you been doing while we were gone? Chop down any trees?"

He was changing the subject and none too smoothly, but Sarah played along.

"Very funny. Actually Daddy and Halley came by. Grandma and Grandpa are going home tomorrow, and Halley wants us to go with her to Grand Coteau. We're supposed to pick her up at 10:00."

He nodded distractedly.

"I'd like to go by Vaughn and Daddy's in a while and spend some time with Grandma and Grandpa before they leave."

He nodded again, and Sarah stopped walking and asked, "What is it?"

"I'm trying to...deal with things."

"It will help to get away."

"Maybe."

After lunch Daniel and Sarah went back to work. Lillian came out periodically to bring hot chocolate, to comment on their progress, and to speculate as to what she should plant here or there. By 3:00, they had accomplished everything they could for the day. Grimy, sweaty, and sore, Sarah and Daniel picked up their tools and brought them to the garage.

"I'm going to the store with Grandma!" Kris announced excitedly as they came into the house. "She said I could help her, and I could get a cookie and a book!"

Lillian momentarily stopped rummaging around in her purse and said, "We'll only be gone an hour." She glanced from her list to her grandchild. "Well, two. I figured it would give us something to do while you got cleaned up. It seems like I'm out of everything except casseroles."

"Is it okay, Mommy? Please?"

"Of course. Be good for Grandma."

They stood on the porch and waved to their son as the car rolled off towards the street. Daniel put his hands on Sarah's shoulders and kneaded the muscles near her neck.

"That feels good. I didn't think I could get so stiff from pulling weeds."

"It's going to be hard to get out of bed in the morning."

Returning to the house, they slowly climbed the stairs to the second floor. Sarah led the way to the guest bathroom where Daniel lit the space heater and adjusted the temperature of the water coming from the tap.

"Sarah, do you want to go first?"

365

"I want to take a shower."

Daniel pulled off his sweatshirt and tossed it on the tile floor.

"The doctor said not until Monday."

"I know. I also know how much I hate baths. A shower is so much easier. I could tape a plastic bag around my arm."

As he unfastened his jeans, Daniel sighed and said, "The water will seep through if we try to use a plastic bag." He dropped his pants on top of his sweatshirt and proposed, "Why don't we take a bath together?"

"Here? What if Lillian and Kris get back?" As the overalls joined the pile of muddy clothes, she said, "We haven't taken a bath together since before Kris was born. I know there was a reason we stopped."

"I think it was because we couldn't find the time. Besides, our tub is just the standard size, and it wasn't very comfortable. This one is older and bigger. Let's live dangerously." He searched underneath the cabinet, as Sarah pulled off the thermal shirt then exclaimed, "Ah-ha!"

"A-ha?"

In triumph, he held out a container of bath crystals.

"*My* husband wants to take a bubble bath?"

"I do if it helps to relax you. Lillian's always loved to soak. She's got a lot of different bath salts and stuff, although I'm not sure that I want to go around smelling like *Whispering Breeze* for the rest of the day."

Sarah came over to him and crouched in front of the open cabinet door.

"Try *Summer Sands*. I think that's what she said Max liked."

"For what?"

Sarah pushed her palm against his shoulder and said, "If they took a bath together, silly."

"Puh-leeze! Sarah, I really don't want to think about them taking a bath together."

"*We're* going to do it."

"What if it were Tristan and Vaughn? Can you honestly say that it doesn't give you a queasy feeling when you think about your parents –"

"Okay, okay. So, use *Mountain Rain* already."

When the tub was full, Daniel eased his aching body into the water, which was so hot that it was almost scalding. It felt wonderful.

Holding onto the edge of the bathtub, Sarah lowered herself with her back to Daniel's chest and dangled her left arm outside the tub. Daniel fished around for the rag, raised it to his wife's hair, and murmured, "You're tense."

"Anxious. I'm having one of those moments. We've been busy all day, and I haven't had time to think about things for a while. Now that we have a break, I feel scared again." She shut her eyes and confided, "I wanted to talk to Max again. I hate feeling like this and crying at the drop of a hat."

"You could come with me next week and see if you like my therapist."

"*You* don't even know if you like him."

She leaned back, turned her cheek, and pressed it against his wet skin. She was trembling slightly, so Daniel wrapped his arms around her and held her securely against him.

"Is that better?"

"A little."

"Don't think about anything right now."

"I can't help it."

"How 'bout if I tell you a story?"

Sarah sat forward and twisted around to give her husband a dubious look.

"Little Red Riding Hood? Goldilocks and the Three Bears?"

"Poland and Echo."

Sarah settled back against him and stared at the ripples her movements made in the soapy water.

"It's a true story," he insisted. "My mother used to tell me about it. She was from Echo."

"Where are these places?"

"Central Louisiana. Interested?"

"I'm enthralled."

"As you can imagine, Poland and Echo are very small towns. During World War II, it was announced that Poland had fallen to the Germans." He paused dramatically, and Sarah smiled in anticipation. "The people of Echo declared: The Germans may have taken Poland, but they'll never take Echo! They put up roadblocks and stood behind the barricades with guns in hand, ready to defend their town against the imminent threat of Nazi domination."

"You are making that up!"

"I am not. It made the front page of the local newspaper. My grandfather was there." He added quietly, "My mother used to tell me stories like that when things were especially bad, which was most of the time. It made her smile. I'm glad it made you smile."

"Me, too. We should do this more often."

"What? Bathe with each other or tell each other stories?"

"Be intimate without having sex."

He kissed the back of her neck and murmured, "Why can't we do both?"

"Daniel –"

"I didn't mean we always have to have sex to be intimate. All I'm saying is –"

"Kiss me."

"Kiss you? But –"

"Just do it."

They made love in the stillness of the afternoon and reluctantly rose from the bed and dressed in time to help unload the groceries.

As they left the Maes' house the following morning, Sarah asked, "Do we have everything? Kris, did you make a pit stop before we left? It'll be over an hour before we get there."

"Yes, Mommy," he said with a roll of his eyes.

"I'll sit in the back with him," Halley insisted, as they prepared to leave.

"Oh, no," Sarah protested. "You sit in the front."

"I want to," she persisted. "Really."

As the car veered onto Interstate 12, Kris began to draw on his Etch-a-Sketch. All at once, he stopped and angled his face up towards Halley.

"I like your sweater. It feels soft."

"Thanks. It has some angora in it, which means it's extra fuzzy."

"I like your Robin Hood shoes, too."

Halley glanced down at her feet. She was wearing lace-up shoes that did, indeed, resemble the footwear of the helpful bandit.

"Thanks. I like your sweater. Who is Thomas the Tank Engine?"

Kris was in his element. He proceeded to explain to Halley all about Thomas and his train friends and their life on the tiny island of Sodor. She listened intently and appeared to be genuinely interested.

"It sounds like a nice place," she commented. "Sort of like in the olden days."

"That's what Grandpa Tristan says, too. What's it like in Colorado?"

"It's very nice where I live. There are lots of trees, hills, and animals."

"How long have you lived there?"

"About two years."

"Where did you live before?"

Daniel spoke across his shoulder and said, "Give Halley a break. She might not feel like answering all those questions."

"Oh, I don't mind. I lived in New York City before that. I think I prefer Colorado."

"Why? Because it has more trees?"

"That and there's this man named Bill, whom I like very much."

Sarah turned to look at Halley and asked, "What's he like? Where's he from? What does he do for a living?"

Daniel smiled and said, "You're worse than Kris."

Ignoring him, Halley confided, "He's fifty-one, divorced with two grown children. He owns his own shop where he sells hand-crafted furniture, rugs, and things. He lives in this log cabin house that sits on a couple of acres."

"A log cabin, huh?" Sarah smiled down at Kris who had already fallen asleep and was propped up against Halley. "Sounds like it might be a long-term affair."

"We're talking about getting married as soon as I get back."

"Why didn't you bring him with you then?" Daniel asked. "Afraid we'd scare him away?"

She laughed and said, "He was coming down with the flu. We thought it might be better if I wasn't exposed to it, and we didn't want to get anyone over here sick, so I came alone. I would like for everyone to fly out for the wedding, if possible. I don't know what your schedule is like the next couple of weekends –"

"The next couple of weekends?" Sarah interrupted. "What's the rush?"

"We'd like to get married before I'm too far along to fit into a nice wedding dress."

"A baby?" Sarah said in disbelief. "Oh, my gosh."

"When we found out last month, we decided we couldn't put off making it legal any longer."

"Daniel, pull the car over so I can get out and hug her," Sarah instructed. When he looked askance, she assured him, "I'm only kidding!"

As Halley reached down and gently removed the Etch-a-Sketch from Kris's hands, she said, "I'm really happy about things. I love Bill and I want so much for everything to go well this time, but I still miss Benjamin. Do you realize our daughter would have been twenty-five this year?"

"We miss Benjamin, too," Sarah said gravely. "But every time I see a lava lamp or a sequined shirt, I think of him."

"Or a beaded curtain," Daniel added seriously. "Or a neon sign."

"He was certainly one of a kind," Halley agreed. "But then Bill is also – in a slightly different way. I can't wait for you all to meet him."

The rest of the drive proved uneventful. As the car cruised over the Atchafalaya Basin, the three friends caught up on a decade of activities and made promises never to lose touch again. As they continued on past Landry's Seafood Restaurant, Daniel relaxed and listened to the two women talk of wedding dresses, infant formula, and the state of the Presidency in modern America.

Soon, he was steering the car away from Lafayette towards Opelousas. It had been twenty-nine years since he had gone that way with his mother for his grandfather's funeral. It was the one and only time that his mother had openly defied Zachary Samuels, who had refused to give her permission to go. Perhaps that was why every detail of their journey had been etched so clearly in Daniel's mind.

Not much had changed in twenty-nine years. There were a few different businesses and some new homes. The Show Town

Drive-In was a wasteland of tangled weeds and grass. Angelle's Restaurant had become the Delta Center. Everything else was more or less the same.

As Daniel drove slowly into the outskirts of the little town of Grand Coteau, Halley said, "That Chevron used to be a locally owned restaurant and filling station. Everybody would stop there for hamburgers and snacks. It's too bad it's gone." Leaning forward, she instructed, "Curve left, then take a right when you reach Main Street. Martin Luther King Drive? Well, it used to be Main Street. Turn here. When you get to the stoplight, go a little further up and pull in at Ivy's. It's sort of a general store. Here! Here!"

Confused, Daniel pulled into a parking lot in front of a place called Catahoula's and declared, "I don't see a sign for Ivy's. Maybe it's another light."

"That was one of the only lights in town. It was the right one." She got out shaking her head. "So much of it's the same, but so much of it is gone. Of course it's only been a couple of dozen years. Why should I think it would stay unchanged?"

Inside the car, Kris stirred awake and mumbled, "Mommy? Are we there, yet? I'm hungry."

"The picnic basket's in the trunk."

"It's so nice again today," said Halley. "Why don't we walk? It's about a mile down that road. It's really pretty."

"I'll get the food," Daniel volunteered. "You sure you're up to it?"

"I'm pregnant, not lame. Things are fine, but thanks for the concern."

"Any time."

"There's the Jesuit seminary," Halley said, pointing to several large, old buildings to the right and its surrounding grounds as they crossed the quiet road. "It used to be a boys' school years and years ago."

They walked casually down Church Street past two churches, two schools, a retreat house, and a small recreational center.

Daniel hoisted the picnic basket from his left hand to his right and asked, "Sarah, what did you pack in this thing?"

371

"Soft drinks, chips, brownies, and ham and cheese sandwiches. There's plenty, but it shouldn't be *that* heavy. I wasn't packing for an all-day hike, just lunch."

"Fine, he grumbled. "It's still damned heavy."

The little group continued down the road past a funeral home and a scattering of isolated houses. They stopped so that Kris could watch some cows grazing in the fields. When the road curved to the right, so did they.

Sarah was buffeted by an unsettling wave of apprehension. There was no reason she should feel anxious. She tried to ignore it as they went on, but the more they walked, the stronger the feeling grew. Something wasn't right. Or, rather, something *was* right. It didn't make sense.

"Horses!" Kris shouted and ran forward across the narrow road so that he could see more clearly through a fence.

Halley came up beside him and said, "Some people have horses at my old school, which we students called *Coteau*. Its actual name is the Academy of the Sacred Heart." She turned and shielded her eyes from the sun and directed, "There, you can see part of the school. Isn't it beautiful? Oh, I should have come back sooner. I always loved this place. It has a personality of its own. You can feel it in the red brick, the columns, the shutters, and the porches."

"Was it always like this?" Daniel asked.

"The school opened with a handful of students in 1821. In 1830 this new building was constructed. The bricks were actually made here on the grounds. I think it cost something like ten thousand dollars to construct the main building. Imagine what you'd get for that amount today."

They entered through the closest gate and meandered across the lawn. Kris ran off towards some swings and an old wooden seesaw.

"Mommy! Look! A saw-see!"

"Seesaw," Daniel corrected. "You stay on those swings for a second. We'll play on the seesaw after lunch."

The adults wandered across the grass to a sanctuary of sorts. Two statues graced the little area.

"This is the Grotto. See the statue of the Virgin Mary and the little child offering her flowers?" Sighing, she admitted, "This is

372

bad. I can't recall who the little child is supposed to be. That's awful." She pointed to a white wooden dwelling that sat demurely on the other end of the lawn and said, "There's the Cottage. It's where the headmistress and some of the other nuns live. Next to it is the chapel on the end of the main building. You can't see the three galleries from here."

"Galleries?" Sarah echoed.

"The porches that run along the front of each floor. I can show you when we come back around. Let's walk this way first."

"Kris!" Sarah called. "Let's go!"

"The stables are behind the Cottage in the old barn if you'd like to take a look," Halley suggested.

Daniel shook his head in amazement as they neared the barn. "Is this the original structure? It looks ancient."

Before Halley could answer, Kris cried, "Daddy! A tomb place! Just like for Grandpa Max!"

"A cemetery," Halley said quickly. "It's where all the Religious are buried."

"Where does that passage lead?" Sarah asked a little too hastily in an attempt to divert everyone's attention away from the graveyard.

"I'll show you," Halley offered.

The group moved *en masse* towards a narrow hallway in between two buildings. As they walked single file through the passage, Sarah could sense the tension in her husband. She wanted to take him aside and talk with him, but there was no place to go and no time to break away from their son and their friend.

"To our right is the main building," Halley was saying. "See, there's another green cistern like the one we passed behind the chapel. I'm glad they never tore them down. I wish that the St. John Berchman Shrine was open. Maybe we can ring the bell later and go inside to see it. It's the only shrine in the United States that's really at the site of a miracle."

To his wife's relief, Daniel said nothing. As Halley took Kris's hand, Daniel reached for Sarah's.

"Here are the gym and the quadrangle. The long building to the left is the high school. Upstairs is where the boarders live. The building on the right is where the classrooms are for the elementary students." She pulled Kris forward gently along the sidewalk and urged, "Let's walk through this breezeway and see the fish pond."

The child happily unfastened the latch on the small gate that opened out onto a circular driveway.

"This is where the administrative offices are." Halley gestured in the direction of the front building, which was adorned with massive columns and huge glass doors. "Over there's the pond."

The little boy darted across the grass towards a huge rectangular cement pond surrounded by concrete benches.

"Kris, no!"

Daniel dropped the picnic basket and raced after his son. As Kris prepared to dive blindly into the pond, his father threw his arms around the child and swung him backwards, stumbling in the process. The pair toppled to the ground, and Kris burst into tears.

"You can't just jump in there! You could have drowned!" Still breathing heavily, Daniel stopped and looked at his son then forced himself to lower his voice before saying, "You scared me."

He glanced over the edge of the raised concrete barrier that ran the length of the pond. There was no water. A sick feeling washed over Daniel as he picked the boy up and put him in his lap.

Halley and Sarah ran up beside them. Daniel looked up at his wife and said shakily, "There's no water. He could have been killed."

She nodded and knelt next to him and their crying child.

"You okay, Kris? Daddy caught you by surprise, huh? He really didn't mean to yell. He was worried about you."

Kris nodded and wiped at his cheeks.

"Why don't Kris and I take the picnic basket up on the first floor gallery and set everything out?" Halley offered brightly. "You two take your time and wander here in front. When you're ready to eat, we'll be waiting."

Kris scrambled to his feet, the fear and the tears quickly forgotten, and asked excitedly, "Can I carry the basket?"

"We can carry it together."

Sarah lowered herself onto the cold concrete edge of the pond. She rested her hand on the side of Daniel's neck, as they watched their son and friend walk back towards the gate. When the figures were out of sight and earshot, Daniel repeated, "He could have been killed."

He stood, paced back and forth for a few moments then sat on a nearby bench. Sarah pushed herself up and went to sit beside him. Daniel put his arms around her and laid his head on her shoulder.

"It's all right," she whispered.

He held her tightly as she rested her cheek against the top of his head. He wanted to cry, but the tears wouldn't come. So, he was still.

Finally, he pulled back. Sarah leaned forward to kiss him and suggested, "Why don't we take the walk that Halley was talking about? Then we can join the picnic in progress."

Daniel stood and helped Sarah to her feet. They went back to the circular driveway and followed the gravel as it returned to the road.

"Look at that," muttered Daniel.

Sarah surveyed an elegant, formal garden area. There were brick patterns laid out throughout the garden – octagons, stars, hearts, circles, and triangles. Within each brick design, roses and other flowers had been planted. Hedges bordered a walkway that led to a statue.

"We'll have to go around and see the front of that statue later," he muttered. "The garden is great. I wish we could get Max's to look this good. I don't think there's a chance of *that* ever happening. How about you?"

Sarah wasn't next to him anymore. He turned and saw her standing about twenty feet behind him. She was staring open-mouthed in the opposite direction of the school.

Daniel headed back to where his wife stood. When she didn't acknowledge his nearness, he moved in front of her and asked, "Is everything okay?"

She raised her hand and pointed then directed, "Look."

He glanced over his shoulder and said, "It's very nice."

"Daniel, *look again*."

He looked again.

Two rows of massive oaks stood before them, their branches intertwined to make an incredible canopy across a large expanse of ground. Their roots swelled up in intricate patterns that went on and on. It was an alley of oak trees.

Sarah turned and went through the main gate that stood behind them. Daniel followed silently, his heart thudding and his stomach in knots.

Crossing diagonally through the garden, Sarah strode purposefully across the grass. When she stopped, Daniel came up behind her and waited. She was facing what Halley had said was the chapel. There were pine trees extending from where they stood to the front steps of the church. The swings were to their left.

"It's exactly like in the dream I had when I was sixteen."

He wrapped his arms around her shoulders and chest and said, "That was half a lifetime ago. Maybe you heard Halley talk about it when you were small." She was quivering in his arms, so he tightened his grip and murmured, "There has to be a reasonable explanation."

"She never talked about this place. She used to say she missed it too much. I've never been here before, but the oak trees, the pines, the swings…" She laughed softly and muttered, "We even have a picnic basket like the one in my dream."

Sarah broke away from him and went towards the statue that had been placed in the center of the garden. She took six halting steps until she stood before it. After several moments of contemplation, she turned and sat on the little hillock that raised the statue of Christ towards the heavens. Daniel sat with his back against the small hill, then guided her onto his lap and cradled her against him.

"Well, here we are," he remarked. He slipped his fingers into her curls and said, "Our moment of truth."

"Here we are," she repeated. "And we still don't believe, do we?"

He brushed his lips across her forehead and said firmly, "We'll sort it out. We'll take it slowly. If it were anyone but you, then I wouldn't hesitate to dismiss this. I can't think of any excuse right now, and I'm too tired to try."

"You mean you're too lost."

"Maybe. I really would like some peace before I die."

"Me, too." She rose from his lap and said, "Are you ready?"

He stood and took her hand, and they began to walk towards the main building. From somewhere in front of them, they could hear Halley's soft voice and then peals of laughter coming from their son. Daniel stopped walking, leaned down, and kissed his wife, who brought her arms up around his neck.

They stood like that for some time and allowed themselves to experience the simple joy of being together. The birds sang; the breeze blew the leaves of the trees; and the clouds floated happily in the bright blue sky. For that moment, it was more than enough, and all was right with the world.

Other Books in This Series:

A Good Man's Life

Mercy

Unfinished Business (Final Chapter)

ABOUT THE AUTHOR

Lauren Cutrera, who also writes under the name Barbara Cutrera, has published over 20 contemporary romance, romantic suspense, paranormal romance, mystery, and fiction novels. Diverse people and plots highlight her works, drawing readers into the characters' unique journeys as they navigate their way through their struggles and triumphs. Lauren and her husband, Budge, are the proud parents of a grown son. They live in southwest Florida and have a cute and naughty Yorkie, Hadrian, who sleeps next to Lauren as she writes each day.

Explore other published works by the author at amazon.com and goodreads.com

Check out all things Lauren (and Barbara) at www.laurencutrera.com

And connect with her there or on

Facebook: https://www.facebook.com/profile.php?id=100063631654302

Instagram: https://www.instagram.com/laurencutrera/

Pinterest: https://www.pinterest.com/laurencutrera/_saved/

OTHER BOOKS BY THE AUTHOR:

The Essential Elements Series

Kindred Spirits
Scorched Creek
Spirits Corner
Memory Lane
Homeward Bound

The Limitless Series

Sight Unseen
Better Left Unsaid
Unheard Of
Under Her Skin
Brain Storm
Out On A Limb

The Seneca & Michael Duet

A Lovely Dream
A Lovely Reality

The Gift Series

The Healer's Gift
Jordan's Way
Bound by Grace
The Nameless

The Real World Series

Over, Under, Across & Through
A Good Man's Life
Mercy
Unfinished Business (Final Chapter)

Standalone Novels/Short Stories

In A Manner of Speaking
Prim & Proper
Lucky
Compromising Positions
True: 3 Short Stories

www.ingramcontent.com/pod-product-compliance
Lightning Source LLC
Chambersburg PA
CBHW061304170626
46817CB00001B/43